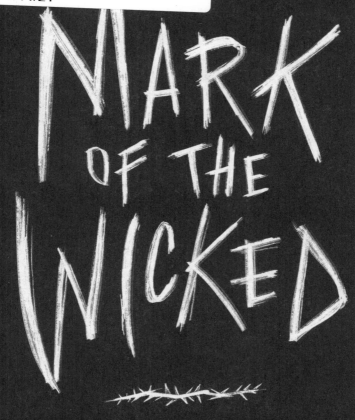

MARK OF THE WICKED

GEORGIA BOWERS

Swoon
READS

Swoon Reads | New York

A Swoon Reads Book
An imprint of Feiwel and Friends and Macmillan Publishing Group, LLC
120 Broadway, New York, NY 10271

swoonreads.com

Our books may be purchased in bulk for promotional, educational, or business use.
Please contact your local bookseller or the Macmillan Corporate and
Premium Sales Department at (800) 221-7945 ext. 5442 or by email at
MacmillanSpecialMarkets@macmillan.com.

Library of Congress Cataloging-in-Publication Data
Names: Bowers, Georgia, author.
Title: Mark of the wicked / Georgia Bowers.
Description: First edition. | New York : Swoon Reads, 2021. | Audience: Ages 13–18. |
Audience: Grades 10–12. | Summary: When sixteen-year-old witch Matilda grows closer
to Oliver bizarre things begin to happen in their town, but as she faces blame for these
strange occurrences, Matilda sets out to discover the true culprit before
anyone else turns up dead.
Identifiers: LCCN 2020038387 | ISBN 9781250773890 (hardcover)
Subjects: CYAC: Witches—Fiction. | Magic—Fiction.
Classification: LCC PZ7.1.B686 Mar 2021 | DDC [Fic]—dc23

LC record available at https://lccn.loc.gov/2020038387

First edition, 2021

Book design by Trisha Previte

Printed in the United States of America

ISBN 9781250773890 (hardcover)

1 3 5 7 9 10 8 6 4 2

For you, Mum;
I miss you with every breath,
and every semicolon.

CHAPTER ONE

Our kind are scarred with the names of those we've hurt with our
magic, to serve as a warning to others to keep their distance. But
every rule has an exception, and we are no exception to that rule.
Only the cunning can hide their true visage, but it comes at a price.

—Grimoire of the Hollowell Women

Sixteen days until Halloween

The first time Matilda swallowed a bee, it hadn't gone well. She'd panicked, which made the bee panic, and Matilda's tongue had swollen up like a puffer fish, impossible to hide from her mother. Only her grandmother sneaking her a brew of witch hazel and aloe vera to gargle had brought it back to its normal size.

The morning sun trickled through the naked branches, scattering spots of light across the wooded ground, the color stuck somewhere between that time when the night retreats and the day takes over. Matilda looked over her shoulder, then back at the hive. She wasn't in the mood for dancing with the bees when they went for her, but she needed that queen.

Matilda's grandmother visited the beehive once a week to tell the bees what had been going on in the family home, a ritual that Matilda still hadn't worked out the logistics of, considering her grandmother had hardly spoken in three years. Nevertheless, Nanna May crept through the trees every Friday morning to respect the bees and keep them informed. Matilda always wondered whether they buzzed in response or stayed silent, like they were right now.

Without her realizing it, Matilda's fingers crept across the gnarled letters on her face, tracing the names of every soul she'd twisted, every person she'd broken. She dropped her hand to her side. *One more won't make a difference*, she thought to herself.

Her eyes scanned the twisted ground for what she needed. A few feet away was a clump of *Urtica dioica*, or stinging nettles to anyone who hadn't been dragged through the woods to learn the Latin names of every single plant they could lay their bored eyes on every day of the school holidays. Matilda pulled off her woolly gloves and bent down and caressed the nettles in both hands, wincing as the hairs rubbed against her skin. It smarted for a moment but was nothing in comparison to what the army inside the hive would do to her once they felt threatened. The nettle sting buzzed over her hands like an invisible force field. Who needed protective gloves when you'd been taught how every weed in the woods could help you, and your fingers twitched with magic?

The burn crept over her hands, and she took a breath and closed her eyes. As she thrust her head into the open arms of the nettles, the crows squawked a greeting to the daybreak and hopped about on the silver birch branches, hustling one another to get the best view of the witch at work. Matilda looked up and frowned, grimacing as the pain seared her forehead.

"Shhhh!" she spat at them.

The squawking stopped, and a black-and-white shadow

swooped down from the trees. Matilda watched the magpie pecking around in the weeds, its orca markings announcing its arrival, bringing along sorrow for whoever needed it. Matilda saluted the lone bird with a nod of gratitude; what others dismissed as superstitions, she had been taught to embrace as gifts, traditional portents of death a perfect foundation for mischief. Her face throbbing, she walked to the opening in the tree, still nothing but thick silence seeping from within the hidden honeycomb.

She reached inside the tree trunk, her fingertips brushing against an army intent on protecting its precious leader. The nettle trick worked, though, and she couldn't feel a single one of the tiny stings as they attacked her hands, not even on her face as they went for her like tiny missiles of wasted death. She swatted them away as her fingers hunted, and the silence of the hive turned up to a howl of terror.

"There you are," said Matilda, a smile as sweet as the honey the bees would never make sliding across her face.

She withdrew steadily, shaking off the persistent workers, and then held her hand up in front of her eyes, a black-and-yellow beauty struggling between her thumb and forefinger. Matilda brought her prize to her lips and kissed it, careful to avoid its barbed stinger, then threw the bee into her mouth and swallowed it, embracing the fire that followed down her throat.

Her bee-swallowing technique had certainly improved since the first time.

⬥

The morning light had changed even in the short walk from the hive at the back of the property to the kitchen. Matilda poked her head around the open stable door, ducking under the elder tree branch her grandmother had hung there to keep evil from entering through the back door. The fire flickered in the arms of the hearth, which meant her Nanna May, whose life revolved around stoking the fire so their ancestors could find their way should they need to, couldn't be far away, and the lingering aroma of mimosa and rich ground coffee meant that she'd just missed her mother. Matilda's stomach growled as she spotted a fluffy dome of bread sitting on top of the scratched kitchen table.

"Sweet," she whispered.

She opened the lower part of the door and stepped into the heart of the cottage, headed straight for the loaf. Her dad had made loads of improvements to the cottage before he left, but her grandmother wouldn't let him touch the kitchen, apart from installing a fridge. Light came from the windows and hanging lanterns, and warmth came from the huge stove that, along with the open fire, made the kitchen the warmest place to be throughout the year.

As she cut the crust off a slice of bread, the back door creaked open, and Matilda spun around and blinked at the visitor peeking around the open door.

"Where'd you trot in from, Victor?" said Matilda, holding out her hand.

A tiny goat blinked its golden eyes at Matilda, its front hooves poised in first position as it watched her spray bread crumbs all over the cracked kitchen tiles. Victor tilted his head to one side and inched into the kitchen with the tiniest of trots until he was at Matilda's feet.

"Here you go." She scratched his chin, then smeared jam over a piece of bread and gave it to the goat. "Who's the most adorable thing on the planet?"

"Thought I'd gone?"

Matilda's mother, Lottie, came down the uneven steps into the kitchen, her white Persian cat, Nimbus, slinking after her like she owned the place. Lottie shook her head and pointed a manicured finger at Victor, then at the back door.

"I know you love him, but you know the rules," said Lottie, grabbing a dustpan and brush from a hook next to a bunch of lavender. "Look at the floor, Matilda. He's gotten crumbs everywhere."

Matilda crossed her arms and watched her mother crouch down in her heels to sweep up the crumbs. Just the sight of her mother made her stomach boil with aggravation. She couldn't be within three feet of Matilda without creating some kind of conflict. If Lottie had come in five minutes later, the goat would have polished off every last crumb anyway.

Lottie looked up at Matilda from beneath the frown that was permanently attached to her forehead. "Tilly? What did I just say?"

Matilda huffed as she leaned forward and whispered into Victor's ear, annoyed that her mom had called her by her childhood name.

"You better get out of here, before you end up in a stew."

She ran her hands over his downy face and kissed the top of his head before he trotted out of the kitchen door.

"Why can't he be in here?" said Matilda, turning back to her mother. "Nanna May has Genie in the house all the time."

"The bird is house-trained, that damn billy goat is not," said Lottie, throwing the crumbs into the sink.

Matilda frowned as she watched Lottie brush nonexistent crumbs off the front of the hideous black poncho she was wearing. It was like she even dressed to annoy Matilda.

A flash of red and brown swooped into the kitchen and darted in and out of the open windows as if to showcase just how much freedom it had in the cottage. The robin circled the room three times, then landed on its owner's shoulder as she shuffled in through the back door and headed straight for Matilda.

Matilda stiffened, averting her eyes from Nanna May's own milky ones, their corners crisscrossed with wisdom. Her hair was pinned on the top of her head in a smooth white knot like it always was, and her long skirt and cardigan trailed across the floor, their colors from the same palette as the robin.

She stopped in front of Matilda. If Matilda stood up, she'd tower over the old woman, but Nanna May didn't feel small when you were close to her. She hooked her gnarled fingers around Matilda's wrist and raised her hand until it was under her nose. She peered at it, shaking her head at the angry red bumps that covered Matilda's skin. Matilda pulled away and Nanna May inched over to the fireplace, where she took an age to lower herself onto the three-legged stool in front of it. She picked up the iron poker, looked at Matilda's mother, then turned to the flames burning by her feet.

"Is that . . . ?" Her mother walked over to Matilda, grabbed both her hands and frowned at them. "Nettle stings? Have you been at the hive, Matilda? Was it the queen? *Again?*"

"No," said Matilda angrily as she batted her mom's hand away and stood up.

"Don't lie to me, young lady! What have you got up your sleeve this time? I'm guessing it's nothing good?"

"Would you even believe me if I said it was?"

"Well, is it? Tell me, are you doing a spell to improve your concentration? Or maybe one of your classmates is unwell? Or maybe you're placing a blessing on this cottage?"

Matilda rolled her eyes. Why would she waste her time with magic to help people who ignore her when she could make them slowly lose their hair instead? Matilda smirked at the memory of Lauren McFadden freaking out as she brushed out clumps of hair in front of the mirror at school.

"For goodness' sake, Matilda, are you even listening to me? How many times?" Her mother opened a cabinet and picked out a small green bottle, then leaned over the sink and yanked leaves from the small pots collected on the windowsill, her anger punctuating the lecture with each plucked herb. "How many times do I have to go over this with you? You don't use death in magic. Whether it's a human or a horsefly, we respect life in our magic. You'd understand that so much more if you were part of a coven. You're nearly seventeen . . ."

"I didn't kill anything. Technically. It's still alive," said Matilda quickly, steering her mother away from *that* conversation about joining a coven. Again.

"And what is it this time?" said Lottie, grinding the leaves under a giant worn marble. "Lead in the school play? Time for a new best friend? Did someone dare to copy your haircut? What petty thing could possibly warrant you distressing those creatures in the middle of the autumn? It's a very simple rule: Never use magic to hurt another, physically or mentally, unless you want the name of your victim scarred on your face."

"But we can hide our scars." Matilda shrugged. "So why not have some fun with our magic?"

For the last three years, Matilda had been collecting the names of those she'd hurt with her magic like it was a hobby. It was fun coming up with creative ways to inflict pain or bring misfortune to her enemies, or just being popular for a few weeks. Unlike other witches, Matilda could do bad but keep the slate clean. Clean in the eyes of others, anyway.

Lottie pursed her lips and shook her head.

"This is exactly why you're not old enough for that spell." Matilda's shoulders slumped, ready for the weekly lecture. "Our bloodline was blessed with the gift to conceal our scars so we could move freely without judgment in a changing world, to give witches a second chance, not so you can use magic to curse your classmates on every whim. Your father had no right to give you that spell; you're clearly not mature enough for it."

"Nice to know what you think of me," said Matilda, folding her arms.

"You give me no choice to think anything else! It's all about balance; you do good, the universe sees that; you do bad, it's written on your face, whether we can see it or not."

Matilda felt like banging her head against the table. From the moment she was aware that Ferly Cottage was a home full of spells and incantations, she had been taught the rules her ancestors lived by and that she was expected to respect and embrace those rules. The first rule was simple: Use magic to cause pain or control the free will of another, and you'll get the name of your victim seared across your skin. Use magic to help others, to further your understanding of the craft, to keep maintaining the balance, and no harm will come to you.

But why have access to an ancient spell that meant every time you *did* use magic to hurt someone else, you could just erase the consequence from your face? Matilda didn't understand it. Why have the spell if it wasn't meant to be used?

"We don't need anything drawing attention to us, not with all those dead animals that keep showing up." A small line of worry appeared between Lottie's eyebrows as she looked at Nanna May. She shook her head and ran her hand from Nimbus's sour face all the way to her bush of a tail. "Cats this time, Nanna May. *Cats.* Plural."

"That's nothing to do with me," said Matilda, putting up her hands in surrender. She turned to Nanna May. "You don't think I would actually kill a cat, do you?"

"I'm not saying that, Matilda," said Lottie. "I'm just . . . unexplained animal death is never a good sign, not for us and not for nonwitches. My coven is rattled; they can feel something approaching, a poison blowing in the wind, and with Ivy's anniversary and Halloween coming up? This is a sacred time of year, and someone is tainting it with these animal deaths. One thing you can be certain of is that when things go wrong, people look for someone to blame, and nine times out of ten that someone will be female. That's how the whole mess with Ivy started in the first place. People around here would love an excuse to knock on that door and start throwing accusations around."

Matilda rolled her eyes again. "Nobody believes in witches anymore, Mother."

"You'd be surprised what people believe if they're desperate enough." Lottie shook her head and poured the ground leaves into the bottle using a copper funnel. "I haven't got time for this. I'm meeting someone." She plucked a strand of raven hair from her head, wrapped it around her finger, slipped it inside the bottle, then spat into it and stuck a cork in the top.

"Date with your precious coven?" said Matilda, folding her arms.

Lottie straightened up and smoothed down her clothes, her jaw clenched tight as she looked at Matilda. Matilda swallowed, reminded of the silence of the hive from earlier. Lottie walked across the kitchen, Nimbus trailing behind her ready for a show. Her mother peered at Matilda's face, seeing the names that weren't there.

"You need to show your magic, and your history, some respect. Stop with the schoolgirl spite before that face of yours is scarred beyond recognition. I may not be able to see it, but I know you, Matilda, I know what you have hidden there."

Lottie swept out of the kitchen, her heels click-clacking through the cottage as she left Matilda and Nanna May to stew in her anger. Matilda looked at the tiles beneath her feet, worn and dull from centuries of her bloodline going about their lives in the kitchen. Her mother could be fierce, but that was the longest conversation she'd had with her in months. The chasm that had grown between them since her dad left, had gotten so big that Matilda didn't have the energy to cross it, and Lottie had stopped holding her hands out to reach over to Matilda anyway. Lottie was so lost inside a daily whirlwind of being a good daughter to Nanna May and a supportive member of her coven that being a mom had fallen down the cracks somewhere.

Matilda turned to Nanna May and stuck out her chin.

"Thanks for sticking up for me," she said. Her grandmother raised an eyebrow, then lifted the poker to tend to her fire. "You know it wasn't me who killed those cats, don't you? You know I couldn't hurt anything like that."

Her grandmother's eyes flicked down to Matilda's stomach, then back up to her face.

"I already said; I didn't kill it. She's still crawling around." Matilda glanced down. "Just . . . in my stomach. It's just a bee, Nanna; they fly around annoying people."

Nanna May frowned at Matilda, then looked at Genie.

"You know what I mean. I'd never hurt Genie, either. Or a cat."

"Wicked Tilly," whispered Nanna May as she watched the flames lick around the poker.

"I told you, Nanna May," sighed Matilda as she bent down and kissed her grandmother's silky hair. "Please don't call me that."

Matilda pulled a chunk from the loaf and went to dip it in the pot on the fire, but Nanna May slapped her hand and shook her head. Matilda shoved the bread in her mouth and rubbed her hand, watching Nanna May pull the petals from a chamomile flower growing in a basket above the fireplace and throw them into the bubbling liquid.

"How can you cook something that smells so delicious and not want to share it with your favorite granddaughter?" Nanna May rolled her eyes, then pointed at the cuckoo clock. She took a pinch of ground cumin from a pestle and mortar and sprinkled it in, too. "I know I'm your only granddaughter, but you know what I mean. When's it going to be ready, then? You've been cooking it forever."

A soft padding sound whispered from the back door and a fat, bark-colored toad waddled across the threshold of the kitchen. Matilda felt her grandmother's shoulders tense, and she blinked at the brazen amphibian crawling over the tiles like he'd been invited for breakfast. Nanna May pulled herself up from the stool and reached for the broomstick leaning by the fireplace.

Matilda sighed and picked up her schoolbag. Next, Nanna May would sweep the toad back into the cold, then spend the rest of the morning picking the herbs and spices she needed to make talismans they'd all have to put under their pillows.

"Good luck, Nanna May," said Matilda, leaving the old lady gently sweeping the toad out of the door, along with any bad luck it had brought with it.

CHAPTER TWO

A green-and-orange banner flapped high above the tables in the cafeteria, black swirled writing reminding students of the Witching Well Festival at the end of the month. Matilda frowned at the banner as she carried her tray across the room. The town started stringing shop fronts with orange bunting and dressing in dark green cloaks as soon as October blew in after the dregs of September summer. It was the only time Gravewick was mildly interesting, bringing people from miles around to take part in the Halloween festival, so there was no chance it wasn't already on people's social radars.

Matilda waited at the end of the table she'd been sitting at for the last few weeks, its occupants turning to look down their nose at her as she smiled at them. They all turned as Ashley Abercrombie sashayed into the cafeteria, her name rippling across the tables in the hushed way it always did. She joined her group at the table in the middle where Matilda was sitting, the perfect stage for her adoring audience, and flicked her blond hair over her shoulder. She surveyed her subjects at the table, her eyes resting on Matilda.

"Why are you sitting at my table, exactly?"

Just to make sure my spell is deserved, thought Matilda. She shrugged and offered Ashley a smile.

"Just having lunch."

"Sorry, are we still friends?" said Ashley, folding her arms. "That was so last week, before you stopped being supportive; I don't need that kind of negativity around me."

Matilda remembered watching Ashley twirl around and around in a new jacket, demanding Matilda tell her whether it was making the right statement. Matilda, who had decided that even a little conjured popularity and companionship wasn't worth the mind-numbing tediousness of hanging around Insta-ready Ashley, told her that it did, if the statement was *I have no taste*.

"I'm over you now," said Ashley, looking Matilda up and down. "Maybe you should go and sit with your friends over there."

Matilda looked at the table Ashley was pointing at. "There's nobody there?"

"Exactly," sneered Ashley, putting her hands out so her minions could tap her palms.

Matilda heaved a sigh for the audience and sat at the table alone just as Sean walked into the room toward Ashley and her disciples. A toothpaste-ad smile gleamed from Sean's perfect jaw, punctuated by two dimples as he slapped the outstretched palms of his soccer teammates and made his way to Ashley, who was pseudo-ignoring him.

Matilda had always assumed Sean was like the rest of the idiot soccer players at her school—bravado and cruelty tied up with a ribbon of cheekbones and swagger. But they'd been paired up on a history assignment the year before, and after spending a few weeks working so closely, Matilda realized she'd been wrong about him.

Instead of kicking back and letting Matilda do all the work, he'd been really proactive about the project they were doing, which was, ironically, on the Salem witch trials. Sean had shown a real interest in the subject and divided up the research between them, then recounted some of the shocking things he'd found with wide eyes. One day, he even broke away from a group of his friends to give Matilda his own copy of one of the books he'd found on the trials. Matilda blushed as he made her promise to read it and let him know what she thought.

For those few weeks, she felt like she was the most important thing in Sean's world. Something was happening to Matilda's insides as she and Sean worked next to each other in the library or Sean hurried after her in the cafeteria, gesticulating as he recounted what he'd read about Samuel Parris or Bridget Bishop. When Sean had turned around in class and high-fived her with one hand while holding up their A-grade assignment in the other, she realized she'd fallen for him. No magic, no potions, just some other ingredient Matilda had never understood.

Why? thought Matilda, her stomach bubbling with anger as she watched Sean heading for Ashley. *Why her?* But Matilda knew why. She knew that like was attracted to like, and Sean, with his perfect, just, *everything*, was the king and Ashley was the queen.

The queen bee.

Matilda lifted her hand to her mouth, a blond strand of Ashley's hair curled around her forefinger. Her father had taught her sleight of hand and the art of distraction, which, he had told her long ago, were necessary when you lived by incantations and spells. Matilda could snatch a strand of hair or whip off a charm bracelet better than the Artful Dodger. With her hand still in front of her mouth, Matilda breathed deeply until everyone fell away from the cafeteria, leaving Ashley sitting in her spotlight.

"Climb from within; my pain is yours," she whispered. The scene

came back to life, and Matilda let out a whistle of breath as she rearranged the contents of her tray, glancing up at Ashley every few seconds. Ashley was front and center at the table, her followers hanging on to her every vapid word as she used her own brand of magic on them. *I love your hair like that; do mine for me? Or I love your winged eyeliner; do my makeup for me?* And *I love your jacket; lend it to me?* At first it felt like you were the center of her world, but you soon realized everything she said and did was for her own benefit.

Having Ashley as a friend had been a good move to start with. It was a thrill when she looped her arm through Matilda's and shared all the latest hookups as they strutted down the halls together. When Matilda watched Ashley rehearse for the school play or run around the soccer field in center midfield, she'd felt proud to be in her circle, even if she'd put herself there using magic.

As the weeks went by, though, Matilda grew tired of following Ashley around. The girl was an overachiever and insisted on dragging Matilda along to every extracurricular activity she'd signed up for, from philosophy club to musical theater. Rather than wanting a friend, all Ashley wanted was more audience members in the Ashley Adoration Society. Matilda was going to end the enchantment with a snuff of a flame, but then Ashley had gone and turned her attention to the one person Matilda felt something real for.

Sean.

Ashley kept looking over her shoulder at Sean before turning away, leaving him shaking his head and biting down a smile. Their blatant attraction made Matilda's skin crawl with rage until Ashley cleared her throat and held her manicured fingers in front of her lips. She frowned, then turned to her neighbor and opened her mouth to say something, but started coughing like a middle-aged mechanic after a pack of Marlboros.

Here it comes, thought Matilda. The first time she'd used magic to hurt someone she'd been a little nervous, but now all she felt was a rush of excitement that her words and actions could have a devastating effect on someone else. Once she'd mastered the spell to hide her scars, there was nothing in the world that wasn't there for her to take for herself.

Lottie tried to steer her down a path of natural magic with no consequences or pain; potions for predictions, spells for healing, incantations for protection, even talismans to ward off the common cold. What Matilda was doing now was way more powerful, but she could hear her mother inside her head. *Use your magic to hurt another, and you'll know that pain threefold with each letter scored into your skin.* Although Matilda could hide her scars, that part was true—she could still feel the pain of each name hidden on her face and carried that pain around day and night.

"Ash? You okay, babe?" one of Ashley's friends asked as she patted her on the back.

Ashley thrust her chair back, her face as pale as the moon, her wide eyes boring into her friend's. The coughing stopped, and her chin wobbled as she sucked in some air.

"I . . . I . . . there's something . . . something . . . UUUUH!!!"

Ashley's hand slammed against the table, crashing the cutlery and plates together. The screech of chairs scraping against the floor pierced through the chatter in the cafeteria, sending all that was normal exiting through the doors as everyone around Ashley backed away from her. She clutched her throat and wretched over the table, her bulging eyes pink and glassy with panic.

A smile twitched at Matilda's lips as she threw fries into her mouth like she was eating popcorn. Seeing Ashley, who was normally so poised and superior, hunched over the table, confused and scared, made Matilda's dark little heart sing with joy.

Sean watched Ashley, his mouth turned downward like he was looking at a slug writhing under a shower of salt. Ashley's body twisted against the table, her face as red as a stoplight, and she retched over and over, clawing her throat until the saliva-soaked thing that was choking her freed itself and flew from her mouth.

A bee. The queen bee.

Nobody moved until a couple of the girls at Ashley's table jumped up and ran out, Matilda guessed to either throw up themselves or get a teacher. Everyone else had frozen in their seats, staring with wide eyes and stomach-curdling disgust as Ashley wiped away the saliva dripping from her chin.

She lifted a shuddering hand to her swelling lips and blinked at her audience. "What . . . what the f . . . ?" she gasped, tears clinging to her long lashes. "What's happening to . . . UUUHH!"

Ashley's white knuckles gripped the edge of the table, her body doubling over as she heaved again, splattering more bees over the lunchtime leftovers. She blinked at the wriggling insects crawling over one another, then her eyes rolled up into her head and she slumped to the floor. The cafeteria gasped, then chairs scraped back and Ashley's remaining disciples ran to her side, while others pulled out their phones to start the gossip that would accompany the photos being taken by people who stared, open-mouthed.

Matilda wiped the grease from her hands and spun around in her chair. She picked up her bag and walked with a spring in her step in the opposite direction from Ashley and her insect vomit. The spring became a skip and then a jog as pain burned up from her soul, heading for her face, and she grabbed the doorway and swung herself into the corridor, bumping into bodies and tripping over feet.

"Move! *Get out of my way!*" she shouted, angry that she hadn't headed to the bathroom sooner.

Matilda squeezed her eyes closed as the first letter tore into her skin. *A* for *Ashley*. She gritted her teeth with each stroke of the letter, then clenched her fists as the agony of the letter *S* started. Matilda could feel her skin splitting open as she weaved between the oncoming traffic, desperate to lock herself in a cubicle before the rest of the letters could form, but she slammed into a lanky senior as he turned from his locker.

"Whoa, sorry," he said as they stepped side to side to get past each other.

"Out of my way," growled Matilda, the letter *H* cutting into her skin and ridding her of all patience.

"I am *trying* to get out of your way. Okay, stop," said Lanky Boy. He put his hands on her shoulders and she looked up, surprised at the uninvited touch. He was hunched over, used to lowering himself down to talk to normal-sized people, and his bouncy hair was brushed forward and coordinated perfectly with his honey-brown eyes. "I'll go this way, and you go . . . shit. I mean, you're *bleeding*. Do you know you're bleeding? Like, really bleeding, a lot."

Matilda's hand flew up to her cheek. The magic that concealed her scars couldn't hide the letters when they first appeared in her skin. As with everything else in magic, it was all about balance and consequence, and that was the price she paid for the gift. Others might not know what she'd done, but she would feel the pain of it.

"Yeah, I . . . ," Matilda said, her eyes darting around. She spotted the girls' bathroom and looked at the boy, the color draining from his face as he stared at the blood on her cheek. "I'm okay, I . . ."

Lanky Boy took a step back and closed his eyes, his face the same color as the gray walls of Gravewick Academy. He breathed deeply, then opened his eyes again, letting them rest on Matilda's face. After a second, he shook his head and put his hand over his mouth.

"Sorry!" he called over his shoulder as he ran into the boys' bathroom.

Matilda bit the inside of her cheek as another letter appeared, and she rushed into the bathroom herself, her hand over her cheek in case any of the mirror-worshipping girls were in their usual spot, contouring nonexistent cheekbones and smaller noses. Her shoulders relaxed as the door closed behind her; the entire room was vacant.

Matilda lowered her hand and surveyed the damage as the rest of the letters claimed her face. Her winged eyeliner was still flawless and her curly black hair flowed over her shoulders, but the flickering light and the blood pouring from the fresh letters on her face made her look like an extra from a horror movie.

The harsh bathroom light blinked in Morse code, telling her *I know what's on your face.*

"No, you don't. Nobody knows," she said to the light. "Nobody except me."

Was it worth it? asked the light.

"Yes," she said. "She deserved it."

For once in her life, Ashley would know what it was like to feel out of control, to not fix a problem by clicking her fingers and having someone else sort it out for her. She would know that bad things happen to bad people and how it feels to have everyone recoil from her instead of worshipping her for a change.

Matilda grabbed a pile of paper towels and soaked them in cold water. She wiped the evidence away, watching her blood swirl down the drain. But what was left on her face would take more than paper and water to get rid of. Retrieving a small green bottle from her bag, Matilda held it up to the light; there wasn't much left, she'd have to brew a fresh batch before next time.

The contents of the bottle, made up of dandelion leaf, goldenrod, peppermint, and lavender, plus a drop of Matilda's blood and a snip of her hair, was the same brown color as most potions, but it was the most powerful and life-changing Matilda had ever used. She looked over her shoulder again, then unscrewed the bottle and took three small, sour sips, then turned back to the mirror. Focusing on her reflection, Matilda licked her finger and trailed the tip of it across Ashley's name, then put her hands over her face and whispered the charm like she had done so many times before.

"What is here I cannot see, what is here I can feel. Take this name and triple my pain so others may not know."

When Matilda looked up, there was a different reflection staring back at her, one whose secrets were hidden away beneath perfectly smooth skin. She felt a tickle in her throat and, remembering her visit to the hive earlier, she coughed a few times and caught the soggy queen bee in the palm of her other hand.

"Thank you," she said, letting it crawl onto the open window.

Matilda stepped away from the mirror, ready to tolerate the halls of Gravewick Academy once again. But when she lifted her hand to push the door open, she felt as though a weight was pulling her down and a cloud of smoke swirled in front of her eyes, consuming the light around her. She fell onto the white tiles of the bathroom floor and deep into the sudden darkness inside her head.

CHAPTER THREE

"Hello? *Hello?*"

Matilda blinked and recoiled, her body shockingly tense after being submerged in pitch-black. It wasn't the voice that had woken her, but the palm that slapped her cheek, and she twitched, ready for another one as she pulled herself up onto her elbows.

"Who's slapping me?" she demanded, the fog lifting from her eyes as she squinted at the person kneeling over her. "How am I on the floor?"

"Oh, good."

"*Good?*" repeated Matilda incredulously.

"Yes, I mean, good that you're okay. I thought you were unconscious or dead or—"

Matilda put her hand up and the girl raised her eyebrows and stopped talking.

"Erin," sighed Matilda. Of all the people to slap her awake, it had to be Erin, ex-best friend and relentless interrogator.

Erin sat back on her heels and frowned. "Yes, *Erin*. Not exactly your fave, but would you rather I'd left you on the floor?"

Matilda glared at Erin, a mess of freckles and red curls hovering just above her.

"Was the slap really necessary?"

"Like I said, I thought you might be dead. I was just about to call someone, but you woke up. Are you okay? What happened? Did you hit your head?"

Matilda rubbed her eyes. That was it; Ashley, then the blood, then the mirror, then the floor. She'd blacked out.

"How long was I out?" asked Matilda, her body feeling as though it were transparent, a part of her disappearing.

Erin shrugged. "Since I came in? Two, three minutes maybe? I thought it was the same as what happened to Ashley just now." Matilda started getting up, ignoring Erin's outstretched hand. "Did you see? She coughed up a *bee*, and then she collapsed. Mrs. Murphy and Mr. Gill are still trying to clear everyone out of the cafeteria before the whole thing ends up on YouTube. Is she okay?"

"Is who okay?" asked Matilda, brushing off her tights. She stood up straight, turning in front of the mirror to check if there was toilet paper stuck to the elbow of her maroon-and-gold school blazer.

"Ashley," Erin repeated.

Matilda smoothed her hair down and shrugged as she looked in the mirror. Satisfied there were no traces of blood smeared on her face, she turned back to Erin.

"How should I know?"

Erin frowned. "I thought you were . . . I mean, aren't you two best friends? I've seen you hanging out together a lot."

A smile twitched at the corner of Matilda's mouth.

"I wouldn't say we were *best* friends."

"Oh. Well, I saw the ambulance arrive, so I guess she'll be okay." Erin picked up her bag and slung it over her shoulder. "Have you fainted before?"

Matilda looked at herself in the mirror. Was that what had just happened? She'd always imagined fainting to be gentler, something you wouldn't be aware of. The shadow she just fell into had more intent, like it was coming to get her, to take something.

"No," she said, then turned to Erin. "I'm fine now. You can go."

"Actually, I . . ."

"Actually, you what?" said Matilda. "I appreciate you waking me up, but this doesn't mean we're friends again, Erin."

Erin folded her arms. "Actually, I still haven't used the facilities, so I'd like to go if that's quite all right with you, your royal highness of the girls' bathroom. And you're welcome, by the way. I could have left you lying on the floor for the freshmen to trip over. I wish I had now."

Typical Erin response, thought Matilda as she picked up her bag from the floor. They'd first met one rainy lunchtime in the school library. The last Percy Jackson book had finally been returned, but just as Matilda reached out for it on the shelf, another small hand grabbed it from right under her nose. After much arguing and mediation from the librarian, Matilda and Erin had agreed to read it together. They met every lunchtime, where they settled down on beanbags, waiting for the other to nod when it was time to turn the page. Their heads got closer and closer as they read, both gasping and crying at the same parts. When they'd finished, they kept meeting to discuss the series and draw terrible fan art together.

That was pre-scars and before her father left. Now it was safer not to get close to anyone. In Matilda's world, there was no place for friendships that weren't created in a cauldron.

"Yeah, thanks a million," said Matilda, turning to leave.

"Matilda?"

"What now?" she sighed.

"What happened?" asked Erin, gently shaking her head as she looked deep into Matilda's eyes.

Matilda frowned at her, then rolled her eyes. "We're not doing this again, are we?" she said, folding her arms. "Like I've already told you, we just grew apart. That happens sometimes." She opened the door to escape, but Erin stepped in front of her.

"Not you and me; I gave up wondering why you suddenly stopped being my friend ages ago. I mean, what happened to *you*? Why are you so . . . mean?"

Matilda looked back at Erin and could feel herself falling back to a few years ago, when they would have been catching up or making plans in front of these mirrors. Matilda looked away before she fell too far and checked her reflection in the mirror again. She shrugged and stepped around Erin through the door.

"Just lucky I guess," said Matilda, stretching a smile across her face.

As soon as the door slammed behind her, the smile dropped from her face and she hugged her arms across her chest. Seeing Erin always rattled her, but waking up on the bathroom floor had sent her into an internal spin. Matilda had dealt out enough dark magic to know what it felt like when someone was trying to take something from you, and as she walked down the halls of Grave-wick Academy she was sure she felt a loss in the pit of her soul.

The bus rumbled off in a cloud of exhaust fumes and prepubescent and pre-Halloween squeals. The sun was nearly down, preparing for the clocks to go back in a couple of weeks by casting the sky with a glorious pink-and-orange glow. Matilda welcomed the cold as it sterilized the stale air from the bus, but pulled her coat around her.

She breathed in, savoring the smell of autumn. Fires burned as people arrived home and peeled off their woolly hats and scarves, and the fallen leaves wafted up their earthy smell as Matilda kicked through them on her way to Ferly Cottage. If the wind blew just right, she was certain she could smell the spiced apples stewing on her grandmother's stove, ready to be enveloped inside a delicious piecrust. The smells, the tastes, and the magic Halloween would bring were all reasons why this was Matilda's favorite time of year.

Nimbus crept out from between the skeletal branches of a hedge and sat in the middle of the path.

"What have you been up to?" asked Matilda as she stroked the cat's fur. Nimbus lifted a paw to clean herself and a gray feather floated to the ground. "Hunting, hey? I wouldn't be surprised if it was you killing all those other cats."

Nimbus turned and slinked ahead, her tail and bottom high in the air. Matilda followed the cat around a wrought iron gate and down a path speckled with shadows and crunchy leaves, her shoulders relaxing as she walked beneath the arch of a yew hedge. The garden's aroma massaged her soul. She could walk home wearing a blindfold and still find the garden gate just by following her nose.

Lottie was always telling her not to use the back door like "some sort of stray," but Matilda loved coming home this way. The overgrown yard was a chaotic explosion of flora and fauna, and a rust-colored palette of pumpkins and squash lined the edge of the cottage, harvested and arranged by her grandmother as soon as October arrived. Stepping-stones led across the grass to the back door of the crooked cottage and Matilda's favorite room:

the kitchen. Her stomach growled as she imagined what her grandmother had been baking in the giant green range while she was at school, but her feet paused over the stone as the window flickered with light and she saw her mother sweeping back and forth.

Nanna May will bring me something later, Matilda thought as she crossed the grass away from the kitchen and her mother. The bubbling pond and singing toads welcomed her home as she passed the basil for salads and belladonna for spells in Nanna May's herb garden. She rounded the back of the cottage, then followed the gravel pathway that was lined with daffodils in the spring and dandelions in the summer.

"Hey, little buddy," she said, crouching down and fussing over Victor as he trotted out of the shadows in the woods. "Missed me today?" He bleated and Matilda smiled. "I know. Me too."

Victor followed Matilda to a cream-colored garden room nestled between naked cherry trees, two flickering pumpkins on either side of the door. As she put her hand on the doorknob, a timer clicked and hundreds of lights blinked on, strung around the roof of the garden room and spiraling around the tree trunks.

Her mother had always encouraged her to spend time in the building to connect with the energy around her, and Matilda soon felt more comfortable being in the garden room among the trees and the wildlife than anywhere else in her life. She often fell asleep on the floor while she read her grandmother's books about magic, so she brought out a beanbag and a lamp so she could read into the night. One day she walked in and the daybed was there, a clear message from Lottie that if Matilda would rather be out in the garden room and away from the family home, then she didn't have a problem with it.

Matilda opened the door and turned on the lamp, smiling as Victor's hooves thumped on the wooden floor toward his cushion at the foot of Matilda's bed. Matilda dropped the blinds on the four windows at the back of the large octagonal room, leaving the ones at the front open, then fell onto the beanbag. She pulled out her phone and checked the last message she'd sent her dad, and sent a smiley face just in case he'd missed it the first time. She smiled as three dots appeared on her screen, then settled down into the beanbag, but the dots disappeared, leaving the deranged yellow smiley staring up at her.

"Let's see what they're saying about Ashley instead, shall we, Vic?" she sighed. Everyone who'd ever come into contact with Ashley had posted their concern and well wishes for her on the school social site. Matilda shook her head as she read. "They're going on about her like she's dead."

She drank in the gossip and photos of Ashley and noted the lack of Sean's presence on any of the posts, when a message popped up from an unknown sender.

Hey. Wanted to say sorry for earlier.

Matilda frowned as she peered at the tiny avatar of a boy staring at her, holding a red Solo cup up to the camera, then replied.

Who is this? Sorry for what?

Oliver. For nearly throwing up all over you. Don't like blood.

Matilda's eyebrows twitched up as she realized Oliver was the boy from the hallway earlier. She sat back and frowned. Had she dabbed an ointment on this Oliver and forgotten about it? She didn't remember doing a love spell recently, certainly not on him. She tapped on his photo. *Oliver Tillsbury.* She squinted at the enlarged image, her pulse quickening and her cheeks warming as she studied his features. How had she not noticed him before?

Oh yeah, right! No worries, had forgotten all about it.

She held her breath, but another message pinged up almost immediately.

Good to know I made an impression.

She pulled her knees up and quickly ran her eyes over his message again, then typed a response.

Ha ha, yeah.

Buy you a coffee tomorrow to make it up to you?

Matilda held her phone to her chest and looked out of the window. Was this a joke? She couldn't see anyone outside waiting to pounce on her for believing someone wanted to ask her out unprompted by magic, so she looked back down and replied.

Coffee?

Yeah, before school?

How do I know you're not going to vomit on me?

Matilda pressed send, then bit her lip.

I can't guarantee anything but I'm hoping there won't be blood this time.

Ha ha. Ok, where?

Grounds? 8.15?

Ok. See you then.

"What the *hell* have you been up to?" hissed a voice from the doorway. Matilda dropped her phone and looked up as Lottie stormed into the garden room, cheeks red and her eyes burning.

"Don't you knock?"

Her mother bent down in front of Matilda like she was addressing a toddler. "Let me handle this, understand?"

"Handle what?" said Matilda, frowning at her mom, then looking up as two police officers crunched up the gravel pathway.

"What the . . . ?"

"Here she is," said Lottie, a smile slapped onto her face as she spun around to greet the two officers.

"Thank you, Mrs. Hollowell," said the man.

"Actually it's Ms., but please, call me Lottie."

"What's going on?" asked Matilda.

"Matilda, I'm Officer Powell and this is Officer Seymour. We'd like to ask you a few questions, if that's okay?" said the female officer.

"Am I under arrest?"

Her mother put a firm hand on Matilda's shoulder but kept her voice light. "Why on earth would you be under arrest, you silly thing. They just want to talk to you."

Officer Seymour looked at Victor, who was still curled up on his cushion, then turned to Officer Powell and raised his eyebrows. Matilda stroked the goat's head and blinked at them.

"Do you like animals, Matilda?" asked Officer Seymour.

Would I have a goat in my room if I didn't like animals, Sherlock? she thought, frowning at them. Her mother nudged the beanbag with her foot and Matilda stood up.

"Yeah, I guess so. Why?"

"I'm sure you're aware there's been a spate of animal deaths in recent weeks? Rabbits, cats, that sort of thing?" Matilda glanced at her mom, who nodded, cuing Matilda to nod, too. "Well, I'm afraid there has been an unfortunate incident at the farm down on Thickthorn Lane."

"Thickthorn Lane? You mean Blossom Farm?" her mother asked, then sat down on the bed as the officers nodded. She looked between the two of them and put her hand on her chest. "An incident? Was someone hurt?"

Matilda swallowed. "Yeah, what kind of incident?"

Officer Seymour hooked his thumbs on either side of his vest. "A number of cows were found slaughtered."

Matilda looked at Lottie. Being honest with her mom didn't come easily, but when she'd said she had nothing to do with the cats that were killed, she'd been telling the truth. Now it was cows, too? Her mom's words from that morning echoed inside Matilda's head.

Unexplained animal death is never a good sign, not for us and not for nonwitches.

"How many?" asked Lottie.

Officer Seymour cleared his throat. "More than twenty."

Matilda swallowed, hoping that the image of twenty slaughtered cows in a field wouldn't hang around for bedtime.

"So, was it a fox or something? I mean, don't they have dogs on that farm? Rottweilers? Could they have done it?"

Officer Powell shook her head. "Unfortunately, they were found dead, too."

"I'm sorry. I mean, that *is* terrible news, but I don't understand what it has to do with my daughter?" Lottie said, looking confused.

The police officers looked at each other, neither wanting to upset the pretty lady.

"Well," said Officer Powell, taking a deep breath, "the carcasses, all of them, had a name carved into their sides."

"What name?" asked Lottie, her mouth tight.

The officers looked at each other and then spoke in unison.

"Matilda."

CHAPTER FOUR

Fifteen days until Halloween

Matilda yawned and checked the time again: 5:38 a.m.

The police had insisted on leaving them to get some sleep, but that was the exact opposite of what Matilda had done. She lay in bed all night as questions fired off in her head. Who'd killed those animals? Why had she blacked out? Would it happen again? Were the animals and her blackout a coincidence? Something in the pit of her stomach told her she was deluded if she thought so. Finally, she decided if she was awake, she might as well make the most of it and get ready for her coffee with Oliver.

Although it was a struggle unfurling herself from her warm bed, Matilda was glad to be out before everyone else had even thought about waking up and the time still belonged to the witches. She tightened her scarf and tucked it inside her coat to keep out the premorning chill as the distant bleats of deer, the gentle beep of midwife toads, and the smell of burning leaves made her feel like she was the only person in the audience of the best show in the world.

She tucked a book of spells under her arm and made her way down the path to Ferly Cottage in search of some extra ingredients. The last couple of days had been unpredictable to say the least, so she wanted to make sure her meeting with Oliver went exactly as she wanted it to, and since she'd lost interest in Ashley she needed a new distraction. She'd found some ginseng and cinnamon in her own stash, but needed catnip and basil. Her mother was bound to have catnip in the larder for Nimbus, and there wasn't an herb in the world she couldn't find in Nanna May's garden.

The frost-covered gravel crunched beneath her feet until she reached the back door. She unclicked the handle and hurried in, the warmth from the stove and the fire doubling up to warm her inside and out. She put the spell book on the counter and turned to the larder just as a lantern flame on the kitchen table flickered to life, illuminating six sets of blinking eyes.

"Shit," hissed Matilda, pressing her hand to her chest. "Sneaky much?"

"I think you'll find it's you doing the sneaking, Tilly. And don't swear in the kitchen," said her mother, watching Matilda along with the other members of her coven. "What are you up to?"

Matilda looked at the coven members sitting in their kitchen, glaring at each of them nursing mugs of herbal tea, their faces as familiar as Matilda's own family members. There were five of them sitting with her mother at the table, as different from one another as strangers waiting for a bus, but all of them women and all with the knowing look of someone who could see the magic in the world with every one of their senses.

They'd bounced Matilda on their laps when she was a toddler or dabbed coconut oil on her grazed knee, but the resentment she felt toward them since they pushed her dad away meant she could barely contain her disdain for them.

"Where's Nanna May?"

"Don't ignore my question, Matilda," snapped Lottie, getting up and reaching for the spell book. Matilda snatched it back and held it to her chest. "What are you up to?"

"Nothing, why?"

"Why? Because you're sneaking around before sunrise clutching a spell book and the police were here last night asking questions about dead animals, that's why."

"I told you," sighed Matilda, trying to cover her own concerns with bravado. "That's nothing to do with me. I don't know how those cows got hurt."

"Not hurt, Matilda, *killed*. With your name on them. There's something going on. We can feel it," said Lottie, looking around at her coven members.

"Why can't you accept it's nothing to do with me? The police did."

As the words left Matilda's lips, she knew that she was addressing herself as much as her mother. Between checking the time and rearranging her pillow all night, Matilda's thoughts kept drifting back to her name carved into those cows. Somehow, she was involved in their deaths, even if she didn't understand why.

"After we left you, I had to give them one of Nanna May's brews so they'd forget why they were here and leave! You're not just brushing this off, Matilda. We don't like using potions on people without their knowledge."

"So, I'm not allowed to use magic to solve my problems, but it's fine for you to use it to get rid of yours?" muttered Matilda.

"What did you say?" said Lottie, folding her arms.

Matilda sighed. "Nothing. Can I go now? I've got stuff to do."

Lottie pursed her lips and nodded. Matilda grabbed the catnip from the larder, then swung through the doorway, letting the door slam behind her, and headed for Nanna May's herbs in search of basil. Around the corner, just past the herb garden, she could see the hunched figure of her grandmother shuffling around with a garden fork nearly as big as she was. A small fire glowed at her feet, and Matilda realized where the smell of burning leaves had come from.

Nanna May dropped the fork and threw a handful of tiny seeds into the fire, peering at the flames crackling at her feet. Matilda smiled as she watched her. The seeds she'd thrown into the fire were pumpkin seeds—Nanna May would chew them first, then spit them into the fire in the kitchen and wait for them to ping out onto the floor. Lottie had banned her from doing it inside after one had hit Nimbus in the eye.

After a few seconds, one of the pumpkin seeds leaped out of the fire and landed at Nanna May's feet. The old lady bent down to retrieve it, and Matilda hurried to her side and picked it up, then dropped it in the soil-lined palm of her grandmother. There was another faint snap, then another and another, and Matilda gathered the seeds up and handed them to Nanna May.

"What are you looking for, Nanna May?" asked Matilda as she looped her arm through her grandmother's and escorted her to the pond.

Nanna May took one of the seeds and threw it into the water. Matilda watched the water ripple out in circles as the seed hit the surface. Nanna May threw another in, her eyebrows drawing together and mouth moving silently. She bit her lip as she shook her head, then turned to Matilda.

"What's it say? What did you see this time?" asked Matilda.

According to Lottie, Nanna May was blessed with divination, a fairly common gift among witches. Matilda had always been respectful toward her grandmother and her belief that she could see the future, but deep down she thought the predictions were more likely just coincidences. Still, she looked at Nanna May with what she hoped was eager anticipation as the old woman clutched Matilda's hand and turned to her.

"Wicked Tilly," she whispered, the words sending a trail down Matilda's spine. Nanna May grabbed Matilda's other hand and looked at the pond, shaking her head as her eyes zigzagged over the surface like she was reading a message. She looked at Matilda again, her eyes grave. "Wicked Tilly."

Matilda squeezed Nanna May's hands and offered her a tight smile.

"What have I told you, Nanna? Please don't call me that."

Nanna May let go of Matilda's hands and reached inside her duffle coat. Matilda looked at the horizon; if she was going to get her spell done by sunrise, she'd need to wrap this up and get back to her garden room. Matilda tried to retreat, but Nanna May gripped her tighter, then pulled an embroidered handkerchief out of her coat. She pursed her lips and tried to tie a knot in it.

Matilda kissed Nanna May on the forehead, then backed away from her, smiling as the old woman's eyes widened and she gestured at the almost knot in the handkerchief, holding it up so Matilda knew who it was intended for.

"You know I love you, Nanna May, but I don't want your used handkerchief, even it does keep evil spirits away," said Matilda, picking some basil from the herb garden. "Got to go now, got to get ready for a date. Wish me luck."

Matilda bounced down the path and blew Nanna May a kiss, smiling at the old woman still holding out her handkerchief. As soon as she rounded the corner, the smile dropped from her face and she wondered what her grandmother had seen in the ripples in the pond. A gust of wind sent a hush through the trees, and Matilda nodded to herself, deciding that maybe, just in case, she'd make a protection charm. One that didn't involve carrying around a secondhand handkerchief.

CHAPTER FIVE

Grounds was quiet apart from the steady stream of customers with bloodshot eyes who couldn't start their morning without caffeine, so Matilda felt right at home after her night of zero sleep. She drank the dregs of her cappuccino, then checked in her phone to make sure there wasn't a foamy mustache sitting on her lip.

Matilda had tried to put the visit from the police and her early morning clash with her mother out of her mind by throwing herself into choosing an appropriate hairstyle and accessories for her meeting with Oliver, but thoughts of dead cows and cats kept bubbling through the piles of discarded scarves, along with a question that she just couldn't seem to silence.

What if it was me?

She shook it away, trying to drown it in more important thoughts like who she would have to mess with to guarantee a position as prefect next term, and how could she get a place on the French exchange trip when she didn't even take French. Then Grounds's door tinkled and Matilda looked up as Oliver walked in, and there was another, important, thought.

Is he worth the potion I got up before sunrise to make?

Oliver pushed the bouncy hair back from his forehead as he scanned the tables. Matilda straightened up and fiddled with the empty sugar pot on the table, keeping her eyes on him. He bit his bottom lip and walked over to her table, ducking beneath the same dangling bats and orange and green streamers that were hanging from every shop ceiling in Gravewick. Hands behind his back, he bent down and narrowed his eyes as he inspected her face. Matilda held her breath as his aftershave and the fabric softener from his pillow floated between them.

"Nope," he said, straightening up and grinning at her. "No blood today. I think we're both safe."

"Guess so," said Matilda, her shoulders relaxing.

He looked at her cup and his face dropped. "You've already ordered? I was supposed to buy that for you."

"I had a late night." Matilda shrugged. "You can buy me another?"

Oliver beamed at her, and Matilda was glad she was sitting down. *What a smile. Dimple to dimple*, she thought, wiping her clammy palms on her thighs.

"What are you having?"

"Um, I'll have another cappuccino, please."

"Cappuccino number two, coming right up," said Oliver, walking over to the counter.

Matilda watched him order their drinks in the reflection of the coffee-shop window and put her hand in her blazer pocket, curling her fingers around the glass bottle that was concealed inside it. Oliver came back from the counter and sat down next to her.

"She's going to bring them over," he said, gesturing to the woman behind the counter.

"Cool, thanks."

"You're very welcome, Matilda."

If he doesn't stop smiling at me, I think my heart is going to explode out of my throat, which will not be good because he doesn't like blood, she thought, breaking their eye contact as she tucked her hair behind her ear. She glanced back at him; he was *still* smiling at her.

"So," she said.

"So," he said, his smile getting wider.

"Um." She tapped her fingers against the side of her cup, then looked at him. "You're a senior, right?"

"Yeah," he said, nodding. "What about you?"

"Junior," said Matilda, shifting in the chair and putting her hand back in her pocket. "So . . . are you new? I mean, I don't think I've seen you before?"

Oliver shook his head. "No. I mean, yes, I'm new to the school, but I started in September. We moved here in the summer but only from Landford. I live on Gallon Street, by the lake?"

Matilda nodded. Nanna May had told her that Gallon Street's original name was Three Gallows, after three witches were hanged there, but the name was changed so people would buy houses and real estate agents could make a fortune.

"How about you?" said Oliver.

"How about me, what?"

"Where do you live?" he asked.

"Oh, right," Matilda said, cringing at how uncool she sounded. It was so much easier to talk to boys once they had your love potion in their system and they thought everything you said was groundbreaking. "Ferly Cottage, on the edge of town."

"Do you have brothers and sisters?" Matilda shook her head. Oliver smiled at her. "Lucky. I have a half sister; she's a pain in my ass."

Oliver thanked the waitress as she set their drinks down on the table.

"I need sugar. Do you need sugar?" asked Oliver. Matilda nodded and pushed her chair back. "Stay where you are. I'll get it."

Oliver picked up the empty pot from their table and walked back to the counter, waving to the woman to refill it with packets of sugar. He looked over his shoulder and smiled at Matilda, and she froze, her hand in her pocket, the glass bottle tight in her sweaty palm.

Oliver turned back to wait for the sugar, and Matilda looked down as she pulled the bottle out of its hiding place, unscrewed the lid, and held it over Oliver's cup of coffee. She gasped as she felt a hand around her wrist. Oliver was leaning over the table, the sugar in one hand and her wrist still in his other, with a crooked smile tickling his lips.

"You don't have to use that on me," he said, taking the bottle from her fingers. "Let's give this a chance the nonwitchy way, don't you think?"

CHAPTER SIX

Matilda watched Oliver put the bottle down on the table, then stared up at him.

"What . . . I . . . what . . . I . . . ," she said, opening and closing her mouth like a koi.

Oliver looked over his shoulder and sat down.

"Witch," he said, nodding at her. "Right?"

Matilda swallowed. "No, I mean . . . What? I . . ."

Oliver held his hand up, then shuffled his chair closer to the table so his elbow was touching hers. "It's okay. I practice, too."

"You . . . practice?"

"Yeah. You know that dudes can be witches, too, right?"

"Of course I do," Matilda snapped. "My dad was a witch. *Is* a witch."

"Really?"

"Yes, he . . . never mind. Back up, back *right* up. You're telling me you're a witch?"

"Yep," said Oliver, sipping his coffee like revealing himself to be a witch was the most natural thing in the world.

"But how'd you know I'm a witch?"

"Your face, when you were bleeding yesterday," said Oliver, pointing at Matilda's cheek. He unzipped his coat and Matilda nearly fainted as he lifted his T-shirt up a fraction to show her the word *Daniel* scarred across his very toned abdomen. "I get mine on my body, not my face."

Matilda shrugged, hoping that her inability to form words after seeing the waistband of Oliver's boxers would pass for nonchalance.

Oliver narrowed his eyes and sat back in his chair.

"That was you yesterday, wasn't it? With Ashley and the bees?" Matilda folded her arms and glanced around the coffee shop. Oliver gently hit the table as he smiled at her. "I knew it! I knew I saw an *A* on your cheek. The bees were pretty intense. I've never even heard of anything like that."

"She deserved it," said Matilda, sticking her chin out.

"Hey, I'm not judging," said Oliver, holding his hands up. "That girl is poison. Just remind me never to cross you, that's all."

Matilda pulled her mug over and blew into it, trying to process what was happening.

"Where's it gone now? Her name?" he asked, peering at her face.

Matilda swallowed. She'd made a basic love spell to use on Oliver mostly out of habit and because she needed a new distraction. What had just happened had completely blindsided her. Not only did he know about magic, but he wasn't intent on lecturing her about upsetting the balance.

"Um, I can hide my scars."

"Really? How do you do that? I mean, not that I want to go around doing horrible things to people, but it'd be nice to be able to take my shirt off in the school locker rooms."

"Sorry, but . . . how do you know about this?" asked Matilda, her cheeks flushing a little.

"How do I know what?" said Oliver, taking another sip of his drink.

"About magic? About being a witch? About getting scars?"

"Well, I don't really know that much about it. I'm quite new to it all, but I know the first rule is that if you use magic to hurt someone else then you end up with a big nasty name scored across your body. I didn't believe it but I learned the hard way."

"You're not a lineage witch?" Matilda asked.

"A what-now witch?" said Oliver, raising his eyebrows.

"Lineage. So, it doesn't run in your family?" Oliver shook his head. "Why did you start, then? Guys don't tend to be interested."

Oliver looked out of the window and let out a long sigh. "I had kind of a rough time before the summer, with my family and stuff, and sort of stumbled across it. I was spending a lot of time in the library, and there was this coven of old ladies who met there."

"I bet they loved you," said Matilda, thinking how much of a fuss her mom's coven would make over Oliver.

"Of course," smiled Oliver. "They'd feed me cake and teach me about magic. And how to knit. I was all about the meditation side to start with, but the more I learned the more I got into it. There was one lady who really helped me learn how to focus, and she could see I was taking it seriously, so she gave me some of her old books. She said she'd learned everything from her mom, so I guess she was a . . . what did you call it?"

"Lineage witch."

Oliver nodded. "The coven taught me some basics just before we moved here, and I've tried to read as much as I can." He looked up at Matilda and smiled. "What?"

Matilda smiled, too, and shook her head gently. "I just can't picture you sitting in a coven in some library."

"Hey, it was exactly what I needed at the time. I needed a focus and to feel in control of something."

Matilda swallowed. Hearing Oliver's words was like reading out a page from her diary. Since her dad left, the only time she felt she had any control in her life was when she was using magic. She couldn't stop him from leaving, but she could make others do what she wanted; the control was a comfort.

"And then I move here, and it's like witch central with girls vomiting bees in the cafeteria and all those dead animals. You heard about that, right?"

Matilda nodded, her shoulders tensing.

"That has to be someone using magic, right? I didn't think you were supposed to hurt anything living, but it seems pretty . . ."

"Odd," said Matilda. She wasn't sure how Oliver would react if he knew the police had been at her house the night before, specifically asking Matilda questions about her possible connection to the latest deaths.

"Yeah, more than odd. I actually heard those cows had writing carved into their skin. I mean, how gross is that?" said Oliver, frowning out the window as if he was trying to piece together a crime scene.

Matilda willed herself to come up with a different topic of conversation that would distract Oliver, but her stupid brain couldn't think of a single thing apart from the image of her own name on the animals. She looked down at her hands, then let out a small sigh of relief as Oliver steered the conversation on.

"But anyway, where were we? Let's not talk about dead animals anymore, shall we? Not the topic of conversation I had in mind for today." Oliver smiled, but there was some fear hidden in his eyes as he tried to change the subject. "What about you? I'm guessing being a witch is a family business?"

"Yeah, it goes way, way back. My family's origins are right here, in Gravewick. You know the story of Ivy-down-the-witching-well?"

"I think it's pronounced *wishing* well," said Oliver.

"Thanks for the mansplain, but around here we call it the *witching* well," Matilda said, smiling at him. "Ivy lived here in Gravewick, like four hundred years ago. Everyone knew she was a witch, but they went to her in secret if they were sick. It was all fine until someone actually said it out loud and all those people she'd helped turned on her, worried that they would be accused of witchcraft themselves. Apparently, they broke every one of her fingers, sewed her lips together, then threw her down a well in the woods and left her to starve to death. It was one of the wettest autumns recorded and after a few days the rain filled the well until she ended up drowning. People throw coins down there now and ask her to grant wishes, so her soul was never able to rest. Have you noticed how much ivy there is growing everywhere in Gravewick?"

"I've never really thought about it."

"Now I've told, you'll notice it everywhere you go. Green, brown, red. Around tree trunks, over walls, up people's houses. That's her, reminding people she's still here. So they say, anyway."

"For real?" said Oliver, his eyes wide as he absorbed the story of Ivy. "Is that what this is all about?"

He pointed to a big green-and-orange poster advertising Gravewick's Witching Well Festival. Matilda nodded and went on, her muscles crackling with the excitement of being able to share such a well-known town secret with someone who'd recently started using magic.

"Everyone knows the story and the festival is fun, but Ivy was a real person. I've seen drawings. She wore a moonstone around her neck and always carried an athame."

"A what?"

"Athame. It's a sort of ceremonial knife. People said she carried it in case she ever came up against the devil."

Oliver swallowed, his eyes wide. "So, do lineage witches, like, worship the devil?"

"It was just a rumor. Real witches don't believe in the devil, Oliver." Oliver nodded, his shoulders relaxing. "You really are new to all this, aren't you?"

"Yeah, and you're a walking encyclopedia," said Oliver, smiling.

Matilda shrugged. "My mother and grandmother have been teaching me all my life, and my dad, before he left. Mom is always banging on about the purity of my magic and how I need to respect it by learning through the right channels."

"When did your dad leave?"

Matilda stiffened. "You ask a lot of questions."

"Do I? You want to ask me anything?"

Matilda bit her lip and narrowed her eyes.

"Why'd you leave your old school? Were you expelled?"

"Yeah, they caught me sacrificing a goat in my dorm and kicked me out."

"Ha ha."

Oliver shrugged. "It was getting too expensive."

"Oh."

"No big deal." The corners of Oliver's mouth twitched and his eyes crinkled. "I'm kind of liking it here."

Matilda took a long drink, hiding her smile behind the cup.

"Do you like living here?" asked Oliver.

"I guess so. I mean, I have no choice really," said Matilda. Oliver frowned and sat forward in his chair. "Because of my lineage, we draw a lot of power by being here. My magic would weaken if I lived anywhere else. It might even disappear altogether."

"But, can't you just do what I do and learn it again?"

"It doesn't work like that for lineage witches. I love the power I have, what I can do with it. I'm not sure I'd like a life without it."

"So that means no travel, no college?"

"I thought about trying a trip to France but—WHAT THE . . . ?!"

Oliver's hand flew up to his chest and he jumped in his seat, spinning around to look at who Matilda was pointing at. He frowned through the window, his chest rising and falling as he took calming breaths, then turned back to Matilda.

"Friend of yours?"

A girl stood at the coffee-shop window, her hands resting on the glass and her face pushed up so close she was giving herself a little piggy nose as she stared at Matilda. Matilda frowned and waited for her own heartbeat to slow.

"No, I don't think so?" she said, peering at the girl. "What's she looking at?"

Oliver cocked his head and looked between the girl behind the glass and Matilda.

"I think she's looking at you. Are you sure you don't know her?"

The girl pulled away from the glass, letting her features fall back into place, and Matilda realized who she was.

"I *do* know her. Her name's Erin; we actually used to be friends. Why the hell is she staring at us like that?" The glass fogged where Erin was breathing against it. Matilda locked eyes with her and mouthed through the glass, "What's your problem? Get lost, Erin!"

Erin's eyes slid from Matilda to Oliver. They both looked at each other until Erin turned from the glass and walked away as suddenly as she'd appeared, her red hair blowing around her face. Once she'd gone around the corner, Oliver and Matilda turned to each other and burst into giggles.

"Jeez, what a weirdo, staring at us like that. I don't understand what she was doing," said Matilda.

"Do you think she wanted something? Why didn't she just come in if she wanted to talk to you?" said Oliver absently, checking his phone. "Shit. She might be a weirdo but she's a punctual one. We better get going, or we'll be late for school."

A wave of disappointment paralyzed Matilda for a moment, and she had to force herself to shuffle forward in her chair and pick up her bag.

"Thanks for the coffee," she said.

"No problem," said Oliver.

Oliver stood up and did a theatrical stretch as he looked at the Witching Well Festival decorations that were dotted around Grounds. He smiled at Matilda, then turned his phone over and over in his palm, cleaning the screen with his sleeve.

"You okay?" she asked.

He stopped rubbing at his phone and blinked at her.

"Huh? No. Yes, I mean yes, I'm okay. Just assessing all this." Oliver smiled and gestured at the empty coffee mugs and the two of them facing each other. "And wondering whether it went well enough that if I asked you might say yes to coming to that party with me Friday night?"

He's asking me out. He's asking me out of his own accord, thought

Matilda. She bit the inside of her cheek to keep from smiling. Matilda surveyed this new boy, wondering where getting to know him the nonwitchy way, as he'd put it, might take her.

"You've been here a month, and you're invited to a party I know nothing about?"

"It's Sean Barker's; we play soccer together. His parents are away, and he's taking advantage. Do you want to come?"

Matilda looked down at the floor, then at Oliver, no longer able to hold back the smile on her face.

"Yeah, sure. I'll come."

"Cool," said Oliver, his shoulders relaxing. "I'll pick you up at eight thirty? Is that too early?"

How would I know? This is officially my first party, thought Matilda.

"Eight thirty is fine," she said.

"Awesome. Ferly Cottage, right?" Matilda nodded and Oliver smiled so widely his dimples were like connect the dots. "We better get to school."

Matilda looked down and put on her coat, beaming at each button as she did it up.

CHAPTER SEVEN

Matilda closed one app and opened another, cross-referencing Oliver's posts to check his story about private school and segueing off to various girls' profiles who might be exes or even current girlfriends. When Matilda was friends with Ashley, one of Ashley's favorite pastimes was poring over boys' profiles to track their movements and see who they were hanging out with. Matilda had always rolled her eyes and shaken her head as Ashley stared at her phone, scrolling, scrolling, scrolling until she found something to obsess over, and now here Matilda was doing the exact same thing.

As Matilda scrolled down the newsfeed, a post someone had shared caught her eye. She sat up and read the headline: "Further Deaths Add to Animal Slaughter Mystery."

Matilda held her breath as she scanned the article; this time it was horses. The hairs stood up on her arms as she read the report, and she pulled her blanket tighter around her. The police had no leads but were treating it as suspicious. There was no mention of any names or words on the bodies.

Who the hell would do this? she thought as she pulled herself up and swung her legs off the side of the bed. Something moved in the corner of her eye and Matilda spun around, sighing when she saw Nanna May shuffling around outside with a pair of rusty garden shears.

"What are you doing, Nanna May? It's freezing. Go inside," said Matilda as she stuck her head out the door. "I can do that."

Her grandmother carried on cutting the twisted branches of a bramble hedge that was growing outside Matilda's windows. Matilda shoved on some shoes and went outside where Nanna May was on her knees yanking at the roots of the bush. Matilda put a hand on her shoulder and Nanna May looked up at her.

"I said, I'll do it. I thought you old people were supposed to be too scared to go out in the cold weather?" Matilda picked up the shears and rested them against the bench. "Come in while I finish getting ready and I'll do that tomorrow. What even is it, anyway? I've never noticed it before."

Her grandmother straightened up (as straight as the weathered old woman could go) and peered at Matilda. She moistened her lips and whispered so quietly that if the wind hadn't dropped just at that moment, Matilda wouldn't have heard her words.

"Wicked Tilly."

"You're not coming in if you call me that, Nanna May."

"Wicked Tilly."

Matilda shook her head, then put her hand under her grandmother's elbow and gently guided her into the garden room.

"You haven't spoken in three years, and now you've decided that's your new catchphrase?"

Matilda set her grandmother down on her bed and wheeled the heater over to her feet. She took Nanna May's hands in her own and tried to rub some warmth into them, just like Nanna May had done with Matilda's frozen hands after she'd run around the garden on crisp autumn weekends. Nanna May pulled one of her hands away and traced Matilda's cheek with a crooked finger, her fingernails caked with soil from tending her herbs.

Matilda recoiled from her touch, guilt slopping around in her stomach.

"She deserved it. I thought she was my friend, but . . . you wouldn't understand." Victor appeared with Genie perched on top of his head and put his chin on Nanna May's knee. Matilda stroked him as her grandmother let Genie hop onto her finger and then her shoulder. "And I already told you, those dead cows are nothing to do with me. Or those horses. And cats. I could never . . ."

Matilda's knees buckled and she slumped sideways, shadows of a blackout swirling at her temples. Her grandmother caught her with quicker reflexes than anyone would expect from an old woman, and as she cradled Matilda's head in her lap, Matilda could just make out the small white pouch Nanna May pulled from inside her sleeve. It tinkled as she smashed it onto the wooden floorboards, then waved it under Matilda's nose.

The black smoke was sucked from the edge of Matilda's vision, and she blinked up at her grandmother.

"I nearly blacked out, didn't I?" Nanna May nodded as she smoothed Matilda's hair from her face. "What's happening to me, Nanna?"

Nanna May's eyes darted back and forth across Matilda's face like she was looking for a fortune to read, then she looked out at the darkness tapping on the window, wanting to come in and play. Matilda swallowed, the look of fear in her grandmother's eyes turning her spine to ice until Nanna May hushed her and raked her fingers through Matilda's hair.

"Okay, but don't get any dirt in my hair." Matilda pulled herself up and helped her grandmother back onto the bed, then sat cross-legged at her feet. She stared out of the windows. The usual calm she felt in the company of the old lady was far out of reach. The whisper of fear that something was hovering, ready to shroud her in darkness at any moment, and the mystery of the animal murders were just too much even for Nanna May's gentle hands to counteract.

CHAPTER EIGHT

Thirteen days until Halloween

Matilda had been ready for the party for hours by the time she gave herself permission to leave her garden room and make her way to the front of Ferly Cottage. Her stomach was bubbling with an unsteady mix of nerves and excitement, so she took long calming breaths as she strode down the gravel pathway.

As always, the night helped to settle her emotions, and she glanced into the woods and drew strength from the secrets and shadows of her ancestors. A figure moved between the trees, and Matilda stopped, squinting into the darkness.

"Hello?" she called.

There was a sharp intake of breath, and Lottie's hair fanned out in a halo as she looked around. Matilda frowned as her mom tried to conceal what was in her hands, something with a handle that glinted in the moonlight. Before Matilda could tell what it was, it had disappeared inside the folds of Lottie's coat. Matilda opened her mouth to ask what she was doing, but Lottie spun around and disappeared between the trees.

"Okay, Mother. Weird, even for you," said Matilda as she carried on down the path, filing the moment away for a future argument.

The sight of Oliver striding across the gravel driveway made Matilda's freezing fingers and toes buzz with heat. The wind whipped around her, excited for her night out, and she kept tucking her hair behind her ears in a futile attempt to control it.

Oliver let out a long whistle, his eyes taking in every brick and crack of Ferly Cottage.

"Nice house," he said.

"Thanks," said Matilda, glancing over her shoulder. "It's been in our family for generations. It's where Ivy lived."

"Ivy-down-the-witching-well Ivy?"

Matilda nodded. "It's been added on to since then, but she lived in the original part of the cottage."

"Wow," said Oliver, raising his eyebrows.

"That's your car?" asked Matilda, biting her lip and nodding at the tiny car in front of her house.

Oliver looked up from his feet and smiled. "That is correct."

"Do you even fit inside?"

"It's like climbing into a big hug," said Oliver, folding his arms as he reached Matilda. "My other car was better, but we had to sell it. Still wheels, though. I didn't know if I was allowed to park in the driveway?"

"Wherever is fine," said Matilda, hurrying to the car and away from the unsubtle curtain twitching that was happening in Nanna May's bedroom windows.

"Whoa, whoa," said Oliver as Matilda reached for the passenger-door handle. "I'll get that."

"Thanks," said Matilda, smiling as she slipped into the seat and looked up at Oliver before he closed the door. "I'm not sure I could have managed it myself."

"Hey, total feminist here, but I would have died if the door fell off before our date even began."

Matilda smiled. She hadn't even gotten in the car yet, and already she was enjoying being with Oliver.

Oliver jogged around the car and pulled his door open with a creak, then managed to slip into the driver's seat.

"Ready?" he said.

"Ready," said Matilda, trying not to laugh as Oliver tucked himself inside like the Big Friendly Giant squeezing inside a Smart car. "How long have you been driving?"

"A year now," said Oliver, checking his mirrors, then pulling away. "Wish I'd learned magic before then—wouldn't have waited until I was sixteen or stressed about passing the test."

Why didn't I think of that, thought Matilda. *Oh, I know, because it's not like I'd have anywhere to go.*

"What would you need for something like that? A, what do you call it . . . glamour on the license so if a cop looked at it, they'd see a fake birthdate?"

"Or a control spell would work," said Matilda, nodding as she looked into the blackness of the night. She glanced back at Oliver, who was smiling at her. "What?"

"This is cool, huh? Talking about spells and witchcraft and stuff."

"Yeah, very cool," said Matilda, biting her lip to stop her smile from breaking her jaw in two. "Although the only conversations I ever have with my mom are about magic."

"That must be good, though? Learning from your mom?"

Matilda nodded. "And my grandmother. It would be nice to talk about something else, though, not that my grandmother actually speaks much."

"She doesn't talk?"

"There's those questions again."

"Sorry, tell me to shut up."

"I'm just kidding. She hasn't really spoken since my dad 'left,'" said Matilda, hating herself for doing the air quotes around the word but not knowing any other way to explain.

"So, he didn't leave?" asked Oliver.

"According to my mom he left. *He* left *us*. That's her story and she's sticking to it."

"But you think otherwise."

"He wouldn't have done that. She made him go; I know she did," said Matilda, looking down at her hands.

"You don't have to tell me this if you don't want to."

Matilda put her elbow on the door and looked at Oliver, his eyebrows set in a permanent frown as he concentrated on the quiet roads. She took a breath, then let it out, along with all the thoughts that had been stuck in her throat since the day her dad disappeared.

"You're lucky that you're not lineage and you didn't grow up in a house that was all about magic. My dad was like you and did everything he could to learn about the craft to try and please my mom, but he was never good enough and she pushed him out further and further until there was no place for him anymore. Do you know much about the difference between lineage and learned?"

Oliver shook his head. "I didn't even know they were a thing until you told me."

"Okay, so there's a lot that a learned witch can do the same as a lineage, but a lot that they can't."

"Like what?" said Oliver, glancing at Matilda.

"Well, lineages always have a familiar." Oliver frowned at Matilda, and she shrugged. "It's tradition. Also, we sometimes have a gift on top of our 'regular' magic, like telepathy or divination."

"Really?" said Oliver, his eyebrows shooting up his forehead.

"That one's still up for debate, in my opinion. My grandmother's convinced she can see the future, but I've only ever seen her guess the weather."

"She probably secretly uses a witchy weather app," said Oliver, smiling. "What else?"

"Um, you don't have your ancestors to guide you, so sometimes a learned's magic can be unpredictable."

"Agreed," said Oliver. "I have a burned pair of new Nikes to prove it."

Matilda smiled. "Lineages always have a grimoire that's passed down through generations."

"Grimoire?"

"The family book, book of shadows, whatever. It absorbs the essence of each witch that writes in it, preserving the bloodline's power for the next generation. Learneds aren't allowed to even touch our grimoires, the power in them is so sacred. Shit, the lectures I've had about that book. *To give up your grimoire is the highest treason a lineage witch can commit; those before you will punish your contempt by stripping you and your family of magic. Give up your grimoire, give up your magic,*" said Matilda, adopting her mother's nagging voice. "A lineage's magic will always be more powerful because of the generations that have built it. Learneds don't have our history; they don't live, eat, sleep, and breathe magic."

"You make it sound like a full-time job."

"It is. Sometimes." Matilda looked out of the window.

"Did your dad learn magic because of your mom?" asked Oliver.

"He told me one of the reasons he fell for her was because

she was a witch and he was thrilled that magic was real. He was pretty lonely as a kid so he lost himself in magic, like magician's magic, card tricks, coins out of ears, that sort of thing. Because he could never be as powerful as my mom, I think he felt like he had to make up for it with all these little tricks up his sleeve. He taught me a few things," said Matilda, smiling at Oliver. "They come in handy when I need to distract someone so I can swipe something personal for a spell. Anyway, when he met my mom, he was blown away by the world she opened up to him, but there was no way he could keep up, and he never felt like he was good enough for her or her coven. He had to work all the time because she spent all *her* time meeting and casting with them instead of getting a job herself."

Matilda's mind reached back to the day before he left, to the last time he took her to her horseback-riding lesson.

"I used to hear them arguing about her coven all the time, then the last time I saw him he made me promise never to join one." Matilda sighed. Oliver looked at her, his face serious. "So now with my seventeenth birthday coming up, my mom is on me about joining a coven."

"Which is the last thing you want to do."

"Exactly."

"When's your birthday?"

"Next week," said Matilda.

"Well, happy birthday for next week," said Oliver with a smile.

"Thank you," said Matilda, blushing.

"Do you still see your dad much?"

Matilda shook her head. "Not really. We FaceTime and message, but it's difficult for him to get away and I doubt he wants to risk seeing my mom. He's coming to see me next weekend, though." Oliver glanced at her and smiled. "But enough about my parents. Tell me about your mom and dad, and your sister."

"Not much to tell really, not compared to your family history, anyway," said Oliver.

"What do they do?"

"They owned a company selling gym equipment but sold it because it was taking up too much of their time. Now Dad's working at the athletic center, Mom doesn't work at all, and like I said, my sister is a pain in my ass." Oliver glanced at Matilda. "I wonder what they'd say if they knew I was driving around with a witch in my car."

Matilda smiled, her shoulders relaxing as they made a silent agreement not to talk about parents anymore.

"Technically, two witches."

Oliver smiled at her, then pointed ahead as he slowed the car down.

"Sean's house is up there, but I'll park back here otherwise I'll be designated driver for everyone tonight." He switched off the engine and looked at Matilda. "Ready?"

"Ready," said Matilda, catching a glimpse of herself in the car mirror and wondering who on earth this very happy-looking person was.

CHAPTER NINE

They followed the thump of music and the hyena laughter until they found themselves standing in front of a detached Victorian house with skeletons hanging out of the upstairs windows and smashed pumpkins on the doorstep. Sean's parents were obviously fans of the legend of Ivy. Someone had spent a lot of time making a life-size model, complete with broomstick and long green cloak, and twisted her up in the ivy that grew over the front wall.

There was movement behind every window and already a few bodies passed out on the front lawn. Oliver put his hands in his pockets, smiled at Matilda, then started down the path to the open front door. Matilda swallowed as she watched him get closer to the party, her feet rooted to the ground. Oliver looked up and turned around.

"Are you coming?" he said, opening his arms and nodding toward the house. "All the good Jell-O shots will be gone."

Matilda stared at the house, the smell of smoke and spirits curdling her stomach and the sound of the music pressing down on her eardrums. She folded her arms and shook her head as Oliver walked back toward her.

"I was kidding about the shots. Literally have no idea what the fuss is about." Oliver tilted his head and frowned. "What's going on? Don't you want to go in?"

Matilda shook her head. "I . . ."

Oliver's shoulders dropped. "I knew taking you to a party was a stupid idea. Do you want to go somewhere else?"

Matilda bit her lip, wishing that being able to magic herself into thin air was really a thing.

"I've never been to a party before, okay?" she blurted, regretting the words as soon as they left her lips. "I'm this freak-of-nature witch who can only make friends if she tricks people into drinking a potion or by lighting a candle for them on a full moon, but I've never stayed friends long enough to get a party invite. Go on, you can laugh at me, I know you want to."

"Seriously?" said Oliver. Matilda turned back to the car, but Oliver grabbed her elbow and gently pulled her around. He looked over his shoulder, then turned back to her. "We don't have to go in. It's probably not even that good." They both looked at the house as a long *woo-hoo* floated out of the windows. "But if we do go in, I won't leave your side, so you don't have to be scared."

"I'm not *scared*."

"I know, I mean, I don't know," said Oliver, sighing as he pushed the hair from his forehead. "Matilda, just tell me what to say so this doesn't end right here on the sidewalk."

"So what doesn't end?" said Matilda.

"Me and you." The October air warmed up between them as Oliver gave her a crooked smile. "So, are we going in?"

Matilda nodded. *I can do this*, she thought as she started toward the house. *It's just like being at school with these idiots.* Something brushed against her hand and her stomach fizzed like a bath bomb when she glanced down and saw Oliver's hand closing around her own.

"Ready?" said Oliver as they got to the front door.

"Ready."

Oliver squeezed her hand and the party pulled them into its noisy, smelly soul. People yelled into one another's ears and nodded along to conversations there was no way they could follow over the music. A boy from Matilda's class demanded everyone watch as he threw himself forward to perform the worm, only to end up a sweaty heap at their feet. They stepped over him as people in pointy witch's hats or long green cloaks shouted Oliver's name, holding out their hand for a slap, and some girls dressed as inappropriately sexy Ivys nudged one another and whispered as they watched Oliver navigate Matilda through the party.

"What's with the cloaks and hats?" shouted Oliver over the music. "They look like hobbits?"

"It's because of the Witching Well Festival," said Matilda, looking back to give the Ivy girls one last disapproving look.

Oliver nodded, and they wove through the revelers into the kitchen, where every surface was occupied by glass bottles and red plastic cups. More guys greeted Oliver and looked Matilda up and down before giving him a nod.

"How do you know so many people," said Matilda over the loud music.

"Easy for guys," said Oliver. "Join the soccer team and you have a ready-made group of friends."

"You make it sound so simple," said Matilda under her breath.

"Do you want a beer or a vodka or something?" shouted Oliver.

Matilda shrugged. "Whatever you're having is fine."

"I'm not drinking, unless you want to walk home later." Oliver pulled a Coke out of a bucket of ice. "This is me for the rest of the night."

"Can I get one?"

Oliver nodded. "Of course."

Matilda's shoulders sagged as Oliver let go of her hand and dug around for another can of Coke for her. She looked at the boys in the kitchen and wondered if any of them knew who she was.

She certainly knew who they were.

The boy on the left, Joe, was the first boy to ever kiss her when she was fourteen. She'd smudged a love balm on his wrist while he sat next to her in French, then that night he'd appeared at her house and asked her to go to the park with him. They sat opposite each other on the merry-go-round and when she leaned forward, he kissed her right on the lips. As soon as they parted, the spell was broken, and he'd climbed off the merry-go-round and run all the way home. She wouldn't usually get a scar from doing a love spell, but Joe had a girlfriend who was crushed when she found out, so because Matilda had caused her emotional pain, even indirectly, she'd ended up with her name on her face.

The boy next to him, Laurence, used to be one of those kids at the top of every class, always had his hand up and took part in every extracurricular activity there was before Joe gave him his first joint. Matilda sat next to him at lunch one Monday and sprinkled a powder onto his pepperoni pizza, and by the end of the week he'd completed all her homework and delivered it to her every night by seven p.m.

The last, but certainly not least, was a boy called Drew, and if Matilda ran a finger over the left side of her forehead she could feel his name etched there in her skin. She looked at him leaning against the counter, his right hand crinkled with silver scars from a freak accident with a Bunsen burner three years ago, after he'd sent a photoshopped picture of her to all the boys in their class.

Whenever she passed these guys in the halls, she'd feel a

smug, gleeful satisfaction that they had no idea they'd been on the receiving end of her self-serving magic. But seeing them all in the same room together with Oliver made her feel uneasy, exposed, like they could all see what was on her face.

"I . . . Do you know where the bathroom is?" she said, trying to keep her voice steady.

"Use the one in Sean's parents' room," said Oliver, opening his drink. "It's probably not caked in vomit and Red Bull yet."

"That's strictly out-of-bounds, dude," said Laurence, his eyelids heavy.

"How come?" asked Oliver.

"She's in there, you know . . . she . . . with the bees."

"Bees?" asked Oliver, glancing at Matilda.

"Lay off the weed for two minutes and let some oxygen get to your brain, man," said Joe, slinging his arm around Laurence, then looking at Oliver. "He means Ashley; she's out of the hospital. *Insisted* on coming to the party, not for the attention or anything."

Matilda's mouth went dry. She didn't know Ashley had ended up in the hospital after what happened, figuring the school would probably just let her rest in the nurse's office or send her home. She told herself not to worry, that Ashley had probably spent her hospital stay taking selfies to post on Instagram, but a nugget of guilt rapidly took up residence in Matilda's head. Annoyed with herself, she turned to the kitchen door.

"Do you need help finding another bathroom?" asked Oliver.

"No, I'll be fine," said Matilda, having no intention of actually going to the bathroom now that she knew Ashley was in Sean's parents' room.

She squeezed through the partygoers and made her way to the

stairs, looking over her shoulder at Oliver, who carried on talking to the guys in the kitchen. As she turned back, she bumped into someone.

"Sorry," said Matilda, looking up and sighing when she realized who it was. "Erin. Didn't see you there."

"Watch it," said Erin, her eyes flashing at Matilda. "Like you haven't done enough."

"What does that mean? What the hell could I have possibly done to you?"

"Trying to push me over as well."

"Push you over?" Matilda blinked. It'd been years since they were friends, but she didn't remember Erin ever being this aggressive. Forceful, yes, but not aggressive. "What are you talking about, Erin?"

"Oh, lucky me, she remembers my name."

"Of course I remember your name," said Matilda, trying to squeeze past Erin but stepping back again when she wouldn't move. "I'm not in the mood for this. Can I just get past?"

Erin folded her arms and took a step back, her eyebrows in an angry line across her forehead. Matilda looked her up and down as she forced her way past and headed up the stairs. When she reached the top, she glanced down and shook her head; Erin was still giving her a death stare.

"Freak," whispered Matilda, then turned to find Ashley.

There had been a time, not even that long ago, that the thought of creeping around in Sean's house would have filled Matilda with such excitement that she would have exploded. It was rare that Matilda actually felt attracted to someone, because the boys in her class were mostly repellent, but there was just something about Sean. He was gorgeous, that went without saying, but his face was open and honest, and he actually made eye contact when he spoke to you instead of checking his phone every six seconds. Not that they'd really spoken much since their history assignment, but when they did, he looked at Matilda properly.

She'd tried a few spells to get his attention and draw him to her, but nothing had worked. Magic was like that sometimes, or he might have performed a ritual that repelled her magic without realizing it (as was common with superstitious boys who played a lot of sports; wearing their lucky socks protected them from more than just a nasty foul).

Matilda looked at an old school photo of Sean on the wall. The anger that had bubbled from her soul when she watched the attraction between Ashley and Sean had consumed her, and now, post-Oliver and a new attraction, a little scratch of guilt was itching at her skin. It was ironic that one of the reasons she'd made Ashley her friend was because of her friendship with Sean, but Ashley having a thing for him was the very reason Matilda hurt her. Now that Oliver was in the picture, she thought that maybe sometimes people just connect, almost like magic.

"Where are you, queen bee?" whispered Matilda as she opened the bedroom door, morbidly curious to see what sort of shape Ashley was in after her bee trick.

The room was still and Matilda slid in, gasping as the darkness in the bedroom crept toward her, dragging familiar shadows across her eyelids as she slumped onto the high pile carpet.

CHAPTER TEN

"Matilda? Matilda?" Matilda opened her eyes, and Oliver let out a long breath. "Oh, thank God. You okay?"

Matilda blinked and looked at a floral lampshade she didn't recognize. She pulled herself up onto her elbows and frowned. Her chest tightened as she realized she'd blacked out again, and now Oliver had found her looking in goodness only knew what state. Heat rushed up her neck as she averted her eyes from his and rubbed her forehead.

"I passed out, didn't I?" she said, her voice shaking.

"I think so. You were gone for ages so I came looking for you and found you like this. Are you okay? Is your head okay?"

"I'm fine. This is so embarrassing," said Matilda. "Why does this keep happening to me?"

"*Keep* happening? You mean this has happened before?" said Oliver. Matilda sat up and put her face in her hands. "Let's get you some fresh air."

"I'm fine."

"You're the color of milk, and I doubt Joe's fumes wafting up the stairs are doing you any good." Oliver stood up and held out his hand. "Come on."

"See?" said Oliver, opening his arms wide as they walked toward a giant of a tree, away from the small (but definitely disastrous) bonfire that a group of kids were daring one another to jump over and smash pumpkins into. "Outside is good."

Matilda took a deep breath, letting the air whistle up her nose and clear out her lungs. She felt like her insides had shrunk and the smell of magic that followed her around had faded with her blackout, but being under the inky night sky was rejuvenating. Nanna May always used to tell her that their family was more comfortable at nighttime, the moon and stars sharing their ancient secrets as owls and bats swooped overhead in protective circles.

Her grandmother, as usual, was right, and Matilda felt like she was in control again.

"Better?" asked Oliver.

"Better," she said, looking over her shoulder at the house as it throbbed with excitement. "Is it bad that I like it more out here? Shouldn't I be doing Jäger bombs and flashing everyone? Isn't that what people do at parties?"

Oliver put his hands up.

"I'm not going to stop you, if that's what you want to do."

Matilda pushed Oliver, her hand lingering on his arm a little longer than it needed to. She looked up at him. He was obscured by shadows, but she already knew every inch of his face, his stubble, his dimples, and didn't need the light to tell her how beautiful he was. He looked toward the tree and nodded.

"Shall we?"

"A tree swing? Really?"

Oliver laughed. "I didn't know it was here, I swear."

"I suppose you're going to offer me your jacket next?"

"Do you know what? I *am* actually going to do that." He pulled his coat off and put it around Matilda's shoulders. "I admit it all. I made you faint just so I could get you outside under the stars and on this incredibly romantic swing and give you my jacket."

"I knew it," said Matilda, grabbing the rope as she sat down on the weathered wood that had probably been Sean's prized possession for a time.

Oliver grabbed the other rope and lowered himself next to Matilda, her breath warming in her chest as the side of his leg pressed against hers. She was thankful for the blanket of night so Oliver couldn't see how red her cheeks were.

"This was such a bad idea," said Oliver.

"What do you mean?" said Matilda, her heart sinking.

"Bringing you to a party. What was I thinking?" Matilda looked at her hands in her lap. "No, no, I don't mean . . . you know that I'm glad we're here, just I wish it was somewhere a bit more private."

"This is kind of private."

Oliver's dimples appeared as he smiled at Matilda.

"Yeah, I guess it is."

The wind whipped around the tree branches, and crisp leaves floated onto the grass. Matilda pulled Oliver's coat around her shoulders, then froze as she felt him lean toward her and put his arm around her to hold on to the other rope.

He blinked, his eyelids heavy as he looked at her and he bit his bottom lip.

"Do you know, I'm feeling a lot of pressure at this precise moment," he said.

Matilda swallowed.

"Yeah?"

"Uh-huh," said Oliver, lifting his hand up to Matilda's cheek.

"No!" said Matilda, pulling away from him violently.

Oliver looked surprised, his eyes perfect circles.

"Shit, what did I do? I'm sorry, I . . ."

Matilda shook her head, her heart panicking against her chest as she watched the confusion ripple over his face.

"Nothing, it's not you. I . . . I . . ."

Matilda felt Oliver's warm hand over hers, and she looked down as his fingers closed around it.

"Go on," he said, "you can tell me, Matilda. What's going on?"

"My face. I mean, the scars on my face from when I've hurt people. You can't see them, but you can still feel them."

"Oh," said Oliver, "I don't care about that. I mean, it's not like you've hurt hundreds of people . . . is it?"

Matilda shook her head. "Not really," she said, not making eye contact with Oliver as she said the words. She was certain she wasn't into triple figures, but she'd stopped counting a long time ago. "I've just . . . I've got a lot of names on my face, Oliver. *A lot*."

"So, nobody's ever . . ."

Matilda crossed her arms.

"I've *been* kissed, thank you."

"But?"

Matilda's shoulders sagged.

"They . . . none of them were real. The kisses I've had, I mean. They didn't kiss me because they wanted to, or because they cared about me, or . . . I guess I've just never known what it's like to be kissed for real, so I've never worried about someone touching my face because I've never been kissed that way."

"Until now," said Oliver.

Matilda swallowed. A branch snapped in the darkness, coming

from somewhere between the tree swing and the bonfire. Matilda had fallen so deep into their conversation she'd forgotten they weren't actually alone. They frowned at each other and turned to where the sound had come from. Oliver squeezed Matilda's hand as they peered at the rustling bushes. He swallowed, then stood up.

"Probably just one of those idiots going for a piss in the bushes," he said under his breath, then called out. "Put it away, dude, whoever you are; we have ladies present."

Someone stepped out from behind the tall bushes and stared at them from beneath a mass of curly hair wilder than it normally was.

"I don't believe this," said Matilda, shaking her head as she stood up. "Erin?"

"Erin?" repeated Oliver, frowning at Matilda, then turning to look at Erin just as she ran down the lawn.

"Hey! Come back!" shouted Matilda, but Erin had already disappeared among the partygoers. Matilda turned to Oliver. "She had a go at me inside as well. What the hell is going on with her? Do you think she was watching us?"

"I have no idea. Who is she?"

"She's the girl who was staring at us outside Grounds a few days ago, remember?"

"Was that her?" said Oliver. "She likes staring, huh?"

"Hmm," said Matilda absently, her mind occupied with wondering what on earth was going on at this party.

"Didn't you say you were friends with her?"

"Used to be friends," corrected Matilda.

"So, what happened?"

Matilda shrugged. "Usual thing, I guess. Just grew apart,"

she said, not wanting to get into the real history of their ex-friendship. She watched Erin's hair disappear back into the throes of the party. "Maybe I should go after her? Find out what the hell her problem is?"

"Forget about our stalker; probably just too many Jäger bombs. You were telling me that you'd never been kissed."

"That's *not* what I said," said Matilda, elbowing Oliver.

"I'm teasing," said Oliver. "So, you can hide those scars but if someone touched your face, they'd be able to feel them?"

Matilda nodded. "And I can still feel the pain from each one."

"Ouch," said Oliver. "How can you hide them?"

"Family secret." Matilda smiled. "Witches are supposed to bear the scars of those they've hurt, so others can see them coming and know to keep their distance. We can hide ours, but we still have to carry the pain of them like they're fresh wounds."

"Cool." Matilda frowned at Oliver as he shook his head. "I mean, it's not *cool*, hurting people. I mean the whole witch thing. It's cool."

"Really? You're not afraid of me or anything?"

"Yes, really, and yes, I think I am a bit afraid of you, but you're not going to do anything horrible to me, are you?" Oliver's eyes glowed from the bonfire light as he smiled at Matilda. "But I'm starting to see why your dad fell for your mom. I know I'm new to all this, but I really want to learn more, Matilda."

"Well, I guess you nearly vomited on the right person then, didn't you?"

Oliver smiled and curled his fingers around the rope.

"I guess I did."

He leaned back and grabbed the rope on Matilda's side, then

kicked his feet across the mud, pushing the swing a few steps backward. Matilda grinned and lifted her feet, letting Oliver steer them both on the swing.

They both looked up and frowned. Instead of swinging forward, they trundled back and forth in a zigzag, forcing Matilda to squeeze up against Oliver as the swing came to a stop, leaving them stranded in an awkward position.

"That was a total letdown," said Oliver. "Feels like there's something caught at the top. Hop off a sec."

Matilda jumped off the swing and watched Oliver pull himself up so he was standing on it.

"Okay. This is probably going to end badly so don't laugh."

He stuck his tongue out of the corner of his mouth, held the rope with one hand, then jumped up with his other hand stretched above him. Matilda sucked air into her chest, grimacing until Oliver landed on the swing with both feet, upright, but staring at her with wide eyes.

"What's wrong?" she asked.

Oliver swallowed, an audible cartoon gulp, only his face said they weren't in any kids' cartoon.

He jumped off the swing and rushed to her, put his hands on her shoulders, and tried to turn her around as she stared between him and the swing.

"Get inside. We need to get inside."

"Oliver, what's . . ."

They both looked up as the branches cracked and the swing juddered under the weight of something. Matilda yelped and jumped back, and Oliver clamped a hand over his mouth as the something fell from above them, landing partially on the swing and on the ground, at an awkward, terrifying angle.

Matilda stepped forward, glad of Oliver as he grabbed her wrist so she couldn't get any closer. She shivered as something icy, something terrible, went through her, the two coats she was wearing powerless to stop it getting into her bones.

"Is that . . . ?" said Matilda, not insulting herself or Oliver by finishing the question.

They both knew what it was.

Or who it was.

"Where did she . . . ?" whispered Matilda, staring at the body in front of her, then looking up into the broken tree branches above them.

"I . . . I felt her arm caught up in the branches when I reached up." Oliver swallowed, waiting a few seconds before he could carry on. "I must have dislodged her."

There was no sound as they both stared at the body, a girl's body, her legs caught on the swing, her torso twisted so she was facedown in the mud. The wind rustled the branches, scattering leaves over her as if there were nothing out of the ordinary and the scene in front of them was perfectly autumnal. Matilda held her breath. Maybe if she held it for long enough, the girl would wake up, pull herself up from the ground, and drunkenly stagger back to the party. But she wasn't drunk.

She was dead.

Matilda jumped as she felt Oliver's hands fumbling over her sides until he pulled his phone from his coat pocket, dropping it twice before he managed to unlock the screen and turn the flashlight on. The beam of light juddered in front of them, and they stared at the girl's carefully selected party outfit: a red plaid A-line skirt with a white fitted T-shirt tucked into it, smudged with blood and grass stains. Matilda and Oliver blinked at her metallic ballet flats, one of them just hanging on, hooked on her stiff, pedicured toes.

"Oh my God," whispered Matilda, tears springing in her wide eyes. "Oh my God, that's Ashley."

"We should call the police," said Oliver, the light shaking in his hand.

"Is she definitely . . . ?"

Oliver looked at Matilda, then crouched down to get a closer look at Ashley. He sucked his breath in suddenly and then spun around and bent over, splattering vomit across the bottom of the tree and all over his shoes. Matilda ran to where he'd dropped the phone, picked it up, and took tiny footsteps closer to Ashley.

"Matilda, don't!" gasped Oliver between heaves. "Please don't look."

Matilda shone the light over Ashley. It wasn't just the blood that had made Oliver throw up; it was what was carved on Ashley's sallow, gaunt face.

A name.

Her name.

Matilda.

CHAPTER ELEVEN

The party was bathed in blue and red as the police and ambulance lights set the night alive with a fear that was getting much, much closer to home. Matilda felt as though the police had taken ages to arrive, but Oliver had told her it was only fifteen minutes. One of the officers checked the body while another spoke to Oliver, and Matilda was certain that Ashley would suddenly start coughing and sit up like in a movie, then spend the rest of the night being the center of attention.

But she didn't.

Matilda flinched again as the officer took another photo of Ashley, the flash adding to the otherworldly feel of the scene in front of her. She watched the detectives work around the body, wishing she could sit down but too afraid to move to search for a chair. Yellow-and-black police tape cordoned off the area around the tree, flapping in the wind as the words the police officer used when he spoke into his radio repeated in Matilda's mind.

One female adolescent, not conscious, not breathing; no signs of life.

No signs of life.

Oliver stood next to Matilda, his jaw clenched against the cold and his shoulders shaking. Matilda dropped the blanket someone had put around her and started pulling Oliver's coat off. He put his hand on her arm.

"Just keep it. Please," he said.

It was all he'd managed to say to her since the murder team had arrived about an hour before. As well as the tape around Ashley, the police also put tape across the garden between the house and the tree in an attempt to stop the drunken partygoers traipsing up and down with their phones in the air, trying to get a view of the scene. They lingered in clusters, wiping one another's tears or whispering theories about the death they weren't allowed to get any closer to.

Crows cawed from the top of the tree as if they'd known what was hiding in the branches. Of all the things she'd inflicted on others—an itch they couldn't stop scratching until their skin wept with blood, visions of spiders the moment they closed their eyes, or a sudden excruciating broken bone—Matilda had never been this close to death. Especially the death of someone she knew and had messed with just days before. She felt like the ground was uneven and she couldn't get her footing, shock and shame pushing against her from every direction.

The paramedics pulled the zipper over Ashley's head.

"Don't catch her hair!" said Matilda, then squeezed her eyes closed. She felt Oliver's hand on the small of her back, and she looked at him, grateful that he was holding her up when he was just as drained and stunned as she was.

"Matilda? Matilda Hollowell?"

Matilda looked over her shoulder, searching in the darkness for the owner of the voice and where she recognized it from.

"I thought it was you. You were here at the party?" said Officer Powell, narrowing her eyes as she leaned into Officer Seymour and showed him a small notepad. He frowned at it, then looked at Officer Powell blankly. "We were at your house the other day, right? Did you report the body?"

"A-actually, I did," said Oliver.

"If you could let Matilda answer the question, I'd appreciate it," said Officer Powell.

Matilda swallowed.

"Yes. I mean, no, I didn't report the body," she said, ignoring the question about being at her house. Maybe her grandmother's brew hadn't worked as well as her mother thought. "Oliver did. But we found it, found *her*, together."

"Right," said Officer Powell. Matilda pulled the blanket tight around her shoulders as the officer watched her. "And it's your name that was found on the body, is that correct?"

"Yes, but, but I wouldn't . . . I mean, am I a suspect or something?" said Matilda, her mouth dry. She looked between the two officers, tears stinging her eyes. "Please, when can I go? I've already given my statement."

"Not yet; you're a significant witness and one of the detectives will want to speak to you." Officer Powell locked eyes with Matilda. "Don't go anywhere."

Matilda opened her mouth, but felt Oliver's hand clasp the blanket and the coat she was wearing.

"Of course, Officer. We'll be here," he said.

"Make yourselves comfortable," called Officer Powell as both officers turned toward the crowd down the garden.

Matilda and Oliver watched them walk away, the groups throbbing with excitement as to who would be questioned first. Matilda exhaled the breath that had been trapped in her lungs since Officer Powell called her name.

"What was that about? How'd she know your name?" asked Oliver.

Matilda shook her head and started backing away from Oliver, away from the images that were seared into her mind ready to creep out in her nightmares.

"Shit, this is too much; it's too much!" said Matilda, feeling panic constricting her chest as she tried to breath.

"Matilda?" whispered Oliver, gently grabbing her wrist. "Stay calm and tell me what's going on."

Matilda rubbed her eyes and turned to Oliver. "You know those dead animals that keep showing up?" said Matilda. Oliver nodded. "Those two came to my house the other day because a herd of cows was found slaughtered."

"Yeah, I heard about the cows. Why'd the police come to your house, though?"

Matilda wondered what the others were telling the officers and what they were writing down. Did they have a suspect already? She looked back at Oliver, who was frowning at her, searching her face for some enlightenment in the darkness they'd stumbled on together.

Trust him, she thought. *You can trust him; he knows what you are.*

"They had a name carved on their sides. All of them did."

Oliver swallowed. "Oh, shit."

"Yes, oh, shit. And now there's a dead girl, a girl *I* was friends with once upon a time, and she's got my name on her face. What the hell? I mean what the *hell* is going on? They're going to think I did this, aren't they?"

Oliver looked at the circus around them, where they'd felt like the only two people in the world just hours before, then grabbed Matilda's hands and shook his head.

"No, no, look; it's going to be fine. They need to take statements from everyone here, but us especially because we found her. There's no way anyone could think it was you, you have, like, a hundred witnesses who saw you at the party, and you have me, too. We've been together the whole time." Matilda looked up at Oliver, her eyebrows furrowed with worry. "What? What's that look? Oh, shit. You went to the bathroom on your own."

"Not exactly."

"What does *that* mean?" Oliver looked at Matilda, his eyes wide. "Matilda, you need to tell me what happened, and you need to talk fast because if you're dragging me into something and we're about to talk to the detective . . ."

Oliver's question hung in the air and Matilda grabbed his words with both hands, knowing she couldn't be in this alone.

"I didn't go to the bathroom. I went to find Ashley."

Oliver's hands went up to his head, but he glanced at the police and dropped them.

"Okay. Okay, so that means you were the last to see her alive."

"No, but I didn't. She wasn't there, in Sean's parents' room. It was empty. And then I . . . that's when you found me. What if . . . what if I . . ."

Oliver shook his head. "What if you managed to find her while you were unconscious, kill her, carve your name in her face, then carry her through the party, past everyone, and stick her up that tree?"

"Not when you say it all like that, but . . ." Matilda's eyes stung every time she blinked, and all she wanted to do was crawl into bed and pull her blanket over this nightmare. "I could have done something while I was unconscious, something terrible using magic, or hate, or something wrong got mixed up in the spell I used on Ashley the other day . . ."

"Matilda . . ."

"Let me finish. You can't deny the facts. Dead animals and now a dead human, all with my name carved into them. I've never felt anything like these blackouts. It's like something is coming for me, and I'm not in control of my body." Matilda watched as the paramedics wheeled Ashley away. She shook her head and looked back at Oliver. "I hated that girl, Oliver. I hated her so much that I swallowed a bee so she would vomit up a hive. What if this darkness is taking over and I'm losing control?"

"Look," said Oliver, putting his hands on her shoulders. "You have nothing to hide. We came together, you used the bathroom, I met you outside, then we came down here. That's all."

Matilda shook her head.

"We'll talk to the police and then I'll drop you off at home, and we'll work this out after some sleep."

"I need to clear this up," she said, "I need to find out what's going on with all these deaths and my blackouts, but right now I need to not get into trouble for this."

Matilda looked over her shoulder and tried to count how many people there were in the garden, as well as the police officers who were hanging around like flies. She turned back to Oliver.

"I can do a spell to change people's perception or just make them forget about things, but I'll need to do it on everyone, not just the police. There are so many people here. I've never . . ."

Oliver straightened up, finally looking more like himself than he had since they found Ashley.

"Maybe I could help you? I mean, I know I'm still learning, but those old ladies at the library taught me a thing or two about witchcraft. Plus, I want to learn more, so it's a win-win."

"Really?"

"Really. I'll do whatever you say. You can be my teacher."

Matilda narrowed her eyes.

"You really don't think it was me?" she asked, folding her arms.

"How could it have been?"

"And you're not worried that people are turning up dead with my name written on them?"

"There's definitely something going on, but I don't think you're behind it, Matilda."

"Okay then."

"Okay then," said Oliver, smiling.

Even though she felt like she was standing in the middle of a nightmare, Matilda couldn't help but smile back at him.

CHAPTER TWELVE

Twelve days until Halloween

"Has anyone ever told you that you mumble?"

Oliver pressed a hand to his chest and slumped back in his chair.

"Ouch. That hurt. Next time you attack my personal character, a warning would be nice."

"You wanted to help, and you can't help if you can't say the spell clearly. *Say it clear, say it true.* That's what my grandmother used to say. Before she stopped speaking."

Oliver sat forward and folded his arms on the table. They'd nestled themselves in a corner at Grounds, their mugs of coffee warming their autumn-chilled fingers and noses. What looked like an old textbook to anyone who didn't know better sat on the table between them, but on closer inspection the swirly hand-writing and intricate drawings scratched in the margin gave it away as one of Nanna May's spell books.

"How can she do magic if she doesn't talk?" asked Oliver.

Matilda rested her chin on her hand and shrugged.

"Because she's lineage and super old? I don't know, when you're seriously ancient maybe you don't need to speak the words out loud. When you're a magic newbie, though, you definitely have to. I've never done a spell that didn't involve some kind of incantation."

"How is that even possible? Has anyone at school heard you saying your spells out loud?"

"Oh yeah, all the time."

"What do you do?"

"I cast another spell so they forget what they've heard. There are enough gaps in their memories to make fishing nets out of their brains." Matilda tapped the book in front of them. "Anyway, you don't have to say it *loud*; you just have to say it *clear*."

"And true."

Matilda smiled. "That's right."

Oliver picked up a long piece of black twine from a tangled pile on the table, then peered inside a paper bag.

"And tell me again what we're making with these?" he said, pulling a hazelnut from the bag. He held it up to his eye and looked through a hole running through the middle of it.

"Witch's ladder," said Matilda, taking the twine and the hazelnut from Oliver. "Or *ladders*, plural."

"I've read about those. Aren't they used for dark magic?"

"They can be, like all magic." Matilda glanced up at Oliver as she started threading the hazelnut onto the twine behind the cover of a menu standing on the table, motioning for him to watch. "Witches used to tie feathers or bones into the twine with the intent to curse or even kill someone. That's obviously not what we're doing."

"Obviously," said Oliver, watching Matilda's fingers.

"We'll tie a hazelnut onto the twine for each person who was at the party so they forget what happened."

"Including the police?"

"*Especially* the police." Matilda stifled a yawn. It was three o'clock in the morning by the time the detective had finished with them and they were allowed to leave the party. "I'll take half and you take half, tying them all on and spacing them apart, just like this. Then you hang them above the candles in the bag; one ladder above one candle."

"Then I say the spell, *clear and true*, and let the candle burn the ladder?" Matilda nodded, and concern flashed in Oliver's eyes.

"What's wrong?" she asked.

"Will we, you know, get each of their names if we're doing this spell?"

Matilda shook her head. "No." She paused. "We shouldn't. Memory spells are like love spells in that way, kind of a gray area. I've never gotten a name from doing one."

"Okay," said Oliver, letting out a sigh. "Good."

"So, start the spell at sunset and stay with the candles until each ladder burns enough to break. The bag of candles is for you; there are five in there, and I'll do the rest. Make sure you're in a well-ventilated room because they'll be really smoky and stinky because of the fat."

Oliver frowned.

"You mean wax," he said.

"No, I mean fat."

"Do I want to know what kind of fat?"

"Probably not." Matilda smiled as Oliver curled his lip.

"Anyway, take all this stuff with you, find somewhere private, with ventilation, then at sunset you say this." Matilda pushed the book toward Oliver, and he leaned over it, peering at the words she was pointing at. "You don't have to memorize it; you can borrow the book."

Oliver's shoulders relaxed.

"Thanks."

Matilda slurped the last of her coffee and pushed her chair back.

"Let's go."

She packed the book in the canvas bag and started wrapping herself up to venture back out into the crisp wind while Oliver looked inside the bag, turning his nose up as he lifted it over his shoulder.

"Gross."

"You need to get used to the gross."

"I don't think I . . ."

Oliver's voice trailed into nothing, and Matilda turned to see what he was looking at. Her stomach plummeted to the floor as they watched the lone figure trudge from the door straight past them. Sean stopped at the counter and stared at the menu, the bags under his eyes and shaking hands making him look more like someone drifting in for a scrap to eat than one of their classmates. Oliver glanced at Matilda and raised his eyebrows. Matilda shrugged, and Oliver walked up and leaned on the counter next to Sean.

"Hey, man." Sean's eyes were transfixed on the menu until Oliver bent down and caught his gaze. "Sean, it's Oliver, from soccer. You in there, man?"

Sean blinked and shook his head.

"Sorry, was just . . . hey."

"I just wanted to say I'm sorry about Ashley. It's just unbelievable. I'm so sorry.

Sean bit his lip and nodded, then frowned at Oliver.

"Wait, you found her, didn't you? Did you see anything?" said Sean, his bloodshot eyes blinking rapidly.

"No, we didn't see anything. We've already told the police."

Sean grabbed Oliver's arm.

"But you might have forgotten something because of the shock. Think again. Was there anyone there? Anybody that might . . ."

"I'm sorry. There wasn't anyone." Matilda watched as something flickered across Oliver's face, and he glanced at her before looking back at Sean. "Do you think coffee is a good idea? You look like you haven't slept. Shouldn't you be at home?"

Sean's head looked like it was too heavy for him as he shook it.

"I don't know. I don't know where to go. We used to come here but . . ."

"Do you want me to drive you home?"

"I just want to be on my own." Sean shook his head again, his red eyes desperate for peace, and he turned away from Oliver, then stared at Matilda. "You."

Matilda flushed and looked around.

"Me?"

"Your name. It was your name all over her. *Matilda*." Sean's eyes flashed, and he charged toward Matilda but tripped into a chair. "Why was it your name? What did you do to her?"

"Nothing, I . . . it wasn't me," said Matilda, backing up to the wall.

"Matilda was with me, Sean. It wasn't her. I think you need to get home," said Oliver.

Sean looked at them both, blinking like he was trying to wake from a nightmare. His head drooped, and he frowned at his feet as he walked out of the door. They watched him walk past the window, his open jacket flapping in the wind, then turned to each other.

"That was horrendous," said Oliver, putting his hands on either side of his head. "I had no idea what to say to the poor guy. He shouldn't be out and about after last night. Could we use magic to help him get over what's happened?"

Matilda frowned.

"All over her."

"What?" said Oliver.

"*All over her*. That's what he just said, right? We only saw my name on her face but was it everywhere? How does he know that?"

"I doubt there's been an investigation yet. Maybe Ashley's parents told him what the police already know."

All over her. Matilda was freaked out when the police first told her about the dead cows, but what happened to Ashley was another level of horrific, and now Sean was painting an even worse picture. She felt like she was being pulled into death's shadows at every turn, and she had nothing to fight back with.

"I need to see her."

"Wait, *what?*" said Oliver, shaking his head.

"I need to see her body. I mean, I just need to know what happened to her, Oliver. I need to know that it wasn't . . ."

"It wasn't you, Matilda."

"Okay, but I need to know if it was magic, if it was a witch."

Oliver glanced at the man tidying up behind the counter, then leaned into Matilda.

"Do you think there are other witches here?"

"Could be. I didn't know about you until you told me," said Matilda.

"I don't know how I forgot about this, but remember that girl, the one who was staring at us when we were here the first time? I remembered just now when Sean asked if we saw anyone else."

"Erin?" said Matilda, her forehead screwing up as she tried to put her and Ashley together in any kind of scenario where Ashley ended up dead. "She was acting weird, I guess, but really? You think it could be her? You think she's a witch?"

"No idea, but it's a bit of a coincidence that she was sneaking around a few minutes before we found Ashley," said Oliver. Matilda frowned and looked out the window. "What are you thinking?"

"I'm thinking Ashley will be at the morgue still, won't she?" said Matilda, swallowing at the thought. "They won't have moved her to the funeral home yet or the coroner's office, not until Monday. I need to see her. I need to get a closer look at my . . . at the marks on her, Oliver."

"Is the morgue in Gravewick?"

"No, it's at the hospital in Oakwell."

"Okay. Okay, I'll drive you if that's what you really want, but I can't be sneaking around looking at dead bodies. I'm sorry, but no."

"That's fine; that's all I need."

Oliver put his hand on Matilda's shoulder and guided her toward the door of Grounds.

"Yeah, you're really low maintenance."

CHAPTER THIRTEEN

"Do you know where the morgue is? How are you even going to get in there?" Oliver ducked down to look at the entrance of the hospital as people holding balloons and magazines marched through the automatic doors. "There isn't going to be a door marked 'dead bodies' waiting for you, you know."

Matilda rolled her eyes.

"You really are a newbie witch, aren't you?" She pulled a small spray bottle out of her bag and shook it in front of Oliver's eyes, the pink liquid shimmering as it splashed back and forth. "A couple of sprays of this and the staff will take me exactly where I need to go. They'll even stay and hold my hand if I want them to."

"What is that? A potion?" said Oliver, taking the bottle and peering at it.

"Technically, it's poison." Matilda took it back. "But if it makes you feel better we can call it a potion."

"Okay, I better go find somewhere to park." Oliver looked over his shoulder, then back at Matilda. "Matilda? Did you hear what I said?"

Matilda stared out of the window, her hand frozen on the handle as Oliver's words faded into the traffic.

"What the hell?" she said to herself, frowning as her eyes followed someone walking through the automatic doors. She turned to Oliver. "That's my mom."

Oliver leaned over Matilda, and despite the bizarreness of seeing her mom hurry through the entrance of the hospital, she took a moment to enjoy the kaleidoscope of butterflies that flapped their wings the moment he was close to her.

"Maybe she's visiting someone?"

"Maybe." Before her dad left, Lottie would have told Matilda if a friend or a member of the coven was in the hospital, but she didn't think she would now.

Oliver turned the car's fan up to try and clear the fog that had formed on the inside of the windows, then he put his hand on Matilda's arm.

"Are you worried there's something wrong with her?" asked Oliver. Matilda looked at her hands in her lap, then up at Oliver. "What's up?"

Matilda swallowed.

"What if she's here for the same reason we are?"

"Same reason *you* are, not *we*. *We* are not going looking for a dead body. *You* are . . . oh. You think your mom is looking for Ashley? Does she even know about what happened?"

"Everyone knows what happened to Ashley. They either picked someone up from the party, or they've read about it online."

"But why would she come here looking for her?"

Matilda looked out of the window again, staring at the spot where her mom had looked over her shoulder and then hurried through the doors just a few minutes ago.

"I don't know," said Matilda, thinking back to the police visiting her house a few days ago. "She was pretty shaken up when the police told us about the cows at that farm, more shaken up than I thought she'd be. Isn't it a bit weird that she just happens to be at the same hospital where Ashley's body is?"

Oliver blinked, letting Matilda's words sink in.

"You think your *mom* killed Ashley? How did you get there? You're joking, right?" Matilda glanced at Oliver, then looked out the window again.

"I don't know. She just seems so angry all the time. She lectures the hell out of me about using magic to hide my scars, but I'm sure she's got way more than she admits. I mean, she doesn't even have a job. How does she pay for everything?"

"But that doesn't make her a murderer."

Matilda wrung her hands together as she stared at the hospital doors. "I saw her, Oliver, the night of the party. She was creeping around the cottage all shifty." Matilda paused. They'd drifted apart since her dad left, but had Lottie really drifted that far, to such a dark place? "She had something with her; she tried to hide it when she saw me. I think it was a knife."

"A knife?" repeated Oliver. Matilda nodded. "And now she's here."

Matilda looked back at Oliver. "And now she's here."

"You really think she . . . ?" said Oliver, letting the unfinished question hover between them.

"I don't know. All I'm saying is, there's a hell of a lot of weird shit happening in this town, and maybe she's gotten caught up in something really dark. Maybe she's getting herself really lost. Maybe there's more to what went on between her and my dad than I thought. Slaughtering a whole herd of cows? That's a big sacrifice. And a human? We don't even contemplate that kind of magic."

"But why your name? Why would she incriminate you?"

"I don't know." Matilda looked out the window again, then turned to Oliver. "Look, can we just go? This doesn't feel like a good idea anymore."

Oliver nodded and turned the key in the ignition, then waited for a space to pull out. He turned on the radio and tapped his hand on the steering wheel as he drove, but it didn't drown out the question that was rattling around inside Matilda's head.

What if she's finally had enough of me?

CHAPTER FOURTEEN

All the late nights had finally caught up with her, so after Oliver dropped Matilda off, she crawled into bed for an afternoon nap. Her tired body fought against the endless questions that were going off in her head and eventually won—she finally fell into a deep, blissful sleep.

Matilda groaned as she slowly woke up, keeping her eyes closed to trick herself into going back to dreamland, but one side of her face was numb and she had pins and needles in her fingers from sleeping at a funny angle. She reached across the bed in search of a blanket but gasped as the unexpected sound of rustling leaves made her eyes flick open.

She was on the ground, her face resting in the mud. She jerked her head up and blinked at the tree trunks surrounding her. Her breaths became shorter and faster, not pulling enough oxygen into her tightening lungs as she looked around, unable to place where she was as she sat up. She looked down at her hand that had felt so tingly and almost wept with relief as Victor looked up from nibbling her fingers. Matilda pulled him into her, covering him in kisses.

"You're freezing, Vic," she said, her throat tight. "How long have we been out here?"

Matilda could tell from the gray light through the treetops and the birds singing their final song that twilight was on its way, so a few hours had passed since she'd gotten into her bed. She looked down and pressed her hands against the legs of her joggers, her chest tightening when there was no sign of her phone. She stood up, her hand on Victor as she looked around trying to get her bearings, a small ball of panic bouncing harder and harder in her stomach.

There was a familiarity to the emptiness she could feel inside, like there was another hole in the part of her that connected her with her bloodline, just like the other times she'd blacked out. The blackouts were frightening enough, but there was something sinister about expecting to wake up in the warm folds of her bed and instead finding herself facedown in the muddy, fallen leaves. It was like whoever was behind it wanted her to know she wasn't the one in control of her body.

They were.

Matilda shook the thought away before it could take hold, looked at the vaguely familiar pattern of trees, and turned to Victor.

"You know the way home?" she said, trying to ignore the wobble in her voice. The goat looked up at her, and she rubbed the spot between his ears. "Come on, then."

The late October afternoon was cold and pushed Matilda forward. Victor kept at her side as they headed toward Ferly Cottage, Matilda determined to get back as fast as she could so she could leave the blackout behind her, deep within the woods. Even as she picked up her pace, the shadows just wouldn't stop nipping at her heels, and she knew she had another reason not to sleep later that night.

Victor stopped eating the sugar lumps out of Matilda's hands, blinked at her, then galloped through the back door into the dusk—a sure sign that Lottie had just gotten home.

Matilda pressed her hands against the mug of lemon-and-ginger tea she'd brewed for herself. Her garden room hadn't seemed so inviting when she got back, so she and Victor decided to have a pit stop in the kitchen instead. She looked at Nanna May, who was stirring the pot over the fire with a long wooden spoon and glancing up at Matilda with every seventh stir.

"What?" said Matilda, pushing her hair over her shoulders. "This is my kitchen, too, you know."

Matilda sat up at the sound of her mother's heels click-clacking across the kitchen tiles and the almost inaudible pid-padding of Nimbus's paws. Lottie's eyebrows popped up at the sight of Matilda sitting at the table, then her chin twitched a fraction, sharing an unspoken secret with Nanna May.

"Good evening, Matilda. Gracing us with your presence? Aren't we the lucky ones," she said, sweeping past Matilda and opening the fridge.

"Do I need an invitation?"

"No, unless I gave birth to a vampire," said Lottie, crouching down to fuss with Nimbus's ears. "And sometimes we do wonder, don't we, Nimbus?"

If it was possible for cats to laugh, Nimbus did, then stuck her bottom in the air and went to find something that wasn't hers to sit on and cover in hair.

"Whatever," said Matilda, glaring at the back of her mom's head. "So, did you have a good day?"

Her mother's shoulders sagged, and she turned to face Matilda.

"What's happened now? Have the police been here again?"

"No, but that's quite a leap, Mother. I'm just asking about your day."

"Which you never do."

"So, maybe I'm making an effort," said Matilda.

Lottie looked at Nanna May, who shrugged and turned to her pot.

"Fine. My day was fine. Thank you for asking, Tilly."

"Where've you been?"

Matilda's mother picked up the cast-iron kettle, filled it with water, then set it on top of the range, keeping her eyes firmly on her hands the whole time.

"Out and about," she said over her shoulder as she turned the gas on, then lit a match and poked it underneath the kettle.

"Out and about where?"

"Just in town, doing a bit of shopping, a few errands."

"In town? You mean Gravewick?" asked Matilda.

"Yes. Gravewick," said Lottie, focusing all her attention on the kettle. "What did you get up to today?"

"Saw a friend," replied Matilda.

Her mother turned and leaned against the kitchen work top, a smile stretched across her face like a mask.

"An actual friend or one of your friends who doesn't know why you've suddenly become so interesting?" The stool that Nanna May was sitting on creaked along with the old lady's knees as she pulled herself up and frowned at Lottie, whose smile wavered. "I'm glad you've got a friend, Matilda."

"Me too. No idea why I find it so hard to make relationships with people the normal way. I have *such* a good role model."

Her mother took a sharp breath and pointed a gelled finger-nail at Matilda.

"What the hell is that supposed to mean? Is this about your joining a coven? You can ignore me all you like, but there's magic you can only access with the support of a coven. If you wanted to invoke the spirit of your ancestors, or—"

"Not everything is about joining a coven, Mother," said Matilda, standing up. "Why would I ever need to invoke a bunch of dead witches? I can access whatever magic I want with none of your rules holding me back, and I don't need anyone's help to do it. When are you going to get that?"

"But, Matilda, when a witch turns seventeen—"

Matilda pushed her fingers against her temples. "You can repeat it as many times as you want, but your words won't change my mind. Your coven broke this family, it drove Dad away, and I will *never* be a part of something so destructive and self-involved."

Lottie flinched as though Matilda had slapped her in the face, then folded her arms.

"Whatever you think you know about what happened with your father, you're completely misled. I couldn't have raised you if it weren't for my coven."

"And you've done *such* a good job," said Matilda, her stool screeching across the tiles as she stood up.

She ignored her grandmother's sympathetic outstretched hand and walked through the kitchen door into the hushing twilight.

"We're stronger as a collective, Matilda," called Lottie through the back door. "I know you think the cloak spell is the only magic you need, but one day that negativity is going to turn on you . . ."

Lottie's voice trailed off as Matilda picked up a lantern and Victor joined her side, letting the croaks and caws of the animals that relished the nighttime silence her mother's warning.

———•◦•———

The smell of apple pie and hot chocolate wove up the path and tickled Matilda's nostrils, complementing the smell of burning hazelnuts and leaves, and masking the rancid smell of the candle. Nanna May trudged up the path toward Matilda's garden room with a steaming mug in one hand and a small-handled basket in the other. Matilda looked up from the freestanding terra-cotta chiminea, its flames warming her as she sat on the bench outside her room with Victor lying across her feet.

"You always know when I'm hungry, Nanna May," said Matilda, taking the warm mug and the basket from her grandmother and setting them on the bench beside her.

Nanna May looked at the chiminea and wrinkled her nose, then glanced up at the inky sky and shook her head.

"Rain?" said Matilda, peering up at the sky just as her grand-mother had. "I can't feel it coming."

Nanna May shrugged and turned away, gesturing at the pie in the eat-it-before-it-gets-cold way she often did when she brought Matilda food.

"I will," said Matilda, lifting the napkin to peek at the wedge of apple pie in the basket. "This definitely won't last long. Thank you."

Nanna May shuffled back down the path, and Matilda wiggled her feet so Victor would let her move and get on with finishing her spell. Inside the chiminea was a fat candle sitting in a cast-iron holder, burning bright and smelling just as bad as she'd warned Oliver it would. Matilda had balanced an old poker across the top of the chimenea, and now the last of the witch's ladders hung from it, dangling just above the candle flame.

Matilda blew on the hot chocolate, smiling into the mug as she smelled a hint of cinnamon and orange. She looked into the chiminea and, certain that the twine was about to burn in two, she set the mug down and knelt down in front of the candle.

"With each knot tied by my fingers and with each fruit that I burn, burn their memory clear of that night so they should forget."

As if by magic, the twine broke halfway down and dropped on top of the candle. Victor bleated, and Matilda smiled at him.

"Yes, you can go in and snuggle up now, Vic."

The goat trotted through the garden-room door, and Matilda blew out the candle, wondering whether Oliver had managed to do his half of the spell. She smiled as she pictured him tying the witch's ladders, then his face as he realized she wasn't joking about the bad-smelling candles. It wasn't the first time he'd nudged into her thoughts since they'd said goodbye earlier, and she knew it wouldn't be the last.

Matilda went to a little shelf under one of her windows where a ceramic bowl was filled with pebbles. She put her fingers inside and tickled the smooth stones, feeling the energy at the end of her fingertips settle down. Once she was sure the crackle of magic had left her body, she went back to the bench and grabbed her hot chocolate and apple pie, then hurried into the warmth of her room, where Victor was already curled up on his cushion. She put her treats next to her bed, then closed the door just as a faint *tap, tap, tap* of rain sounded on the roof.

She looked out of the window as the rain became more insistent and extinguished the last glows of the chiminea. Her bed called to her, inviting her to crawl into where she would read while she ate her pie, snug and dry out of the rain that her witch grandmother had predicted would come.

CHAPTER FIFTEEN

Eleven days until Halloween

"But just because she lied about where she was doesn't mean she was creeping around checking on her handiwork at the hospital."

Matilda watched Oliver shuffle through the kissing gate and then followed him through.

"No, I guess not," said Matilda. "But for all the issues we have, she's never really lied to me about anything like that. Until now."

They headed across the field, following the path worn out for them by dog walkers and families, their own mission a little different from the normal Sunday strolls. The sun was so dazzling that the sky seemed higher than normal, and the crisp wind almost blew away Matilda's worries as it flicked her ponytail back and forth.

"I'm not seeing any animals out here. I don't know if that's good or bad," said Oliver, frowning as he squinted across the fields. "To be honest, I don't know what we're looking for."

"This land belongs to the same farmer who owned the cows that got . . . you know," said Matilda, swallowing hard.

"Slaughtered?" said Oliver. Matilda nodded and caught her breath. "It really bothers you, doesn't it? Hey." Oliver grabbed Matilda's wrist, and she stopped and looked up at him. "You don't still think it might have been you, do you?"

"I . . . I don't know. It's definitely someone using magic, and it was my name carved on . . . ," said Matilda, closing her eyes but still seeing Ashley in the darkness. "I need to see where these animals were killed, in case it triggers a memory. These blackouts have been getting longer, and yesterday after you dropped me off I . . . I . . ."

"You what? What happened?"

Matilda sighed, torn between sharing her worry with Oliver and not wanting to admit the blackouts might mean that she was losing her mind or her magic.

"I don't know what happened. One minute I was in my bed, and the next I was lying facedown in the woods, Victor nibbling at my fingers."

Oliver blinked.

"Sorry. Victor?"

"He's my goat."

"Of course he is," said Oliver, smiling.

"A witch needs a loyal pet, Oliver, for when the world turns against her."

"Sorry, you were telling me you were unconscious in the woods, and I got distracted because I thought you were with someone. Carry on."

Oliver started walking again, and Matilda closed one eye against the bright sun and watched Oliver's silhouette ahead of her until he turned around.

"What?"

He got distracted because he thought I was with someone, she thought. She smiled and walked to his side, her feet squelching on the mud underfoot from a night of heavy rain.

"Nothing. The first time it happened I'm sure it was just a

few minutes, but they're getting worse and I just feel so drained afterward. If I can get from my room to the middle of the woods at the back of our property, maybe I could kill a herd of cows or even a person without realizing it?"

"You're not a werewolf, Matilda." Oliver put his hands on her shoulders, and Matilda felt like he was holding those paddles paramedics use to shoot volts through someone's heart. "Right?"

Matilda shoved Oliver, and he looked down at her, a smile as bright and open as the sun on his face. He dropped his hands from her shoulders, and Matilda's heart deflated with disappointment as he carried on striding across the field.

"Oh, shit," said Oliver, stopping still like a scarecrow.

"What's wrong?" asked Matilda, turning to see what he was looking at.

"Those," he said, pointing ahead.

Matilda frowned, then looked back at him.

"The sheep?"

Oliver nodded and started walking back the way they'd come. He looked at Matilda and stopped.

"Come on, then," he whispered.

"Why are you whispering, Oliver?"

"In case."

"In case what?"

"They're wild animals, Matilda. Let's just go back."

"They're not *wild* animals. Don't worry, they'll just ignore us. We can get to the farm just over the next field, and we'll look less suspicious if we use the public paths. Come on. I used to come here all the time with my dad."

Oliver squinted at the sheep, then sighed and shook his head.

"Well, if we get trampled by a pack of sheep, then you owe me big."

"Deal," said Matilda as she looked at the gate on the other side of the field, then glanced back at the sheep, several of which had stood up.

"So, your dad used to bring you up here?" asked Oliver, his voice tight.

"Every Sunday we'd go for a walk, just the two of us. I used to spend all day Saturday with my mom or grandmother in the woods, where they tested me on the Latin names of plants or which birds carry the souls of the dead or which flowers you never bring into the house."

"Normal kid's stuff, then," said Oliver.

Matilda smiled. "Dad knew how much I hated it, so when we used to walk together we'd just talk about how pretty everything was, and that's all I had to do."

A sheep bleated from across the field, and they both looked up. All the sheep had stood up and were facing their way. Oliver looked at Matilda.

"Don't panic; they're just watching us," said Matilda. "People walk across here all the time."

"Then why are you walking fast?" said Oliver, easily keeping up at her side.

"I'm not," said Matilda, squinting at one of the sheep that was walking in their direction.

Oliver looked over his shoulder.

"Let's just go back."

"Nothing is going to happen, Oliver."

"Well, maybe not, but sheep kind of freak me out, okay? Most animals, in fact."

Matilda swallowed as she counted ten, then eleven, then twelve sheep walking toward them, as if they were possessed. She'd never given them any thought during the dozens of walks she'd taken with her dad when the sheep would meander around living their best life, chewing grass and lying in the sun. But the way they were looking over at her and Oliver, dozens of eyes homing in on a target, they were more like predators setting their sights on an injured gazelle than harmless farm animals.

The wind dropped, and Matilda took some calm from the quiet, then as it whipped up again a screaming sound drifted over them, so loud that Matilda put her hands over her ears. She looked at Oliver, who was doing the same thing, then back at the sheep in disbelief that a sound more at home in a horror film was coming from them.

"What the hell?" she shouted. "The farm can wait. Let's go back."

She gave them one last look before she turned and started walking back to the gate, her blood running cold and her feet slipping in the mud as their screams seemed to get louder.

"*Thank you.* That's not normal, is it? They're all walking over here? No, no, forget that," said Oliver, looking over his shoulder as he started to jog. "They're *running*. They're running, Matilda! They're coming for us!"

"They're sheep, Oliver; they don't *come* for people," said Matilda, looking back.

She froze as more than twenty sheep ran toward them, their black heads pointing at Oliver and Matilda like poisoned darts, their bleats like guttural screams that belonged in nightmares, a far cry from the woolly animals people imagine leaping over their heads at bedtime.

"Shit," said Matilda. "Shit! They're coming for us! RUN!"

Oliver nodded, his face the color of their pursuers, and grabbed Matilda's hand as she caught up with him, both of them glancing over their shoulders as the cloud of sheep closed in on them like a thundering storm. A couple at the front of the flock lost their footing in the mud and tumbled onto their sides, bleating and kicking their legs helplessly as the rest trampled over them.

Matilda focused on their escape, pinpointing the gate in the corner of the field. She momentarily dropped her pace as she noticed a figure standing behind it, then ducking behind the bushes.

It wasn't the first time she'd seen a mane of curly red hair disappear into bushes.

"Matilda!" shouted Oliver, pulling Matilda back up to his pace.

"Did you see her?!" panted Matilda, pointing at the hedge where she'd just seen Erin. "Did you?"

Oliver ignored her and gasped as he looked over his shoulder. Matilda didn't need to look to know that the sheep had gained on them—she could practically taste the dampness of their coats in the back of her throat.

"Nearly there!" panted Oliver. "Go!"

Matilda knew what he meant; she'd go through the gate first. She'd worked the gates hundreds of times and could slip through in a flash. She let go of Oliver's hand and pounded across the thick mud, panting as she grabbed the catch with quivering fingers, adrenaline making her fumble before she released it and squeezed through. Oliver heaved a grunt and clambered over the low fence, collapsing in a heap on the grass.

Matilda backed away from the gate, her eyes wide with shock as the sheep kept coming, ramming into one another and climbing up on their front legs, their yellow teeth sticking out from their bottom jaws as they wailed at the escapees. She stumbled to where Oliver lay on his side, staring at the almost demonic black heads that didn't look like they were going to let some wooden fence posts and wire stop them from getting to their victims. Matilda shrieked and spun around as she felt a heavy hand on her shoulder.

"What the bloody hell have you two done to my sheep?" barked a tall man with a black beard, his eyes wide under two very thick, very angry-looking eyebrows.

"Hey," panted Oliver, pulling himself up, "don't touch her!"

The man pulled his hand away from Matilda and held it up as if in surrender, but he still looked angry. He turned to the sheep as one of the mob shoved its head between a gap in the fence, its tongue lolling out of its mouth and its eyes rolling up as it pawed at the ground, trying to break through the wire.

"I was shouting from back there, but you idiots couldn't hear because you've riled up my sheep." The man, apparently a farmer, was shouting over the bleats of the sheep. He looked them up and down; they both looked like they'd come last in a mud race. "Which brings me back to my original question: What the *bloody hell* have you done to my sheep?"

"We were just walking and . . . we . . . I literally have no idea what happened," said Matilda, her body shaking with adrenaline. "They just started chasing us, and they were screaming like . . ."

"Screaming?" The man looked between Oliver and Matilda. "Have you been doing drugs?"

"What? No, she's right; that's what happened," said Oliver, looking over his shoulder at the sheep. "They tried to attack us."

The man frowned harder until his eyebrows were pointing

downward like an angry arrow. Matilda and Oliver gasped when he suddenly stepped forward, and they both stumbled out of his path as he strode to the fence and leaned over the sheep. He reached into his pocket and threw a handful of pellets over the flock. They quieted down as they turned away in search of whatever he'd thrown them.

"What's that?"

The man turned and glared at Oliver as he threw another handful. "Alfalfa pellets," said the man, throwing another handful over the sheep's heads. "Now get out of here."

Oliver looked at Matilda and whispered, "What the hell?"

"Let's just go," said Matilda.

They turned and started jogging down the path, looking over at the mass of dirty white-and-black fleeces slowly dispersing from where the man stood.

"Did you see Erin by the gate?" said Matilda, still catching her breath.

Oliver stopped and looked over his shoulder.

"That's who that was?"

Matilda nodded. "I think it's safe to say she's got something to do with this."

She looked farther down the path but couldn't see Erin. Oliver looked at Matilda, shaking his head as a smile snuck in at the corner of his mouth. He pushed his hair off his glistening forehead and bit his lip.

"What? What could you possibly be smiling about now?" asked Matilda, her hands on her hips.

The smile broke out on Oliver's face, pushing his eyebrows high on his forehead, and he put his hands together as he bent down a little.

"You owe me."

"What?"

"Don't you *what* me; you *owe* me," said Oliver. "I said if we were attacked by a pack of sheep, then you'd owe me big."

Matilda rolled her eyes, but the switch to Oliver's banter was comforting and her heart fluttered in equal parts sheep-induced adrenaline and the fact that he was flirting with her.

"It's a flock of sheep, not a pack."

"However you want to say it," said Oliver, slinging his arm over Matilda's shoulders and, quite possibly, stopping her from floating off. "You owe me."

They walked down the dirt path, and the thought of what Oliver might want from her almost distracted Matilda's mind from what had happened and why Erin had been there.

Almost, but not quite.

CHAPTER SIXTEEN

Ten days until Halloween

The Witching Well Festival banners in the cafeteria flapped high above as everyone caught up over lunch. What had happened to Ashley at the party was still the hottest topic of conversation at Gravewick Academy, and that, along with dead animals, had increased the regular festival and Halloween buzz so Matilda's classmates were rowdier than normal.

She didn't blame them. A dead body and slaughtered animals were way beyond what anyone should be worrying about right now, and Matilda had sleepwalking into the woods and being chased by a flock of sheep to throw into the mix, too. She frowned as the noise echoed from the high ceiling and looked over Oliver's shoulder, her eyes flicking from table to table in search of the only person who seemed to be connecting all the events of the last few days.

"Hello? Matilda?" said Oliver, waving his hands in front of her face. "Are you in there?"

"Hmm?" said Matilda, blinking at him.

"You are literally the least subtle person I have ever met," said Oliver, shaking his head.

Matilda watched Oliver look over his shoulder and then fold his arms.

"Huh?" she said.

"You've been sitting there all through lunch saying 'hmm' every twenty seconds. I haven't even been talking for the last five minutes."

"Sorry. I'm looking for someone."

Oliver rolled his eyes. "No shit, Sherlock. You're looking for Erin. Like I said, subtle."

Matilda leaned forward and crossed her arms on the table, her tray of food untouched in front of her.

"Don't you think we need to talk to her?"

Oliver wiped his hands together and leaned forward so they looked like they were playing a game of chess.

"I think we should just keep to ourselves. Have you looked around? Everyone is still talking about us."

Matilda looked over her shoulder. At first glance, the cafeteria was as it always was, laughter and shoving across tables, frantic homework getting scribbled before the bell rang for the next class, and chatter and heartbreak echoing between the tables and chairs. But when Matilda looked around, there were conversations behind hands and averted eyes as she caught people looking their way.

"Stupid Instagram," said Matilda, folding her arms. "There's no point in trying to change a perception if it's all *hashtag Matilda's a murderer.* The spell was a total waste if everyone's still talking about us."

"Maybe I did it wrong?" said Oliver, rubbing the back of his head. "I mean, when is sunset, technically?"

"Hmm?" said Matilda, pushing herself up as her eyes followed Erin walking to the counter.

Oliver looked around.

"No. Matilda, sit down. Just leave her," he hissed.

Matilda ignored Oliver as he frantically waved her back to their table. Not caring that half the room was probably still watching her and suspecting her of murder, she took a deep breath and walked over to the counter where Erin was choosing her lunch.

"Erin," she said, the memory of the sheep chasing them surging through her. "Hey! Erin!"

Erin stared through the glass at congealed pasta and rubbery burgers, her eyes widening when Matilda grabbed her arm and spun her around. She looked into Matilda's face and her expression switched from benign indifference at the lunchtime offerings to poisonous hostility. Matilda had gotten used to Erin watching her from a distance when they stopped being friends, but she'd done it less and less as time went on and their friendship became just another childhood memory. Erin might glance at her in the hallway, but she had never looked at Matilda with such hate before.

"Get away from me," she snapped, yanking her arm out of Matilda's grip.

"Not until you tell me why you were following us yesterday."

"I've told you before; I've got nothing to say to you."

"Why were you there? What did you do to those sheep? Why were you watching us at the party?"

Everyone in the room heard Erin's palm slap across Matilda's face before she felt its sting burn her cheek. She gasped, her mouth turned down in shock as she blinked at Erin.

"What the . . . ?" said Matilda, her voice wobbling like her trembling hands. "You *slapped* me. How could you slap me?"

"I *said* I have nothing to say to you," said Erin as she turned away, put her hand on the counter, and started tapping her fingers on the glass as she studied the food.

A pretty girl with a nose ring and long braids rushed toward Erin as Matilda felt Oliver's hands on her shoulders. He steered her away from Erin and the girl, who was gripping Erin's wrist and whispering into her ear, past the sniggering and the smartphones and out of the cafeteria with her hand and her shock plain on her face.

They pushed through the doors, and Matilda turned to Oliver.

"That just happened, right?" said Matilda, her wide eyes blinking as she gestured over her shoulder.

"Are you okay?"

"Do you have eyes? No, I'm not okay! That bitch just slapped me. I got slapped! In my face!"

"I know," said Oliver, his eyes filled with concern as he shook his head. "What was that about, do you think?"

"I don't give a shit what it was about. Nobody does that to me."

Matilda tried to shove past Oliver, shuffling side to side when he jumped backward and got in her path.

"Whoa," he said, putting his palm on the wall and blocking her. "What are you doing?"

"I need my bag. It's got my spell book in it."

"Your spell book? That's cute, Sabrina."

Matilda glowered at Oliver but felt her anger getting extinguished by his flirting.

"It's just where I keep my notes and spells."

"Is that different from the grimoire?"

Matilda nodded. "The grimoire is passed down through the bloodline, and it's the source of our power. My book is just what I carry around with me for everyday spells."

"Should I have a book? Is there an app instead?"

Matilda blew a lock of hair out of her eyes. "You can't distract me with this crap, Oliver."

"I know," said Oliver, folding his arms. "But, has your desire to go and turn Erin into a frog waned a little?" Matilda rolled her eyes and nodded. "Good, then I'll leave you to keep cooling off and *I* will go retrieve your bag, then we're going to skip and decide what to do about all of this.

Before Matilda could respond, Oliver had turned and disappeared back into the cafeteria. She folded her arms and fell back against the wall, trying to make herself believe that the bubbles in her stomach were from her anger at being slapped and not at the anticipation of skipping school and spending the afternoon with Oliver.

⋅•●•⋅

"What does it look like again?"

Matilda sighed and turned to Oliver, who was peering at a crooked tree branch like he was expecting something to suddenly unfurl from its skeletal limbs. Green ivy covered the trunk he stood at, and Matilda wondered if Ivy herself had been close by during one of her rumored trips out of the well. She pulled her book from her bag and showed him the sketch of a plant. Again.

"This. *Solanum dulcamara*, also known as bittersweet or woody nightshade. It looks like this, with reddish berries, and you're not going to find it growing on a silver birch tree."

"And why are we looking for it again? In the woods. In the cold," said Oliver, adjusting his scarf and shoving his hands in his pockets as he squinted at the plants and fallen leaves.

"I need Erin to be honest with me," said Matilda.

"That's right. That's what you keep saying."

Matilda pushed a branch out of her way and crept through the woods. She knew the area like the back of her hand, having spent so much of her childhood in the woods memorizing the names of the flora that grew there and learning to respect the fauna that made their homes there.

Erin's hand slapping across her face echoed through Matilda's head. She balled her hands into fists and took down a lungful of air, letting her woods ground her. Oliver had been right to stop her from lashing out. Matilda would have felt some gratification at first, but then the emptiness would have come crawling back after she gathered another name on her face.

Especially Erin's name.

Now, with some distance from the slap, Matilda was determined to find out what Erin was up to.

She scanned the camouflage until the fire-colored berries caught her attention, like tiny little bull's-eyes among the scrambling green vines. She pushed through the weeds, not caring that the dampness of the undergrowth soaked her jeans up to her knees.

"Found some," she called over her shoulder, hearing Oliver's footsteps trail after her, tiny clouds of his breath puffing by her ear when he stopped behind her.

"That's it?" he asked, and Matilda nodded, slipping her backpack from her shoulder and pulling out a latex glove. "Looks tasty."

Oliver reached out to the berries that dangled down in little bunches and huffed when Matilda smacked his hand and glared at him.

"No. Looks poisonous. Very poisonous."

"Oh." Oliver swallowed, then widened his eyes. "I don't think poisoning Erin is the answer, Matilda. She's not going to be very honest if she's dead."

"We're not poisoning her," said Matilda, putting the glove on then pulling a small glass jar from her bag. "She's hardly going to ingest any of it."

She plucked three of the deadly berries from the bunch and dropped them into the jar.

"Now what?" he asked.

Matilda held up the jar and swirled it around, making the berries inside chase each other around and around. She smiled at Oliver, relishing sharing the preparation of a spell in someone else's company for a change.

"Now, Mr. Private School Witch, let's see what you can do."

Twilight had come, but under the shadows of the trees the time could pass for midnight. The crows called out, protesting that they weren't ready for rest, wanting to see what the witch and her companion were cooking up in the sooty cauldron on the glowing pile of twigs and dry, curled leaves.

Matilda picked up a handful of dirt and held it above the cauldron, rubbing it between her hands before it fell into the purple liquid. She glanced at Oliver, shadows dancing over his face but not hiding his features enough that Matilda couldn't see the excitement in his eyes.

"Why the mud?"

"To honor the earth. It's where all the elements of the spell began."

"Oh."

Matilda's lips twitched as Oliver nodded.

"What do you think goes in next?"

An owl hooted and Oliver looked up, then back at Matilda, his face in a grimace.

"Not the owl?" He jerked his head around as a chorus of frogs started ribbiting. He swallowed. "Or the frogs?"

"We never use the energy of a living creature," said Matilda, dusting the last of the dirt off her hands.

"Energy?"

"Life force. Spirit. Whatever you want to call it." Matilda looked up, her cheeks warming in the glow of the fire bubbling under her cauldron. "Blood."

"Really?"

Matilda cocked her head and frowned at Oliver.

"You seem surprised?"

"I guess I am," he said. Matilda raised her eyebrows, and he went on. "I've read loads about how animal blood in witchcraft is . . ."

Oliver swallowed, his eyes searching the darkness for the right word.

"Powerful?" Matilda offered. "It's true. Blood, the force of a living thing, would make any spell more powerful, but we don't do that."

"We?" Oliver swallowed. "So, some people do?"

Matilda nodded. "People who haven't been taught about the origins of our magic, the importance of respecting what we share this earth with."

Oliver smiled. "People like me, you mean."

"I didn't say that," said Matilda. "From what I've heard, though, witches who do go down that route tend to be self-taught."

"You mean amateurs," said Oliver, raising his eyebrows play-fully.

Matilda smiled back at him. "However you want to put it. But normally, because they're not rooted naturally in the magic, they don't have the discipline or experience to handle that sort of power." She picked up the jar of bittersweet berries. "So, no to the owl, no to the frog. Next we add this."

"But you've seriously never used, like, eye of newt, toe of frog?" said Oliver, watching Matilda pour the berries into the liquid.

"I couldn't," she said, shaking her head. She thought of the thin line she danced on but never crossed. The spell she used on Ashley was probably the closest she'd ever gotten to that kind of magic, but she knew in her heart that she hadn't ended the bee's life. "I've ingested living things before but, and I know it's gross, they always come back up. If I find a feather on the ground or a snake skin, I'd use them because they're gifts from the living. My mom is always going on about balance and she's right about that at least; magic is like fire, pretty on a birthday cake but deadly if you set fire to something you shouldn't. I don't tip the scales with what I do; I might cause someone pain, but I feel that pain physically on my face."

"So, if Erin really killed all those animals, or even Ashley as well . . . ," wondered Oliver.

"Death in magic is a dark path, one you can easily get lost on. If Erin used all the death from those animals in a spell . . ." Matilda widened her eyes and shook her head. "I can't imagine the kind of power or control she would have felt. That would be some high-level shit. Where do you go after that?"

"On to human life."

"That's what I'm thinking." Matilda crossed her legs and pulled her ponytail out, shaking her hair over her shoulders.

"What if it's not her, though?"

Doubt blew a gentle breath on Matilda's ear and she suppressed a shudder as two other faces swirled into her thoughts: her mother's and her own.

She swallowed. "That's what we're going to find out. You ready? Are you grounded?"

"Grounded?" said Oliver, watching Matilda as she turned her neck side to side as if she were warming up before a race.

"When you practice witchcraft, you're using all that's around you to work your will, and you need to become part of it, to ground yourself."

"Okay," said Oliver, raising an eyebrow.

"Don't believe me if you want, but young witches spend hours alone in the woods or in fields listening to the heartbeat of what's around us, what we need to tap into when we're using magic. A good witch should be able to ground herself in the blink of a billy goat."

"Or himself," said Oliver, mirroring Matilda's seating position and stretching his arms over his head.

Matilda smiled. "A witch should be able to tap into the energy that turns the world, not just when they're practicing but at any time, like sticking your finger in the air to check the direction of the wind. So, make yourself comfortable and listen to the breath of my ancestors inviting me to draw on their souls."

"Sounds kind of . . . intimate."

Matilda met Oliver's eyes. "It is. There's nothing more intimate than the connection between a witch and her bloodline. Nothing close."

"I'm not sure I agree with that," said Oliver, a smile twinkling in his eyes.

Matilda silently thanked the nighttime for concealing her flushed cheeks from Oliver, then pulled a photo from her jacket pocket and handed it to him.

He frowned as he opened it up, tilting it toward the glow of the fire so they could both see the photograph of Erin.

"Where did you get this?" asked Oliver.

"Like I said," said Matilda, looking at the photo she'd torn down the middle, removing herself from the image but not the memory. It'd been taken a lifetime ago at a theme park after they'd been on the Big Dipper for the sixth time, which explained Erin's even wilder than usual hair. "We used to be friends."

At Matilda's nod, Oliver stuck the corner of the paper into the fire, then held it up as they both watched it burn, blue flames licking at Erin's smiling face. He held on to the paper, his fingers creeping away from the flames until, at the very last minute, he dropped it into the cauldron with a fizz.

The wind whooshed through the trees, sweeping down to tickle the leaves on the ground with its wispy fingers. Matilda took a long breath and looked at Oliver from under her heavy eyelids.

"Can you feel that?"

Oliver frowned and glanced side to side and then locked onto Matilda's eyes, a smile on his face as bright as the embers bubbling in the cauldron's contents.

"I feel it," he said, nodding.

Matilda could feel the magic approaching on the air, in the plant's stems pulsing down to their roots, and in the blood pumping through the hearts of the nighttime creatures they were sharing the floor of the woods with. Animals often visited her during her magic, so Matilda wasn't surprised when she and Oliver were joined by a white rabbit. She smiled as it hopped over, its eyes as black as the smudges of dirt that striped over its fur, fixed on the magical proceedings.

Something in the air nipped at Matilda, whispering to her that she wasn't in control of her spell, that there was something pushing her aside with crooked elbows. Matilda's eyebrows pinched together as she tried to gain control of her surroundings, to ground herself in the same way she had told Oliver to just minutes before.

"Matilda?" said Oliver.

Matilda ignored him and watched the rabbit as it twitched its nose and peered at her. Movement caught her eye, and she squinted into the darkness as another dirty white rabbit emerged from a hole deep in the muddy ground. It moved across the ground, not hopping like the first one, but hobbling. It came to a clumsy stop next to its companion, and she gasped when she saw why it hadn't hopped like a cheerful woodland creature.

Its front paw was at an angle, a tiny gnarled foot under its dull white body. Matilda's muscles poised to rush to its aid and save its unlucky foot, but the breath froze in her lungs as her eyes met its own.

Its own, one eye.

A gash dripped from the side of the rabbit's face. Matilda gasped as it was joined by a third rabbit, with one ear poking up like an antenna, the right side of its body matted with blood. It hopped to join its companions, the three of them twitching their noses and blinking as if they were just cute little pet-shop bunnies and not like something that had escaped from a slaughterhouse.

"What the hell?" Matilda said, her voice barely audible as she gaped at the rabbits and then at Oliver, who was frowning at her.

"Matilda?" said Oliver, pulling himself onto his knees and edging around the fire toward her.

"No!" she shouted as Oliver edged closer to the rabbits. They glanced at him, then looked at Matilda again, shuffling closer to her until the first one was sniffing at her knee.

"No, what?" Oliver looked over his shoulder, then back at Matilda, who'd frozen as the rabbit with one eye hopped into her lap. "You've gone gray."

"Get it off me," she whispered, holding her hands up in case her fingers brushed its dirty fur. "I can't . . . get it off me, Oliver."

Oliver's eyebrows drew together, and he shook his head a fraction, his eyes running up and down Matilda's body. "Get what off you? You're really scaring me, Matilda."

"That makes two of us," she said, swallowing a scream as rabbit number two joined its friend in her lap. "You don't see them, do you?"

Oliver was on his knees by her side, his eyes wide and searching her face.

"See what, Matilda?"

Matilda closed her eyes as tiny little paws climbed over her legs and rested on her stomach. She opened her eyes and looked down at the one-eared rabbit on its hind legs with its front paws on her chest, its nose twitching wildly as if it were talking to her in some silent rabbit language.

The shadows were coming again, but for the first time Matilda was happy to let them swoop their cape around her and pull her down into the darkness. She took one last look at the three faces staring up at her, then lifted her head and focused on Oliver before he was consumed from her vision.

"Death," she whispered, slumping on her side.

CHAPTER SEVENTEEN

Matilda opened her eyes and blinked up at the pitched roof of her garden room. She looked around and her shoulders relaxed; she was lying on her bed with a teal crocheted blanket draped over her, the one Nanna May had made for her, and there wasn't a single wisp of white fur to be seen. Movement caught her eye, and she shifted her head, checking that one of the rabbits hadn't come back for an encore.

"What are you doing?" Matilda said, her voice soft and slow from sleep.

Oliver looked up from her bookcase, a flash of relief in his eyes followed by a crooked smile that brightened his face. He glanced back at the shelves and picked up a worn book, its spine cracked and blue cover torn from years of Matilda carrying it in her schoolbag or reading it by flashlight under her duvet.

"Just looking at your little book collection," said Oliver, holding the book up. "*The Worst Witch*?"

"It's a classic for all young witches." Matilda stretched out and smiled, too comfortable on her bed to pull herself upright.

"As are *Winnie the Witch* and *Meg and Mog*, obviously," he said over his shoulder as he read the spines hiding behind glass jars and stubby candles. "Is there a witch reading list that I don't know about?"

Matilda felt like she was getting a warm bear hug just from

hearing the titles of her beloved books. Oliver left the bookcase and moved to the side of her bed, crouching down so his face was level with hers.

"My mom got them for me. She didn't want me to think that the whole world thought all witches were green and evil."

"That's pretty cool of her."

"I guess," said Matilda. She remembered curling up with her mom and reading each of the books at bedtime, loving the fantasy plus the pebbles of truth making up the witches' worlds. Something tugged inside Matilda's chest as she thought how different her and Lottie's dynamic was now. "Plus, she always said there were little seeds of truth about our kind in all those books."

Oliver perched on the side of her bed and studied Matilda's face. "You're not the color of my sports socks anymore, so that has to be a good sign. How do you feel?"

Matilda nodded, then pulled herself upright. She grabbed a cushion and tucked it between her back and the wall, then smoothed her hair out of her eyes. She was still pretty shaken, but not so much that she wasn't aware of how close Oliver was to her, in her room.

On my bed, she thought, praying to the goddess of wild things that she didn't have a trail of drool on her chin.

"I feel okay," she said, pulling her knees up to her chest and trying to ignore the growing blank spot in her magic.

"Good," said Oliver, nodding. "So maybe you can tell me what the hell happened?"

"It was another blackout," said Matilda.

"Bullshit," said Oliver. "It was more than that. You don't need to cover up this stuff from me. Tell me what it was."

Matilda sighed. "I don't know for sure. I could see these three white rabbits, but they were, like, rotting, disfigured."

"Rotting rabbits?" Oliver said, his mouth turned downward. "Gross. What do you think it was?"

Matilda looked out of the windows and shook her head.

"I don't know. I need to do some research, but I think it was a warning."

Oliver's eyebrows drew together, and he inched closer to Matilda, pulling his feet up in case whatever the warning was about might grab his ankles from under the bed.

"A warning?" he asked, swallowing.

Matilda nodded. "About everything that's been happening, with the animals and Erin." *Or my mom*, thought Matilda. "Just before I passed out, when we were doing the spell, I could feel something in the air, something, like, nagging me, scratching at me. It was darkness, but not like nighttime. A hollow shadow."

"What was it?"

"Something not good," said Matilda. Oliver blinked at her, his eyes brimming with concern. "Are you okay?"

Oliver shook his head. "Not really. This is a side to witchcraft I haven't experienced. I've been picking and choosing the cool bits of practicing. I've never had a rabbit corpse warn me about something."

"Oliver, this isn't my life, either," said Matilda, shuffling forward. "I've never seen anything like this, not so much all happening at once anyway."

"What do we do?"

"We still need to talk to Erin." Matilda looked around the room. "What did you do with my spell stuff?"

Oliver stood and walked over to the door where the cauldron and Matilda's bag were sitting.

"I managed to pack everything up."

Matilda stood and joined him. She crouched down and peered into the glossy liquid resting in the bottom of the cauldron.

"I didn't spill any," said Oliver. "I got everything, and everybody, back safely."

"How *did* you manage to get me back?"

The muscles in Oliver's jaw relaxed, and he bit his lip as he crouched down opposite Matilda.

"Broomstick."

"You think you're joking, but there's some truth in all that," said Matilda, tucking her hair behind her ear and raising her eyebrows.

"What? Flying broomsticks? Come on."

Matilda nodded. "In a way. Witches used to rub themselves with ointments made with plants that had hallucinogenic qualities, and then they felt like they were flying."

"On a broomstick, though?"

"Every good witch has a broomstick, Oliver. We have one in the house. They're a symbol of cleansing, infused with the essence of the home, life, family. Anyway, when they used the ointments, they'd feel and see things, like an out-of-body experience. They felt like they were floating through the air, above the earth, flying past the moon."

"You really know a lot about all this, don't you?"

"I have to. It's my heritage. I'm just glad all the books my grandmother made me read and all the stories she's told me have actually stuck."

Oliver nodded gently as he smiled at her. "Well, I'm impressed."

He bit his lip again, gently, then locked his eyes on Matilda's as the space between them got smaller and smaller. Matilda held her breath, watching Oliver's mouth as it got closer to hers. She almost forgot they were in her garden room until a jangle of breaking glass startled them both. Oliver stood up.

"What was that?" he whispered.

Matilda's eyes darted around her bedroom, seeking out the culprit that had interrupted her potential bliss. *If Victor is in here, he's in big trouble*, she thought, then spotted glass shards twinkling on the floorboards.

The black bramble bush that Nanna May had been trying to hack back outside Matilda's garden room had grown up the sides of the building and was now creeping across the windows. A gnarled tip was tapping against the weathered wood where it had just pushed one of the diamond-shaped panes of glass out of the frame. Matilda jumped up and stormed over to the window.

"This stupid weed, whatever it is, has been growing outside my room," she said, furious with the bramble for disturbing her and Oliver. "And now it's started growing through my window! Look. I mean, *how?*"

Oliver joined her and frowned at the glass on the floor, then the space where the bramble was poking through.

"Maybe the wind blew it?" he said, gesturing for Matilda to follow him outside.

They walked around to the broken window outside and Matilda put her hands on her hips as she peered at the overgrown bush.

"Nanna May keeps cutting it back, but it doesn't seem to stop growing." Matilda sighed. "Oh well, just another thing to add to the list of weird."

Oliver nodded. "The ever-expanding list of weird," said Oliver. He looked at the window, then at Matilda, his eyes moving across her face. "Hey, listen, what're you doing tomorrow?"

Matilda shrugged. "It's Tuesday, so school."

"It's not just Tuesday, though, is it?" Matilda frowned at Oliver, then rolled her eyes. "Thought I'd forget it's your birthday tomorrow?"

"I never do anything on my birthday," she said, folding her arms.

"Until this year," said Oliver, smiling. "Let's skip again. I think we deserve it."

"What're we going to do?"

"Leave that to me. I think I have a plan, birthday girl."

CHAPTER EIGHTEEN

Nine days until Halloween

"Excited?"

Oliver glanced at Matilda as he drove, his window open a crack, letting the crisp autumn breeze ruffle his hair. Happy to be hanging out with another witch, especially because that witch was Oliver, Matilda mirrored his smile and looked back at him.

"I'm not sure excited is the right word. Maybe if I knew where we were going?"

"And ruin the surprise? No way, birthday girl. We're nearly there anyway," said Oliver, looking between the map on his phone and the road ahead.

They drove down twisty-turny lanes on the outskirts of Gravewick, where lone cottages on crocus-lined tracks hid behind ancient wooden gates. It felt good to leave school and her mom and the blackouts behind and let the natural beauty of her surroundings distract her.

"So what did you get for your birthday?"

"Nothing," said Matilda.

Oliver whipped around to look at her so quickly Matilda felt the car move.

"Nothing?" he asked. Matilda shook her head. "Why not?"

"Some witches don't celebrate their birthday until the first new moon after."

"Is that what you'll do?"

Matilda let out a long sigh and nodded. "It's what my mom and my grandmother want to do. They like tradition. I'll receive gifts, there's a big deal about passing the family grimoire down to me, and then there'll be a feast."

"So, what sort of stuff's in this grimoire, then? Why's it so special?"

"I don't actually know, as I've never seen inside it, not until they give it to me on my 'birthday,'" said Matilda, doing quote marks with her fingers around the word.

"Why not?"

"A witch isn't considered responsible enough to access the family grimoire until she turns seventeen. Lineage magic is powerful, and its source is the grimoire. The idea is that if you learn everything you need about the craft before you turn seventeen, then you can be trusted with it."

Oliver glanced at Matilda, narrowing his eyes as he looked between her and the road ahead. "You're not telling me something."

Matilda flushed. "What do you mean?"

"You're holding back on me, I can tell. Come on, birthday girl, spill."

"Well," she said, looking out of the window, "I *have* seen a part of it."

"Ha! I knew it. What did you see? Love spell?" he said, waggling his eyebrows.

"You can find a basic love spell in most books on witchcraft."

"Good to know, thank you." Oliver's eyes crinkled as he glanced at Matilda. "So, what was it, then?"

Matilda took a moment to look at Oliver's profile as he drove them toward whatever birthday surprise he had in store for her.

She felt so light when she was around him, not having to drop a potion into his drink or snatch a piece of stray hair from his shoulder. Talking to him was so different from whispering incantations behind her hand from a dark corner, and the more time she spent with him the more she realized how isolated she'd felt before she met Oliver, creating friendships instead of building them.

"The spell to hide the scars on my face," said Matilda. "My dad found it in our grimoire and left it for me before he left."

"That was cool of him," said Oliver.

"My mother certainly doesn't think so," said Matilda, folding her arms.

"So, what is the spell anyway? I'd love to hide mine."

She shook her head. "I can't tell you; it's a family secret, and I would be betraying my bloodline."

"Fair enough," he said, checking the rearview mirror as he put his turn signal on. "It's a day of secrets and surprises, then. And speaking of surprises, we're nearly there, *and* I've got you another little surprise. It's just in there."

Oliver kept his eyes on the road and waved his hand in the general direction of Matilda's knees. Her heart fluttered as she looked around to see what he was pointing at, then, guessing he must mean the glove compartment, she reached forward and opened it up.

"In here?" she said, opening it up.

"No, the side pocket in your door, next to your seat," he said, driving the car over into a small pull off on the side of the road.

Matilda nodded and went to close the glove compartment, but noticed something inside among the sunglasses and car manuals. She reached in and pulled it out.

"Did you make this?" she said, holding up a small doll made

from thin pieces of rope tied onto one another to make arms, legs, and a body. A large knot at the top formed the head and frayed knots at the ends of the arms and legs made little splayed hands and feet. "It was in your glove compartment."

"Um, *no*," said Oliver, frowning at the object as Matilda turned it over in her hand. "What the hell *is* that? And what the hell's it doing in my car?"

"A poppet," said Matilda. "It's not yours?"

"No, it's not mine," said Oliver, recoiling from it as Matilda held it up to him. "It looks like one of those voodoo dolls." Matilda looked at Oliver, then slowly put the poppet back into the glove compartment. "No! What are you doing? Don't put it back! It *is* a voodoo doll, isn't it?"

"Similar, although they're not always used to hurt people. They can be used for healing, too. You sure it's not yours?"

"I think I would remember putting *that* in my glove compartment, don't you?" said Oliver, his eyes blinking wide. "Do you think someone put that thing in my car?"

Matilda's eyes searched his face and nodded gently. Oliver sucked air in through his nose and gripped the steering wheel.

"Have you been feeling okay?"

"What? *Why?*" said Oliver, almost hyperventilating.

Matilda shook her head. "It's probably not even real, Oliver. It's nearly Halloween and the Witching Well Festival is soon. Maybe it was one of your friends? Have you had anyone else your car?"

Oliver stared at Matilda, then bobbed his head up and down. "Yeah. Guys from soccer, all the time."

"There you go, then," said Matilda, then a thought flashed in her head faster than she could hide it from Oliver.

"What? What's wrong?"

Matilda bit her lip. "Remember when we saw Erin in the field? Maybe she put it in your car?"

Oliver swallowed. "You think it was her? You really think she's messing around with magic? Why me, though?"

Matilda looked at the little figure tucked inside the glove compartment. *Why would Erin target Oliver, and how did she even know about poppets and that sort of magic*, Matilda wondered. They'd been friends since elementary school, and Erin had never spoken about magic or witches. She took a deep breath and slammed the glove compartment closed.

"Look, honestly? I don't think it was her," said Matilda. "But . . ."

"But?"

"Just in case, you need to submerge that thing in moving water, then bury it in your garden before sunset tonight, okay?"

Oliver kept his eyes on the closed compartment and nodded. Matilda's stomach was bubbling with anger. She still felt like Oliver wanting to spend time with her was some kind of fluke, and a dead body at the party and a possibly cursed poppet hidden inside his car were surely going to snap him out of whatever act of goodwill his interest in her was.

"So," said Matilda, watching Oliver, who was still staring at the glove compartment and its sinister contents. "Do you want to just take me home?"

"What?" he said, his eyes finally resting on her face. "No! Unless, do you want to go?"

"No," said Matilda, "not if you don't."

"Good," said Oliver, a small smile warming his face. "Because I don't."

He turned the engine off, and they sat in the sudden quiet, smiling at each other, until Oliver leaned forward. Matilda held her breath, sure that he could hear her heart beating against her rib cage as he got so close she could smell his shower gel, until she realized he was gesturing for her to retrieve the box from the side compartment.

In all the poppet excitement she'd forgotten what she'd originally been looking for. She turned and made a big fuss of fishing out the item so Oliver couldn't see her red cheeks, then turned back with the small black box in her hand.

"Happy birthday, birthday girl," he said. "Open it up, then."

Matilda looked at the small box in her hands. Her fingers shook as she gently pulled the lid off, conscious that Oliver was watching her. Inside was a bracelet made of perfectly round gemstones that shimmered when she lifted it out of the box and closer to her eyes.

"It's nothing much," said Oliver, the nervous anticipation of a gift giver clear in his voice. "I just wanted to get you something to open. Although, should I have waited until that new moon thing?"

Matilda bit her lip. "No, it's fine. I mean . . . thank you; you didn't have to get me a present."

"You know what it is?"

Matilda held it up to the window and turned it over in her hand, the black surface revealing peacock greens and blues as it glistened, like water mixing with oil.

"It's labradorite," she said, smiling. "Helps to aid tranquility and peace of mind."

"Thought you could use some of that in your life right now. We both could," said Oliver, taking the bracelet from Matilda and fastening it around her wrist. She felt tiny volts of electricity shooting from where the tips of his fingers kept brushing her skin and was almost relieved when he let go. "Oh, and it's good for your digestion, too."

"Well, that's always a good thing," she said, turning her wrist over to admire the bracelet, then dropping her hands back into her lap. "It's perfect, Oliver. Thank you."

"You're welcome. But the birthday fun doesn't end here, so out you hop and onto surprise number two. Or if you count the little guy in there," said Oliver, "surprise number three."

As Oliver got out of the car and stretched his long limbs, Matilda said a little prayer to the goddess that the poppet in the glove compartment was just one of Oliver's friends joking around and not someone putting the only guy she'd ever felt truly comfortable with in danger.

CHAPTER NINETEEN

The autumn wind kept flicking Matilda's hair around until she tied it in a loose side braid as they walked along, bouncing questions about magic and school and family back and forth like a game of pro table tennis. The morning sky reflected Matilda's mood, bright and promising, and the hedgerows they passed offered a warm hug against the cool wind, accompanied by a soundtrack from the birds, the distant smell of fires warming households, and, as Matilda had noticed for the last few minutes, the sound of rushing water.

"Nearly there, birthday girl," said Oliver, beaming at Matilda as he kindly took shorter steps so she could keep up. If he was still worried about the poppet, he was doing a good job of hiding it. "You didn't eat before you came, did you?"

Matilda frowned. "I had breakfast."

"How long ago?"

Matilda looked at her phone. "About three hours. Why?"

Oliver raised his eyebrows. "You'll see."

They came to the end of a path, and Oliver put his hands on Matilda's shoulders to steer her to the left, leaving two throbbing patches of heat where his palms had been. The muddy path opened up to a narrow road sloping upward, and Matilda took a long, cooling breath as she walked alongside Oliver, her legs starting to feel the pinch from all the walking and now trudging uphill.

"So, I've been thinking about you a lot, and, correct me if I'm wrong, but the last week has been pretty tough on you, right? With what happened at the party and the blackouts and those sheep? Oh, and the zombie rabbits." Matilda nodded, reluctant to let those thoughts muscle in on such a beautiful morning and mute the fact that Oliver just said he'd been thinking about her. "The other thing I thought was that, and I hope you're not offended by this, you're one hell of a control freak."

"Hey," said Matilda, jabbing an elbow into Oliver's side, "you hardly know me."

"Oh, I'm getting there, though, and this adorable personality trait just radiates from you, like, all the time. The witchy part of you loves to keep things in control, am I right?"

"Maybe . . . ," said Matilda, biting the inside of her cheek.

"And you never switch it off. I see you watching everything around you all the time, wanting to jump in and take control. So, we're going to give you a little distraction from all that."

She'd never felt quite as exposed as she did right now, not knowing what Oliver had in store for her but also because he saw things in her that she tried to ignore in herself. Oliver nodded at something ahead of them, and Matilda realized they'd been walking toward a stone bridge.

The bridge was just wide enough for two cars to drive across at the same time, although they hadn't seen a single vehicle during their walk. As they reached it, Matilda noted the beautiful red ivy growing along the old stone and took some comfort knowing that her ancestor's presence made it all the way to the outskirts of Gravewick. A shallow river babbled beneath the bridge, its grassy banks home to a flock of ducks waddling around, then diving into the water, bobbing under the surface in search of midmorning snacks.

There was movement on the bridge, and a woman wearing a red cap with a black ponytail poking out the back pushed herself off the waist-high wall and waved to them. A red van with yellow writing emblazoned down the side was parked on the other side of the bridge opposite, and someone wearing the same red cap was leaning against the driver's door. Matilda's mouth went dry as she read the word ADRENALINE on the van, and she realized why Oliver had asked if she'd eaten before they came.

"Oliver?" said the woman, shielding her eyes from the sun.

"Yeah," said Oliver, stretching his hand out to the woman. "Rebekah?"

Rebekah grabbed his hand and smiled brightly as she shook it.

"I wasn't sure whether we could park up here, so my car's back there. I hope that's okay?" said Oliver, pointing over his shoulder.

"That's fine, we'd rather not have too many vehicles on the bridge so that works for us."

"I figured that," said Oliver, then he looked at Matilda. "Plus, I kind of wanted to build up some birthday excitement for Matilda."

Rebekah turned to Matilda, her eyes crinkling as she smiled ever wider.

"So, you're the birthday girl, then?" Matilda nodded and looked at the man by the van. "That's my buddy Pete, he'll be giving me a hand today. Matilda, you ready to have some fun?"

Rebekah grabbed Matilda's limp hand and pumped it up and down as Matilda looked at some scaffolding that was attached to middle of the wall. She swallowed as she craned her neck to see the metal poles and joints fastened together holding a mesh platform that stuck out of the side of the bridge.

"Um . . . yes?" Matilda managed, her voice already retreating.

"Has Oliver told you what we're doing today?" Matilda shook her head and swallowed, eyeing the platform on the bridge. "A surprise—even better! So, what we've got set up for you is a bridge swing. You know what that is?"

"I think I can guess," said Matilda, already struggling to get her words out, as her mouth had dried up.

"Okay, well, I'm here to make sure you enjoy yourself and keep you safe at the same time. Pete and I will grab you a harness and get you all strapped up, talk about safety, and then we can get you out onto the platform there, ready to jump." Rebekah put a hand on Matilda's elbow and smiled. "You still up for it?"

Rebekah had such a warm smile and open face that Matilda didn't feel that she could tell her that no, she absolutely did not want to do anything that involved the words *bridge* or *swinging* and why would anyone put them together and think it was a good idea? Instead she nodded and concentrated on trying not to hyperventilate and the fact that Oliver had organized the activity for her.

"Great," said Rebekah, clapping her hands together. "Let me get the gear, and we can get started."

"Cool, huh?" said Oliver, smiling as he put his hands on the wall and leaned over. "I did bridge swinging on vacation when I was a kid, and it was awesome."

"They let *children* do this?!"

Oliver laughed, his mouth so wide Matilda could see his back teeth. "Yes, it's perfectly safe, and I've checked Rebekah's company out: total professionals. And hey, we're not that high up, maybe only like seventy feet?"

"That's *way* higher than we need to be," said Matilda. Her heart pounded as she tried to work out how she would even get onto the platform, and she backed away shaking her head at the thought of climbing over the wall. "I'm sorry, but there's no way I can do this, Oliver, no way in the world. It was a nice thought, but I'm not going anywhere near that thing—let alone jumping off it. This isn't what bridges were invented for. This is the *opposite* of what bridges were invented for."

Oliver put his hands on her shoulders, the heat from his touch not doing anything to settle the butterflies already flapping their wings inside her stomach.

"Come on, you're a badass witch, remember? You can do this, and I promise once you come up, you'll want to do it again."

Matilda shook her head, craning her neck to look at the ducks who were very safely waddling around on the bank.

"Yes, but *I* do the scaring; I don't go around looking to scare myself, thank you." She shook her head as she looked at Oliver. "I can't, Oliver. I'm really sorry, but I can't."

"Fair enough," he said, disappointment rippling across his forehead. "I'll tell Rebekah before she hauls out the equipment."

"You can still do it? I'd love to watch."

Oliver shook his head, offering Matilda a small smile. "It's okay, we can go and find something else to do."

The disappointment in Oliver's eyes was unbearable. Matilda bit her lip as she looked out at the platform, then back at Rebekah, who was unpacking the equipment from the van. Matilda clenched her shaking fists and turned to Oliver, clearing her throat as if she were about to recite an incantation.

"I've changed my mind. I'll do it."

"Matilda, it's okay," said Oliver, brushing his hair up from his forehead. "This was a stupid idea."

"No, it wasn't, and you're right, I do need to let go. I need to not think about what's been happening with everything, and if dangling from a bridge is the way to do it, then that's what I'll do."

"Matilda . . ."

"I'm ready," said Matilda as Rebekah walked over with a black harness covered in buckles and loops hanging over her shoulder and a small metal scale in her hand.

"Great," said Rebekah, holding the harness out in front of her. "Let's get you nice and tight in here, and I'll go through the safety instructions."

Matilda nodded as she cooperated with Rebekah, stepping on and off the scale, then focusing on her every word as she went through exactly what was going to happen and what Matilda needed to do. Every now and then, Matilda would glance at Oliver, whose eyebrows were drawn together in deep concentration. Matilda made Rebekah go through it all one more time, just to make sure.

"You ready?" asked Rebekah.

"What do you think, birthday girl? Still up for it?" said Oliver.

"Yes," said Matilda, taking a long calming breath. "I'm ready."

Rebekah led Matilda to the side of the bridge and connected her harness to the end of a rope that was curled up in a loop on the platform. She turned Matilda around a couple of times and checked her harness, giving Matilda a good shake and a pull from all directions, then helped her climb over the wall.

Matilda planted her feet onto the mesh platform as her senses suddenly tripled in awareness and she could hear the sound of rushing water much louder than from the safety of the bridge. She took another breath, the normally cleansing smell of the elements below her doing very little to calm her wobbling legs, but she gripped the rope and closed her eyes, sending a silent prayer out into the open.

Sisters forgotten, keep me safe. Mothers beyond, keep me safe.

"Matilda? You ready?" called Rebekah.

Matilda tried to swallow, but her mouth was as dry as sand. She turned her head a fraction, hardly daring to move in case she lost her balance, and called over her shoulder.

"Yes . . . ," she croaked, "yes, I'm ready."

"Okay, girl! Now it's all on you," shouted Rebekah, each of her words swollen with belief in Matilda. "Do you want me to count you in?"

"Y-yes!" called Matilda, squeezing her eyes shut as her heart pounded through her eardrums.

"On one, okay? Here we go . . . *three* . . ."

Matilda opened her eyes, the river below suddenly seeming much farther away than it had a few seconds before. The wind whipped at her legs, and she felt sure it was strong enough to tip her over the edge before she was ready.

". . . *two* . . ."

She shuffled forward, gasping as the platform shook under her movement. Her body was doing everything it could to keep steady against her shaking limbs, but standing still had become the most alien thing in the world. She held her breath, knowing what was coming next, and she looked ahead at the horizon, the branches of the trees in the distance holding their limbs up as if they were cheering her on.

You can do this, Matilda. You can do this.

". . . *one!*"

Without giving a single beat for a negative thought to enter her head, Matilda leaped from the platform, a scream from the very core of her soul reeling out of her as she went. Wind whistled past her ears as she descended, feeling like she was plummeting through the air with absolutely nothing to stop her, her white knuckles clinging to the rope. She was sure she was going to hit the ducks below until suddenly the rope took up the slack and she swung right underneath the bridge, through the shadows, and out of the other side, her screams echoing against the damp stone each time she swung under the arch.

The swinging started to slow, and Matilda stopped screaming and let go of the rope, swinging back and forth, her arms and legs stretched out like she was a starfish. The smell of the river rushed past her, and she was sure her wide smile would be plastered to her face for eternity by the wind rushing past her. Back and forth she went until she was moving at a pace where she could see the same bricks under the bridge each time she swung beneath it and make out the different markings of the ducks that were still ignoring her.

Finally, she stopped moving, and she heard a metallic clunk before she was winched upward. She held on to the rope and looked all around her, the rusty browns and oranges of the autumn the most perfect backdrop for the euphoria that was glowing from her red cheeks.

"Okay?" asked Rebekah as she reached the platform, a knowing smile on her face. Matilda bobbed her head up and down, still smiling ear to ear, certain that she'd left her voice under the bridge somewhere. Rebekah nodded. "Excellent." She helped Matilda back onto the bridge where Oliver was waiting for her, a huge smile tickling his bright eyes. Matilda beamed at him as Rebekah unbuckled the loops and connectors on her harness. She felt like a different person from the one who stood in the same spot before, refusing to jump from the bridge and out of her comfort zone. Now she felt a hundred times lighter, as if being able to fly back and forth under the bridge meant that she could float off into the sky whenever she wanted.

"So," he said as Matilda stepped out of her harness, "what did you think?"

Matilda shook her head as she beamed at Oliver. She couldn't believe that she'd been soaring through the air just minutes before, feeling nothing but the wind on her face as all her worries were flung from her soul into the water each time she swung under the bridge.

"It was . . . it was . . . exhilarating," she said, her voice shaking from adrenaline. "And you were right."

"Right about what?" said Oliver.

Matilda let out a long sigh and looked over her shoulder at the edge of the bridge. "I want to do it again."

*　◆　*

Oliver switched the engine off as they pulled up outside Ferly Cottage, and Matilda realized she hadn't stopped smiling the entire journey home. She looked out of the window; the house was still, so she and Oliver wouldn't have an audience.

"Here we go," said Oliver, "delivering you home in one piece."

Matilda's cheeks ached as she smiled again. "Thank you, and thank you for today. I never thought I'd have so much fun swinging under a bridge. I mean, I never thought I would actually swing under a bridge at all."

Oliver smiled back. "Glad to hear it."

"So, I guess I'll see you at school tomorrow? Unless you want to come in for a bit?"

Oliver glanced at the house, then shook his head. "I better get going. Got some stuff to do today, then there's that poppet to drown and bury later before sunset, remember?"

Matilda's heart sank into the pit of her stomach. She'd had such a wonderful time with Oliver that she'd forgotten about the poppet. She looked at the glove compartment and everything else came rushing back and pressed down on her shoulders: Ashley, the sheep, the rabbits.

The blackouts.

"Good point." She looked at Oliver, willing him to say something to keep her in the car, but there was silence. "Well, I'll leave you with your poppet, then."

Oliver nodded. "Bye."

"Yeah, bye."

Matilda turned as slowly as she could and clunked open the door handle. She gave him a tight smile and got out of the car, wondering whether she'd misread him all along or maybe even that she'd imagined he was going to kiss her the day before in her room.

She turned to close the car door, her heart fluttering as she looked up and he was standing on the other side of the door.

"Hey," he said, resting his hands on top of the door.

"Hey."

"Sorry, I . . ." Oliver paused, biting the inside of his cheek as he looked at his feet. "I was kind of feeling the pressure in there."

The world held its breath and tiptoed backward as Oliver locked eyes with Matilda. Fireworks spun inside her stomach as he took a step closer to the open door between them. She was caught between his eyes and his lips, stuck in an unbearable moment of anticipation that she wanted to speed up and never end at the same time. They both moved closer to the door until she could smell his shampoo mixed with the scent of the river. He leaned down and finally his lips were on hers, switching her entire body up to ten. She felt his hand on her neck, heat rushing across her skin at his touch, and they fell into the kiss together until Matilda could sense it coming to an end. Oliver pulled away, breathing deeply, and gently pressed his lips against hers again, once, twice, and a third time.

He straightened up and beamed at her.

"Happy birthday."

"Thanks," she said, smiling back at him.

Matilda left Oliver standing by his car and tried not to skip back to her garden room as she thought that this was possibly the best birthday she'd ever had in her life.

CHAPTER TWENTY

Eight days until Halloween

Matilda checked her phone again, then craned her neck, trying to look past all the uniforms that were congesting the hallway. If it was possible, she felt even happier than she had last night. Her dad had texted her on the way to school, checking to see how she was and that he could still come and visit for the weekend. She told him she was fine, and she was looking forward to seeing him, then he must have gotten distracted again, because he forgot to say goodbye.

"Looking for someone?"

She turned around and couldn't stop the smile from erupting on her face. Oliver was leaning against the lockers, his arms folded as he smiled back at her. They'd been messaging each other all night, but she still refused to believe it was real until she saw him at school.

Oliver leaned down and gestured with his chin, enticing Matilda into him until she was close enough to kiss, his lips bringing her to life a hundred times more than a shot of espresso. She felt his hand close around hers and let him lead her down the hall.

"So, how you doing?" said Oliver, leaning into her ear.

I feel like my heart's about to explode, thought Matilda.

"Fine."

"Any more blackouts, dead animals, bodies?"

A black cloud shaded Matilda's internal sunshine as Oliver reminded her of the not-so-romantic events of the last week or so.

She shook her head.

"That's what I like to hear. And also, I got rid of that creepy poppet thing so I think that's cause for celebration, don't you agree?"

Matilda shrugged. The idea of celebrating seemed a little too much like tempting fate, but Oliver was practically bouncing with excitement and she was glad to see him as happy as she was.

"Come on, Matilda. We need this. Our first almost kiss ended with a dead body falling on top of us, and you kept fainting whenever we spent time together, although I still believe that was purely due to your overwhelming attraction to me." Matilda elbowed Oliver, and he pulled her into his side again. "Our romantic countryside walk turned into the sheep version of *The Walking Dead*, but now? We celebrated your birthday together, I finally kissed you without anything going wrong, and I'm getting pretty good with the witch stuff. I think that's definitely cause for celebration."

Matilda looked down the hall. Green and orange streamers zigzagged the ceiling and a dummy of a witch on a broomstick hung just above them, her green hooded cloak flying out behind her.

"There's the Witching Well Festival; it starts tonight. We could go to that if you like?"

"See, I knew there was an idea in that pretty head," said Oliver, kissing the top of Matilda's head.

"Thanks," said Matilda, frowning as Oliver pulled away. "It's a wonder I have the brain space for ideas considering all the cooking and cleaning I should be thinking about, right?"

"Sorry," said Oliver sheepishly. "Your head is pretty, though."

"If you say so," said Matilda, smiling a little so Oliver knew she was messing with him.

"So it's a date. A death-, blackout-, and crazed-sheep-free date."

"Well, the whole festival is celebrating someone's death, so . . ."

"Blackout-and-crazed-sheep-free date only, then," said Oliver.

Matilda smiled. She didn't care what kind of date it was. It was a date.

"This is perfect, Matilda."

Oliver squeezed Matilda's gloved hand as they walked beneath a fern-green banner strung between two trees, *Gravewick Witching Well Festival* spelled out in gold swirly letters across it. Two scarecrowlike figures loomed over them on either side of the entrance, holding flickering lanterns in their scrawny hands, their bowed heads shrouded in tattered green cloaks that hung all the way to the ground.

"They look like they're real," said Oliver, looking between each of the figures. "They can't be, though. They're not, are they?"

Matilda smiled. "They're not real, but there'll be lots more inside, and you'll see people wearing the green cloaks, too. That's what Ivy used to wear, apparently."

Oliver craned his neck until they left the cloaked figures behind them, then beamed at Matilda as they steered through huddles of people waiting for hot apple cider or bonfire toffee served by witches and devils. People walked past wrapped up head to toe in anticipation of a long night in the cold arms of autumn, dragging broken chairs, pallets, and other wooden items to the pile of wood in the center of the field where Boy Scouts directed them to dump their furniture.

"What's going on there?" asked Oliver.

"There'll be a massive bonfire at the end of the festival, but then they'll remove all the Ivy stuff and do it all again on Halloween."

"What's that?" said Oliver, pointing to the right of the bonfire.

Matilda turned to see people milling around a fake stone structure, a pair of black-and-white striped legs with black lace-up boots sticking out the top of it.

Matilda sighed. "That's supposed to be Ivy."

"What are they all doing?"

"They're throwing coins in and making wishes. It's like a whole thing for the festival. Nobody gives a shit that she was an actual real person who died a horrible death because they give all the money collected to charity at the end of the festival."

Oliver frowned as he watched people throw their offerings into the fake well, the coins shimmering in the fairy lights like magic dust.

"Do you come every year?" he asked.

Matilda shook her head. "It's bigger since the last time I came. It used to just be a day, but now it goes on for three."

She watched two girls from her class check that the pompoms on their woolly hats were just right before they held up mugs of hot chocolate in fingerless gloves and smiled for a selfie.

"You don't come every year?" asked Oliver. Matilda tore her eyes away from the girls and shook her head. "Why not?"

"My mom doesn't like it," said Matilda. "My dad snuck me out for it a couple of times, though."

Oliver put his arm around her neck and pulled her closer, kissing the top of her head.

They stopped in front of three cloaked figures that looked as though they were hovering above a pile of pumpkins.

"Are pumpkins just a Halloween thing or a witch thing?" asked Oliver.

"Both. Halloween is when the veil between the now and after is pulled back, so the scary faces keep the evil away but the flames inside guide our dead back to us."

"And," said Oliver, "do you want the dead to visit?"

"Sometimes," said Matilda, peering up at the wooden signs in the cloaked figures' skeletal hands.

"Okay," said Oliver, reading the words on each of the signs, "what do you want to do first? Food? Games? Maze?"

"I don't mind; you choose."

"Let's start with food, then see what these games are about so I can impress you with my athletic ability."

Hollowed-out apples stuffed with LED candles lined the path toward the food stalls, and their stomachs growled as the aroma of bacon rolls, baked potatoes, and burgers beckoned them to line up for hot food on the chilly autumn night.

They strolled past the stalls, reading the menus outside each until Matilda felt Oliver head toward a large tent with green and black ripped material hanging in front of its entrance and pumpkins piled on either side. They pushed back the frayed curtains into the tent, where people sat on blankets on top of bales of hay, drinking from steaming mugs as they chatted and laughed. Oliver rubbed his hands together.

"What would you like?"

Matilda looked at the blackboard by their feet and her stomach growled again. "Can I get some fries? And a hot dog? And a hot chocolate?"

"Sounds good. Do you want to wait here and I'll get it?"

Matilda nodded and sat down on one of the hay bales. Oliver left her and joined the line for food as she checked her makeup on her phone, not daring to take off her woolly hat for fear of the flat hair that would be plastered across her forehead. She turned to put her phone back in her bag, glancing at the strings of golden leaves and fake crows and owls circling above them. The atmosphere warmed her insides, and she looked around at everyone curled up on the hay sofas and smiled, then froze as she noticed someone in the far corner.

A man with a beard who Matilda recognized was gesticulating as he leaned down, speaking quietly into the ear of a woman who was looking away from him and shaking her head. Matilda narrowed her eyes until she pinpointed where she knew the man from; it was the farmer who owned the sheep that had tried to attack them.

The woman he was talking to was her mother.

Matilda gasped, her cheeks flushing as she grabbed her bag and stood up. Her mother looked at the man, then glowered as she pointed her finger at him. He shook his head, neither of them looking her way as they were so engrossed in their argument. Matilda hurried outside into the welcoming cool air.

"Hey, where'd you go?" said Oliver, juggling an armful of food and a drinks holder as he came up behind her. His smile faded as Matilda looked at him. "What's up?"

Matilda glanced inside the tent just as the wind blew, flapping the black material like waving fingers before it concealed her mom from view. She opened her mouth to tell Oliver that her mom was in there, that she was there even though she never let Matilda go, and that she was with the angry farmer who owned the sheep and the slaughtered cattle, but the look of disappointment etched on Oliver's face made her close her mouth and smile at him instead.

"Nothing, just, I wanted to get some fresh air," lied Matilda. "Got my fries?"

Oliver smiled and handed her a cardboard tray and cup of hot chocolate, steam swirling up through the tiny hole in the cover. It was worth the lie just for his dimples, and she resettled herself into the festivities, closing the drawer on the questions about her mom, ready to open it later.

* * *

"This is *literally* impossible."

Matilda stifled a laugh as she watched Oliver stab at the red apples floating in the barrel, swear words exploding from his mouth each time he tried to catch one with the small, pretend, black-handled knife in his hand.

"You just have to kind of get it right above," said Matilda, her tongue in the corner of her mouth as she set her sights on an apple bobbing at the side, "and *stab*."

She smiled and held up her pretend athame with the apple stuck on the end of it.

"Cheat. You've done this before."

"Four years ago!"

"You're using witchcraft, then." Oliver looked up at the others by their barrels and put his hand to the side of his mouth. "Witch! We've got a witch here, and she's using magic to cheat at this ridiculous game!"

Matilda shoved Oliver, then pulled her apple off the knife and put it in a small basket.

"Do you want to do something else?" she asked.

"No way. I'm not going anywhere until I've got one of these bastards," said Oliver, his eyebrows pulled together in concentration.

"It's not a competition, Oliver."

"Yes, it is; it's a competition between me and these apples."

"Competitive much?"

"I am. I'm the first to admit it." Oliver paused, his hand poised to stab into an apple, then leaned into Matilda and whispered, "That's how I got my first scar."

"What did you do?"

"My best friend at my old school. We were super tight, but when we got on the soccer field that all went out the window because we were just as good as each other, so we were always going for captain. One game, he was being seriously aggressive, barging me, pulling me down when I was going in for a header, and then he went in for a really dangerous tackle and ended up busting my ankle."

"And he's your friend?" Oliver nodded and Matilda rolled her eyes. "I will never understand boys."

"Oh yeah? Don't go thinking this is a one-way conversation," said Oliver, gently pinching Matilda's waist until she giggled. "You're telling me how you got your first scar after this."

"Fine. So what did you do?"

Oliver's eyes twinkled. "I made him mix up his left and right."

"Seriously? Not bad. Very subtle."

"It was hilarious watching him from the sidelines on my crutches. He didn't know what the hell was happening, and everyone was shouting at him, even the coach thought he was messing around. Anyway, that's when I got my first." Oliver shrugged. "I didn't think what I'd done to him was that bad."

"That's how it works. However small, however petty, it comes back at you."

"It was the first thing that coven warned me about."

"Where is it, your scar?" asked Matilda.

Oliver lifted his arm and pointed down his side. "Down there."

"What name?"

Oliver smiled. "Davis."

Matilda grimaced. "S's are bad."

"You're telling me. I've got Susan here," he said, pointing at the left of his chest.

"Why?"

Oliver shook his head. "Uh-uh, you have to tell me yours now. What was your first?"

Matilda flushed as she went back to her first scar, her first spell against someone, but skipped over that memory for one she was prepared to share with Oliver. "The name was Beth. I made her hair fall out."

"What? Why?"

"Because her mom did it in a French braid and I was jealous."

"That's cold, Matilda." Oliver put a hand up to his own head. "You're not jealous of mine, are you?"

"At least she wasn't my best friend."

Oliver smiled and bit his lip. "You're telling me you've never used magic against a friend? I don't believe you."

"I haven't," lied Matilda, not ready to share the name etched in the skin just under her hairline with Oliver. "So, what about Susan?"

Oliver's face dropped. "She was the worst. I was getting cocky because of Davis and I'd managed a few other little spells as well, so thought I'd try magic to get myself some extra cash. Susan was behind the desk at the bank and, well, she ended up getting fired, so I deserved the two S's."

"Yes, you did," said Matilda, giving Oliver a stern look before she stabbed another apple.

"Like you're so innocent," said Oliver, swearing under his breath as an apple bobbed away from him. "How many names have you got hidden on your face, anyway?"

"Enough," said Matilda. "Do you have many more?"

"Just the one I showed you." Matilda held her breath, hoping that Oliver would unzip his jacket and lift up his hoodie to show her *Daniel* carved across his abs. Instead he just pointed.

"You next. Who else do you have?"

Matilda traced her fingers over the names hidden on her face, trying to decide which name she would reveal to Oliver until she found the letters along the top of her forehead.

"Natalie—she couldn't stop biting her nails, not even when she'd eaten them away and was chewing on her nail bed."

"Gross."

"She deserved it."

"Why?"

Matilda frowned. "I can't even remember now."

Oliver shook his head, a smile twitching on his lips. "Who else is there?"

Matilda traced the names of the boys who'd ignored her or made fun of her, deciding not to share those with Oliver. She ran a finger down her cheek. "Sophie."

"Don't tell me; you can't remember what she did, either?"

"Oh, I remember," said Matilda, stabbing at the apples with a bit more force. "That girl made my life an absolute misery for as long as I can remember. First it was name-calling, then as we got older it got more sophisticated and she'd start rumors about me, bombard me with abusive messages on my phone. She made up a profile on the school site once, using my name and a photo of me, and said I was a witch."

"Really?"

Matilda nodded. "I don't know if she actually believed that, but it definitely stuck and made it harder for me to fit in or make friends. She was such a nasty piece of work."

"What did you do to her?"

Matilda took a deep breath. She hadn't thought about Sophie for a long time. Out of all the people she'd hurt, Sophie was one that Matilda had a slight tinge of regret for.

"I spent every night lying awake in bed worrying about what she was going to do next. Even when she lost interest in me for a bit, my anxiety got even worse because of the anticipation. I wanted her to know what it felt like, not being able to sleep because of the worry and the fear, so I gave her night terrors."

"Night terrors?"

"Yeah, you know, like nightmares but with screaming, or kicking and lashing out, even sleepwalking. She was supposed to have them for a week or so, and I knew it'd worked because she looked terrible: bags under her eyes and her hair wasn't all perfect like it normally was. She was obviously completely exhausted and too tired to bully me."

"Glad she got what she deserved, then."

Matilda fiddled with the athame. "It kind of went wrong, though."

"What do you mean?" said Oliver, dropping the knife in the barrel and turning to Matilda.

Matilda shrugged. "I don't know what I did, but instead of the night terrors being temporary, they went on for weeks and weeks until she ended up having to leave school."

"What happened to her?"

"I don't know for sure, but I think she changed schools. I went over what I did to try and undo it, but I wasn't great at recording my spells back then."

"Shit," said Oliver, frowning at her. "That's pretty harsh, Matilda."

Matilda nodded, then looked down at the pretend athame in her hand; she didn't like the way Oliver was looking at her. "It's one I feel pretty bad about."

The cool wind carried the cheery sounds of the festival over their heads for a few seconds as they stood in silence. Matilda clenched her jaw, angry with herself for sharing the story with Oliver and making him see what kind of monster he'd been spending time with, until she felt his fingers find her hand.

"Sounds like she really did make your life hell, though. Where did you say her name was?" Matilda ran her finger across her cheek and held her breath as Oliver did the same with his thumb. "Just remind me to stay on the right side of you, okay?"

Matilda's heart almost burst open as she looked into Oliver's eyes.

"Okay."

Oliver put his arm around her and kissed the top of her head.

"It's getting pretty crowded. Let's find somewhere a bit quieter."

CHAPTER TWENTY-ONE

The night twinkled with stars and string lights, and Matilda was swept along with the merriment of the festival as families and groups of friends enjoyed the annual reminder that a witch had been sent to her fate down a well. She was pleased to see Oliver enjoying himself as much as she was, and having not recovered from his apple-hooking failure, he decided they should try the maze and split up to see who got to the center first.

They'd started off calling each other's name, giggling when the other responded on the other side of the hay, but getting more and more distant the farther they went through, until there was no answer. Matilda stopped and jumped, but not high enough to see over the bales of hay stacked up to make the walls of the maze. She sighed and kept on walking, stepping over howling pumpkins and fake black cats as she followed the path, fairy lights strung all over the hay, lighting her way.

"Oliver?" she tried, pausing in case her footsteps drowned out his response, but there was still nothing.

Matilda turned a corner and gasped as a tall cloaked figure hovered over her, its clawlike hands reaching out to grab her. She stepped around a half-open trunk with a mummy arm sticking out of it, pausing when the fairy lights strung above flickered, then turned off. For a heart-stopping moment, Matilda was submerged in claustrophobic darkness until they pinged back on and she headed forward.

"Oliver?" shouted Matilda as she pulled out her phone.

The lights blinked out again, and she gasped as her phone was smacked from her hand. She crouched down and stretched out to search for it. Something brushed her fingertips and she yelped, pulling her hands into her chest when the lights returned and she was face-to-face with a blinking pair of eyes she could recognize anywhere. Victor peered up at her, like he was waiting for a handful of sugar cubes.

"How the hell have you followed me in here, Vic?" Matilda said, tickling the spot between his ears as her heart raced in her chest.

Victor responded with a bleat as the lights flickered again, and Matilda felt him disappear from beneath her fingertips. The lights came back on and Matilda squinted at the spot where the goat had been just before, her hand flying up to her mouth in horror as her eyes adjusted to what she was seeing.

Victor was lying on his side, one dull eye wide open and staring right through her. A dark pool of blood crept closer and closer to Matilda's shoes, trickling from the gash that glistened across his neck. Matilda reached out to him but froze as she saw her hands smeared with the blood of her beautiful boy, one of them grasping a carving knife.

"N-n-no . . . ," she whispered, falling back against the hay. "This isn't real . . . this isn't happening . . ."

The lights blinked off and Matilda moaned, not knowing whether it was better to stay in the darkness or to try and find her way out. When they came back on, Victor was back to standing and looking at her with empty, soulless eyes, and he trotted forward, leaving tiny little hoofprints in the blood. His coat was matted with blood, and the smell of rotting flesh hit Matilda's throat as she stumbled back and vomited.

Victor jumped up so his front hooves rested on her thighs, smearing blood on her jeans. He bleated at her, but it sounded more like the screams from the sheep than her precious goat.

Matilda closed her eyes and shook her head. "No! Please no, leave me alone!"

Fingers tightened around her wrists, and Matilda thrashed side to side until a voice made her freeze.

"Matilda? Shit, Matilda?! Whoa, whoa, whoa, it's me; it's Oliver."

Matilda's eyes flew open, and she gripped Oliver's coat.

"Oliver!" she sobbed.

"It's okay. It's okay." Oliver helped her sit, glancing at the vomit glistening on her coat. "What the hell happened?"

Matilda took a napkin from him and wiped her face.

"H-how did you find me?"

"I heard you; I think everyone at the festival heard you," said Oliver, then held up Matilda's phone. "I found this back there." He put a hand on her cheek, his eyebrows drawn together as he looked her up and down. "Are you okay? What happened? Was it a blackout?"

Matilda looked around. The blood, the knife, Victor. It was all gone, just the haystacks and the twinkly lights of normality surrounded her again—the horror had all been in her head. She looked back at Oliver, her bottom lip trembling as she clenched his sleeves tight in her fists.

"Something's happening to me, Oliver," she whispered, feeling the familiar black cloud coming to pull the shade over her again, "something terrible."

CHAPTER TWENTY-TWO

Matilda sipped the sweet liquid and sighed as the warmth trickled through her body toward her soul. She sat with her legs pulled up and a knitted blanket around her in the comforting aromas of the kitchen with Victor curled up on the floor, Nanna May shuffling back and forth to a small saucepan warming on the stove.

"This is just tea, isn't it, Nanna May?" she said, warming her hands on the mug. "I told you; I'm fine."

Her grandmother patted Matilda's shoulder as she moved past her, opening the larder and replacing small jars of powders and leaves, all telltale signs that what she'd just brewed for Matilda was definitely more than just herbal tea.

Despite what she'd said, Matilda was grateful to receive help to calm down. She hadn't stopped shaking since the maze and felt such overwhelming relief when she saw Nanna May and Victor waiting at the door of her garden room that she'd burst into tears, leaning on the old woman as they walked to the warmth of the kitchen instead of the isolation of Matilda's room, and covering Victor with kisses every few steps.

Matilda's phone buzzed, and she picked it up from the table and smiled. She replied to Oliver, telling him she was okay, then took another sip of the drink and sighed. She turned to Nanna May, who was back at the fireplace, her wrinkled face glowing from the flames.

"It won't make me forget?" she asked, her shoulders relaxing as her grandmother shook her head without looking up from the pot she was stirring.

"Good," she said, taking another sip.

Matilda's hands hadn't stopped shaking on her way home in Oliver's car. What she'd seen in the maze was terrifying, and she had to squeeze her eyes closed every time her precious goat's body flashed inside her mind. But she didn't want to forget.

Someone was using magic against her, but not the type of magic she would ever access. The blackouts kept leaving her with holes in her magic, but they also left a sour aftertaste of something very dark and very dangerous. Matilda knew she tiptoed on the line with the things she'd done to people, maybe even accidentally stepping over it a couple of times, but whoever was messing with her had the line so far behind them it wasn't even a speck in their rearview mirror. Whoever it was would be sorry they started this dance with her. She tickled Victor's head again, then brushed her cheek with her fingertips. The letters were so gnarled into her skin that one more name wouldn't make a difference, whoever's name it was.

The front door slammed and the faint kissy-kissy sounds of Lottie greeting Nimbus drifted through the cottage. Matilda straightened up and fixed her glare on the entrance to the kitchen, the clip-clop of her mother's expensive boot heels getting louder until she appeared at the top of the steps, her frown lines deepening across her brow as she laid her eyes on Matilda.

"What are you doing here?" she asked, sighing as she adjusted her navy pashmina, then picked the kettle up from the stove.

"Surprised to see me?" asked Matilda, her eyes not leaving her mother for a second.

"Well, yes," said Lottie, letting Nanna May take the kettle from her but refusing as Nanna May tried to usher her to a wooden stool. She leaned against the counter and folded her arms, her usual stance when she was conversing with her daughter. "You're normally holed up in your room. Too good for us, right, Nanna May?"

Nanna May frowned and shook her head as she filled the kettle with water and set it on the stove. Matilda glared at Lottie, angry that she was trying to draw her grandmother into the hatred she so clearly had for her.

"So," said Matilda, leaning down and stroking Victor's downy head, "it's pretty late. Where've you been?"

"Out," said Lottie, looking down and twisting a silver bangle on her wrist.

"Out where?"

Lottie looked up from fiddling with her jewelry. "Excuse me, do I have to report my movements to you, little one?"

Matilda smiled. "Just showing an interest in my mother, that's all. Mother."

Matilda's cheeks ached from smiling, but she let the quiet push down on her mother until she responded.

"I went to see a movie."

"Who with?"

"A friend."

"What kind of friend?"

Something flashed across her mother's face, her features taking on slightly sharper edges than before.

"Just, *a friend*, Tilly. Is that okay with you?" snapped Lottie.

"Okay, okay. Very quick to anger there, Mother." Matilda lifted her hands up. "So, do you want to know where I've been tonight?"

Her mother shrugged. "Sure. Where have you been?"

"The Witching Well Festival."

Red crept up Lottie's neck and flushed her cheeks like a warning light that she'd been caught in a lie. She cleared her throat.

"Really?"

Matilda nodded. "And it was a very interesting night, for lots of reasons. Somebody tried to scare me."

Her mother frowned. "Who did? Who tried to scare you?"

Matilda stood up, letting the blanket fall from her shoulders, her eyes fixed on her mother's.

"Doesn't matter. They'll get theirs."

"Matilda, I . . ."

"You what?" Lottie opened and closed her mouth, her eyes darting around the room. Matilda shook her head. "I didn't think so. Come on, Victor."

Matilda opened the door and walked out, Victor at her side, the whistle from the boiling kettle ringing into the dark night.

CHAPTER TWENTY-THREE

Seven days until Halloween

The girls ran up and down the field, shouting to one another as they got into position, their hockey sticks poised and ready to receive the ball. Matilda watched them speeding beneath the gray clouds bulging with rain, not having to think about anything apart from scoring against the opposite team. Matilda recognized each player but couldn't place any of their names, all of them in her class but not in her life.

Matilda turned from the window and looked around at everyone in her biology class, the majority of whom were covertly checking their phones behind textbooks or in their laps as the teacher talked through the parts that make up a cell.

Why am I here? she thought to herself, feeling more disconnected from her fellow students than she ever had before. Why bother with high school when she could never leave Gravewick anyway? What would be here for her when everyone else moved on to college or to travel the world? Would she live with her mother, who apparently wanted her dead, and Nanna May for the rest of her life?

The only good thing in her life was Oliver. She had completely fallen for someone who wouldn't stick around in Gravewick longer than he needed to. Could she go with him? Could she live a life without magic?

I may have no choice, she thought to herself as she doodled stars on the cover of her notebook. She'd tried a spell to see the truth in her mother, to find out what was going on with her, but it hadn't worked. Matilda couldn't focus; she was rattled from what had happened in the maze and found it impossible to ground herself enough to do a spell that she'd used a hundred times before.

The monotonous droning stopped, and Matilda looked up at the teacher, who was frowning as she looked out of the windows that ran down the side of the classroom. Matilda followed the teacher's gaze, impatient shouts coming from the field. About fifty feet from where she sat in the classroom stood a girl holding a hockey stick, ready to strike the ball at her feet. Of all the girls she was watching before, she was the only one whose name Matilda knew.

Erin.

Matilda shifted in her seat as she locked eyes with Erin, her blue eyes shining out from her red face like diamonds ready to cut through glass. The teacher tried to settle everyone in the classroom, and some of the girls on the field jogged toward the rogue hockey player, while Erin kept her eyes on Matilda like there was nobody else around them.

A smile slid across Erin's face, and Matilda gasped as Erin surged forward, sprinting toward the classroom and expertly controlling the ball in front of her until she stopped, looked up, then swung the hockey stick over her head.

"Get down!" shouted the teacher as the class screamed and ducked under their desks.

Matilda fell from her chair and shuffled under the desk, panting as she turned back to watch. A single pane of glass in the ancient classroom was no match against the speeding hockey ball and the screams deafened Matilda as the ball smashed into the window, sending shards of glass showering across the room.

The screams turned into whispers, then into confused chatter, and the glass crunched as everyone crept out from under their desks. Matilda poked her head out and slowly pulled herself up, then looked out of the window.

Erin stood with her legs apart, her hockey stick in one hand like she was a warrior who'd just slashed her way through an army. Thunder cracked from above and rain crashed down from the clouds, drenching Erin as she stood as still as a statue, a smile slashed on her face, staring at Matilda, oblivious to the two girls and PE teacher who were charging at her like rugby players.

They tackled Erin to the ground, and Matilda watched, her heart beating like a bass drum and her stomach twisted with confusion, as Erin let them pin her arms behind her back and hold her down on the slick grass, her eyes still on Matilda like a leopard on a gazelle.

CHAPTER TWENTY-FOUR

"So, she's been suspended?"

Matilda watched Oliver as he nodded and blew into his cup. He'd messaged her after the news of the window had traveled through the school's halls and made her agree to meet at Grounds for to-go coffee before they went for a walk. The whole school was buzzing with what had happened, photos of Erin soaking and red-faced as she was marched away in the rain popping up on social media. Everyone had their theories (Erin hadn't been picked for the school hockey team and was trying to prove her worth; the biology teacher had given Erin a bad grade and she was pissed because she wanted to study zoology in college; people with red hair are naturally weird, etc., etc.), but Matilda only caught snippets of conversations, as nobody talked to her, and Oliver was her only direct source of school buzz.

Oliver took a sip of his coffee and glanced at her as they made their way through the trees, their feet squelching in the rotting leaves and rainwater from the storm.

"Apparently, yeah. For a week, according to one of the guys on the team. His sister is friends with her."

The gaps between the trees grew smaller, and Matilda edged ahead of Oliver, using her free hand to steady herself against the trunks, her coffee sloshing in her other hand.

"Did she say why she did it? Erin, I mean?" asked Matilda.

"She just said she doesn't know, apparently."

"She doesn't know why she tried to decapitate me?"

There was a pause, and Oliver sighed. "Matilda . . ."

Matilda whipped around. "Don't tell me that she wasn't, because I was sitting right there, Oliver. She had her eyes on me, like some kind of deranged Olympic medalist about to take a penalty, and she did not take them off me, not even when she swung the hockey bat over her head and smacked it right at me and then when they were holding her down on the ground. How can you not think that? With the slap as well?"

"Stick."

"What?"

"It's a hockey stick, not a bat."

"I don't give a shit what it's called," said Matilda, both of them looking up at the sound of wings flapping away from the danger of her loud voice. "How is there any other explanation apart from she was trying to hurt me? Again?"

Oliver looked at her, his eyebrows angled and his mouth in a stern line.

"I just . . . I just don't like the idea of it, okay?"

"What do you mean?"

"That someone's trying to hurt you. First your mom and now Erin? It's too much, and I don't feel like I'm doing a very good job of protecting you. Can't I just pretend that Erin had it out for whoever was sitting next to you?"

Matilda's heart rolled over like a puppy waiting for its tummy to be scratched. She moved toward Oliver and looped her arms around his waist, careful not to spill her coffee, and pressed her cheek against his jacket. She looked up at him.

"You don't have to protect me. I can protect myself."

"I know you can, Wonder Woman." Oliver lifted the edge of Matilda's woolly hat and kissed her forehead. "But we can still look out for each other."

Matilda went up on her tiptoes and kissed Oliver, biting her lip as the warmth from his lips traveled through her veins.

"So you believe me, then? That Erin's out for me?"

Oliver nodded. "Of course I believe you. She's violent. You need to watch yourself. I wouldn't be surprised if she did have something to do with Ashley."

Matilda turned away from Oliver and started pushing past the branches again. There were a hundred spells she could try to find out who'd hurt Ashley or what was going on with Erin, but not when her magic was still so shaky.

"You really think so?"

"Sean told me that the police are saying the party compromised any evidence they found, so they haven't been able to arrest anyone. Another guy on the team's mom works at the station, and she told him that's actually bull and really they just didn't find a single shred of evidence, no DNA, no fibers, hair, nothing." Matilda frowned and looked back at Oliver, who raised his eyebrows. "That's got witchcraft written all over it, don't you think?"

Matilda pulled her coat tight around her, the chill creeping down her spine nothing to do with the cool autumn air. The possibility of an unknown witch in town made her feel uneasy, especially considering the trail of carnage that was getting more and more wicked the farther it went.

"Well, if that's true and it is Erin, then she's going to a very dark place," said Matilda, wondering how she'd never known that Erin was involved with magic even if it was after they were friends. It just showed how getting mixed up in dark magic could turn a person inside out. They'd spent so many lunchtimes and sleepovers sharing secrets with each other, but this was obviously something Erin had hidden deep in the dark shadows of her soul. It was hard to believe she was the same person who Matilda had spent so many years joined at the hip with.

"So, we need to make sure she doesn't hurt anyone else. We need to make sure she doesn't hurt you."

Matilda let herself smile. Having Oliver on her side chased the chill away, and the gentle flap of butterflies in her stomach puffed warm air inside her. The tree trunks began spacing farther apart until the two of them could walk side by side again, finally opening up onto a round clearing.

"We're here," panted Matilda, smiling at Oliver as she took his hand and led him away from the trees.

The quiet of the woods seemed like a brass band compared to the silence that embraced them, the tree branches reaching over to their companions around the clearing and shielding them from the outside world. The grass was lush, springy under their feet without the boggy patches they'd avoided in the woods, and dotted with weeds and wildflowers, the fallen leaves awaiting the next stage in their life cycle.

"What's that?" asked Oliver, pointing to the center of the clearing.

Small animals zigzagged across, pausing and peering at their visitors before darting into the safety of their woods. In the middle was a crumbling well, its stone sides obscured by ivy creeping around it. Wings flapped, sending feathers snowing down on them as they walked toward the well, and Matilda looked up at the silent audience members settling themselves on the branches overhead. She blew them a kiss, then squeezed Oliver's hand as they reached the edge of the well.

"This," said Matilda, letting go of Oliver's hand and putting both of hers on the ivy covering the well, "is why we're here."

Oliver peered at the well, his eyebrows creeping up over wide eyes.

"Is this the well? Like, *the* well?"

"This is where they say Ivy was murdered," said Matilda.

"Why don't they do the festival here?" asked Oliver.

Matilda shrugged and looked around. "It's not big enough, I guess. That or they're scared Ivy might come crawling out of the well and curse everyone for disrespecting her. That's what I'd do."

"Hey, you weren't complaining when you were wolfing down those fries at the festival the other day. Or when you were cheating at stabbing those apples."

"I wasn't cheating," said Matilda, smiling.

"I believe you," said Oliver, winking.

Oliver gripped the side of the well and leaned over the opening, whistling as he peered down into the shadows. He pulled out his phone and shone the flashlight down the well as if Ivy might still be down there waving at him.

"You really think she's down there?"

"Maybe," said Matilda. "I don't think anyone wants to risk finding out whether the whole thing is a myth or not, though."

"Don't want to wake the witch from her eternal slumber." Oliver swallowed. "It doesn't look that deep. She didn't try and get out?"

"Depends who you believe. People say she crawls out sometimes and creeps around town, leaving her mark so we won't ever forget her."

"The ivy. This stuff is everywhere," said Oliver, rubbing a green leaf between his fingers. "So why are we here?"

Matilda took a deep breath. She was struggling to accept that her magic was waning, let alone admit it to Oliver.

"Do you remember when I showed you how to ground yourself? There are places in Gravewick that are like hot spots of energy, especially to my family, but I'm wondering whether a non-lineage witch can feel them, too."

"And this is one of the hot spots?"

"If she's really down there, I'd say it's *the* hot spot."

"Where are the rest of them?"

Matilda shrugged. "All over. Nanna May said the spots are where death and magic shake hands, where they strike a deal. I think I might have felt it in my garden room and the house. I'm not sure." Guilt rushed over Matilda as she realized how little she'd worked to seek out the energy of her ancestors, especially for the last few years. Instead of listening to her mother when she talked about their bloodline, Matilda would automatically switch off and roll her eyes. "Do you feel anything?"

Oliver closed his eyes, a tiny line of concentration etched between his eyebrows. A minute passed before his shoulders sagged and he shook his head.

"That's a shame. I thought we could try and draw on the energy here, and it might have helped with these shadows in my power so we can do some casting. A protection spell, from Erin," said Matilda, wringing her hands.

"Hey," said Oliver, putting his arm around Matilda. "We can still do that. Two witches are better than one, right?"

Matilda nodded weakly. *Especially when one practically feels like a beginner*, she thought.

"I guess so. I like being here, anyway. Reminds me of my dad."

"It does?"

"Yeah. He used to take me horseback riding at a farm near here. I rode the same pony, every time. Checkers. She was beautiful, black and gray. God, I loved that pony." Matilda felt something pressing down on her heart, and she looked at her boots before she could carry on talking. "Mom didn't want me wasting my time learning to ride a horse, so Dad used to bring me here on the way so we could say that I'd been studying magic. 'Let's drop in on Ivy, shall we?' he'd say."

"You don't ride anymore?"

"Not since he left," said Matilda, her lip wobbling. She wiped a warm tear from her cheek. "I'm sorry. I didn't bring you here to cry all over you."

"Hey, come here." Oliver pulled Matilda into his chest and squeezed her tight. "It's okay. I'm sorry about your dad. I wish I could do something."

Matilda relaxed into Oliver's arms, the assault of her memories retreating into the distance as she breathed in, his familiar smell calming her like a magic spell. He put his hands on her arms and looked down at her.

"Did you want to try the energy drawing thing now?"

Matilda shook her head. "I feel kind of drained. I'm not sure it would work. Can we try another time?"

"Sure," he said, adjusting Matilda's pom-pom hat. "That kind of works out well. I've got a little something planned for us."

———•◆•———

The sun was on its way to bed, but not before it had diluted the sky with its glow, dyeing the clouds into pink, floating puffs of cotton candy. Matilda followed Oliver down a path, ducking as it took her between crooked limbs of trees that grew so close together they'd formed a tunnel overhead. Oliver stopped suddenly and turned back to her.

"You wait here and don't move until I call you, okay?" he said.

"Why do I . . ."

"*Okay?*" said Oliver, smiling at her.

Matilda nodded and watched Oliver carry on ahead of her between the trees. Once he was out of sight, she listened until he called her name and then she hurried forward, peering through the slim gap in the trees and hedges at the end of the path. She could see sparkling ahead, and when the smell hit her she realized exactly where they were: the lake. She pushed through the last of the hanging branches and, after her eyes adjusted in the waning light, she couldn't suppress her smile.

The beauty of the sky shared its image on the water, bathing the surroundings in a warm radiance. Straight ahead of Matilda was a short jetty that stretched out over the water with a wider section at its end. Tiny glass jars with flames flickering inside each one lined the jetty up and down, plus there were two little glowing pumpkins. At the end was a checked blanket with cushions scattered on top, and sitting with his legs crossed at the ankles was Oliver.

Matilda bit her lip as she made her way down to the water and stepped onto the jetty, beaming at Oliver as he smiled at her. He pulled himself up and walked to meet her halfway, taking her hand as he led her to the blanket, its edges dotted with more candles.

"Hungry?" he said, putting his arms around her.

Matilda nodded, her stomach growling at the sight of the large picnic basket that sat on the blanket. Oliver pointed to the cushions and a bundle of blankets, and Matilda sat down, her cheeks aching from smiling.

"Good," he said, picking up the basket and sitting next to her. He lifted the lid and unzipped an insulated bag, a glorious aroma of fries escaping and floating up to Matilda's nose. Oliver pulled out a cardboard container and a foil parcel and handed it to Matilda. "I didn't know how to transport mac and cheese, so I got takeout instead. I hope that's okay."

Matilda nodded as Oliver beamed at her, then retrieved the same two items for himself.

"So, we have here hot dogs accompanied by the best fries in town." He glanced at Matilda, then went back to unwrapping his hot dog. "I found the people that ran that food tent at the Witching Well Festival. You said it was the best hot dog you've ever had, so . . . um, are you okay? I mean, is this . . . ?"

Matilda blinked at Oliver as his question hung in the air. "Yes, of course."

"Are you sure? That's the first thing you've said since you got here."

"It's . . . it's . . . wonderful, Oliver. I can't . . . I can't believe you did all this. It's just so completely perfect I guess I'm a little speechless."

Oliver let out a little whistle and grinned at her. "Good. Okay, that's good."

"Why did you do all this?"

Oliver shrugged. "Just because of everything that's been happening. I really wanted to do something nice for you."

Matilda held her breath, not wanting her emotions to overflow and become tears. She leaned into Oliver and he turned to her, accepting her kiss as appreciation in the absence of coherent speech.

"Eat up, before it gets cold," he said, tossing a fry into his mouth.

·—•◦•—·

Matilda blew into her mug and looked out onto the lake, sighing as the stars mirrored on the water twinkled when the wind tickled its surface. Oliver had poured them both hot chocolate from a flask, and they'd nestled into the cushions and thrown a couple of blankets over their legs to keep the October night from chasing them away before they were ready.

"All good?" asked Oliver.

"All good," said Matilda, stretching out her limbs and smiling. Being with Oliver surrounded by the warm glow of candles made Matilda feel safer than she had in weeks.

"I love the candles."

"Me too," said Oliver. "I can stare at a candle flame for ages. Really helps me wind down."

"You're sounding more and more like a lineage witch," said Matilda, resting her head on Oliver's shoulder as she watched the pumpkin's face blink and wink in the wind.

"What do you mean?" asked Oliver.

"Candle magic is one of the first kinds of magic we learn, and the first lesson is using a candle for meditation."

Matilda watched the candle flicker and could feel herself falling into the pumpkin's burning orange eyes until she sat up suddenly.

"You okay?" asked Oliver.

Matilda shook her head, realizing that the frowning pumpkin face was trying to tell her something.

"I'm so stupid," she said, pulling her bag onto her lap and rooting through it. "*So* stupid! I should have thought of this before. Candle magic. It can be used for all sorts of spells and casting, but it can also be used for insight or visions."

Oliver frowned at the candles on the jetty. "Candles can do that?"

"Candles help witches do that. It's ancient magic, what the first witches used. Using the candle flame to meditate connected them with the natural forces of the universe."

"Right," said Oliver, frowning at Matilda as she stopped rifling through her bag and turned to him.

She pulled a small glass bottle out of her bag, then jumped up and grabbed the pumpkin. She sat down cross-legged in front of Oliver, blew the flame out, then took the stumpy candle out of the pumpkin and held it up.

"Want to give it a try?"

CHAPTER TWENTY-FIVE

Oliver took the candle from Matilda, frowning as he turned it over in his hands. He looked at Matilda, then took the bottle from her, shaking the clear liquid inside as he held it up to his eyes.

"What is it?"

"Salt water. Another lesson for a young witch: You never know when you need to cleanse something for a spell," she said.

Matilda opened the bottle and poured some salt water onto her scarf, then gently wiped the small candle as Oliver watched.

"Have you done this before?" he asked. Matilda glanced at him, then shook her head. "Why not?"

Matilda shrugged and looked up at the stars, a little nail of guilt scratching the back of her neck.

"Never really needed to. Normally I just do the magic and get what I want that way. But I know what I'm doing. I think." Matilda remembered her mother teaching her about candle magic, drilling into her the importance of being able to access another plane in case she ever needed answers she couldn't find in the usual places. She looked at the picnic basket. "Is there a knife in there?"

"A knife?"

"To scratch what I want from the flame into the wax."

"Oh, right." Oliver opened the lid and pulled out a butter knife. "Will this do?"

Matilda nodded and took the knife from Oliver, then scratched the letters into the candle wax as well as she could. She could feel Oliver's breath as he watched her wipe the tiny curls of wax away, leaving the jagged word INSIGHT in the candle. She put the candle back into the safety of the pumpkin and got comfortable on a cushion.

"So, what do we do now?" asked Oliver.

"I'm going to light the candle, then clear my mind and focus on what I want."

"Which is?"

"Answers," said Matilda, shaking her hands and shoulders to loosen her muscles. "Then I'll stare into the flame until it's burned all the way down. Do you have a lighter?"

Oliver pulled a lighter from his pocket and handed it to her.

"We could be here awhile, until the candle burns out," she said, lighting the wick.

"I can wait," he said, draping a blanket around her shoulders, then holding her hand.

Matilda had never had anyone to hold her hand while she cast her magic, and Oliver's presence made her feel more determined to make the spell work. She crossed her legs and watched the candle burn, remembering everything her mother had taught her about connecting with the fire and falling into its light. The wind blew gently on her face, and as she stared at the beckoning flame, Matilda felt as though she and Oliver and the croaking frogs were the only beings on the planet.

———

"It's not working," sighed Matilda after a few minutes. "I can't see anything. Nothing at all."

She frowned at the orange flame dancing in the breeze, mocking her. The weather had changed from a crisp autumn evening to a threatening prestorm chill in the short time she'd been staring at the candle, and the water lapped against the jetty more urgently than it had before.

The rushing wind turned from a whisper to a hiss, and Matilda looked around, her blood freezing as if there were something sweeping toward them, caressing the surface of the lake with its long, sharp fingernails. The water was choppy, splashing over the sides of the jetty and making the boards judder like they were trying to buck her and Oliver off. Matilda put her hands down on the wood to steady herself and blinked at Oliver as he tried to keep upright, too. The surface of the lake grew angrier, and the wind lashed around them, snuffing out the candle and whipping Matilda's hair around her head.

"What's happening?" said Oliver, raising his voice over the cracking branches and howling wind.

"Must be a storm," cried Matilda. "Get to the car!"

They got up, hunching over to keep their balance as they collected the blankets and cushions of their now distant perfect lakeside picnic. The wind pushed against them from every direction until Oliver dropped the picnic basket and turned to Matilda.

"Forget the stuff, let's just go!" he shouted.

Matilda nodded and dropped the blanket as a blast of wind forced her to stumble backward and tangled it around her legs.

"Oliver!" she shouted, panic strangling her vocal cords as she tripped over the blanket and lost her footing.

She fell backward, her arms flailing as she tried to get her balance, but the wind was forcing her away from Oliver and closer to the edge of the jetty. She gasped as he tried to reach her against the elements, his eyes wide as they both realized what was about to happen.

Matilda's fingertips brushed against Oliver's as she plunged backward into the freezing October lake. She inhaled water and tried to catch a breath. The lake muffled her screams as she thrashed around, kicking against the blanket that was still clinging to her and weighing her down. She blinked hopelessly in the darkness, unable to tell which way the surface was as the water stung her eyes and tried to suffocate her along with her panic.

Fear tightened its arms around her chest, choking her with every panicked, ragged breath. Something brushed against her skin, light and gentle, but ominous and dangerous in the depths of the lake. The moon peeked out from behind the clouds and gave her a touch of light to see by. Matilda looked down at a long fringe of reeds waving up from the lake bed, beckoning her to sink deeper into the lake's shadows. A shrieking sound came toward her from the distance, getting louder and louder until screaming filled the lake and Matilda's head.

The reeds waved against her skin as she desperately tried to swim upward toward the moonlight, but something stung her palm. She inhaled, and more water shot up her nose as a reed curled around her wrist and pulled at her. Another snaked around her other arm, and she pulled against it until suddenly it broke free and sprouted four legs and a tail, then skittered up her arm and across her chest. The lizard scampered around her neck as the reed on her wrist loosened and scuttled up her arm and over her face to join its companion.

More reeds curled around her ankles before turning into long, thin lizards and twisted around her legs, gripping her with tiny claws, each lizard piercing her ears with their unnatural screams. Matilda thrashed around, trapped under the water as they slithered over every inch of her, pulling her downward until the terror was too much and she opened her mouth to scream.

"Oliver!" she shouted, sitting bolt upright on the jetty, her voice echoing between the trees. She looked down at her crossed legs and the blanket that Oliver had put around her shoulders just before she'd lit the candle, and she felt his hand around her own. She was safe and dry, and her vision, or nightmare, was over.

"I'm here!" said Oliver, pulling her into his chest. She held on to him, blinking into his sweater, her eyes flicking around as she took in the jetty and the dry blanket and cushions they were sitting on. "Jesus, Matilda, you're shaking. You completely zoned out, then started screaming. What happened?"

Oliver tightened the blanket around her shoulders, then looked at her, his eyebrows angled over his wide eyes as they searched her face.

"They . . . they were pulling me under the water," gasped Matilda, adrenaline shaking her limbs as her body refused to accept she was safe on the jetty.

"What were?"

"I don't know. I . . . I was trapped and there was screaming and . . . and these . . . lizards . . . all over me, just all over . . ." Matilda's voice cracked and she sobbed, her hands shaking as they gripped Oliver's coat. She blinked at him, tears clinging to her eyelashes as her lip wobbled. "I can't take any more of this, Oliver. I can't! I feel like I'm losing my mind."

"Hey, hey, I've got you. You're safe. You're safe," he said as she slumped against him.

Matilda cried into him, feeling as though she would never stop shaking from the fear, from the cold, from the constant threat of somebody or something that was out to get her. Once she'd run out of tears, she leaned into Oliver, taking his arm and pulling it around her until she was nestled into what felt like her only safe space in the world. He took Matilda's hand and brought it to his lips, closing his eyes as he kissed her palm. She looked up at him, the water casting an otherworldly reflection on his skin, then nestled back into his arm.

"I'm right here, okay?" he murmured, his fingertips gently tapping where her heart was beating beneath her ribs, his other hand gently stroking her hair. "I'll always be here, Matilda."

His words weaved their own spell on Matilda's tired soul, and she let the warmth of his body lull her into a much needed, restful sleep.

CHAPTER TWENTY-SIX

Six days until Halloween

Matilda smiled at the woman in the booth as she took the toffee apple from her, passed her some money, then turned to join the crowds milling around at the Witching Well Festival. Oliver had dropped her off at home in the early hours of the morning, and she'd crawled into her bed, her thoughts still full of lizards. Their plan to meet at the Witching Well Festival bonfire was the only thing that managed to put her head into a fuzzy enough place that she could fall asleep.

People bumped into her as she moved through the crowd, pushing past so they could get a good spot at the bonfire. Couples took selfies around her, smiling and kissing in front of the firewood and festive decorations, letting the world know that they were together, and they didn't have to face it alone, just as she didn't have to anymore. They'd arranged to meet after Oliver had run some errands for his dad, and her stomach flopped at the thought of seeing him again.

Matilda nudged her way to the edge of the firewood. Two men wearing luminous vests and carrying red buckets pushed through the crowd and gestured for everyone to step back. Matilda shuffled back with everyone else, craning her neck to look out for Oliver, hoping that he'd be there to see the bonfire ignite.

The men whispered important health and safety business to each other as they inspected the firewood, and the crowd rubbed their hands together and tightened their scarves. Matilda bit into her apple, crunching through the sharp toffee and juicy fruit as she watched the scouts scuttle back and forth, setting down more buckets of sand and water, then shifting the large stones that surrounded the firewood. Finally, there was a nod from one of the men and the crowd whooped with excitement as the men lit firestarters and circled the bonfire, crouching down and sticking them through the crooked gaps in the firewood.

Crackles popped through the noise of the crowd, and Matilda squinted as smoke filled the air, the fire catching and growing brighter as it forced her to shuffle backward. She took another bite of her apple and watched the flames grow stronger; her eyebrows pinched together as she missed the feeling of Oliver's hand in hers. She lost herself in the orange flames and floated into the memory of the night before, when she had woken up in Oliver's arms all snuggled under a blanket, hiding away from thoughts of lizards and drowning.

Matilda stared at the smoke rising up from the flames, but the warmth from the fire and her thoughts of the lake were extinguished by long icy fingernails prickling a trail down her spine—she could see Oliver's image in the smoke. Her breath caught in her throat and she blinked to clear her vision, but she could still see his face twisting and dancing above the flames.

"Oliver?" she whispered, dropping her toffee apple and stepping closer to the fire.

"Miss, you need to step back, please."

Matilda ignored the voice and frowned into the fire, her eyes darting around, searching for the image in the smoke.

"Miss?" said one of the luminous-vest men. "Miss, are you okay?"

"No," she whispered, shaking her head. "No."

The smoke swirled into the sky like a gray dragon twisting its body in and out of the stars, stretching Oliver's face until it vanished. She knew nobody else could see what she saw, that only a witch could read the smoke rising above the fallen branches of elder trees and know that it was a message from her bloodline. Matilda felt as though she were being pulled away from the laughter and clapping around her, the revelry and the happiness getting farther in the distance as she realized that Oliver was in grave danger.

The vest man looked at her, waiting for her to confirm that she was okay, but she ignored his concern and backed away, barging past the happy attendees to the exit of the festival, fear driving her legs faster than she'd ever run before.

───◆───

Matilda slowed to a jog and tried Oliver's phone again, holding her breath as it rang and cut through to voicemail.

"Shit! Oliver, answer the phone, please!"

She'd run back to her house in the hope that she'd misunderstood their arrangement, but he wasn't there. She ran into the night, past stragglers on their way to the bonfire, completely oblivious to what the flames had shown Matilda.

The sign for Gallon Street glowed in the moonlight, and Matilda surged toward it despite the elastic band that had tightened around her chest. Ignoring the voice in her head that was hissing *if he's not there, then what?*, she ran down the street, slowing in the dim light coming from the only functioning streetlamp on the road.

She looked past the overgrown gardens and broken bicycles abandoned on sidewalks and held her breath as she got closer to the end of the cul-de-sac, then saw movement in front of an open garage door. She froze, recognizing Oliver's car with its hood open, and then, safe, oblivious to any danger, a line of concentration across his forehead, out walked Oliver from the garage and leaned over the engine.

"Oliver!"

He looked up, squinting into the darkness as Matilda ran toward him, then smiled as he wiped his sleeve across his forehead.

"Hey," he said. "I'm so sorry. This heap wouldn't start and I couldn't find my phone and I'm all sweaty so was going to take a . . . whoa, are you okay?"

"Are *you* okay?" she asked, barely able to get the words out between the running and the fear that had driven her.

"Pissed off with this hunk of junk that thinks it gets to choose when it runs, but apart from that I'm fine. Just sweating like a pig," he said, shrugging out of his hoodie. He threw it onto an old chair in the garage, then undid a couple of buttons on his shirt and flapped some air down it, his eyebrows drawing together as he locked eyes with Matilda. "Hey, what's going on with you?"

Matilda looked up and down Oliver's body, checking for injuries or a sign that he'd been attacked, but there was nothing but a few smudges of engine oil. She took a deep breath and launched herself at him, clamping her arms around his back. Tears pooled in her eyes and she pressed her face against his chest, warm and musky from sweat and engine oil.

"I thought you were . . . I thought something had happened to you," she said, looking up at him. "I saw you, in the smoke from the bonfire."

"You saw me what now?" he said, kissing her on the top of her head.

Matilda shook her head and pressed her face back into his chest. "I saw your image in the smoke. A warning, a warning that . . ."

Matilda froze, a sense of déjà vu bubbling in her stomach like a cauldron full of shadows. She frowned at Oliver's chest, his shirt spotted with oil stains and damp with hard work. Something peeked out of the neckline. She shuffled backward, staring at the spikes of silver scar tissue on his skin, and looked up at him.

"What's that, Oliver?" she asked, nodding at his chest. "I thought you only had three scars?"

Oliver frowned and glanced down for a few seconds, then straightened up and looked back at her, shadows from the trees above waving their crooked fingers across his face.

Matilda blinked as he undid another button and pulled his shirt open, where a tangle of names were whittled across one side of his body, but she couldn't focus on any letters but the ones that were carved across his chest, spelling out her name.

Matilda.

Oliver bit his lip, trying to keep down a smile that didn't belong on his face.

"Caught me," he said as the smile slid across his jaw and Matilda recognized what it belonged to.

A viper.

CHAPTER TWENTY-SEVEN

The moon and stars shuddered in the sky, and the horizon see-sawed. Matilda lifted her hand to her face and swallowed.

"What . . . caught you? Caught you doing what, Oliver?"

Matilda could hear herself saying the words, but she didn't know why, and her voice didn't sound like it belonged to her. The feeling of dread in her stomach, the look on Oliver's face, nothing of the last few moments felt like it belonged to her.

Oliver wiped his hands on a rag, then sat on the edge of the car and crossed his ankles.

"So, I may not have been totally honest with you when we were trading our scars. I actually have a lot more than I said, but this," he said, pointing at his chest, "this is my favorite one."

"I still don't—" Matilda said.

"You can read, right? It's your name," Oliver interrupted. "You know how it works. I do something bad and then the recipient of the badness gets their name scarred on my body forever."

Matilda shook her head, but closed her eyes and stopped, the motion making her queasy. She stared at Oliver, waiting for him to reveal a sick joke she didn't understand, but he just looked back at her, his usually warm eyes flashing with something she'd never seen in them before.

Danger.

"I don't under—What is this, Oliver?"

"What is this?" he said, folding his arms as he looked up at the moon. "I guess, technically, it's revenge, but it's kind of *graduated* into more than that."

"Revenge?" said Matilda, the word like a foreign object in her throat.

Oliver smiled. "You're *so* confused. Makes a change from the patronizing bullshit I've been smiling through for the last few weeks. *Every witch has a broomstick, Oliver. Witches don't believe in the devil, Oliver.* God, I'm not going to miss pretending you were enlightening me with all that shit. I'll fill you in; I know you think I'm some clueless amateur, but I'm not. I've been practicing magic for nearly two years."

"What?" said Matilda, feeling as though her brain had been mis-wired. Her hands shook in the autumn air and Oliver's cold, wicked truth. The wind swirled around her and whispered in her ear that she should back away, but she couldn't move.

"Two glorious years of magic. Seriously, it's all that's kept me going since my life was torn away from me, thanks to you. Magic was my salvation, and then I realized I needed to come back and share it with you."

"Come back?"

"That's right. I used to live here."

"What?" Matilda shook her head and blinked down at the ground, desperately trying to make sense of what Oliver was saying. "Please, I don't understand what . . ."

"My sister," said Oliver sharply. Matilda flinched, her heart sinking, as she knew that Oliver's sister could be any number of her victims. "You still don't have a clue, do you? Well, take your finger and run it across your head until you find Sophie. Remember her?"

Matilda's stomach plummeted. "She's your sister?"

"Half sister," said Oliver, picking up a rag and wiping at his fingers.

Matilda stepped forward. "Oliver, I really don't know what's happening right now, but I didn't know Sophie was your sister. I told you that I tried to—"

Oliver laughed and shook his head. "I don't give a shit about her. I told you she's a pain in my ass, and she is. This is about me." Oliver dropped the rag and tapped his chest with his finger. Matilda recoiled at the anger that sparked in his eyes and set his jaw rigid, like he was a statue carved from stone. "Remind me again what you did to her."

Matilda looked down at her hands, wringing her fingers together like she was trying to twirl back time.

"Night terrors."

"Yeah, that was it: night terrors. For eternity." Oliver picked his hoodie up and put it on. "Do you know what it's like to live in a house with someone who starts screaming the second they fall asleep? All day and all night? Screams rattling through my house, through my walls, through my pillows until they became *my* night terrors, Matilda. It was like living in a torture chamber."

Matilda shook her head, shame flushing her cheeks as she stared at the ground and listened to Oliver.

"My parents spent every moment orbiting around Sophie, while *my* life was disappearing with each one of her episodes. They took her to doctors, therapists, tried everything, until they ran out of the money they were spending on *my* education at the school she was too stupid to get into. They sold our house and their business and moved us closer to the city where she was admitted into a sleep clinic."

"I was ripped out of my school, my future was snuffed out, and I was then *homeschooled*, which meant packing me off to the local library every day while they sat by her bed and held her hand. I was so desperate I read everything I could find on night terrors, but nothing seemed to match up with what was happening to her until I found a book on a subject I never even considered."

"Witchcraft," whispered Matilda as tears streamed down her cheeks.

Oliver nodded. "If science didn't have the answers, then maybe magic did, and that's where I learned all about hexes and curses. You know, your favorite things."

Matilda's head spun as she tried to connect the lies to the truth.

"So, you didn't really meet a coven?"

"Oh no, I did. I was being Nice Oliver, so they fell over themselves to teach me, just like you did. But then one of them took me aside one day because she said she could sense something dark around me." Oliver shrugged. "That's the first time I siphoned magic from someone . . . learned not to take too much, otherwise you leave a body. Oops."

"This can't be real," Matilda said slowly. She felt the toffee apple she'd been eating travel up her throat.

She watched as Oliver, *her* Oliver, Oliver who had held her when she cried in desperation at the lake the night before, revealed his true face to her. His true, manipulative, murderous face. Matilda focused on her breath whistling up her nose and out of her mouth as he broke her heart and her mind with each of his words.

"Anyway, after many months of living in a disgusting apartment and tests and therapies that didn't work on Sophie, yours truly came to the rescue, and she could finally sleep again, so we moved back here. I was so pissed when my parents said they'd spent all the money for my school, but then I realized that the little witch who'd done this to me must go to the same school as Sophie, so I was happy to slum it at Gravewick Academy. Didn't take me long to work out it was you; you're not as subtle with magic as you think. Plus, nobody likes you because of the witch rumors so you were easy to find." Oliver shrugged. "Then I saw the blood on your face after that outstanding bee performance, and I knew I'd definitely found my girl."

Matilda wiped her cheeks and looked at her feet. "This isn't real."

"You keep saying that, Matilda, but I assure you it is. And I really must thank you. I was doing pretty well by myself, but one or two of the things you've taught me have come in handy. Made being around you tolerable. That, and having a front-row seat when you were convinced someone was trying to steal your magic."

"What?"

"God, I didn't think you were *this* slow," said Oliver, putting a hand on his hip. "Your blackouts? That was me. You took everything from me, so I've been taking from you. I've been siphoning your magic while you were blacked out."

Matilda felt as though she'd been punched in the stomach.

She shook her head. "That was you?"

"Yep, all me. The more scared you were, the more I could take from you. The maze was *excellent*."

"How?"

Oliver tapped his nose. "A magician never reveals his secrets."

"I can't hear this. I can't hear this," said Matilda, shaking her head violently.

"Truth hurts, Sabrina."

A chill rattled Matilda's bones. "You hurt all those animals, didn't you?" she swallowed, backing away from Oliver. "And Ashley. Oh my God. Ashley."

"Ding ding ding!" Oliver clapped his hands together. "I was just trying to get your attention and rattle you up a bit. Worked pretty well, huh? Don't tell anyone, though, will you?"

Oliver winked at her, and Matilda swallowed down the hot, bitter liquid at the back of her throat. She thought back to the moment Ashley's body fell from the tree and shook her head, trying to shake the memory out of it.

"How . . . how did you . . . ," she started, not sure she wanted to know the answer.

"I went to the party before I picked you up, persuaded her to go down the garden to the swing with me so we could talk about what happened," said Oliver, shrugging like he was talking about bad weather. "She was loving all the attention because of your little bee thing, so she was practically begging for a new audience to share her *hashtag trauma* with. Everyone was wasted, even early on, so nobody noticed when she didn't go back inside."

Matilda pictured Oliver and Ashley sitting on the exact spot where Matilda had hoped he might kiss her. She shook the thought away, knowing now that it hadn't been real, but it was rooted in her heart.

"How could you?"

"What I've done is no worse than anything you've ever done, and you know it."

"I would never kill anyone!"

Oliver lifted his index finger and frowned. "You use your magic to get whatever you want, and you've got the scars to prove it."

"But I . . . that was before . . ."

"Before what? Before you met me?" said Oliver. "Like I said, it's no different."

Matilda's breath puffed in front of her face, then disappeared into nothing as she tried to make sense of what was happening.

"What do you want from me, Oliver?" she said, wiping her wet cheeks with her shaking hand.

Oliver smiled the crooked smile that Matilda had spent so many nights dreaming of, then fixed his eyes on her.

"Well, I've been taking your magic already, so I guess that leaves . . . your grimoire. I know you're getting it at your little witch birthday party."

"I can't. We'd lose everything."

"That's kind of the idea," said Oliver, folding his arms.

"No." Matilda shook her head and wiped another tear from her cheek. "I can't let you have it."

"I was kind of hoping you'd say that." Oliver stepped forward and put his hand on Matilda's cheek. She recoiled. He was the only person who knew what secrets she kept hidden on her face, and before Oliver had cracked her world in half, his touch had felt intimate, but now it just felt like an assault. She jerked away and he smiled at her. "Let the fun continue, then."

Matilda pulled back and whirled around, her footsteps pounding away from Oliver in time with her broken heart. The cold wind blew in her face, turning her tears into sharp little pellets, blurring her vision as she ran.

"See you in your dreams," shouted Oliver, slamming the car hood down.

Matilda didn't stop running until she got home.

CHAPTER TWENTY-EIGHT

Five days until Halloween

Rain pelted the windows and beat down on the roof of Matilda's garden room, but it couldn't silence the thoughts that wailed inside her head. She rolled onto her side and pulled her phone out from under her pillow, her eyes stinging and puffy from a night of tears and no sleep.

She squinted at the photos as she swiped through them, staring into Oliver's face for some clue or sign that she'd missed. Her stomach churned as the memories of being with him were frozen in front of her: eating at the Witching Well Festival, snuggling under the blanket on the jetty, all of them frozen in lies.

The images blurred behind her tears, and Matilda's shoulders shuddered, the same way they had been periodically through the night. She turned and cried into her pillow, wailing his name and gripping the sheets in her hands. Finally, she quieted, her body tiring and allowing some respite until the next time the reality of what was happening began to crush her.

She rolled onto her back, staring at the ceiling with her phone clasped against her chest. Was this real? How could any of this have happened? Maybe he'd planned to hurt her but then fell in love with her? Maybe he felt bad about what he'd done?

Matilda held her breath as she swiped through her photos of

Oliver again, looking for some clue, something hidden in his eyes that might have given her a warning, but he just smiled back at her. She opened the school social site and checked his profile to see whether he'd changed his photo from the selfie they shared at the Witching Well Festival. Her heart leaped in her chest when she saw it was still there. She stared at the image, taken just before they played the apples-in-the-barrel game. Matilda was beaming, and Oliver was kissing her on the side of the head—a perfect couple for the camera.

"What the hell is *wrong with you*?!" she screamed at herself, throwing the phone on the floor, her stomach twisting at the thought that she was wishing herself back to that night, back into the arms of that Oliver. But he was never that Oliver. He was a murderer. "He *killed* someone!"

Even saying the words out loud didn't make it seem real; she felt like she was stuck in a nightmare. The Oliver she'd bumped into in the hall was a monster hiding beneath a smile and curly hair—he was a promise that didn't exist. She put her hands over her face, pressing her fingers on her eyelids, trying to feel something else that wasn't despair. She should have known that no one would ever truly feel that way about her.

Tiny footsteps trotted toward her, and she looked up.

"Don't worry, Vic. I wasn't screaming at you," she whispered, managing a weak smile as she tickled his chin. He bleated, then bobbed his head and nibbled the edge of her phone case. "Hey, no. What have I told you about eating my stuff?"

It took all she had to haul herself off the bed and pull the phone away from the goat's mouth. "Don't look at me like that. I'm mad at you for making me get out of bed."

Victor blinked at Matilda as she looked down at her phone,

pain squeezing her eyebrows together as she looked at Oliver's profile again. She scrolled through the comments on his page, people inviting him to parties and banter from his teammates. Should she have known she couldn't trust him? How had she let herself fall so far, so deep for him? Tears fell again, one dropping off her nose onto her phone. She wiped it away, then frowned at one of the comments on the screen, then another, and another.

Make it a hat trick at the next game, Tilly.

Tilly for captain!

Won't be a party without you, Tilly.

"Tilly? *Tilly?*" Matilda whispered, then looked at Victor. "Tillsbury. Oliver Tillsbury."

She yanked on her boots, threw open the door, and ran out into the pouring rain. Victor bleated after her, telling her she should be wearing a raincoat, but she ignored him and stormed down the path, her hair plastered to her face and her leggings soaked in puddle water.

Thunder rumbled as Matilda pushed the kitchen door open, her eyes like a missile on her grandmother at her usual spot by the fire. Matilda stomped over to her, holding her phone up.

"You knew, didn't you?" The old woman glanced at Matilda, then looked back at the pot she was stirring. "Wicked Tilly? You knew this was going to happen?! That's what you saw in the surface of the pond, wasn't it?!"

Matilda snatched the wooden spoon from her grandmother's crooked fingers. "Look at me! *Oliver Tillsbury.* He's Wicked Tilly, isn't he? That's who you've been talking about all this time?"

Nanna May sighed and looked up at Matilda with sad, moist eyes.

"Do you know what he's done? To me? To other people? I . . ."

I thought *I* was Wicked Tilly, like, like I was going to lose it and . . . how could you let this happen?"

Nanna May held out her hand, palm up, and nodded her head as she peered at Matilda. Matilda frowned and batted it away.

"If you'd have . . . if you'd have just *told* me, then I wouldn't have . . . none of this . . ."

Matilda shook her head, now certain that Nanna May had seen Oliver in the ripples in the pond weeks ago. She'd tried to warn her in the only way she could and tried to protect Matilda from Oliver's darkness with her knotted handkerchief, superstition and magic all rolled into one, but Matilda had ignored her grandmother's gift of sight.

Nanna May lifted her hand again, her eyebrows angled in concern, the lines on her ancient face telling so much without having to say any words. Matilda glared at her, then slowly put her hand into hers, her shoulders sagging as she felt her grandmother's knotted fingers squeeze around her own. She could feel her grandmother sharing something with her, a warmth throbbing through her paper-thin skin, and Matilda gave in to it.

Her face screwed up and Matilda cried, her sobs rattling her whole body as she squeezed her grandmother's hand and sank to her knees. Nanna May shuffled around on her stool and held her other hand up as Matilda rested her cheek in her lap, the smell of lavender and basil from the old woman's long dress calming and comforting her.

"Why, Nanna?" she whispered, her eyes heavy as her grandmother's calloused fingers stroked her hair. "What am I going to do?"

Matilda let herself fall into the darkness, even though she knew the answer wasn't hiding in the shadows of sleep.

CHAPTER TWENTY-NINE

Four days until Halloween

The night had barely handed itself over to the morning light when Matilda stirred in bed, but there was no way she could get back to sleep, despite her puffy eyes and aching heart. The universe hadn't righted itself, and Oliver hadn't knocked on her door in tears over the huge mistakes he'd made. Matilda lay on her back and stared at the ceiling. Her entire body was mourning the loss of what wasn't real, but there was a small voice whispering in Matilda's ear: *Get up, do something, because even though you might still have feelings for him, that witch is dangerous.*

Matilda counted to ten, then heaved a massive sigh before she managed to peel herself from her bed. She put her coat on, pulled a woolly hat over her bed head, slung a scarf over her shoulders, then searched for what she needed in her dresser. She heard the clink of quartz crystals and picked up the velvet bag they were in, carrying it over to the fresh jug of water Nanna May had snuck in during the night. She poured the water into a bowl and dropped the crystals in, swirling them around and rubbing them between her fingers, then picked them out and dried them.

She put them into a smaller bowl, pulled on her boots, and left Victor sleeping on his cushion. The air was crisp, and Matilda breathed in the solitude the early morning brought. She looked up and headed east into the woods.

Once she reached the boundary of the property, she knelt down next to a fallen tree and set the bowl of crystals on the ground. She dug a hole with her hands and put a crystal inside, then covered it and closed her eyes.

"Keep that which is wicked from my heart and from my house," she whispered.

She would need to bury the rest of the crystals around the property, but if Oliver was capable of murder, the basic protection spell should keep everyone within the boundary of the crystals safe, even with her magic as shaky as it was.

There was a rustling from above, and a magpie swooped down and landed at the end of the tree Matilda was sitting on. She held her breath, hoping for another one to join it, but the sorrowful bird was just as alone as she was.

She'd retreated back to the garden room after she'd completed the spell and settled herself into a day of hiding out. She listened to music that made her feel worse and watched TV shows that were just mind-numbing enough to make her feel bored instead of devastated, if only briefly. Nanna May brought her some lunch, but Matilda let Victor eat it—the sick feeling twisting in her stomach had stolen her appetite.

There was a tap on the window, and she looked up, frowning, as she gestured for Lottie to come in. She sat up straight on her beanbag and pulled out her earphones, bracing herself for her mother to berate her about something.

Lottie undid her duffle coat and loosened her scarf, looking around the room as she stood in the doorway and adjusted her oversize sweater. Matilda frowned as she waited for her to say something, but Lottie looked as though she'd just walked in from the street and was surprised to find herself alone with Matilda.

Matilda sighed. She was still exhausted from her early morning and was in no mood to talk, especially to her mother. "What do you want?"

Lottie blinked, suddenly remembering that Matilda was there. "Oh, um. Well, I needed to talk to you about something."

"I don't feel well," said Matilda, folding her arms as she watched her mother's eyebrows draw together. "Not that you care."

"Please, don't start with me." She looked at the bed, then back at Matilda. "Can we sit, please?"

"I'm fine here."

Lottie nodded. "Of course you are. Why would I think you'd want to make this easy?"

Matilda frowned and leaned forward. "Make what easy?"

Lottie stared at her, her chest moving up and down as she breathed in steadying air, then looked down at her hands, her fingers twisting and fiddling with her jewelry. Suddenly, fear for her mother twisted in Matilda's stomach as she watched Lottie's eyebrows pull together.

"Mom? What's going—"

"I'm pregnant," Lottie blurted, her cheeks flushing as blood rushed to her face.

Matilda stared, the words she'd just heard not making a connection with the person who'd just said them. The fear that Oliver had done something to Lottie or Nanna May was elbowed aside so confusion and something else could slosh around in her stomach instead, but Matilda wasn't sure what the something else was yet. She looked around the room for a camera crew, but they were the only two people there. Her and her mother.

Her apparently pregnant mother.

"*What?* How much? I mean, how pregnant are you?" Matilda paused, shook her head to make sure she hadn't fallen asleep, then frowned at Lottie. "I mean, *what?*"

"Four months," said Lottie, putting her hand on the bump that was just noticeable under the camouflage of her baggy sweater.

Matilda swallowed, trying to moisten her dry mouth. "Is this some weird joke that I totally don't get?"

Her mother shook her head. "No. It's true."

"So then, what the actual fuck?"

"Don't swear at me, Matilda," said Lottie, putting her hand on her hip.

"I think it's warranted on this occasion, Mother. I mean, you've just come into my room and announced you're pregnant. I literally have no other words."

Matilda stared at her mother and realized the other feeling in her stomach was anger.

Lottie put both hands up. "Look, I didn't come here to fight, and fighting isn't going to do anything to change this. I just . . . the baby's father and I—"

"Stop, please stop," said Matilda, putting her hands over her ears. Lottie folded her arms, and Matilda dropped her hands to her sides. "I don't want to know who the poor bastard is or what twisted magic this is all about."

"This has nothing to do with magic, Matilda."

"Oh, so you *can* do things without involving your precious coven, then."

"It's nothing to do with my coven, either."

"Are you sure?! They're responsible for all the other shit that ruins this family!"

"Matilda," sighed Lottie, shaking her head gently.

"What?" shouted Matilda, a tear falling down her cheek as Victor bleated, then ran out of the door at the sound of her voice. "I don't know what you want me to say. Do you want me to lie and say I'm happy there'll be another reason you keep me pushed out of that house, hidden down here so you don't even have to look at me?"

Lottie blinked and sucked her breath in.

"Tilly," she said, shaking her head and stepping toward Matilda. "Why on earth would you . . ."

Matilda pulled herself up in the most dignified way a person could when they're sitting on a beanbag. She wiped the tears from her face and pointed a finger at Lottie, her hand shaking as she glared at her mother.

"Don't call me that. Don't you *even dare* drop this life-altering shitstorm and then talk to me like I'm a child. You can't come into my room, tell me you're pregnant, and expect me to be all okay about it. What did you think I was going to say? Does Nanna May know?" Her mother nodded, and Matilda bit her bottom lip to keep it from wobbling. "I can't . . . Why? Why would you do this?"

"It wasn't exactly planned, but I love him. This feels different; it feels right."

"You mean different from Dad?"

Lottie folded her arms. "That's not what I meant, and there's absolutely no reason to bring him into this."

"There's every reason to bring him into it because he's your husband and you're having a baby with someone else!" Lottie folded her arms and looked through the window. Matilda's breath caught in her throat. "What? What was that look?"

"Your father and I have been in touch."

"No," said Matilda, putting her hands up to her hair. "No, you never speak to him."

"We've agreed to get a divorce."

Matilda's chest grew tight, and she wanted to scream and cry all at the same time, but all she could do was try to breathe.

"You are the most selfish person I've ever met," she said, her voice shaking. "How could you do that to me? To Dad?"

Lottie shook her head and looked at the floor. "I knew there was no point in trying to talk to you like an adult about this."

Matilda gaped at Lottie.

"Are you serious? What part of this conversation could have gone any other way than it has?" Matilda watched her mother look everywhere but at her, then she crossed her arms. "Who is he anyway?"

"You don't need to know right now."

It hit Matilda square in the eyes. "That man I saw you with at the festival. It's him, isn't it? That farmer? And that's why you were at the hospital. That's why you lied." Her mother stared at Matilda, her eyes full of confusion as Matilda pieced everything together. "Well, thank you *so* much for introducing me to the man you've decided to procreate with. I've literally never felt closer to you."

Matilda looked away from her mother and rubbed her hands over her eyes as if she were trying to wake up from a bad dream. There wasn't any space left inside her to process what her mother was saying, and she felt like she was going to scream. She ran her hands through her hair, pulling at the roots so she could feel something other than anger for just a split second.

"I just don't think it's the right time. I know there's something going on with you and . . ."

"Wait, what were you doing the other night out there in the woods?" said Matilda, remembering Lottie creeping around the trees the night of the party. "Was that about this, too? You had something in your hands, a knife or a . . ."

"It was a mirror," said Lottie, looking at her feet again. "The moonlight and the mirror predicted the sex. Do you want to know—"

"Of course I don't want to know!" shouted Matilda, her eyes wide in disbelief. "What the hell is wrong with you!"

"I'm sorry, Matilda, this isn't exactly . . ." Lottie's voice trailed off as she looked around the room for the end of a sentence.

"What? Isn't exactly what?" said Matilda, raising her eyebrow as she looked her mother up and down. "You can leave now."

Matilda dropped back onto the beanbag and watched Lottie turn and walk through the door, slamming it behind her without looking back. Matilda's stomach did flip-flops as she tried to ignore the fact that her first reaction was to call Oliver. Victor trotted back in and rested his head on her leg. Matilda lay back in the beanbag and threw her arm over her eyes, wishing she could escape for just a minute from the emotions that were choking her. There was a tap on the glass, and Matilda sat bolt upright, glaring at the door.

"What now? Is it twins?" she spat.

Her mouth dropped open as she looked up, and she tensed her legs, pushing herself into the beanbag as she stared at the door. She swallowed a lump in her throat and frowned at the person outside, just a weathered door and a thin pane of glass between them. She put her hands on either side of her and braced herself for whatever was about to happen.

"What the hell are you doing here?" she called.

The person on the other side of the glass, who was the last person she expected to see beneath the naked cherry trees, tapped on the window again, then squeezed her arms around her body.

"Please, let me in. I know this is, like, *so* weird, but it's frigging freezing out here," said Erin, her breath fogging the cracked panes of glass.

Matilda pulled herself up and approached the door side-on, Victor hiding behind her legs. She didn't take her eyes off Erin as she stopped in front of the door and glanced down the gravel path.

"Did you just see my mother?"

Erin nodded. "Yeah," she said, looking over her shoulder.

Matilda rushed forward and grabbed the doorknob, the end of her nose tickling the glass. "What did you do to her?!"

"Nothing." Erin's eyebrows drew together. "I'd never hurt Lottie. Why would you say that?"

"Maybe because you have a tendency to slap people or shower them with broken glass."

Erin's shoulders sagged. "Look, that's why I'm here, Matilda. Please, you have to let me in. I just want to talk, I promise."

"You can talk out there."

Erin sighed and folded her arms. "Fine. Look, I totally get why you're being shitty with me, after the slapping and the hockey thing and the following you everywhere, but—"

"I knew it! You *have* been following me!"

Erin bit her lip. "Like, I said, the slapping, the hockey, the following. But it's not my fault."

"Not your fault? How could this be not your fault?"

"Just shup up and let me finish, okay? This is so hard because

I've literally hated you for days, like deep, death-plotting hatred."

"Oh, in that case, please, wipe your feet before you come in and murder me," said Matilda, her hands shaking with anger and, she hated to admit, fear.

"That's what I mean, though, I don't feel like that now. It's like a fog cleared or something, and I realized what was happening." Erin smiled hopefully. "And I don't want to slap you anymore."

"Well then, my day is just getting better and better," said Matilda.

Erin took a deep breath.

"Look, I know what you are, and I know you can help me."

Matilda folded her arms. "What do you mean?"

"I know you're a witch, Matilda, same as I know that Oliver's a witch, too, and he's put me under some sick love spell and that's why I was so consumed with jealousy that I wanted to kill you," said Erin.

"Oliver?" Matilda put a hand on the doorframe to steady herself. "How do you know he put you under a love spell?"

Erin rolled her eyes and put her hands on her hips. "Because I've had a poster of Katy Perry above my bed for the last five years, and it's not because I like her music."

"What?"

"Oh for . . . I'm gay, you moron. The only way I'd ever have a crush on a guy is if he used magic on me."

"Oh."

"Yeah, oh. Now please open the door."

CHAPTER THIRTY

"It's open," said Matilda over her shoulder as she walked back to her bed.

Erin opened the door and stepped inside.

"Since when did you live out here?" said Erin, her eyes flitting around the room as she wiped her feet and closed the door.

"If you're looking for a broomstick, it's not in here."

Erin raised an eyebrow. "So, I'm right, then? You are a witch?"

Matilda sank onto her bed and barely nodded her head.

Erin smacked her hands together. "I knew it! How could you not tell me? We were friends all that time. I always wondered about Nanna May, though, how she was always talking to the bees and giving me little crystals to take home."

To keep you safe, thought Matilda. She sat up. "How, exactly? How do you know? Who else knows?"

"I mean, I've heard rumors, but most people at that school are as self-absorbed as you are," said Erin, rolling her eyes as Matilda frowned. "Oh, come on, don't be so sensitive. Oh shit." Erin froze as her eyes rested on Victor. "What is *that*?"

"My goat."

"Is it for a . . . are you going to kill it?"

"It's my goat; why the hell would I kill it?" Matilda looked up at the ceiling and held her breath. "I don't use that kind of magic. You still haven't told me how you know I'm a witch."

Erin walked around the room, peering at bottles and sniffing candles. "Like I said, I had my suspicions about Nanna May." Erin put down the crystal she'd picked up and looked at Matilda. "And, I still notice what you're doing at school. We were friends so long I can't help it. You have these phases of being alone, then, bam! You're best friends with someone you have nothing in common with, or you're seeing a guy who's never looked at you twice, then it always ends suddenly and you're all anonymous again like it never happened. You've had all these friends, hung out with the popular crowd, and dated some of the best-looking boys in our school, you know, if you like that sort of thing, but you've never fit right, with any of them."

"What do you mean?"

"I know you, Matilda. You get nervous talking to someone new, and you'd rather hide away in the library than be around people."

"That was ages ago," said Matilda, folding her arms.

Erin mirrored her and raised her eyebrows.

"So, you're telling me that when you got together with Oliver, you marched right up to him and said *hey, I like you*, and there was no, like, magic potion or something involved?"

"I don't want to talk about that," said Matilda, her stomach bubbling at the mention of Oliver.

"See? I knew it. There had to be a reason why people would become so obsessed with you. No way were they just drawn to you all of a sudden, especially the guys."

"Thanks a lot. Are you always this pleasant?"

"You know what I mean. You're obviously pretty, but not the normal Insta-hot type those kinds of boys parade around like a new pair of sneakers." Erin shrugged. "I'm just telling you how I came to my conclusions."

"Fine," said Matilda, irritated by Erin's perception of her. "But how did you get to witches and magic from that? How do you know it's all real?"

"Duh, hello?" said Erin, dropping onto the end of the bed and leaning back on her hands. "We live in Gravewick, home of the one and only Ivy-down-the-witching-well and the best Halloween festival for miles. Everyone knows there were witches around here. And, my girlfriend just happens to be a witch, too. We were brought together by a mutual admiration of all things witchy."

"You have a girlfriend?"

"Yes, although it was pretty touch and go when I kept ditching her to follow you two around. Luckily, I was acting so weird she realized it must be magic"

Matilda sighed. "Fine. Now what the hell do you want?"

"I told you. I want out of this spell."

"Get your girlfriend to help you, then."

Erin leaned forward on the bed, glancing at the bookshelf before she looked at Matilda.

"She's tried, but she says she hasn't been doing it long enough."

"Great," said Matilda, "another learned witch in town."

"A what?" said Erin, but Matilda had turned away from her. "Look, I figured he's your boyfriend so . . ."

"He's not my boyfriend," said Matilda, the words tasting like poison.

"Oh," said Erin, grimacing. "Shit, sorry. I didn't know you'd broken up."

"We didn't. I mean, we were never really . . ."

Erin cocked her head and looked to the side like she was listening for something. "Hey, do you think that's why I've stopped wanting to strangle you? Because you're not together anymore? Bonus!" She paused again, her curls bobbing around as she shook her head. "Now, if I could just stop thinking about him all the time, that would be great."

Matilda frowned, a thought tapping her on the shoulder.

"Why would he use a love spell on you, though?"

Erin shrugged. "Because of the patriarchy? Because I'm awesome? Because he's insane? All of the above?" She shuffled onto her knees closer to Matilda. Matilda crossed her arms. "So, will you help me? I don't like not being in control and what Oli—"

Erin clenched her teeth as Matilda twitched at the near mention of his name. "*He*, what *he's* done to me is fucking creepy, and I know it is but I just can't stop *thinking* about him and *being* with him. I feel sick because I can't see him and I don't know what he's doing right now. It took me forever to realize what was happening, and I want *me* back and Katrina does, too, plus I'm worried that he could do this to someone else."

The blood rushed from Matilda's face, and she felt as though there wasn't enough air in the room for both of them.

"Are you going to faint again?" asked Erin. Matilda closed her eyes and shook her head. "Oh, whoa. Do you think he put this shit on you, too?"

Matilda's eyes flicked open and she glared at Erin. "Stop talking."

"Sorry, just, if he—"

"I said, stop talking."

Erin swallowed and looked around the room, waiting for the storm that was raging in Matilda's eyes to pass.

"Look, I'm really sorry about whatever's happened, but I really can't go on like this. Please help me."

Matilda sighed. "Fine."

"Yes!" Erin clapped her hands together like she was applauding a miniature poodle. "Can I help? I mean, with the magic?"

"You *have* to help, otherwise it won't work. I bet he's just gone basic love spell." Matilda took a deep breath and gestured toward her dresser. "Get that bag of salt and grab that cauldron."

Erin jumped off the bed and skipped over to the dresser, her eyes flying over the surface for what she needed.

She shook her head. "I can't believe you said cauldron. This is *so* cool."

Matilda rolled her eyes as Erin put a small bag of salt into the miniature cauldron and picked it up. "Do you have a photo of yourself?"

"On my phone, yeah," said Erin.

"And you're happy to set fire to your phone?" Erin looked as though Matilda had just asked her to spill a pint of her own blood. "Didn't think so."

"Do you have a printer out here?"

Matilda shook her head and glanced out of the window. "We'll use the one in the school library." She stood and pulled Erin's scarf from around her neck, then took the cauldron and wrapped the scarf around it. "Keep this with you all night. Sleep with it in your bed, and we'll do the spell tomorrow."

"For real?"

Matilda nodded. "Noon is the best time. And then you can leave me alone. Okay?"

Erin nodded and walked to the door, then turned around, her eyes wide and honest.

"I really am sorry, Matilda, about you-know-who."

Matilda folded her arms. "I'll see you tomorrow."

Erin buttoned up her coat and opened the door, leaving Matilda alone in her heartbreaking silence once again.

CHAPTER THIRTY-ONE

Three days until Halloween

"That's it?"

Erin was clearly disappointed at how smoothly the spell had gone, but Matilda was relieved. She was feeling weaker and weaker with each passing day, and her magic seemed to be so hit-and-miss it was making her feel uneasy about casting.

Erin looked up at the clock in the science lab. "I mean, that wasn't even five minutes. That's all it takes to remove a love spell?"

Matilda didn't look up as she tipped the ashes and salt from the cauldron onto Erin's scarf and tied it into a pouch. She handed it to her, then blew out the candles that were dotted around Erin in a circle.

"You tell me. Do you feel like you're still in love with him?" said Matilda.

A smile broke out between Erin's dimpled cheeks. "No . . . no, it's gone." She threw her hands above her head. "Thank you; I'm gay again!"

Matilda handed the pouch to Erin. "Keep this with you for the next week. Sleep with it, carry it around, and you should be fine."

Erin nodded and put the pouch in her backpack. "You want to go get some lunch?"

"No."

"Come on, you must be hungry?"

Matilda stood up and glared at Erin. "Look, I did the spell, now just leave me alone."

Erin blinked at Matilda like she'd just slapped her. "I just thought . . ."

"Just think nothing. This doesn't mean we're friends again; I did what you asked so now we can both move on," snapped Matilda as she shoved things into her bag.

Erin flinched but didn't back down. "I know you're hurting, but you don't have to go about things like this."

"You don't know anything."

"Well, look at my two girls having a little fight." Matilda and Erin jumped and looked at the doorway where Oliver was leaning with his arms crossed. "Although, one of you isn't my girl anymore, are you?"

"How did you find us in here, asshole," said Erin, curling her lip as she looked Oliver up and down.

Oliver shrugged. "I could sense you were both in here, up to something. Matilda and I have a connection, isn't that right?"

Matilda's heart beat in her throat, and her blood rushed to her cheeks. The longing she felt for Oliver made her sick, and she looked at the spot just in front of his feet before he could see the tears forming in her eyes.

"Prick." Erin marched up to Oliver. "Don't ever mess with my head again. Thank God I won't be seeing your fuzzy face and bad perm in my dreams anymore."

Oliver shrugged. "The spell was actually meant for Matilda, but you were a great test subject. The way you followed me around, sending me messages, trying to get her out of the picture." Oliver grabbed Erin's wrist as it flew up from her side, her hand balled into a fist. "Watch it. Play nice."

"Like you, you mean?" spat Erin.

"I can play how I want." Oliver turned to Matilda and pulled something out of his pocket. "You can have this back now that I'm done."

Matilda recognized the necklace Oliver was holding up: a chain with a silver leaf dangling from it.

"Take it, then. It's yours, isn't it?" he said.

"Where did you get that?" asked Matilda, folding her arms as she glanced at Erin.

"Took it from your bag while you were in PE," said Oliver.

Erin stepped forward and took the necklace from Oliver, then looked at Matilda.

"You still wear this?" said Erin, her face softening. "I lent this to you, like, five years ago."

Matilda frowned at Erin and snatched the necklace from her hand. There was too much emotion flying around the room, and she just wanted to crawl into one of the science cabinets and hide.

"Oh, *wait*," said Oliver, looking from Matilda to Erin. He clapped his hands together and smiled at Erin. "The necklace was yours? That's why you ended up under my spell instead of my sweet Matilda. I knew it wasn't because I'd done it wrong."

Erin glared at Oliver. "So glad you've cleared that up."

"Whatever," said Oliver, shrugging, "but I'm actually here to talk to my girlfriend, just quickly. Can you give us some privacy?"

Erin's face softened as she looked at Matilda, then shook her head. "I'm staying."

Oliver rolled his eyes. "Fine. Matilda, have you thought about what I asked you? About what I want you to give me?" Matilda risked a look into Oliver's eyes. She nodded, clenching her fists so he wouldn't see her hands shaking. "And?"

Matilda swallowed. "You're not getting anything from me."

Oliver nodded. "Thought so. Something else, then." Despite herself, Matilda's heart leaped. "Will you meet me later? I have something to show you."

"Where?"

"At the well," said Oliver. Matilda nodded; if she wasn't going to give him the grimoire, then she needed to know what he had planned. "There's my girl. See you there tonight at seven."

Erin stared at Matilda. "You're not actually going to meet him, are you?"

"Course she is," said Oliver, biting his lip as he cocked his head and looked at Matilda. "She can't resist me."

Erin looked at Oliver like he was something she'd scraped off the bottom of her shoe.

"Whatever," she said, shaking her head as she picked up her bag. "Thanks for your help, Matilda."

Oliver moved out of the way so Erin could get through the door, then winked at Matilda.

"Yeah. Thanks for your help, Matilda."

CHAPTER THIRTY-TWO

The sky was ink with a scatter of stars thrown across its surface as Matilda made her way through the woods. At least the shadows of night would hide her pain from Oliver.

The crows cawed as Matilda ducked under the branches and stepped over the tall grass at the edge of the clearing. She'd spent the last few hours preparing herself for being alone with Oliver, knowing that it was better to find out in person what he had in store for her rather than waiting for him to twist the knife from the shadows, but seeing him leaning against the well made her stomach spin.

Oliver looked up at the sound of Matilda's feathered comrades, a smile sliding across his face as he watched her walk toward him. The wind whistled past, and Matilda frowned as she picked up the smell of something that didn't belong, something tainting the aroma of the surrounding woods. She took a long breath, trying to place the smell, then stopped when Oliver opened his arms wide.

"You came," he said.

Matilda paused for a split second, losing herself in the previous few weeks spent with him. He stood up, his eyebrows drawn together in over-the-top concern.

"Something wrong?"

"Was it real?" she blurted out. Oliver frowned at the question. "Us? Was it real or was it magic?"

Oliver smiled. "What do you think?"

Matilda swallowed and looked down, willing her tears to make their way back to her broken heart. "I . . . I . . . I . . ."

"It was real, Matilda. On your part, anyway. The love spell was a backup, but I didn't need it in the end. You fell for me the old-fashioned way."

Matilda's insides crumbled as though she'd been punched in the heart all over again. She took a deep breath to steady herself, then put her hand in her pocket and squeezed the pouch hidden inside. She'd asked Nanna May to grind her a powder and she'd obliged, without any questions. Feeling it in her palm lessened Matilda's anxiety, but she still needed to know what Oliver wanted.

"Why am I here, Oliver?" she managed, her stomach lurching as she looked around, still unable to place the smell.

Oliver rubbed his hands together. "Thought you might need a little more persuading to give me what I want, so I've got a surprise for you."

An icy trail crept down Matilda's neck as Oliver put his fingers in his mouth and whistled. Uncertain steps came from the other side of the clearing, and Oliver's surprise emerged from the trees.

"No," she whispered, shaking her head. Tears prickled her eyes as a beautiful black-and-gray horse stared at them from the edge of the trees. "No! Oliver, what are you doing?"

"What?" Oliver frowned as he walked over to Matilda. "Aren't you pleased to see Checkers?"

"Oliver, please," said Matilda, blinking as the horse from her childhood watched her from the trees. She looked at Oliver, searching his face for some glimmer of humanity but seeing nothing but danger. "What are you going to do?"

"Well, it's not really what I'm going to do, it's more what *you're* going to do." Oliver whistled again, and the horse eagerly cantered around the edge of the clearing, its head bobbing up and down as the wind tousled its hair. Matilda watched it run, the beauty of the horse overwhelming her like it did when she was a child. "Come here, girl."

The horse broke away from the tree edge and trotted over to Oliver, nuzzling his outstretched hand. Matilda's shoulders clenched around her neck as she watched and waited for the destruction to begin. She hurried toward the horse, but Oliver lifted a finger and she stopped in her tracks.

"You stay there," he said, then pulled a bag out of his pocket. "I'm giving you one more chance; give me your grimoire."

Matilda bit her lip, her breath ballooning in her lungs. Oliver stroked the horse's neck as he watched her, his eyes as dark as the night. He sighed and dropped his head for a moment, then looked up and shrugged.

"Your choice. But know that what's about to happen, and what happens to anyone else, is all on you."

"Oliver, please don't. Whatever you're going to do, whatever you think you want, it's not worth it. You can still come back from this," said Matilda, pressing her hands together as she pleaded with him.

"Come back? I've always been here, Matilda, and I like it here."

A sob caught in Matilda's throat as she looked at Oliver; his face was the same one she'd fallen for but his features were different, tinged with danger and death. She shook her head, still unable to believe she was in her own life and not a nightmare.

"There must be something else you want?"

Oliver sighed. "It's quite straightforward." He paused, waiting for her, then nodded. "Remember, this was you."

Oliver undid the small bag and whispered into Checkers's ear as he upended the contents into his palm.

"What's that?" asked Matilda, fear squeezing her vocal cords.

"Grain, plus a few extra things," said Oliver, holding up his palm.

"Checkers, don't! Don't eat that!" shouted Matilda as she ran toward them.

"Stop where you are," shouted Oliver, "or I'll gouge her eyes out, right now."

Matilda froze, her muscles fighting to run to Checkers but her heart knowing that Oliver was so far into the shadows he was capable of anything. She clenched her fists as the horse stepped forward like the trusting, beautiful idiot she was and started munching from Oliver's hand. She swallowed its last mouthful, then lifted her head and backed away.

Flapping rippled from the outer trees right into the clearing, turning into a chorus as the birds thrashed their wings in premonition. Checkers snorted, then bobbed her head up and down and trotted from side to side, like she was standing guard on a drawbridge, then turned to Oliver.

"Here we go," whispered Oliver. "Checkers, beautiful girl, turn your head to the left."

The horse snorted, then moved her head to the left, following Oliver's command perfectly. Matilda's breath quickened as Oliver raised his eyebrows at her, then looked at the horse again.

"Checkers, lift up your front left leg." The horse obliged, and Oliver patted her side and looked at Matilda. "Not bad, huh? Now, Checkers, give me a bow."

Dread squeezed its bony fingers around Matilda's heart as she helplessly watched Checkers edge closer and closer to something deadly. She wiped a tear from her cheek as the horse dipped her head down and lifted it up again.

"Good girl. Now, Checkers, run across the clearing and jump over the well on your way back."

"Oliver," said Matilda, lifting her hands as if she were pulling Checkers's reins. "Please, just leave her alone. I'm begging you. Please don't hurt her."

"Shut up," spat Oliver as Checkers cantered across the clearing. She turned around at the tree line and galloped back.

Matilda held her breath as she watched the horse cross the grass. She dug her fingernails into her palms as Checkers got closer to the well, then almost wept with joy as the horse leaped clean over the stone wall, then circled back and joined Oliver's side.

"Now, Checkers," said Oliver, pointing to just beyond the well, "trot over to that patch near the well."

Checkers did as Oliver said, looking back at him to check she'd followed his command properly. Matilda's eyes flicked from the horse to Oliver, unable to see what invisible danger she was heading into. The horse stopped under the moonlight, and Oliver pulled a small silver item from his pocket. He locked eyes with Matilda and grinned as he held up the lighter, and Matilda's throat closed as she realized what she could smell when she arrived at the clearing.

Gasoline.

Matilda charged at Oliver, her screams echoing between the trees. He ignited the lighter and threw it on the grass just as Matilda tackled him. They tumbled to the ground, Oliver's laughter and Matilda's screams spiraling up to the stars, and she watched in horror as a trail of fire snaked from their feet to where Checkers stood.

"No, no, no, *no!*" she screamed as their stage in the middle of the clearing lit up the night.

Matilda scrambled up, Oliver's laughter assaulting her ears as she tripped toward Checkers and the bright orange flames blazed between her and the horse.

"Relax," said Oliver as he stood up and brushed himself off, "she's perfectly safe as long as she stays inside the ring of fire. You didn't think I'd actually set a horse on fire, did you?"

Matilda held her hands up against the heat, squinting through the flames until she saw Checkers moving back and forth, whinnying for someone to help her. Everything in the woods screamed for the horse; even the nocturnal animals were woken by the smell of burning hair and fear drifting on the wind. Matilda sobbed as she tried to get to the horse, hoping that Checkers would know someone was trying to help her, but her mind raced with panic and helplessness.

"You're right; I totally would. I don't give a shit about animals." Oliver laughed, the flames making shadows dance gleefully across his face. He clapped his hands together suddenly and Matilda flinched. "For our next trick, Checkers is going to take a few steps forward until she's standing in the flames."

"No!" shouted Matilda, tears from the heat of the fire and for Checkers rolling down her cheeks. "No, Oliver, you have you stop this. Please, *please* don't hurt her."

Oliver crossed his arms. "Not until I hear the magic words."

"Anything, please, I'll give you what you want." Matilda pressed her hands together. "Just, please, let her go."

"Finally," said Oliver, rolling his eyes. He walked to the well and picked up a backpack. "I knew you'd come around."

Matilda willed her heart to slow down as Oliver pulled out

a gray blanket and walked past her. He stopped in front of the flames and dropped it over the fire so there was a gap in the flames surrounding Checkers.

"Checkers, come," he said. The horse whinnied and trotted over the blanket. Matilda held her breath until Checkers was clear of the flames, and she ran over and put her hand on her side. The heat from the horse's coat burned Matilda's palm, but she didn't pull it away. She stroked Checkers's side and hushed into her ear, tears falling for the terror the horse had been dragged into.

"Good girl." Oliver smiled. "You *and* the witch."

Matilda looked at Oliver, wishing that she had her full quota of magic at her fingertips so she could punish him for what he'd done. Now that she was close to Checkers, she put her hand inside the pouch in her pocket and grabbed a fistful of the powder hiding inside.

She would settle for some of her grandmother's magic instead.

"So sentimental for animals, aren't you?" said Oliver. "Maybe your little goat could help me next time."

Anger flashed in Matilda's eyes as she glared at Oliver.

"Don't you ever touch a witch's familiar," she said, her jaw tight. She pulled her hand from her pocket and opened her palm, blowing the dust into Checkers's face. "*Let this powder be your shield.*"

Oliver lurched forward and smacked her hand away, his cheeks flushed with anger, but he was too late.

"Checkers, step into the fire!" he shouted.

The horse swished her tail but didn't move. Matilda's heart soared as Checkers blinked and looked at Matilda.

"Run home, Checkers," she shouted, stumbling back as the horse reared up and galloped into the safety of the trees. Matilda turned to Oliver.

"You didn't think I'd come here without a protection spell, did you?" she said, braver now that Checkers had escaped.

Oliver's nostrils flared, and he ran at Matilda, grabbing her arms and swinging her around.

"But if you used it to protect the horse," he said, his lips pressing into her hair, "what's going to protect you?"

Matilda panicked as the woods whooshed by, her tears and Oliver's madness making everything blurry. She struggled against him but tripped over her feet and stumbled back until she could feel the stone well against the backs of her thighs.

Oliver grabbed the front of her coat and pushed her back until she was hanging over the well. Her eyes bulged and she shook her head, her voice lost in disbelief. She clawed at his hands as he bit his bottom lip, looking over her shoulder into the dark abyss of the well. A smile tickled the edge of his mouth and he loosened his hands, pinning her against the edge of the well with his legs.

"Just once in case you don't make it out."

Matilda winced as Oliver pressed his lips against hers, then let go of her. Her arms flailed as she tried to grip the stone, her eyes widening when he stepped back and kicked her feet from under her, his smile getting farther away as she tumbled down into the darkness.

CHAPTER THIRTY-THREE

A groan echoed through the darkness, and it took Matilda a few seconds to realize that it was coming from her. Ragged breaths clawed out of her mouth as she opened her eyes and searched her pockets, her throbbing head adding to the disorientation of being submerged in the shadows.

"Hey, phew. You're alive," called Oliver. "If you're looking for your phone, I've got it here."

Matilda looked up at the rectangular light waving around high above her, then felt her way around the slick stone of the well, her ankles sloshing through the shallow water as she stumbled around.

"I'll leave this up here for when you get out, not that you have anyone to call. You can have this, though. Heads up."

Matilda felt something drop by her shoulder and into the water with a splash. She crouched down and felt around, her fingers freezing as they disturbed the coins resting in the well, until she felt a large handle. She picked up the flashlight and flicked it on, aiming the beam upward. Oliver squinted and put his hand out to block the light.

"Right. I'll leave you to have a little think about things," he said, then pulled away.

"O-Oliver!" shouted Matilda, her eyes locked on the tiny sliver of moonlight above her. She held her breath and listened for movement. "Oliver?"

Matilda waved the flashlight with a shaking hand, her ragged breaths the only sound in the well. It was bigger than she expected, too wide to touch either side at the same time. She shuffled around the edge, peering at the stone and looking for holes or steps or maybe a secret trapdoor, but there was nothing.

She trained the flashlight just above her head and turned as she followed the beam of light, stopping when she spotted a lone piece of stone protruding from the rest about halfway up the well. Farther up was another stone, then a hole, then the top of the well.

Hope surged through Matilda's veins, and she rushed to the side under the protruding stone, then pointed the flashlight down at her feet. Beneath the water were dozens, maybe hundreds, of grubby coins resting on top of the witch who'd been cast into the shadows of the well.

Ivy.

Matilda peered at the old coins, then bent down and ran her fingers over them, wondering whether any of the wishes had come true. How far down did it all go? Matilda shuddered. How far down was Ivy?

She shoved the handle of the flashlight into the coins so it pointed upward and shook out her limbs, ignoring the buzzing creeping around her head.

"Okay," she whispered to herself, trying to steady her breathing. "You can do this."

With her eyes firmly on the protruding stone, she bent her knees and sprang up, her hands stretching high above her head. She fell back down into the water, but pulled herself up and jumped again, splaying her fingers out as if she were trying to touch the moon, but she fell against the other side of the well.

"Come on!" she shouted, panic making her voice shake. "Try and be a bit athletic for once in your life!"

Matilda put her foot against the wall and tried to jump up, but her toes slipped and she fell to her side, the coins and the rainwater not offering the slightest of graceful landings. She pulled herself up and looked upward. She could feel panic rising in her chest, poised to take control of her the moment she gave up. Matilda shook her head, trying not to acknowledge that death was probably leaning over the well, waiting for her, just like it had for Ivy.

"Hello?! A little help, please!" Matilda looked down at her feet. "Ivy, if you're really down here, now would be a good time to prove it."

The sound of tree branches cracking against each other in the wind was joined by the distant roll of thunder, and Matilda could smell the rain before she felt wet drops on her upturned face.

"No," she whispered, her mouth turned down in a grimace. "No, rain is definitely not going to help! Please! Someone help me!"

A fork of lightning illuminated the sky and rain plummeted down the well, fat drops drenching Matilda's hair in seconds and soaking her coat and jeans. She bit her lip and looked down at her already soaked feet sloshing around in the shallow water.

Shallow for now.

Matilda kicked at the coins with the toe of her boot, trying to create some drainage so the water could escape. Another furious crack of lightning lit up the pit of the well. Matilda could see that her efforts had achieved nothing, and the water level was already creeping up.

The rain soaked through to her socks, but Matilda ignored the ice in her toes and jumped up again, her fingers miles from reaching the stone. Her heart leaped as she remembered she was wearing a scarf. She pulled it from her neck, then, holding one end of it, threw it up at the stone.

After the fifth time her scarf landed over her eyes, Matilda tore it from her face and threw it into the water. Her eyes darted up and down, zigzagging the slick walls as she turned on the spot, biting down the tears that were more than halfway to making an appearance. The air felt as though it was getting thicker, and Matilda's breaths rasped in and out as she tried to pull enough oxygen into her lungs.

Lightning flashed again, bedazzling the bottom of the well. The water was past her ankles now and she dropped to her knees, plunging her numb hands into the water over and over, furiously shifting coins deep under the water, until her hand caught something sharp.

Matilda clenched her teeth and peered at the long red line on her palm. The rain washed away the blood that sprang from the cut, cleansing it with each drop as if there were nothing there at all. Thunder roared and rain crashed down as Matilda was hit with a realization like the bolts of lightning in the sky. She thrust her hands into the water again as she searched around the bottom of the well, feeling for what she needed.

She felt a scratch again, but instead of withdrawing her hand, her fingers carefully felt out the shape. Her nose almost touched the surface of the water as she clasped her fingers around what was the true piece of treasure in the well, camouflaged by the coins and the cover of history.

Ivy's athame, rusty and old, but sturdy and ready for action.

Rainwater trickled down her face as she pulled at the knife handle, grabbing handfuls of coins and chucking them over her shoulder as she fought to break it free.

"Ivy, if you're listening, please don't be holding this in your hand," she whispered, and sat on her backside, her feet pressed against the sides as she clenched her teeth and strained.

The knife shifted, and Matilda relaxed for a few seconds and caught her breath before she pulled again. She could feel it straining in her hands, but it felt like something was holding it down. Matilda clenched her teeth and yanked it with everything she had left, and it came free as she fell back against the wall.

Matilda laughed a little, the alien sound echoing up the slick walls. She rested her head on the brick and looked up.

"Ha," she panted, then looked at her hands and gasped when she saw what had anchored the knife down so well.

Wrapped around the knife was the thickest and oldest looking vine of ivy Matilda had ever seen. She slumped against the wall and looked at the vine trailing from around the knife in her hands back into the water, then up a long, thick crack in the wall, a crack that snaked up past the protruding stone Matilda was trying to reach. She'd managed to pull the vine free of its camouflage when she'd freed the knife it was wrapped around.

Matilda stared at the athame, overwhelmed by the closeness she felt to her history sitting at the bottom of the well, her long-dead ancestor helping her to survive. She felt as though the metal was melting into her skin, seeping through to her blood and giving her soul a charge of electricity that sparked with magic. The hole that had been tearing wider and wider since she started having the blackouts seemed to pull back together inside her chest, just a little, gleaming golden strands crisscrossing the shadow and tightening gently.

"Thank you," she whispered, the energy from her bloodline bubbling in her veins as she pulled herself up.

Something in the now knee-deep water twinkled and winked at her as she stood. Matilda put the knife in her pocket and bent down to fish the item out. Her breath caught in her chest as it became visible beneath the surface of the water. She lifted it out and held it up to her eyes.

A misshapen stone dangled from a thick silver chain. As it twisted and spun, Matilda could see tiny flashes of blue hidden beneath its white surface. Finally, she let out her breath.

It was Ivy's moonstone.

Matilda put it around her neck, then waded over to the vine of ivy, tugging at it gently as she looked up. She curled her fingers tight around the vine and closed her eyes.

"Please hold, *please*," she whispered. "I just need to get to that stone."

Matilda bit her lip as she heaved herself up, grabbing the ivy above and climbing steadily, glancing up at the protruding stone that got closer and closer and closer until she was level with it.

Thunder crashed its applause as she scrambled onto the ledge and looked up at the next one. The ivy had run out, so Matilda pulled the knife from her pocket and swung it over her head, aiming for a crack in the brickwork. She clasped her other hand around the handle and tried to pull herself up, her feet slipping against the stone. She wobbled but managed to throw her weight against the brick and stop herself from falling, her arms stretched out to either side and her fingers clinging to the cracks.

The bottom of the well was farther down than she'd thought. She swallowed and looked upward, squinting at the next stone and then the hole above it. Matilda looked from the hole to the top of the well, wondering how on earth she would make the final part of the climb.

"We'll work that out when we get there, hey, Ivy?" she panted, and held on to the knife as she found her footing and braced herself to climb.

Light that wasn't coming from the moon suddenly waved over the top of the well, accompanied by a sound that wasn't thunder.

"Hello?"

"Hello?!" shouted Matilda, almost choking on the word as she blinked at the opening of the well.

The light grew brighter until it shone down the well.

"Jesus, it's her. She's here," said a male voice, getting louder. "Hold on! We're getting you out of there!"

The figure disappeared, his voice joined by another as they murmured back and forth, then a figure leaned over just above her. It kept leaning until Matilda realized they were actually being lowered into the well by whoever was holding on to them.

"Reach up to me!" she called, and Matilda recognized Officer Powell's voice. "Reach up!"

Matilda put the knife in her pocket and reached up with her other hand, holding her breath until she felt fingers around her wrist.

"Hold on!" she shouted as Matilda grabbed ahold of her wrist. "I've got her; pull us up."

Matilda held her breath as she was pulled upward, all three of them in the human chain grunting as she was hauled to the top of the well, where another hand appeared above her head.

"We've got you. We've got you," said Officer Powell, helping her out of the well. Matilda looked up at the moon, both officers rushing to her side as she stumbled backward on shaking legs.

"I'm calling in an ambulance," said Officer Seymour, gripping his radio.

"No," panted Matilda. "No, please. I just want to go home."

The officer shook his head. "We need to get you checked out. Your lips are blue."

"Please," said Matilda, her lip wobbling. "I'm just cold, and I want to go home. I'm not injured."

The two officers looked at each other, communication rippling across their eyebrows. Finally, Officer Powell spoke.

"Let's just get you to the car for now. We've got blankets in there."

Officer Seymour unzipped his coat and put it around Matilda's shaking shoulders. He crouched down and picked up a flashlight, then the three of them began walking away from the well.

"H-how did you find me?" asked Matilda through quivering lips.

"Your friend came to the station and told us she was worried for your safety," said Officer Powell.

"Who?"

"She's waiting in the car."

The rain was still pounding down as if it wanted to drown the night, and Matilda was glad for the rumbling thunder because it meant nobody had to say anything. The cold had numbed her bones, but she felt something else inside her, something that roared in her stomach and singed the edge of her soul.

Something that felt like family.

CHAPTER THIRTY-FOUR

Erin's wide, earnest eyes were visible through the back-seat window as Matilda trudged through the rain to the police car waiting on the side of the road. Officer Powell opened the other back door, and Matilda ducked inside and collapsed against the dry seat, gratefully pulling a blanket up to her chin. She closed her eyes as the door slammed shut and was certain the sound of the rain and the engine running would send her off to sleep immediately.

"Um, *hello?*" said Erin from her side. Matilda opened her eyes, silently waving any rest goodbye. "Are you okay? What the hell happened?"

Matilda leaned back and rolled her head the other way, looking at the rain battering the window.

"Why are you so wet?" tried Erin again. She put her hand on the driver's seat and tried a different audience. "Where did you find her? Who was she with?"

Officer Powell looked in the rearview mirror.

"I'm sure Matilda will tell you what happened when she's ready, Erin," she said over her shoulder. "Oh, we found this, by the way. I'm guessing it's yours."

Matilda took the phone from Officer Powell, then watched the officers look at each other, nodding and grunting in some secret police language. Finally, Officer Seymour shifted around in his seat.

"You're sure you don't want us to speak to anyone about how you got down that well?"

Matilda stuck out her chin. "I fell down."

"Right, yeah, that's what you said before; you just fell down," said Officer Seymour, glancing at his coworker.

Officer Powell leaned over and whispered something. Officer Seymour looked at Matilda, then turned back in his seat, shook his head, and sighed.

"Oh, it's one of *those* calls is it?" he said, folding his arms. Officer Powell glanced at him. "Fine. Drop me off at home, then; my shift finished ages ago."

Matilda frowned at Erin, but Erin shrugged in response. They drove on in silence for another few minutes until Officer Powell pulled over and Officer Seymour got out.

"Hey, Seymour?" called Officer Powell.

Officer Seymour bent down and ducked his head back in the car. "Don't tell me; you want me to update dispatch and close the call? Say we didn't find anything?"

Officer Powell smiled. "You read my mind."

He rolled his eyes and slammed the door closed, then hurried through the drizzle, disappearing into the darkness of the late hour.

Officer Powell turned to Matilda.

"How are you feeling?" she asked. Matilda shrugged, the blast from the car heater not doing anything to thaw out her bones. "Matilda, I think it might be a good idea if we—"

"Please, you don't need to speak to my mom."

Officer Powell shook her head. "I do think we should speak to her, but that's not what I was going to say."

"Oh," said Matilda, folding her arms.

Officer Powell searched Matilda's face, looking for something she knew was there, but not quite knowing what it was. She glanced at Erin, who was watching the exchange like she was glued to her favorite TV show.

"The boy you were with at the party? Oliver, wasn't it?" Matilda's stomach twisted at the mention of his name. "He your boyfriend?"

"Yes. I mean, no. He was."

"Okay." Officer Powell nodded. "He's not around anymore?"

"No, he . . . we . . ." Matilda's voice cracked as she fought to say the right thing.

"Matilda, if you're trying to cover for him . . ."

"I'm not," said Matilda.

"Matilda," said Erin, "maybe you should—"

"I'm not," snapped Matilda again, glaring at Erin.

The officer lifted her hands. "I said *if*. Sometimes people present a version of themselves they think will help them get what they want. People like that can have a gift for twisting up others' lives."

Matilda looked at her hands as the truth of the officer's words sank in.

"You know about Ivy, right?"

Matilda straightened up. "What?"

"Ivy, as in Ivy-down-the-witching-well? What they did to her was just . . . anyway, some of the things I've seen, I always wonder whether there's a little of that left in this town, the ruthlessness of people, of men, to get what they want, to feel like they're in control. Seymour thinks I'm irrational, but I really believe it."

She looked into Matilda's eyes, then turned and put the car in gear.

"Right," she said, "we have another stop to make before I get you both home."

⎯⎯⎯•⎯•⎯•⎯⎯⎯

Matilda stared out of the window as Officer Powell drove them through the quiet streets of Gravewick. They passed hushed houses, all closed up and tucked in for the night, and Matilda's stomach knotted with resentment at the warm glow from upstairs windows, cozy beds soothing their inhabitants to sleep, not a care in the world.

She looked down and unfolded her arms again, holding her hands out in front of her. They were still trembling, and she folded her arms across her chest, hugging herself in a hopeless effort to warm her bones, but she knew the cold wasn't the only reason she was shaking. Matilda could still feel something deep in her soul, something magic that had come out of the well with her, but she couldn't stop thinking about how she'd gotten down there. Had Oliver planned to push her down the well when he asked her to meet him? Was that why he'd brought a flashlight? Had he stayed and watched as the police helped her climb out or did he value her life so little that he'd just gone off and left her?

Officer Powell slowed the car down and pulled over. Matilda looked around and recognized the street as one of the older parts of Gravewick. It was a short cul-de-sac and wouldn't get much traffic unless people wanted to visit one of the small boutique shops that stood shoulder to shoulder with the terraced houses.

"We're here," said Officer Powell, glancing back at Matilda and Erin before she turned off the engine and opened the door.

"Where do you think we're going?" whispered Erin as she undid her seat belt, watching Officer Powell walk around the car.

Matilda sighed. She wasn't sure she had the energy to open the car door, let alone go on some secret expedition around Gravewick's forgotten streets. She shrugged at Erin and looked out the window as Officer Powell opened her car door.

"Thank you," said Matilda, swinging her legs around and pulling up.

"Don't thank me," smiled Officer Powell. "These doors don't open from the inside, guys."

Erin followed Matilda out of the car, then slammed the door shut behind her. The sound made Matilda jump, and she frowned at Erin, who mouthed the word *sorry*. Both girls stood and blinked at the police officer, awaiting the next instruction. Officer Powell hooked her thumbs inside her vest and looked between both of them and narrowed her eyes.

"Can I trust you girls?" Matilda and Erin looked at each other, then back at Officer Powell, and both nodded. "I thought so. Follow me."

Old-style lights dotted either side of the road, humming as they cast shadows on what felt to Matilda like the only three people in the world. She pulled the blanket tight around her shoulders and followed Erin and Officer Powell as they walked silently down the path. Her feet were frozen. If it weren't for the sound of her footsteps squelching across the pavement, she wouldn't have known whether her legs were working properly.

They turned left, and Matilda followed Officer Powell into the relative warmth of an alley beneath an archway that protected them from the biting wind. Matilda put her hand out to feel her way along the brickwork in the dim light, her other senses picking up the sound of trickling water. The alley opened up into a small, square courtyard that had a round brick wall sitting in the middle of it, ivy tangled over the sides and a small but determined fountain bubbling in the middle of it.

There were three doors and three shop windows on each side of the courtyard, and Officer Powell walked to the red door next to a window that was crisscrossed with streamers in the Witching Well Festival colors, as well as books sitting on top of pumpkins and sticking out of cauldrons. Déjà vu tapped Matilda on the shoulder, and she turned to look around the courtyard again, wondering whether she'd seen it before or maybe her senses were all over the place from the trauma of the well.

"In here," said Officer Powell, her voice making Matilda jump.

"Is this a bookstore?" asked Erin, pushing her face up against the window. "How did I not know there's a bookstore in Grave-wick?"

Officer Powell pulled a bunch of keys from her pocket and unlocked the door with a clunk. They all filed through, and immediately the smell and quiet of the books in the shop enveloped Matilda like a warm hug. There was a click, and Matilda squinted as the small shop floor was bathed in light. She turned around to take it all in, the long wooden desk with posters of children's books stuck to the front of it and the rows and rows of books with cracked spines down one side of the shop. At the front were shelves beneath the window stuffed with a rainbow of books in different sizes. On the floor was a big, book-shaped rug, well-worn and well-loved where hundreds of children had probably thrown themselves onto the beanbags and spent Saturday afternoons flicking through the books before begging their parents to buy them.

Officer Powell gestured for them to follow her to the back of the shop, but Matilda was rooted to the spot.

"Hey, Matilda, you with us?" asked Officer Powell.

Matilda walked over to the counter and ran her hand along its wooden front, her fingers exploring the dents and scratches that crisscrossed it as if she were searching for a message hidden in the grooves. She looked up as Erin put her hand on her shoulder and managed to retrieve her voice back from where it had been hiding, along with some misplaced memories.

"I . . . I think I've been here before," she said.

"Really?" said Erin, looking around with wide eyes, still in disbelief that there was a bookshop hidden in Gravewick.

Matilda nodded. "I think . . . my mom used to bring me here."

Officer Powell smiled. "Well, she has good taste," she said. "This is the finest bookstore in town. And also the only. Shall we go through?"

Officer Powell turned to a small door at the back of the store, and Erin followed, leaving Matilda alone in the memory she'd uncovered. She remembered bounding through the door with her mom on a Saturday and throwing herself on the big book rug, sitting on her knees as her hungry eyes searched for books that hadn't been there the last time. She swallowed a lump, the closeness to her mom in her memory like an intruder, then turned just as Officer Powell opened the door with a creak, revealing a whole other room. Matilda left the smell of secondhand books and hurried after them.

She craned her neck to see past Erin and realized why she hadn't moved any farther forward. They stood in a small room with a scratched wooden table in the middle and four worn chairs tucked beneath it. A green velvet armchair sat in the corner with a cushion and crocheted blanket of black, green, pink, and blue draped over it, ready to embrace someone's tired bones, and a table with a pot of lavender stood next to it. Four small windows lined the wall opposite them, set just below the ceiling, each of them a jigsaw of stained glass. Matilda looked at each one, losing herself in the colors and black lines, each depicting one of the elements in the form of an animal: a mole for the earth, a butterfly for air, a snake for fire, and a seahorse for water.

A lamp next to the armchair cast the room with a warm glow and sent shadows up the cast-iron staircase that curved up from the wooden floorboards. Dark timber shelves snaked around all four walls of the room, the knots on the shelf edges staring out at Matilda like tiny little eyes. The books around the walls and the rug the table stood on seemed to soundproof the room, keeping any whisperers or secrets from being overheard.

The books weren't facing spine out as they would in a book-shop or library. Instead, their spines faced inward as if they were keeping their subjects secret, and the battered corners and yellow curled pages of the books faced outward. Matilda pushed past Erin and glanced at Officer Powell, who nodded, and Matilda reached out to one of the long black chains, following it from an iron loop attached to the underside of the shelf all the way up to another iron ring pierced through the corner of the book. It jangled as Matilda let go gently, her eyes tripping over themselves to take in the rest of the books on the shelves, all chained just like their neighbors.

"Um," said Erin, her voice as quiet and measured as Matilda had ever heard it. "What is *that*?"

Erin was staring up at the ceiling, and Matilda followed her gaze. There were five shapes painted in thin black lines curving across the ceiling: a circle flanked by two more circles, each one with half the space inside it blacked out, and two more crescent shapes on either end.

"Phases of the moon," said Officer Powell.

Erin blinked at her. "Oh, of course," she said, rolling her eyes a fraction. "How silly of me."

The room felt alive with a heartbeat, and Matilda could feel its energy seeping into her pores until her heart beat along with it. She felt heavy; her knees started to buckle as if something was pushing down against her. She swallowed and lifted a hand to her head.

"Matilda?" said Erin, moving to her side.

"Whoa, sorry," said Officer Powell, rushing to Matilda and putting an arm around her waist. Matilda gratefully gave up trying to stand and slumped against them as they walked her over to the armchair. "I'm so used to this place I forget how it can affect us. Sit down for a minute. You've had a big night and now this. It's a lot to process."

"Now this? What *is* this?" asked Erin, looking around the room. "Why are the books all chained up like that? And why do I feel like I'm standing next to a magnet?"

Matilda let her head fall back into the armchair as Officer Powell unfolded the blanket and tucked it over her knees. Between the cold from the well and the energy in the room, her body felt as though it needed to hibernate for a year.

"They're spell books. Right?" said Matilda, looking at Officer Powell, who nodded. "That's what I can feel, like I've walked into a cloud of magic, ancient, powerful magic. I can feel it on my skin. Nonwitches can feel it, too?"

"Those without our gifts can also feel the magic in this room," came a voice from the top of the spiral staircase. Matilda managed to look upward as the owner of the voice traveled down each step, her pink manicured nails trailing along the handrail. "A secondhand book can be a powerful thing, its owner leaving a part of themselves between each page: a thought, a revelation, a first love. But a book of spells, the magic from the fingertips of our ancestors on every page, in every curve of their handwriting? Even your nonwitch friend can feel that kind of power."

She stepped off the bottom step and walked over to Matilda. Long white hair hung to the woman's shoulders, and her orange skirt swished across the floorboards as she walked, making her look like she was floating. She stopped at the chair and bent over, and Matilda looked into the woman's bright blue eyes and felt something soft drop into her cold hands.

"Put these on; I've just finished knitting them," she said. Matilda looked down to find a pair of purple socks in her hands. She looked back at the woman, who winked at her. "It's Shetland wool; your toes will soon warm up."

As the woman embraced Officer Powell and kissed her on the cheek, Matilda noticed a small tattoo of a pentacle on her left hand.

"Hello, darling. How's the crime fighting going?"

"Fine, Mom," said Officer Powell, unzipping her bulletproof vest and taking off her belt. "Long day."

Officer Powell hung the vest and belt on one of the chairs, and Matilda noticed the same tattoo peeking out from one of her sleeves.

"And who have you brought with you?" said the woman.

"This is Erin and her friend Matilda. I thought they could do with a visit," said Officer Powell, looking between the girls. "This is my mom, Maura."

Maura peered at Matilda, her eyes twinkling in the orange glow of the lamp. "You're a Hollowell, Lottie's girl." Matilda blinked but didn't respond. Maura nodded. "She's a good witch, part of a good coven."

"You know my mom?"

"I do. She comes to the shop from time to time, not as much as she used to, but she's always welcome." Maura peered at Matilda and raised an eyebrow. "You come from a strong bloodline, but you go down your own path, don't you? Be careful you don't get lost."

Matilda swallowed, unprepared for such insight, and decided to ignore the question.

"How . . . I mean, how do you know her?" she asked.

"I know all the witches in this town," said Maura, then gave a small smile. "Those who want to be known, anyway. Tell me, my dear, you must be of coven age?" Matilda nodded. "I take it you're yet to join one?"

"I just . . . I haven't decided yet," said Matilda, folding her arms awkwardly.

"Well, it's your decision to make, but joining a coven not only makes you part of a powerful group, it connects you with our wider fabric of magic."

"How many witches are there in town, then?"

"You wouldn't need to ask me that if you were part of a coven, my dear, but I'm not just talking about the witches in Gravewick. I'm talking about much farther and wider than that. Now, it's not my duty to lecture young witches—" Officer Powell coughed and Maura raised an eyebrow at her. "It *is* my duty to lecture, my dear daughter, but as I was saying, I don't wish to lecture you, but the strongest move a witch can ever make is joining a coven."

"Thank you, but I . . . I have all the magic I need," said Matilda, shrinking down in the chair.

Maura narrowed her eyes as they ran across Matilda's face. She held her breath, sure that Maura could see all the names hidden on her skin.

"So it seems, or so you believe, anyway." Maura lifted a finger. "But a coven is about so much more than magic, my dear, so much more. Wisdom, support, safety. The list is endless. We are misunderstood, but our power is desirable. A witch always has a target on her back. Your coven would help you look over your shoulder."

Matilda shivered at Maura's words and pulled the blanket tighter around her.

"Officer Powell, what is this place?" asked Erin.

Matilda was glad of Erin's incessant questioning for once, as Maura finally turned her attention away from Matilda. Her head was firing with her own questions, but she didn't have the energy to ask them. She felt as though she and the room were still getting to know each other, and the socializing was exhausting.

"Please, call me Emily," said Officer Powell. "And it's just a place. Our place."

"You're a witch?" said Erin.

"That's right, my dear. A living, breathing, not-so-wicked witch," said Maura, glancing back at Matilda.

"Cool. Sorry, I'm not a witch, but my girlfriend is, so . . . ," Erin babbled.

"You are very welcome here," said Maura, her eyes crinkling as she walked over to Erin and squeezed her shoulder. "Both of you. Now, what is it that brings you here?"

"Well, technically, Officer—sorry, Emily—brought us here after Matilda's psychopath ex-boyfriend threw her down the well," said Erin, shrugging when Matilda glared at her. "What? I know that's what happened. He did, didn't he?"

"I picked them up and thought they could maybe do with a little detour before they went back home alone," said Emily.

"So, Emily, are you a witch, too?" asked Erin, not noticing Emily's neck muscles tensing at the question.

"I am, technically, I mean, by blood, and I do practice, but . . ."

Matilda recalled being surprised that Emily remembered questioning her in her garden room about the dead animals, despite Lottie giving her a brew to make her forget. Emily must have known exactly what she'd been given to drink and dumped it the moment Lottie turned her back.

"Not as she should and not as I wish she would, but she has chosen her path and I accept that," said Maura.

"I just focus my energy on the job. There are a lot of bad people out there, magic or otherwise, but there's no way the department has the knowledge or the open-mindedness to know what they're dealing with half the time. I keep my ear to the ground and volunteer to attend any cases where I suspect magic is at play. I can usually spot when someone's misusing the craft a mile off and we stand half a chance of putting a stop to it."

Matilda nodded. It was almost comforting to see that butting heads with your mother seemed to be a universal witch thing, and not just restricted to the confines of Ferly Cottage. She gripped the arms of the chair and shuffled forward, managing to pull herself up. She was used to the magic in the room now, as if her heart had gotten in sync with its pulse. She walked to the shelves and peered at the crinkly pages sandwiched between the book covers, then turned to Maura.

"They're spell books, aren't they?"

"Yes, sorry, my dear, back to your original question before I came and interrupted. Spell books, diaries of our sisters, grimoires of families where our craft has petered out."

"Where do you get them?"

"Some of them are gifted to us. Some of them I come across when I'm at an estate sale for the store or at secondhand book markets." Maura moved to Matilda's side and took one of the books from the shelf, placing the leather-bound book in Matilda's hands. "Some of them Emily has taken back from those who have no business being in possession of them. All in all, we keep them safe."

Matilda looked at the book in her hand, then glanced at Maura, who nodded at her. She slowly opened it, her eyes widening at the curled handwriting across the yellowing page: *Here be the spells of Ivy Hollowell.* Matilda's eyes widened, and she clutched the moonstone that was still hanging around her neck as she read the rest of the words. *My power will never snuff out like a flame. I am the wind that blows that flame, and I am here for my daughters and my daughters' daughters.*

Matilda sucked a breath deep into her lungs and handed the book back to Maura as if it were a baby about to cry. Erin moved to Maura's side and peered at the book.

"Whoa," she whispered. "Ivy, as in Ivy-down-the-witching-well? And she was a Hollowell? So, she really was real?" Maura nodded. Erin punched the air. "I knew it! I always knew she was real. My dad said she was invented by the town council so tourists would come for the festival. But I knew what they said happened to her was so horrible it had to be true."

Maura looked grave. "She was indeed a real woman who was murdered by the very people she helped. Her spells, her charms, her discoveries, even her doodles are all in here." Maura offered the book to Matilda again, but she backed away. Maura smiled and put the book back in its place. "Another time then, but know she is here should you need her. Now, enough. It's late and we've taken up enough of each other's time."

"I'll drop you both off," said Emily, picking up her vest and belt and heading toward the door.

Erin took another look around the room, then followed her out. Matilda went to follow them, then paused, and turned back to Maura, who was watching her.

"Thank you," said Matilda, her voice soft, "for sharing this with me."

"You're very welcome, my dear. And look." Maura pulled a chain from around her neck, a key dangling on the end of it, and glided over to Matilda. She lifted it over her head, and Matilda could smell Maura's shampoo as her hair wafted back down on her shoulders. She took Matilda's hand and lowered the key and chain into it, firmly closing Matilda's fingers around it. "This belongs to you, too, to all of us. Come here whenever you need to."

"Th-thank you," said Matilda, biting back tears that had sprung from nowhere.

"You must promise me one thing, though, above all else."

"Yes?" said Matilda, her eyes wide as Maura put her hands on her shoulders.

Maura fixed her eyes on Matilda. "Never, ever misuse this place, or I will turn you and your friend into toads, understand?"

Matilda nodded slowly as she watched Maura's crinkled eyes start to twinkle, joined by a wide smile. She patted Matilda's shoulder and winked.

"Just kidding, dear. You need to lighten up; you've got a rough road ahead of you."

They dropped Erin off first, after she filled the entire journey with questions about witches and magic. Once she was gone, they carried on in silence and finally arrived at Ferly Cottage. Emily got out of the car and opened Matilda's door. Matilda got out, her shivering limbs yearning for her bed.

"Well, I'm going in," she said, offering what she hoped was something like a smile to Emily. "Thanks again."

"You're welcome," said Emily. "And sorry about my mom; she reads people. Can get kind of intense. And infuriating when you're fifteen years old and planning to sneak out."

Matilda smiled and headed to the gate, then paused, something nipping at her soul, and turned back to Emily.

"Um, Emily?" she said. Emily looked up. "Did they ever find out who killed Ashley?"

Emily shook her head. "Investigation's still ongoing, but I have a feeling they won't find the murderer, even though I have my own suspicions."

Matilda shivered as a gust of wind sent curled leaves floating down on both of them. Officer Powell looked up at the branches, then flicked a leaf from her shoulder. Matilda swallowed as she looked back at her.

"I'll let you get to bed now, but can I give you this?" Matilda took the business card from Emily's outstretched fingers. "If you need anything, if you feel like you're in danger or you just want to talk, please call me. Okay?"

Matilda nodded, and the officer stared into her eyes one last time before she turned and left her standing alone beneath the moonlight.

CHAPTER THIRTY-FIVE

Two days until Halloween

The climb up the well had made every small movement agony, so Matilda hid in her room, wrapped up in her duvet like a human sausage roll. Her phone buzzed again, and she slid it from under her pillow, rolled her eyes, and slid it back again—another message from Erin checking that she was okay, and in Erin's words, *not down a well somewhere*. There was a tap on the window. Matilda opened an eye and sighed.

"Go away," she called, ready to send Victor over to the door to headbutt her mother until she left. She frowned and lifted her head. "I said, go away."

Lottie opened the door and stepped inside, the frown that was scored into her forehead whenever she and Matilda spoke deeper than usual and Nimbus curling around her expensive boots.

"Are you alive?" sighed her mother. Matilda scowled and rolled over. "Is all this sneaking out about the baby?"

Matilda sighed. Her trip down the well had faded their last conversation. "No."

"I know you don't want to hear this right now, but it's the new moon tonight. The receiving of the grimoire is an important step on your path as a witch, and it means a lot to your grandmother and—"

"Fine," said Matilda. At least if she had the grimoire herself, she could stop worrying about what Oliver might do to Lottie or Nanna May to get to it.

"What?" said Lottie, inching closer to Matilda.

"I said, fine," said Matilda, hauling herself up so she was sitting against her bed frame.

Lottie nodded, then looked at something she was holding, clasping it with both hands as if she was deciding what to do with it, then walked over to Matilda's bed and held out a small green bottle.

Matilda frowned. "What's that?"

"It's to get over a broken heart." Matilda blinked as she watched the contents swirl inside the bottle. "I figured that might be what's going on with you?" Matilda swallowed, unable to look Lottie in the eye. "Anyway, take it and remember to use it on the next full moon."

"I . . . thank you," whispered Matilda.

"You're welcome, little one. I know you were supposed to see your dad this weekend, too, but I'm guessing he canceled again?"

Matilda looked at Lottie, then picked up her phone and checked her calendar. With everything that had happened, she had completely forgotten about her dad's planned visit. She deleted the reminder, certain that he would cancel just as he had all the other times.

"Mom?" said Matilda as Lottie turned to leave.

"Yeah?"

"Why did he go? Was it because of me?"

"You? No, of course not, why would you . . ."

"Then was it you? And your coven? Did you make him leave?"

Lottie blinked at Matilda with wide eyes, her body still as if she'd been frozen. She sighed and sat on the edge of Matilda's bed.

"Pass me one of those cookies Nanna May brought you, would you?"

"But they're . . ."

"Please, Matilda, you've got loads there. I'll tell you what happened, but I can't if I faint from hunger."

Matilda rolled her eyes and took one of the apple-and-cinnamon cookies from the plate next to her bed and gave it to Lottie, who wolfed it down in two bites.

She wiped her hands together. "Thank you."

"So, what happened?"

Lottie turned so she was fully facing Matilda.

"Life with your dad was exciting. He was so eager to learn magic and I was happy to teach him, but we were very young when we had you, too young really, even though it's what we both wanted. It just felt like the right time for us; what could be more magical for a couple than a beautiful baby girl." Matilda rolled her eyes, and her mother shrugged.

"Anyway, your dad was a lot of fun, but he wasn't much help with the day-to-day parenting. He'd much rather be throwing you in the air than changing your diapers. I had to lean more on Nanna May and my coven for help, and he went off to practice the craft more as a way to escape the never-ending diapers and the feeding and the screaming. I guess that's when we started drifting."

Her mother nodded at the plate of cookies, and Matilda handed her another. "We stopped being in love, then we stopped being friends and started living separate lives, so I found a rhythm that worked for you with the help of my support network. Every now and then, I'd try to talk to him about it, but we'd argue about the coven and secrets I shared with them, and he took it all so personally. He just couldn't see that I needed them even more because he wasn't there. He would disappear for days, trying new spells by himself. He became obsessed with magic and couldn't maintain the balance, so he lost his job and the coven had to support us financially, too. We passed each other after he'd had a shower one day, and I noticed a handful of names scrawled down his back and one right there on his neck. I knew he was following magic into the shadows, but by then he'd lost any respect for me and wouldn't hear it."

Lottie looked out of the window, shaking her head at the memories.

"He knew I had you and the coven and Nanna May, and all he had was the magic, so he made it his sole focus. Ferly Cottage is such an easy house to live separate lives in, and we went on like that for years. He resented me sharing things with the coven that I wouldn't share with him. I played my part in that, but I invited him to join more than once and he always refused."

Matilda frowned at her mom, her heart beating fast in her chest. "You make it sound like he was never around."

"Hey, he loves you, Matilda, and he always did. Thankfully, we had a sort of unspoken agreement that you would never witness what was happening to us, so he was there for you in his own way."

Matilda swallowed a lump in her throat as she remembered the horseback-riding lessons or the tiny fireworks he could make using candles and some herbs plucked from Nanna May's garden. The memories of her life with her dad were sparked with love and color, but they were also punctuated with overheard arguments about Lottie's coven and resentment toward their secrets.

"One day I caught him looking through our grimoire," said Lottie, her mouth set in a line.

Matilda's chest tightened. "But learneds aren't supposed to touch it?"

Lottie nodded. "He knew that. Who knows how many times he'd looked at it, but he was so angry there was even more I was keeping from him. There was one particular spell that he was adamant I should share, and he wanted to give it to you."

Matilda instinctively touched her cheek. "The witch's cloak spell."

Lottie nodded. "He was *obsessed* with it, Matilda. Badgered me to show it to him again until one day he used it, and I knew he'd been through the grimoire again. He'd still bring it up every now and again, saying that he wanted you to have it."

"Why do you think he wanted me to have it?"

Lottie sighed. "Control, maybe? I think he realized that he'd pushed himself out of this family, but he was still trying to show that he should make decisions for you. His scars disappeared, so he was obviously taking full advantage of the spell and finding out how easy life was to use magic to get what you wanted, to manipulate free will, or just to cause pain. In a way, I think he wanted you to have an easy life. I told him I wanted to wait until you were seventeen, but he had to give it you. He had the final word the day that he left."

"So, he was looking out for me?"

"In a way, Tilly, that's true. But he soon learned, and you will, too, at the rate you're collecting those scars, that the more of them you get, the more painful they are to carry around, and keeping them covered gets harder and harder."

Matilda looked back at her mother and tried to ignore the

scorching pain that prickled her face from the moment she woke up to the moment she managed to fall asleep.

"You have them, too," said Matilda.

Her mother paused midbite of her cookie. "A few, and I regret and accept each one of them. It's all about balance and respect, Matilda. Isn't that what we've been trying to teach you all this time?"

"So, he just had enough of the coven being here all the time and left?" said Matilda, ignoring her mother's question.

"Partly," said Lottie, finishing her cookie and watching Matilda, trying to decide something. "But partly because of Nanna May."

"Nanna May?"

Lottie stood up from the bed, stretched, and sat on the chair. "When your grandmother stopped speaking, it was a total mystery to me and to the coven, what had happened. Your dad said it was old age, but there was a sort of . . . magical aftertaste in the weeks after it happened, so I had my suspicions. The other thing that was lingering in the air was a new perfume, and the coven sensed that your dad was spending time with another woman. I confronted him, and of course he denied it, but not before he added it to the long list of reasons why he hated my coven."

"What's that got to do with Nanna May?"

"At one of our meetings, Nanna May was invited to use the voice of the coven to tell us what had happened so we could help her. Her voice came from each of us like we were a choir, telling her story as one; she had seen your dad with a woman in town, she'd confronted him and told him if he didn't tell me then she would."

Matilda watched her mother, waiting for her to go on, but Lottie sighed, pain etched into her forehead.

"Mom?"

"He took her voice, Matilda. He cursed her so she couldn't tell me, even in writing."

"No," said Matilda, shaking her head. "He did that to Nanna May? That's why she can't talk?"

Lottie nodded. "I've spent the last three years begging him to tell me what spell he used so I can help her, but he won't." Lottie shook her head and took a deep breath. "Why do witches have scars on their face, little one?"

"To warn others to stay away from them," whispered Matilda, staring at the blanket over her legs through glistening eyes.

"That's right. That's their consequence for hurting others, but we, the Hollowells, were gifted a veil by one of our ancestors and we should use it with respect. Instead, your dad was running around upsetting the balance, still is for all I know, and now he's got you on the verge as well. He's shown nothing but disrespect for our ways, our family, and to magic itself."

"I . . . I . . . ," stuttered Matilda, the information Lottie had just shared almost making her lose her own voice.

Lottie lifted her hands and shook her head. "I didn't want this to become a lecture, Matilda, but it scares me so much when I see how frivolous you are with that spell. I'm scared where it's going to take you. Magic has rules for a reason."

Matilda knew her mother was right, and all the nagging and the lectures had come from a place of fear. When the blackouts had first started coming, Matilda thought it was the darker side of magic coming to pull her into their shadows.

"Do you think Nanna May will ever be able to speak again?"

"She has a few words now. When it first happened, she was totally silent. Do you remember?" Matilda nodded. The silence came just before her dad left, but she never thought the two things would be linked. "It's been very difficult for her, but the power rooted in the soil beneath us continues to help her heal, and she's a very powerful witch."

"That's why you made him go?" said Matilda.

"That's why I made him go."

"You never told me any of that."

"You never asked, little one." Lottie pushed herself out of the chair. "I know you've always thought I was the villain, but between raising you alone and looking after Nanna May, I've just been doing the best I can."

"You should've told me."

"You and your father were so close, and I didn't want to . . . you're probably right, but I was trying to protect you from it all, from what he'd done, what I had to do, but I guess I ended up keeping you at a distance from everything, including myself. I just . . . I didn't know how to fill the hole that your dad left, and I was trying; I'm still trying."

Matilda watched her mom get up and turn to leave her alone.

"Mom?

"Yes?" said Lottie, looking back at Matilda, tears glistening in her eyes.

Matilda nodded at Lottie's belly. "Is it a girl?"

Lottie put a hand on her stomach and nodded. Matilda opened her mouth to speak, but the silence hanging in her bedroom said enough for both of them.

CHAPTER THIRTY-SIX

The sun was on its way down, but not before it left its mark on the sky above, casting it in oranges and pinks that would let the shepherds know they could expect good weather the next day. Matilda sat on the bench outside her garden room, listening to the calls of those animals that preferred to hide in moonlight shadow, much like witches of old did.

Footsteps crunched down the path and Matilda stood up, a figure in a black cloak carrying a lantern approaching her. She brushed a leaf from the front of the long black velvet dress she was wearing, its bodice lined with black pearl buttons, the neckline and sleeves made from intricate black lace her grandmother had spent months making. She pulled the hood of her own cloak over her head and picked up the lantern from beside her, then joined her mother, Victor watching from the warmth of his cushion. Her mother looked her up and down, a small smile hidden beneath her hood.

"Ready?" she said. Matilda nodded. "Thank you for doing this, Matilda."

"I'm doing it for Nanna May; I know it means a lot to her."

Lottie nodded gently, then turned and headed into the trees, holding her lantern up as she stepped over the weeds and bushes. Matilda followed her, the last of the day's light blinking over her beneath the tree branches, avoiding stinging nettles and fallen branches. They didn't speak as they made their way deeper into the heart of the woods, and Matilda's soul seemed to hush as it recognized the familiarity of the ancient trees.

Light flickered ahead, and Matilda knew that's where they were heading. She stepped over a fallen tree with toadstools speckled over it, home to something watching her from deep inside its hollow, ready to witness the ceremony with its fellow spectators perched on branches and peeping out of burrows and nests.

Nanna May stood in the middle of the clearing, surrounded by a circle marked out with white pebbles. Four items on the edge of the circle represented the four directions of the earth and the four elements: a small crate with a chrysanthemum grow-ing out of the earth inside it, a long white feather resting on the ground, a lantern with a burning candle inside, and a small caul-dron half filled with water.

Her grandmother wore a long black skirt and a crocheted black shawl swept around her shoulders, pinned with a sparkling brooch. A wide tree stump level with her knees was just in front of her, something concealed on top of it under a piece of black cloth. Nanna May nodded an invite for Matilda and Lottie to enter the circle. As Matilda stepped over the pebbles, wings flapped from the high branches, sending fluffy white feathers raining down over her as she walked toward her grandmother.

The flames in the lanterns burned brighter, and Nanna May smiled at Matilda as she got closer, opening her arms and grab-bing hold of Matilda's hands. She looked up and down at her dress with moist, sparkling eyes, and Matilda smiled back, letting her enjoy the beauty of the outfit she'd made with her own hands for her granddaughter's birthday.

Nanna May let go of Matilda and nodded at Lottie, who

showed her where to stand, then moved to the left of Matilda, leaving a space in between them so they stood in a line in front of the tree trunk. Lottie looked at Nanna May and then at Matilda and lifted her arms, her palms facing outward. Nanna May did the same, her old fingers like the crooked twigs on a tree branch.

"Guardians of the quarters, elementals of earth, air, fire, and water, mothers of our mothers, and sisters of our sisters, we come here for the seventeenth birthday of your daughter and the passing of the Hollowell family grimoire," called Lottie.

As soon as her mother began calling out to the unseen forces, Matilda felt an energy rising from where she stood in her lace-up boots, making her dress ripple and her hair crackle with static. She had spent so long as a solitary witch that she'd forgotten just how much power they had access to when it was called on collectively. Years had passed since she'd stood with her mother and grandmother in this way, conversing with their ancestors, and she was certain that if she stuck out her tongue she would be able to taste the energy in the air.

Nanna May bent over and uncovered a thick, leather-bound book and lifted it from the tree trunk. Lottie turned to her, and Nanna May placed it in her outstretched hands, nodding to her before Lottie turned to Matilda. Matilda wasn't lying when she told her mother she was just going along with the ceremony for Nanna May, but from the moment she entered the circle with her family, the intensity of what they were doing made her hands shake. She could feel eyes on her, watching her take the next step on her journey as a witch, and the shame she felt at exploiting their ancient ways for her own gain was almost choking her.

Matilda looked into her mother's eyes, practically a mirror image of her own, struggling to remember the last time they had stood so close together. Lottie nodded, and Matilda held out her shaking hands as her mother placed the family book into her palms. The three women watched the edges of the circle respond; a petal fell from the chrysanthemum, a snowy owl swooped from the shadows and circled them three times, the candle burned so hard it cracked the glass in the lantern, and the cauldron tipped onto its side, spilling its contents into a puddle.

Matilda held the book to her chest, feeling its warmth and familiarity as though she had fallen asleep with it in her bed every night, this precious book that someone with such a dark heart was trying to snatch from her family. Her mother gestured for her to put the book back down where it had started and Matilda did so, bending down and gently placing it on the tree stump. Nanna May opened her arms, and Matilda stepped into her embrace, squeezing her tightly and resting her cheek on the old lady's hunched shoulder. Matilda smiled into the darkness they felt so comfortable in, a lost piece of a puzzle finally filling her heart.

A small sob escaped her smiling face and a tear trailed down her cheek. Nanna May stroked her hair and Lottie stepped closer to them, one hand over her mouth and the other on her chest as she watched her mother and daughter bond after a precious rite. Her eyes glistened with tears as she turned to leave, but Matilda reached out and grabbed her hand. She pulled her closer and squeezed her hand as hard as she could in the hope that Lottie would understand all the things she wanted to say but could never find the words for.

CHAPTER THIRTY-SEVEN

One day until Halloween

The atmosphere in the cafeteria was charged with the buzz of chocolate consumption and excitement for Halloween parties and hookups, but none of it touched Matilda. Her macaroni and cheese had sat so long on the tray that it had grown a rubbery skin. She stopped poking it and dropped her fork on the table. If she wasn't surrounded by people, she would have slid the tray onto the floor and slumped over the table, burying her head in her crossed arms. As it was, she kept upright, watching Oliver at the table on the other side of the hall as everyone leaned toward him and threw their heads back and laughed at whatever story he was spinning.

The girl sitting next to Oliver touched his shoulder with one hand and put her other hand on her chest as she beamed at him, then turned away to get something out of her bag. Oliver reached out and upended the contents of a tiny bottle into her drink, quicker than a card dealer at a blackjack table, then looked up at Matilda and winked.

Heat slapped Matilda's cheeks and before she realized what was happening, she was marching over to the table. Oliver sat back and folded his arms, his eyebrows high on his forehead, and one by one his groupies turned to look at their visitor, protesting as she lifted her hand and whacked the girl's drink across the table.

"Hey!" The girl jumped up and looked at her sodden jeans, then glared at Matilda. "What the hell?!"

"What's your problem, loser?" spat another girl.

Matilda's face was like a beacon for the rest of the table's insults, but she stood where she was, her eyes fixed on Oliver as a smile twitched on his lips. He pushed his chair out and put a hand on the girl's shoulder.

"Come on, let's find you some paper towels."

The girl uncurled her lip and smiled at him. "Thanks, Oliver. What's her problem, right?"

"Don't worry about it," he said, leading her away from the table. He looked over his shoulder at Matilda. "Probably just jealous."

Matilda backed away from the laughter and turned to escape the cafeteria but slammed into someone.

"Sorry . . . oh, sorry," she mumbled, blinking at Sean.

"Why'd you do that?" he asked, a harsh line between his eyebrows.

"Sorry, I turned and I didn't see you."

"Not that," he said, then grabbed her wrist. "The drink. Why did you knock her drink over?"

"What? I . . . ," she said, looking at her wrist.

"Did he put something in her drink?" asked Sean, squeezing her. "Did you see something? Was he trying to do something to her?"

"Sean, you're hurting my arm."

"Did he do something to Ashley? Did he use something to hurt her?"

Sean's eyes were bloodshot with sleepless nights, and the shadows of unanswered questions pulled his face down. His usual fade was hidden beneath a forgotten visit to the barber and his creased clothes hung off his shoulders. Guilt coursed through Matilda, but she pulled away and rubbed the throbbing spot where he'd gripped her.

She shook her head. "I don't know. I just . . ."

"Liar!" shouted Sean.

Matilda shrank back, and he blinked at her for a moment, then rubbed his eyes with a shaking hand, turned, and barged past a couple of his friends who'd come to check what was going on. Matilda retrieved her bag from the table and hurried out of the cafeteria before anyone else could shout at her. She looked over her shoulder to make sure Sean wasn't following and, for the second time, slammed into someone.

"Watch yourself, speedy. Oh, hey, Matilda," said Erin as she closed a door with a DO NOT ENTER sign on it, along with the nose-ring girl whom Matilda recognized from when Erin had slapped her. Matilda frowned and tried to get past them, but Erin held out her hand. "Glad to see you're alive and skulking."

"What?" asked Matilda.

"You didn't answer a single one of my texts," said Erin. "Has Oliver done something else to you?"

Matilda shot a sideways look at Erin's companion.

"It's cool; she knows everything," said Erin.

"What?! Why does she know everything? You don't even know everything." Matilda turned to the girl. "Who are you?"

"Uh, I'm Katrina, Erin's girlfriend."

"Well, Katrina, this is none of your business," said Matilda.

Erin put her arm around Katrina's waist. "Actually, it became her business when she got a little confused when I started ignoring her and obsessing over a guy, if that's okay with you. And, also yes, because she's a witch, too, I thought maybe she might be able to help. That's right, you don't have the monopoly on being a witch, Matilda," said Erin, her eyes wide. "Oh, and you're welcome for calling the police and rescuing you by the way, a simple—"

"Erin . . ."

"It's fine, Katrina. She thinks she's the only one affected by his behavior, but—"

"Erin," said Katrina, nodding at Matilda, who was looking at the floor, wringing her hands.

Erin sighed. "Look, I'm sorry. I didn't mean to get angry. It's just, you clearly need help, but you won't let me help you."

"I don't . . . I just . . . seeing him is . . ."

Katrina took a step closer to Matilda and ducked her head down. "You look like you need quiet. Here." She took a step to the side and nodded at the door. "You can use the music room. There's nobody in there."

Matilda frowned. "Music room?"

Erin pulled the door wide open. "Technically, it's the space under the stage where they store all the music equipment and the stuff for school plays. We use it all the time when we want some . . . privacy." Matilda rolled her eyes. Erin folded her arms. "Fine, don't go in then. Stay out here and piss off everyone you bump into."

"Erin," said Katrina, "go easy."

"Sorry." Erin shook her head and her features softened. "You obviously don't want to talk, so just let us do this for you."

Matilda looked at them both, leaning against each other, shouldered up like they could take on the world. She nodded.

"Thank you."

"You're welcome. Now don't go thinking it's an open invitation, though. Like I said, it's our *private* place."

"I think she gets it, Erin."

Katrina smiled at Matilda, then put her arm through Erin's, and they walked down the corridor, disappearing around the corner and leaving Matilda in the hallway to get jostled by passers-by. A couple of girls from the table Oliver had been sitting at walked past and looked her up and down.

"Loser," they said. They carried on glaring at her until they disappeared into the bathroom. Excitement rattled the halls, and Matilda turned to see where the whooping and shouting was coming from, just as a basketball bounced off the wall and hit her in the ear. A group of boys bounded past her, one of them offering a casual apology while his friends laughed like hyenas.

Matilda sighed, stepped through the music-room door, and slammed it behind her. She trod down the wooden steps and paused at the bottom, closing her eyes and breathing in the dusty isolation of the junk-filled room.

"And . . . quiet," she whispered to herself, opening her eyes.

The tiny rectangular windows were so caked in dust that they hardly let any light through, so Matilda reached up and flicked on the lamp that was tied to one of the low wooden beams above her. Erin and Katrina weren't wrong about the room. Anything Matilda had ever seen on the stage was crammed into the space ready for recycling for the next school play.

Stacks of dusty chairs, cracked painted scenery, giant plastic mushrooms, and disassembled drum kits lined the walls. Metal shelving stuffed with leather cases, dented musical instruments, and mix and match costumes divided the room in two. A memory of watching Ashley in the school production of *Grease* swirled up from a pink jacket hanging on a nail. Ashley couldn't sing, but she'd made up for it in confidence and had been an amazing

Sandy. Matilda shook the image away and ventured farther into the room.

A pile of beanbags was fluffed up in the corner in front of some wooden shelves, lovingly created as a little haven from the outside halls. Matilda walked over and dropped onto them, the beanbags sighing as she let them mold to her tired body. A trail of wires and bulbs curled around rusty nails sticking out of the wood, and she flicked the switch on the plastic box and multicolored fairy lights blinked awake.

She leaned back and closed her eyes, her muscles relaxing as she sank into the solitude of the room. After a minute of slow, calm breathing, Oliver flashed in her mind: him kissing her, then at the lake, then the look on his face before he pushed her down the well. Matilda pulled herself up and sighed. It still didn't feel real, the time they spent together before he revealed his true self or that the whole thing was an illusion to get her back for something she did in a fog of spite a few years ago. She closed her eyes again, wondering how long she could hide among the props and scenery.

Her eyes flew open as a clacking sound floated from the other side of the shelves. She held her breath and listened, her heart jumping up her throat as it came again.

Clack, clack, clack.

With any shred of calm now completely dissolved, Matilda scrambled up and charged across the floor, then flew up the wooden steps. She reached for the door handle with a shuddering hand, but her mouth went dry when there was nothing to grab hold of. She checked the other side of the door but there was nothing, not a handle, a doorknob, not even a hole to shout through for help.

Matilda crept down the steps and tried to ignore the dead eyes of theater masks and the crooked puppet of an old man, his head at an angle like he'd just been pulled from a noose. The sound carried on, over and over, clacking along with her heartbeat as it sped up and pumped blood through her body at double speed. She hovered at the end of the shelves and glanced at the window straight in front of her, a stack of wooden chairs the perfect ladder directly beneath it.

"Get through the window; don't look around. Get through the window; don't look around," she whispered.

Sweat glistened on her forehead as she tripped over her feet to get to the chairs, reaching out and catching herself on them as the sound seemed to echo inside her head as well as in the room. The window was just above her, but as she looked up, she sensed movement in the corner of her eye. Curiosity overwhelmed her fear, and she turned to the source of the sound.

A girl sat hunched on the floor. She looked up, her dirty-blond hair parting like a curtain on a nightmare, and grinned at Matilda as she clacked her teeth together.

Matilda fell to the ground, her eyes wide in terror as her breath felt as though it was trying to choke her. The skin on the girl's face hung off her skull like melted wax, her eye sockets hanging down to her cheekbones revealing muscles beneath her unblinking eyes. Her jawbone was completely free of skin, and Matilda could clearly see where the sound came from each time she clicked her decaying teeth together.

Clack, clack, clack.

Matilda shuddered. It wasn't the ripped plaid skirt or the scuffed metallic ballet shoes on the girl's bony feet that made her instantly recognizable; it was Matilda's name carved on her face.

Ashley, dead and decomposing, sat with one leg stretched in

front of her, the other knee lifted up as if she was just relaxing on the school field on a sunny day. One hand rested on her knee, her red manicure chipped and grubby, her other hand absent of any nail polish, as well as any skin or muscle. Matilda couldn't move, frozen by the horror in front of her until Ashley stopped making the hellish sound and tucked her matted hair behind her ear with a skeletal finger.

"Do my hair for me, Matilda," said Ashley, the words clawing out of her rickety jaws as she combed a hand through her lank hair, clumps of it pulling away.

"N-n-no . . . ," whispered Matilda, shaking her head and recoiling from the horror movie in front of her.

"Do my hair for me, Matilda. We were friends once. Do my hair."

Ashley started crawling toward her like an injured wolf clinging on to its last breath of life, determined to drag its prey down to hell. Matilda grabbed one of the chair legs and tried to pull her paralyzed body up, but her sweaty hands slipped and she slumped to the ground. Ashley crept closer and closer, until she curled her skeletal fingers around Matilda's shoe.

"No!" cried Matilda, shaking her leg. "No, please! I'm sorry!"

Ashley reached her hand up to her head and grabbed a handful of hair, pulling part of her scalp away. She clacked her jaw at Matilda again.

"Do my hair for me, Matilda," she hissed, grabbing Matilda's hand and pulling it toward her lank patches of hair. "Stay with me, Matilda."

"Please, no!" wailed Matilda, falling back and closing her eyes. "NO!"

"Jesus Christ! Jesus Christ, Matilda. Stop it! Stop screaming!"

Matilda's eyes flew open, and she blinked at Erin crouching down and staring at her.

"It's just us. Erin and Katrina."

She pulled herself up and lifted a trembling hand to point at Ashley, but she was gone. Erin held out her hand and Matilda took it, allowing her to pull her to her feet. She leaned against the stack of chairs and put her shaking hands over her eyes, willing her heartbeat to slow down.

"What the hell happened?" asked Erin.

Matilda dropped her hands and glared at Erin. "What happened? What *happened*? You sent me down here with no way to get out, that's what happened!" Matilda squared up to Erin. "Did you do this on purpose? Did you do this for *him*?"

"Do what for who? For *Oliver*? You're joking, right?"

Katrina put a hand on Erin's arm. "Erin, she's shaken up. Go easy. What happened, Matilda?"

"You're a witch," said Matilda, her eyes blazing at Katrina. "Did you do this to me?"

"Matilda, tell us what happened!" said Erin, ducking between her and Katrina.

"You locked me in here!" shouted Matilda, tears clinging to her eyelashes as she blinked at Erin and Katrina.

"What are you talking about? You get out the way you came in," said Erin, pointing at the open door, a black handle visible on both sides.

Matilda blinked at the door, then looked at Erin's and Katrina's puzzled faces as she wiped a tear from her cheek. She threw her hands in the air and shook her head.

"Do you know what? I can't do this anymore. He wants that fucking book; he can have it!"

Erin frowned. "What book?"

"It doesn't matter. Nothing matters."

"Not your grimoire? I read that . . . ," started Katrina.

"Oh, you're an expert, are you? How long have you been using magic? A month? Two?"

Katrina took a step back as if Matilda had slapped her.

"If he's trying to make you give him something, whatever it is, don't give it to him, Matilda," said Erin.

"Why not? I can't take this anymore! I'm losing my mind waiting for blackouts or dead things to come after me. I just want him to leave me alone."

Matilda pushed past them, ignoring Erin calling after her as she stormed up the steps. She squinted as her eyes adjusted to the light in the corridor and turned toward her locker, stopping in her tracks as Oliver stood just ahead of her, his arms folded as he leaned against the wall.

Matilda wiped the tears from her cheeks and walked up to him, looking at her feet.

"Everything okay?" said Oliver, his voice oozing with mock concern.

Matilda looked up at him, her lip wobbling as Ashley and the blackouts and her weakening magic all pressed down so hard on her shoulders she felt like she could just fall down at his feet.

"Please, I can't take any more," Matilda whispered. "I need it to stop; I need it all to stop."

She looked into his face, wondering how much worse he could make her life, what other corpses he would haunt her with, how much more of her magic he would tear away. Her soul felt as though it was riddled with holes, and everything Oliver had inflicted on her had battered and bruised what was left of it.

"You know how to make all this stop. Just say the words, and we don't have to go on like this anymore."

"You win," she whispered, shame and desperation tightening her chest as she said the words.

Oliver smiled and put a hand to his ear. "Sorry, didn't quite catch that."

Matilda watched a tear as it fell from her cheek and landed on the floor. She squeezed her eyes and bit against her lip, pushing the tears back so she could look him in the eye.

"I said, *you win*. You can have the book."

"Good girl. Although I'm going to miss all this fun we've been having, aren't you?"

"Screw you, Oliver," said Matilda, clenching her shaking hands. "Come to my house tomorrow, and you can have it."

"I know you love me really," said Oliver, winking at her. "It's a date; see you tomorrow."

CHAPTER THIRTY-EIGHT

Gray clouds sucked the color from the sky, and the bonfire smell that used to invoke memories of raking leaves with her dad just made Matilda feel sick. She had walked all the way home with her hands tucked under her armpits after her encounter with Ashley, and only now as she arrived at her garden gate did she remove them.

They'd finally stopped shaking.

She glanced up at the sky, her heart as gray as the clouds. How had she gotten here? Why had she fallen for Oliver? He hadn't used a love spell, but the way he'd manipulated her made her feel like her free will had been taken away, like she'd done to so many other people over the years. She had the scars as proof of her own wrongdoing, but she'd never contemplated death or the kind of destruction Oliver had been raining down on her. What would he be capable of once she gave him the grimoire?

Matilda stopped in her tracks, biting her lip as she shook the thought away. Whatever it was, it wouldn't be aimed at her anymore and she could just get on with her life. Her fear-and magic-free life.

She dragged her feet as she walked beneath the arch and followed the stepping-stones across the grass. There was movement in the kitchen window, and she picked up speed, keeping an eye on Lottie standing in the kitchen looking down at her bump. Matilda didn't feel like explaining why she wasn't at school, and she couldn't look her mother in the eyes knowing what she was about to do to the family. That the baby wouldn't know the joy of blowing on a dandelion and watching in wonder as her mother manipulated the breeze to return its downy seeds to one piece again, or peering at falling sycamore leaves to predict the weather before setting off to the beach.

The baby wouldn't know those things, but she wouldn't know the pain, either.

Matilda put her hands in her pockets and trudged up the gravel path. A crow cawed and Matilda looked up from her feet, a sharp breath stabbing her lungs. The black bramble hedge that had been growing at the front of her garden room had tripled in size and sprouted branches that reached up in knots toward the roof. The building looked like one of those pirate ships in the deathly arms of a giant kraken, but that wasn't what froze Matilda in her path.

Nanna May sat on the bench in front of the garden room, hunched over with a hundred extra years pressing down on her quivering shoulders. Matilda dropped her bag and ran to her, crouching at her feet as she looked into the old lady's face, tears getting lost in the tracks of her wrinkled skin.

"Nanna May?" whispered Matilda. "Nanna, what is it? What's wrong?"

Her grandmother's bloodshot eyes met Matilda's, then looked back down at her lap. Matilda followed her gaze and peered at the shape cupped in her hands, frowning until she realized what it was and then put her hand over her mouth, her own eyes springing with sadness as she understood her grandmother's grief.

The tiny feathered body of Genie, Nanna May's beloved familiar, rested in the soil-stained hands of her owner, its once bright red breast dull as though someone had turned its light off.

Matilda reached out and ran her index finger along its smooth brown feathers, a small sob escaping her mouth at the coldness of its lifeless body. Its entire head was encased in yellow wax, hardened drips of it caked around its neck.

"Wicked Tilly," whispered Nanna May, lifting the bird closer to Matilda's face.

Matilda closed her eyes, blinking warm tears down her cheeks, then looked at her grandmother.

"I'm sorry, Nanna. I'm so sorry," she said, putting her hand on her grandmother's soft cheek.

She stood and took Genie from her grandmother's hands, then pulled the scarf from around her neck, ignoring the chill that breathed against her skin.

"She can stay out here, with me. Okay?"

Her grandmother nodded and watched Matilda wrap the bird in her scarf, then give it back to her before she picked up a spade and started digging at the other end of the bench. She took a deep breath and looked up at her grandmother as she worked.

"He's not getting away with this," she said, pausing to wipe away her tears. "I promise you."

***

After burying Genie, Matilda walked Nanna May to the warmth of the kitchen, where she sat her down at the table and made a pot of tea. Her mother walked in just as Matilda was scooping the ground valerian powder into the tea ball infuser, and Matilda explained, without disclosing full details, that Genie had passed. She left her with Lottie and hurried back into the cold and into the crooked open arms of the woods.

She ran as far as she could, her mind racing with the events of the last few hours, days, and weeks. She couldn't give Oliver their grimoire, not after finding Nanna May mourning her precious Genie. Oliver may have taken Matilda's magic and terrorized her every waking moment, but how scared Matilda felt was nothing compared to the sorrow in her grandmother's wrinkly face. Matilda wouldn't let Oliver take anything else from her family.

She needed a plan to stop him, but there was something she needed to do first. She slowed down and stopped at the bottom of a thick tree truck, its branches reaching out to the rest of the trees in solidarity. She stuck her hands in the wet soil and started to dig.

Once the hole was deep enough, she lifted Ivy's moonstone from around her neck and gently placed it into the hole, then pulled the athame from her pocket and placed that inside, too. She covered the hole up, then put her hands over the mound of earth on top.

"I'm sorry for what they did to you, Ivy," she whispered as she closed her eyes. "You can rest now."

She stood and headed down a trail to her garden room, the blackbirds squawking their indignance at being disturbed. She mentally ticked off what she would need to do when she got back and what she'd say to Erin, when something that didn't belong in the woods caught her eye.

Deeper between the trees she could see something swaying, something that could be mistaken for broken tree limbs or vines dangling from the branches. Slowly, she crept toward the movement, hairs prickling on her arms as she got closer and saw what it was.

A dozen witch's ladders hung from a tree, moving gently in

the wind, waiting to be discovered. She caught one in the palm of her hand and looked at the black feathers tied into the twine, then let it swing away as something else on the tree trunk caught her eye.

A small poppet, the one she found in Oliver's car but now with strands of dark hair wrapped around its head, was tied to the tree with a long length of rope. Matilda looked at the witch's ladders hanging from the trees again. Oliver had made them all long enough to reach the poppet, caressing it with their dark feathers every time the wind blew.

Matilda yanked the rope away and snatched the poppet from the tree. She hadn't needed anything more than seeing Nanna May hunched over her precious Genie to stop Oliver, but now he'd given her enough to want to crush him.

CHAPTER THIRTY-NINE

Matilda hurried down the alleyway and rushed into the court-yard. The sound of bubbling water trickled past her ears, and she slowed herself, willing the adrenaline and anger to flow past her and change into something bigger, more powerful, just like the water.

She lifted the key on the chain around her neck and unlocked the door. She turned the handle and pushed it open, calling into the dark shop as she stepped inside.

"Hello? Maura? It's me, Matilda." She waited a few beats, then tried again. "Emily? Is anyone here?"

Matilda crept through the door and pulled out her phone, certain that Maura was going to appear suddenly and throw her out, taking back her invitation to come anytime she wanted. She turned her phone light on and headed to the door at the back of the shop, letting the smell of the books caress her soul and level her mind.

She pushed the door open, relieved to find that the lamps were turned on, as if the room was ready and expecting her. As she stepped inside, she could feel the power of the books, whispering to her and inviting her into their open arms, but this time it didn't overwhelm her; it sparked certainty and courage within.

The book she wanted was almost beckoning her, set slightly

farther forward than the rest of its shelf mates. Matilda took off her coat and put her bag down by the table, then walked across the creaking floorboards to the shelf where Ivy's book of spells was waiting. Waiting, she was sure, for her. She pulled it from the shelf and looked at it again, just as she did when Maura had first handed it to her. The power she felt from it was undeniable then, and now she was sure it had tripled. The chain pierced through the bottom of the cover curved down and back up to the shelf, and Matilda frowned as she looked at the table and the length of the chain, wondering whether it was long enough to reach.

"I don't want to stand here all night," she muttered.

"Don't, then," said a voice from the doorway.

Matilda jumped so suddenly she almost dropped the book. She gathered herself and gently put it back on the shelf.

"You scared the life out of me!" she snapped at Erin, who raised an eyebrow and folded her arms. "I mean: Thank you for coming."

"That's better," said Erin, walking into the room and closing the door behind her. "Although there was no way on earth I *wasn't* going to come and meet you in the middle of the night at the secret room with all the spell books."

Erin took her coat off and put it over one of the old chairs, then joined Matilda in front of the shelves. She peered at the book that Matilda had just returned, then looked back at her.

"Is that the one you want to look at?" asked Erin.

Matilda nodded, looking at the book then back at the table. "Yeah, but I'm not sure whether . . . how . . ."

"My guess is all these chains are long enough to reach to the table. Look," said Erin, reaching toward the book, then freezing, her hand in midair. She looked at Matilda. "Is it okay that I touch them, do you think?"

Matilda shrugged. "It's just grimoires you shouldn't touch. I'm not sure about these. I can't tell what they are from their covers."

"Maybe only you should touch them, just for now," said Erin, biting her lip and sticking her hands under her armpits like she was standing in an expensive china shop.

Matilda nodded and pulled Ivy's book from the shelf. She walked slowly, the thin chain jangling with each step, until she reached the table. The chain was still slack enough to give her plenty of movement, then she looked at the tabletop and the book in her hands.

"Can you get my bag? It's on the floor," she said, gesturing with her chin. Erin looked around, then picked up Matilda's bag and put it on the table. "You can open it. There's a velvet bag inside, can you get it out for me?"

Erin nodded and unzipped Matilda's backpack, then pulled out the drawstring bag. She looked at Matilda, who nodded at her, then put her hand inside and pulled out a folded blanket.

"I want to put Ivy's book on top of that on the table. Can you unfold it and spread it out?"

Erin nodded and Matilda's lip twitched as she thought this must be the longest Erin had ever gone without asking a question. Her eyebrows pulled together in concentration as she unfolded the blanket, careful to smooth out its folds and wrinkles until it covered the entire tabletop. It was a blanket Nanna May had knitted for Matilda's thirteenth birthday, made of fifty-two individual squares, one for each of the seasons that had passed since Matilda was born. It was her most precious possession, love and wisdom intertwined with every stitch. It was around her shoulders in the winter and tucked under her chin whenever she was sick in bed, the smell of her grandmother giving warmth and strength whenever she needed it.

Erin finished straightening it out and took a step back, looking to Matilda for confirmation that she'd done a good job. Matilda nodded and Erin sighed, her shoulders relaxing.

"I remember this blanket," she said, smiling as she looked down at the rainbow of colors and patterns.

"Do you?" said Matilda, still holding on to the book.

"Of course I do. We used to sit on the floor with it over our knees while we played cards." Erin looked up at Matilda, her eyes sad. "You don't remember that?"

Matilda's eyes misted as a memory she had hidden in a bottom drawer materialized as easily as if she were looking at a photograph. She nodded.

"Yes, I remember," she said, then swallowed. "Now, can you put . . . do you want to put your scarf on top of the blanket?"

Erin looked like a deer in headlights as her hands flew up to the plaid scarf hanging over her shoulders.

"This? Yeah, I mean if you need it I guess that's—"

Matilda took a deep breath. "Erin, I am really bad at this, but this is my way of asking you to help me. Will you help me?"

Erin bit her lip, then pulled her scarf off and approached the table. She swallowed, her eyes wide with sincerity.

"Of course I'll help you."

Matilda felt some of the muscles in her body loosen as Erin gently spread the scarf across the table on top of the blanket. She fussed with the corners and once she was happy it was straight, she stepped away and watched Matilda place Ivy's book on top of the sacred space they had created together. Matilda sat down in the chair and nodded at Erin to do the same.

"So, I take it you changed your mind about giving that psychopath your grimoire?" asked Erin, pulling out the chair next to Matilda so they shared a corner of the table. Matilda nodded as she angled the book so they could both see it. "Good! Katrina told me what would happen to you and your family if you did. We're here because of him, though, aren't we? Did he do something else?"

Matilda opened the book, her soul swirling in wonder as she looked at the black curled letters that had flowed from the fingers of her ancestor, a witch so notorious that there was an entire festival celebrating her terrible fate.

"I have to stop him, Erin. I have to. I thought I could give it all up, my magic, when he was just coming after me and I couldn't take any more, but now? He's gone too far, and I have to stop him before he hurts anyone close to me."

The image of Nanna May holding Genie in her hands was so clear in her mind that Matilda knew she would carry it with her for the rest of her life. She blinked at Erin, not afraid to let a tear for Genie spill down her cheek.

Erin's own eyes sparkled with tears, and she nodded vigorously.

"Okay," she said, tucking her hair behind her ear, then pulling her chair in closer to the table. She looked down at the open book, then up at Matilda, her mouth set in a serious line. "What do we need to do?"

"I don't know," admitted Matilda, relieved that Erin had agreed to help her but anxious that she didn't know where to start.

"Oh," said Erin, then, sensing Matilda's disappointment, she nodded in encouragement. "But we can find something, right?"

"We have to," said Matilda. She looked at Ivy's book, then turned to the rows of books that must have contained thousands of spells and secrets from hundreds of years back, maybe even before Ivy's time. "My magic is so shaky, and I don't know how to stop Oliver, but I think we can find help in this room, in these books. Witches look after their own, and I just feel like they want to share with me, especially Ivy. I felt it the moment I held her book in my hands; it was like she was trying to tell me something."

"Well, of course," said Erin, leaning over and reading Ivy's words, still too afraid to touch the book herself. "I mean, Ivy's got to be like some kind of Merlin-type figure in the witch community, right? I bet she can help us."

Matilda looked at Erin's face, her freckles and green eyes so familiar to her that sitting at the table together felt like the most natural thing in the world, only she couldn't remember the last time they'd done it. Erin looked up from the book and frowned at Matilda.

"What's up?" she asked.

"I just . . . ," said Matilda. "I don't deserve anything from you, let alone getting you caught up in all this, not after how I treated you. I just wanted to thank you."

"It's okay, Matilda," said Erin, smiling gently and letting her eyes roam around her old friend's face. "Can I . . ."

"Can you what?"

"Can I ask . . . what did I do?"

Matilda didn't think it was possible for her heart to break any more than it had, but she felt a little tinkle as a long-hidden part of it shattered with pain. She wasn't surprised that Erin had asked the question, but that didn't dissipate the shame Matilda felt as she sat in a room filled with books written by women who held honesty and loyalty so close to their hearts. She took a deep breath, then turned in her chair so she was facing Erin, and Erin did the same.

"So, I'm not using this as an excuse, although I guess I am because otherwise I wouldn't have said that, but it was literally the week after my dad left. I was all over the place, in shock, I think, that he'd suddenly just gone and left us, left me, but I was going through the motions, getting up, doing school, coming home, doing my spells."

"I remember," said Erin, the moment clearly fresh in her calendar of memories. "Not the spells part, obviously, but I remember when it happened."

"The day he left I went up to my bedroom and found an envelope with my name on it on my bed. I tore it open, sure he'd written me a letter about where he was going and when he was coming back to get me . . . but it wasn't."

"What was it?" asked Erin, her voice soft.

"It was a piece of paper, folded up, not even neatly. I opened it up and didn't recognize the handwriting across the page; it wasn't his."

"Whose was it?"

Matilda looked down at the book in front of them. "Well, now I think it was Ivy's writing."

"What do you mean?"

"I don't know how much Katrina told you, but the family grimoire gets passed down through generations so our craft can continue and our knowledge is shared. Each daughter receives the grimoire when she turns seventeen, so I'd never even seen ours."

Erin nodded. "She's read up on grimoires and what they mean

to witches like you, that nobody else is supposed to touch them."
She looked around the room. "Are these all grimoires?"

"Some of them, I guess," said Matilda. "We keep our own diaries or spell books, but the family grimoire is where our power is held."

"Which is why Oliver wants it."

"Exactly. Katrina is right about nobody touching a family grimoire. Only lineage witches should handle them, for a learned or a nonwitch to touch one is disrespectful. What my dad did, I should have known then . . . he found my family's grimoire and took a photo of one of the spells and left it for me."

"Why would he do that?"

"At the time, I thought it was because he thought I deserved it, but now I think it was because he knew how much it would piss off my mom and Nanna May."

"That's pretty messed up of your dad, Matilda," said Erin. "So, what was the spell?"

Matilda took a deep breath. "You probably know from Katrina that when a witch uses magic to hurt someone else they get a scar of that person's name on their body?"

Erin nodded. "Katrina has a small one running down her spine."

"Well, the spell my dad had left for me was a way to cover those scars, meaning whoever has the spell can basically—"

"Do whatever they want to anyone with absolutely zero consequences, and the more bad they do the more they become a numb, coldhearted bitch?" said Erin, giving Matilda a knowing look. "I take it you've used the spell?"

Matilda nodded, feeling ultraexposed to Erin but knowing she had to share this with her. "All the time."

"Okay . . . ," said Erin, straightening up in her chair a little.

"I knew what the spell was since I'd heard my mom talking about it with my dad before and the name of it was at the top of the page. *A Spell for a Witch's Cloak.* My head was really messed up and without thinking, I got everything I needed to try it out. You know Eric Walsh, how much of a dick he was?"

"Still is," said Erin, curling her lip like she'd smelled something nasty.

"At the time, he was taking my lunch money every single morning, and—"

"You didn't tell me that!"

"Sorry, kind of had a lot of stuff going on, I guess," said Matilda, Erin's fiery loyalty warming her. "Anyway, he was the perfect test for the spell, so I wanted to get him where it really hurt."

"His soccer skills?" Erin rolled her eyes. "The boy thinks he's David Beckham."

"Once I'd done the spell to hurt him and got the scar, then I could see whether the spell my dad left me actually worked."

"Had you never done a spell to hurt anyone before that, then?"

"No," said Matilda, shaking her head, "I was always way too scared. Anyway, in PE the next day the boys were playing soccer on the field while the girls were playing hockey. I'd planned it all out the night before and had a small branch from a rowan tree that I'd snuck out and left on the sideline with my water bottle."

Matilda paused. She could feel the energy between her and Erin changing, pushing them apart. She stared at the scratches on the table and carried on.

"I watched Eric score his third or fourth goal and run back down the field, his hand held out to all his friends like he was some pro athlete, and I'd had enough of his stupid, smug face. I dropped my hockey stick, ran to the side to where my bottle was, and crouched down facing Eric." Matilda blinked back the tears that were welling up from the memory of what she'd done. "I whispered the incantation and snapped the branch in half."

She looked up and Erin was staring back at her, her eyes wide and brimming with tears.

"I heard the scream the moment the branch was in two pieces, but it came from behind me and Eric was still running around. I turned around, and everyone was running toward someone who'd collapsed on the ground." Matilda shook her head, her voice full of shame. "I'm so sorry, Erin."

"You did that to me?" whispered Erin. "You broke my leg? I mean, it wasn't just broken, it was clean in half . . ."

"I know, and the moment I saw you on the ground I knew it had gone wrong and later I realized it was because of the rowan tree branch. It represents friendship and . . . and I was wearing your hoodie when I got the spell ready, so it was all misdirected, and *Erin* sounds like *Eric*, and with my head all over the place it just all . . ."

"You didn't even come and see if I was okay," said Erin.

Matilda shook her head. "I know. I got up to run over when I saw what happened, but then the scar started searing into my skin. There was blood everywhere and I was so ashamed and I . . . I just ran away."

Matilda's words sank like quicksand into the silence between them. Erin looked down at the table and suddenly felt much further away from Matilda than she ever had before. Matilda looked at her hands, letting them tremble for the terrible thing she'd done to her friend before she abandoned her.

"I couldn't play hockey for a year, Matilda. I missed the county tournament, and it was because of you?" said Erin, shaking her head. "I was in the hospital for weeks . . . You never came to see me and I was so confused, and that's why? Because you were the one who did it to me?"

"I'm so sorry, Erin. I just couldn't be around you after what I did, and I couldn't tell you what I was. I was so confused, and so hurt . . . I'm sorry. Please, I understand if you don't want to help me after this. I don't deserve your help."

Matilda bit her lip and squeezed her eyes shut against the sobs that were rising up in her throat, but she didn't deserve to be the one in pain and she bit them back. In the years since she'd cut Erin out of her life, she'd walked the hallways alone or charmed someone into being her friend, but there was never any substitute for a real friend, for someone like Erin. Matilda braced herself, waiting for the chair to screech across the floorboards as Erin left the monster she was sitting at the table with, but instead she felt Erin's soft hand on top of her own.

Matilda looked up and Erin leaned closer.

"We all make mistakes, Matilda."

"W-w-what?"

"Am I thrilled that my best friend literally broke my shin into two pieces? No, not exactly," said Erin, her eyebrows set in a line above her sad eyes. "And then said best friend abandoned me when I was writhing in agony and ignored me when I got back to school? Not great, either. Not great, in the slightest. But . . . we all make mistakes and I know you would never have hurt me intentionally and, honestly, I'm just relieved to know what the hell happened."

"Really?" The word came out as a sob, along with a snot bubble that Matilda wiped with the back of her hand.

"Gross," said Erin, pulling out a pack of tissues and sliding them to Matilda. "But, yes, really. And hey, bright side? I had no school for weeks, and it didn't affect my hockey game in the long term. Did it?"

Erin raised her eyebrows, and Matilda remembered Erin slamming the ball through the classroom window when she was under Oliver's love spell.

"Thank you," said Matilda.

"It was a long time ago. Okay?" Erin watched Matilda until she nodded. "So, did it work?"

"Did what work?" said Matilda, wiping her nose.

"The spell. To hide the scar."

"Oh, yes," said Matilda, looking into Erin's eyes, feeling some of the weight lift from her shoulders. "But not that time."

"What do you mean?"

Matilda shuffled forward and tilted her head as she pulled her hair back so Erin could see her neck. Erin's eyebrows pinched together until Matilda took Erin's hand and ran her finger along the skin where her hair met her neck. Erin leaned in and trailed her finger across the four letters Matilda kept hidden from sight, her face crumbling as she realized what they spelled.

Erin.

"It's the only name I ever kept," said Matilda, still holding Erin's hand. "I wanted to remember what I did to you."

Matilda watched tears spill down Erin's cheeks as they both reached over the table and collapsed into an embrace, squeezing each other for all memories and love that they'd shared and all the laughter and sleepovers they'd missed. Matilda buried her face into the familiar tickle of Erin's long curls and knew that even after years apart from her best friend, this was exactly where she belonged.

CHAPTER FORTY

Halloween

As the clock ticked them further into the early hours, Erin had grown more confident and decided that they had more chance of finding something helpful if she actually touched some of the books, too. She flicked through the diary of a witch from seventy years ago, while Matilda still pored over Ivy's book.

It was a fascinating read: part spell book and part diary, detailing little tricks and magic shortcuts along with sketches of plants and arrangements of objects for casting spells. Each spell had a name, but Matilda hadn't found much that might help them.

"There has to be something," she whispered to herself.

"We'll find something; don't worry."

But Matilda *was* worried. While she was looking through books, Oliver was off doing goodness knew what. Her stomach turned over at the thought of her mom and grandmother and Victor back at Ferly Cottage, not knowing what sort of predator was on the loose. The crystals she'd buried around the property should help keep them safe, as long as her magic could cope with a basic protection spell, although she still couldn't forgive herself for not figuring Genie wouldn't stay within the confines of the crystal's protection.

Matilda stood suddenly, her chair scraping against the floor.

"Whoa!" said Erin, her hand on her chest. "Please don't do that to a person while they're reading about the history of witchcraft, Matilda. What're you doing?"

"I'm not finding anything," said Matilda, rubbing her forehead. "There's nothing here, and I should be with my family. What if Oliver does something to them while I'm not there?"

Erin leaned over the table so she could peer at the notebook next to Ivy's book. She frowned and looked at Matilda, pointing at the words scribbled down in pencil.

"But you've written loads of stuff down?" she said. "You must have found something?"

Matilda shook her head. "No, I mean yes, I've just been writing stuff down that seems . . ."

"Important?" Matilda nodded. "Show me, then. What have we got?"

"Nothing, it's just random crap."

"Random crap you felt needed writing down." Erin pulled the notebook in front of her and cleared her throat. "*Use the weapons of our enemies against them.* Well, that sounds promising. How do we do that? Use the weapons, I mean. Like, what weapons?"

Matilda shrugged.

"Okay, that's fine. We can find out what these mystery weapons are, somehow," said Erin as though she were reading out someone's homework. "What else do we have? *A spell for a statue of stone.* That sounds good, like turning him to stone? He can't do magic if he can't move, right? Let's do that; you've got all the ingredients listed here."

"We can't. It takes a year to brew the potion, and you need a coven for that spell," sighed Matilda, flopping back into her chair.

"Right, we don't have a year or, I'm guessing, a coven, so that's a no go . . . okay, so the other things you have here are the words *why*, over and over, *bracelet*, *hair*, and *poppet*." Erin looked at Matilda, her eyebrows getting higher and higher as Matilda folded her arms and glowered back at her. "I'm so confused. What the hell is a poppet? And why, why, why what?"

"Oh, I don't know," Matilda sighed. "Why is this happening? Why did he do this to me? Why didn't I see what he was up to?"

"No," said Erin, making Matilda jump as she smacked the top of the table. "We are *not* doing this. You are not blaming yourself for what that psychopath has been doing to you."

"But there have been signs! So many signs that something was coming, that he was coming for *me*. Not just my grandmother but the rabbits?" Matilda flicked through the book, then pointed at a page. "*A rabbit's young are born with their eyes wide open, making these creatures recipients of the gift of second sight. To see a rabbit in a dream is a sure warning that something wicked is on its way to your door.* See? And those lizards that were crawling all over me in the lake?"

"I'm sorry, what?" said Erin, looking confused. "Rabbits? Lizards?"

Matilda turned the pages of the book again, her hand shaking as she followed Ivy's words with her finger. "*A lizard is a master of trickery and camouflage, deceiving those who look upon them. A lizard coming to you in your dreams is a caution that someone close to you is your enemy.*" She looked up at Erin and shook her head. "And I saw loads of them, *loads*, so you'd think I'd have gotten the message, but apparently not. Then his face in the smoke?"

Erin held her hands out like she was taming a wild horse.

"Matilda, take a breath . . ."

"But I should have known! Everything he did was to get me to let my guard down so he could siphon my magic. The stone on the bracelet he gave me? Labradorite to help feelings of anxiety and induce calm. And my hair? He was always brushing back my hair, which I thought was the sweetest thing ever, but he was actually collecting bits of it to use on the poppet he'd made of me, which I found tied to a tree in the woods along with some witch's ladders that I showed him how to make! Even the bridge swinging was to get me to let go. I've been so stupid! Why would anyone actually like me unless it was because I've made them using magic or they're pretending to so they can ruin my life?"

"Wow," said Erin, taking a deep breath. "There was a lot of that that I did not understand, which I will get back to you about, but for now you need to step back and give yourself a break, Matilda. Oliver has manipulated the hell out of you, not just with magic, and he wears one hell of a good nice-guy mask. Don't waste your energy directing blame at the wrong person." Erin leaned across and squeezed Matilda's shoulder. "Don't you dare do that to yourself."

"I just feel so . . . weak." Matilda looked at Erin and shook her head. "I've spent the last few years doing whatever I wanted to people, taking whatever I wanted from them, their friendship, their knowledge, their hard work. Now I know what it's like. I deserve this."

"No, Matilda. Okay, true, you *are* kind of mean, but, no, you don't deserve it."

Matilda smiled weakly at Erin, grateful for her honesty. "I've been taking my magic for granted, and now that he's stolen part of it from me I can't focus properly. I'm scared I can't stop him, Erin."

"We'll find a way," said Erin, her face serious. "We'll stop him."

Matilda nodded and took a deep breath just as footsteps started tapping down the spiral staircase.

"Sorry to interrupt." Matilda and Erin looked up as Maura glided down the spiral staircase, holding a round tray in her hands. "I thought I heard your voices. Thought you could do with some refreshment."

Maura stepped off the bottom step and walked around the table, placing the tray far away from the books. There were two tall mugs with plastic covers over the top of them and a plate of chocolate-covered cookies.

"Now, I'm very happy to have you girls here, but if you spill anything on these books or I find any crumbs inside the pages, I'm afraid I'll have no choice but to, as Emily would say, lose my shit with you." Matilda and Erin glanced at each other, both of them trying to suppress a smile. "Nevertheless, our craft requires sustenance, and here it is in the form of pumpkin spice lattes, with a little sprinkle of rosemary for focus and concentration, and dark chocolate cookies, with a bit of ginger for your taste buds." Matilda's stomach growled, and Maura smiled at her. "You're welcome, my dear."

Erin was the first to stand and go to the snack tray, making a big show of slowly lifting the mug to her mouth and blowing into the hole in the top before she took a sip, her eyes widening as she carefully put it back down.

"That's officially in my top five of the most amazing things I've ever tasted," she said.

"Well, keep a space for those cookies," said Maura, turning back to the stairs. "How's it going?"

Matilda opened her mouth to answer, but Erin jumped in first.

"My eyes are aching from all the tiny writing. Why'd they have to write so small in olden times? Or is it a witch thing?"

Maura smiled, lifted the tray back up, rested it on one of the chairs, then gestured for the girls to pick up their books and the blanket. She gripped the underside of the table and Erin and Matilda shoved backward as she suddenly lifted the tabletop like a lid on a hinged box. There were dozens of tiny compartments snug in the hollow of the table, each with a piece of colored fabric nestled inside and a different item sitting on top. Maura picked up a gold magnifying glass, its handle made of shiny mother-of-pearl, then handed it to Erin.

"Maybe this will help your young eyes."

Maura lifted her hand to close up the table again and Matilda looked, her eyes taking a quick inventory of the objects that were hidden inside. There were brown knives and small ceramic pots, two poppets tied in an embrace, a lace handkerchief, a brass-handled mirror, crystals, and cracked green bottles with cork stoppers. Maura pressed the lid down firmly, then put the tray back on top, smiling at them both as if secret table compartments were the most normal thing in the world.

"Maura," said Matilda, helping Erin replace the blanket and scarf, then gently putting the books on top of them, "what was all that stuff?"

"You've seen objects like that before, in your own home I expect?" said Maura. Matilda nodded. "That is all they are, items belonging to witches, probably some of them who wrote the words in these books."

"Why do you have them?" said Matilda, reaching across the table and taking the magnifying glass from Erin.

"Hey!" said Erin. "Get your own magic magnifying glass."

Maura watched Matilda turn the magnifying glass over in her hands. "These are the tools of witches that once were, Matilda. They were each infused with the soul of the witch who owned them, helping them along their path. I found some of them on my search for these books; others have found me. Some items I was able to reunite with the witch's family, but some remain lost. I keep them here, safe in the company of the books. Maybe that's where they belong, if nowhere else."

Matilda remembered finding Ivy's athame, the connection she felt as she held it in her hand at the bottom of the well. It was almost as if it had wanted to be found so Matilda could use it. Ivy seemed to keep speaking to Matilda, but she just couldn't quite make out her words. She leaned back in her chair and stretched her tired shoulders back, looking around at the hundreds of books that surrounded them.

"Not going well?" said Maura.

Matilda looked at the woman, her open face and long skirt reminding her of her grandmother when her body wasn't too frail to chase Matilda around the herb garden and she still had her voice. Matilda shook her head.

"This is an amazing collection, but I don't really know where to start because I don't really know what I'm looking for."

"Well, are there any books in here that speak to you, Matilda?"

"Yes, Ivy's does."

"Of course," said Maura, smiling. "She speaks to all of us."

Matilda frowned at the open book, then looked at Maura.

"Maura, do you know anything about stealing magic from another witch?"

"Siphoning magic?" confirmed Maura. Matilda nodded and she went on. "To take a witch's power for yourself is an extremely dark deed. Someone siphoning is positively wrapped up in the most negative kind of magic there is. It's unforgivable."

"Siphoning!" exclaimed Erin. "That was one of the words I didn't understand."

"What about the person they've taken the magic from, can they get it back?" said Matilda, ignoring Erin.

"Impossible," said Maura, then, after Matilda's shoulders sagged, she added, "almost."

"So, a witch who's had her magic siphoned *can* get it back?"

"Not quite, my dear, but perhaps a witch could borrow some magic from someone else."

"But isn't that the same as siphoning?"

"Not if the other party is willing and you ask nicely. It really is just borrowing, though; the witch will want it back."

Matilda folded her arms, trying to make sense of Maura's words. Magic was the only way she could stop Oliver, and if her own magic had weakened, perhaps borrowing it from another witch was the only way.

"But I don't know any other witches," she said, more to herself than the others, thinking she couldn't possibly go to her mother or explain this to Nanna May.

"What about Katrina?" said Erin.

Matilda straightened up and nodded, looking at Maura.

"Lineage?" Maura asked. Matilda shook her head. "Then no. I have no issue with the learned, but their magic doesn't flow through them in a constant the way it does for lineage witches. Ours is there all the time. A learned has to make their own."

"Doesn't seem very fair; they can take from you, but you can't take from them." Erin looked at Matilda. "There must be someone else?"

Matilda shook her head and looked at Maura.

"Oh, there is, Matilda. You just need to ask them. Or invite them."

"You mean, you?" asked Matilda hopefully.

Maura put her hand on her chest and laughed. "Oh, my dear, I need all my magic, I'm afraid."

"I don't understand, then," said Matilda, starting to feel like she'd actually get more sense out of Nanna May.

"You will, my dear, and I will say one more thing, for some secrets are made to be discovered and not passed on by others: Should you find another who is willing to loan you their magic, you must be absolutely honest with them."

"Honest with them?"

"They like to see who they're sharing with. You must show them your true face."

"My true face?" said Matilda, glancing at Erin's own completely confused face before she looked back at Maura. "I still don't understand."

"You must let the mask drop, Matilda," said Maura, smiling gently at Matilda as her eyes ran across her face. "Enough from me; this is your journey. I will leave you to it."

"Um, thank you, Maura," said Matilda.

"You're welcome; mind what I said about the crumbs, though," said Maura, winking at Matilda before she ascended the staircase and left them alone with their research.

Erin waited a few seconds after the swishes of Maura's long skirt had disappeared into the shadows before she turned to Matilda, her face a picture of utter confusion.

"Did you get any of that?" asked Erin.

Matilda let Maura's words swirl around her head, not quite

settling into any kind of logical order but also feeling somehow familiar.

"I'm not sure. I think, maybe?"

"So, what does she mean?"

"I think we need to keep looking."

"Well, I definitely require cookies, then," said Erin, picking one up from the plate and taking a massive bite, her eyes rolling back in ecstasy. "Number one. This cookie is number one in my top five. I should have four more to give them all a place, too. It's the least they deserve."

Matilda smelled her latte, the aroma of Halloween and autumn twirling its fingers around the smell of rosemary, an herb she had used as a young witch to improve her memory for math tests, a purer use of magic before she started gathering hidden scars to get what she wanted. She shook her head at the thought, knowing that her lack of respect for the rules of her craft and selfish use of her family's gift was exactly what got her into the situation she was in.

She took a sip of the latte, closing her eyes and letting its warmth travel down into her soul.

"Good, huh?"

"*So* good. But come on. We need to keep looking," said Matilda, shoving a whole cookie into her mouth as she went back to her seat.

"It would help if we knew what we were looking for," said Erin, a sigh escaping as she looked around the room.

"I'll know when we find it. Just keep looking."

"Is that what he was doing to you, then? Stealing your magic?"

Matilda nodded. "Among other things."

"Asshole," muttered Erin. She closed the book she'd been looking at. "Well, I don't think there's anything in this one. It's just some old woman going on about her pet ferret. I mean, it's all she ever writes about. There's drawings of it, too."

"It was probably her familiar," said Matilda, turning the page of Ivy's book, wondering what Ivy's familiar was.

"Familiar? I thought they had to be cats? Katrina got a cat. Called it Fairuza."

"Your learned witch girlfriend thought she needed a familiar? That's cute," said Matilda, rolling her eyes.

"Hey, watch it."

"Sorry," said Matilda, "just a little oversensitive about the amateurs, I guess."

Erin stood up and returned the book to its place, then walked along the shelves until she found another. Matilda tried to ignore the sound of the chain jingling as her eyes ran over Ivy's words, tripping over the curls and curves of handwriting from a different time. A few beats of silence past before Erin's chair scraped back again and Matilda looked up, her lips pursed.

"What now?"

"It's the smell of the lattes. I need another slurp." She went around to the tray and took another drink, then hurried back to her chair. "Seriously, *so* good and Maura was right; I really feel like it's helping me focus."

"Right," said Matilda, raising her eyebrows and looking back down at the book.

"What's this?" asked Erin, sliding the book around so Matilda could see a sketched figure on the page.

Matilda sighed and looked at the drawing, obviously a woman from the dresses and curves, with crosses drawn over her hands and a zigzag across where her mouth would be. She looked at Erin, then back at her own book, rubbing her temple as she tried to concentrate.

"It's what they used to do to witches around here." Matilda could feel Erin watching her, about to pounce with more questions. "They would break each one of their fingers so they couldn't prepare a spell, sew their mouth shut so they couldn't speak any magic, and then they would kill them."

"Oh," said Erin.

"Yeah. Oh."

Erin turned another page, and there was a minute of quiet until something on the page prompted another question.

"Why pumpkins for Halloween? I mean, where did it all come from?"

"Oh my God, *Erin*, stop, please," said Matilda, pressing her palms together and looking at Erin with wide, pleading eyes. "I'm really trying to concentrate, and this isn't exactly helping."

Erin put her hands up. "Sorry, sorry, I'm just, like, so intrigued by all of this. Didn't mean to get off topic."

"Thank you."

Matilda rubbed her eyes, trying to ignore the cookies that were staring at her and continued to leaf through Ivy's book, Maura's words still lingering in the back of her mind each time she turned a page. She was certain there was something hidden between the sketches and notes that would help, but she just wasn't seeing it. A few minutes passed until Erin's voice nudged into her concentration again.

"So, this is from, like, two hundred years ago and this witch, Doris something, is obsessed with the first of November. The day after Halloween?" said Erin. Matilda nodded, not looking up from her book. "I thought Halloween would be a biggie for witches?"

Matilda sighed. "It is; it's just more like Christmas Eve. The next day is just as special."

"So, you do celebrate Halloween?" asked Erin. Matilda nodded, trying to concentrate on Ivy's words. "Like we do? Non-witches, I mean."

"Of course, mainly. Everything you do to celebrate has some of our traditions at its core. We have pumpkins everywhere and there's a big meal but we spend it as a family rather than going out with friends," said Matilda, yearning to be back at Ferly Cottage being fed by Nanna May at her favorite time of year.

"That's why you would never come trick-or-treating with me?" asked Erin. Matilda nodded—she had always been sad that she never got to join in with the other children, but her dad said the way they played with magic at Halloween was embarrassing. "So, what happens on the first of November, then?"

Matilda sighed, thinking that asking Erin for help wasn't a good idea after all. "I haven't got time for this, Erin. Maybe you should get Katrina to learn about this stuff and then you can quiz her."

Erin fixed Matilda with a look of disappointment, then bent back over the book. Matilda took a deep breath and looked down at her own when Erin's voice floated across the table.

"*At the stroke of the witching hour on the first day of November, the veil of death floats away on the autumn winds and we may converse with our long dead shadows. The spirits are free to visit as they did in breath and we embrace them as they are family.*" Erin juddered in her seat. "Urgh, creepy."

"Well, you wanted to know what it was all about."

"So, witch spirits actually come back on the first of November?"

"Yes, but, Erin, seriously, *please* can you just . . ." Matilda froze, hairs standing on the back of her neck as if Ivy herself were leaning over her shoulder. Matilda sat straight in her chair and looked at the book in front of Erin, her eyes wide and her fingers twitching as adrenaline coursed through her body. "Keep reading."

"But you said . . ."

"Keep. Reading," said Matilda, sparks flying in her head.

"Okay, okay. Jeez," said Erin, bending over the book again. "*We ask of them on this day to share their guidance and protection, for they know of our struggle and our enemies. As the night bathes us with its hour of protection, this is when we call them, this is when we seek them, this is when we ask them.*" Erin sat back and looked up at Matilda, her eyebrows pinched together. "What's old Doris going on about?"

Matilda leaned over Ivy's book and flicked back to the page at the front she'd seen when Maura handed it to her the first time. There were her words, written down almost as if they were a message from the past. *My power will never snuff out like a flame. I am the wind that blows that flame, and I am here for my daughters and my daughters' daughters.*

Sparks set off inside Matilda's head, and she held her breath as she put the pieces of a shattered mirror back together in the hope she would be able to see. Her shaking hands turned the pages of the book, gently but quickly trying to find another page that she had absentmindedly flicked past, dismissing it as old magic that was irrelevant to her.

But it was all relevant to her. She realized that now. She was connected to all the books in the room and the words inside them. *A wider fabric of magic*, as Maura had put it. She found the page, the adrenaline coursing through her body making it impossible to read logically as she kept jumping ahead by a word or a line. She took a deep breath and focused, then finally read the spell.

"Erin," she said, a smile spreading across her face, a smile that had been so alien in the last few weeks she wasn't sure it fit properly anymore. "You are a genius."

"I am?" said Erin.

"Yes," said Matilda, pushing her chair back and throwing herself onto Erin. She let a very shocked Erin go, then turned to check the time on her phone. "Okay, we need to work fast. Do you think Katrina would be up for helping? I was kind of rude to her."

"Kind of?" laughed Erin, but she nodded. "Absolutely."

"Excellent. Call her and get her to come and meet us at my garden room. I'll go back and try to put this all together," said Matilda as Erin pulled out her phone. "Oh, and does she have a car?"

"No, but I do," said Erin.

"Perfect. You go and pick her up, then, and bring pumpkins," said Matilda, leaning over Ivy's book again and ignoring Erin's puzzled face. "Lots and lots of pumpkins. Oh, Erin?"

"Yeah?"

"Happy Halloween."

CHAPTER FORTY-ONE

There was a tap on the glass, and Matilda jumped up from the floor and bounded to the door, trying to read the faces on the other side of the glass. How up for this were they? She opened the door and stepped back.

"Morning," she said, hugging her arms around her shoulders. "Jeez, it's freezing. Come in."

"You have coffee, right? Say you have coffee," said Erin, closing her eyes and resting her head on Katrina's shoulder, who peered at the brambles suffocating the garden room.

Matilda shook her head. "No coffee, but I've got dandelion, or I could go pick some fresh mint from the greenhouse?"

Erin opened an eye. "I've been up all night with you, Matilda. What would I do with that? Chew on it?"

"No, sorry, I mean, I can make some tea with it. It'll wake you up."

Katrina squeezed through the door with Erin still resting on her. "If it'll stop her whining, let's give it a try." She walked into the center of the room, looking around at the crystals and the herbs that grew beneath the windowsill, then her eyes rested on the open book on the floor surrounded by Post-its and torn notepaper. "This is your room?"

Erin held up her hand before Matilda could answer.

"Enough *have-some-tea-isn't-my-room-Instagram-worthy* bullshit. Just tell us what you need us to do and where the hell we're supposed to put all those pumpkins?" Erin looked around the room, suddenly noticing the brambles at the windows. "Also, in other news, you need to do some serious weeding, Matilda. What's with the fairy tale shrubbery?"

Erin and Katrina watched Matilda, their eyebrows waiting high up their foreheads. Matilda looked at the brambles. Erin was right; they did make her garden room look like something from an old storybook.

"I didn't think it was anything, but now I think it's a message," she said, looking at their puzzled faces.

"Huh?" Erin groaned. "I can't cope with any more cryptic shit, Matilda."

"I'm sorry. You deserve an explanation, especially since you're both here to help me." Matilda looked at Katrina. "But first, Katrina, I want to apologize to you. I've spent so long assuming I was the only witch at school that it made me act kind of . . ."

"Bitch-like?" offered Katrina.

Matilda nodded. "I shouldn't have been so rude to you. I'm really sorry."

"It's okay, Matilda. I get it. I just want to help."

"Thank you, I'm so glad you're here; I wouldn't be able to do this without you."

"Okay, let's wrap up the mutual witch appreciation society," said Erin, smiling at Matilda. "You were all wired and mysterious back at Maura's. What's the plan?"

"I think I've found a way to stop Oliver from using magic."

Erin tipped her head to the grimoire. "Is that your grimoire?"

Matilda nodded. "It is, but it's so much more than that, Erin. It's my family's lifeblood, our essence. To give it away would mean handing their magic over, and I can't do that. I can't let him take that from them. He's not taking any more from them."

"A hundred percent agreed," said Erin, taking a step closer. "So, what's the plan?"

"He's coming here, tonight. He thinks I'm going to give it to him." Matilda paused, adrenaline making her hands shake. "But I'm giving him something else."

Erin chewed the inside of her cheek as her eyes ran across Matilda's face. She shared a look with Katrina, then finally she spoke.

"Is this dangerous? I mean, we're not summoning the devil or some shit like that, are we?"

Matilda shook her head. "No, it's not dangerous. Not for you, anyway. I don't know how it'll turn out for me, but if it works, Oliver won't be able to hurt anyone anymore."

Katrina knelt down and picked up a piece of paper covered in scribbles and drawings. Her eyebrows drew together as she read what was on the page.

"This is how you're going to stop him?" she asked. Matilda nodded. "I'm no expert, but this doesn't look like you'll get your magic back."

"I don't care. I need to stop him. *We* need to stop him."

There was a tap on the glass, and they all looked around. Matilda smiled and nodded at the person standing in the doorway.

Erin frowned. "What are you doing here?"

Sean stepped through the doorway and put his hands in his pockets.

"I guess I'm part of the *we*."

Matilda watched Sean smear a quarter of the pot of jam onto a piece of warm bread, then stuff the entire slice into his mouth. He rolled his eyes back as he chewed, then turned to Matilda.

"What?" he said, spraying her with crumbs. "It's incredible!"

Matilda raised her eyebrows. "Hey, I brought it in to be eaten. You guys have been here for ages, the least I can do is feed you."

She looked at Erin and Katrina lying on their stomachs on her bed, their feet entwined as they carved pumpkins and tested each other on what Matilda had given them to learn. She couldn't work out if they kissed each other each time they got it right or when they got it wrong. Either way, they kissed each other a lot.

There were more papers and Post-it notes spread across the floor, along with crumb-covered plates and teacups (they'd all agreed that dandelion tea wasn't that bad), and at one point Erin had filled the room with her snoring because she couldn't fight the hours she'd been awake any longer. Victor sat at Matilda's side, and she tickled his ears as she watched Sean lean over her notes, his eyes wide as they flew across the handwritten words.

"Sean?"

"Yeah?" he said, not looking up from the book.

"Why did you agree to all of this? I mean, you seemed to take the whole thing pretty well."

Sean sat up and rubbed the back of his head. "For Ashley."

Matilda nodded. "I figured that. But you seemed to accept the witch stuff like it wasn't a big shock."

Sean shrugged. "It's not. I mean, my grandma is into it all."

Matilda leaned forward. "Really?"

"Really," Sean said, a smile dancing around his lips. "When I was born, she buried a witch bottle at the front door of our house. Said it would protect the most beautiful baby in town from love spells and curses."

"A witch bottle?"

"Yeah, you've heard of those, right?"

Matilda smiled. "Oh yeah, I've heard of them."

Sean went back to looking at Matilda's notes, and Matilda smiled and shook her head at her own stupidity. No wonder none of her spells had worked on Sean. She glanced at Katrina and realized how naive she'd been to think she was the only one at school with a connection to magic.

"Hey, Elphaba?"

"Don't call me that, Erin."

"Why not? You're Elphaba from *Wicked*, all misunderstood and vulnerable, and we're Willow and Tara, just completely adorable," she said, giving Katrina a peck on the cheek. "Who do you want to be, Sean?"

"I'll just be Sean."

"Fine, don't play the game, then," said Erin, pulling a face at Sean. "Matilda, I'm confused about something. How will you do your thing if you're helping us with our thing?"

Matilda jumped up and walked to her bedside table, stepping over the pumpkins waiting to be carved. "I'm not going to be helping you."

Erin peered at the book in front of her, then looked at Matilda. "But it says there should be four of us?"

Matilda nodded. "That's right: four for the elements, the seasons, and the directions. I'll take care of the fourth, don't worry," she said, rummaging through the drawer, then glancing at the clock. "Are you okay to start setting things up out there?"

"But the bread?" said Katrina, gazing at the half-eaten loaf sitting next to Sean.

"Take it with you, and your jars and candles. Oh, and do you have a compass on your phone?"

"Yes." Erin rolled off the bed and pulled Katrina up, then

picked up three candles and three green jars, handing one of each to Katrina and Sean. "Are you okay?"

Matilda nodded, picking up the business card from her drawer and reaching for her phone. She watched them traipse toward the door, candles in one hand and slices of bread in the other. Her mouth went dry as a sharp pain clawed at her heart.

"Guys." They all turned around. "Thanks."

One by one they nodded, then left Matilda alone. She looked at the business card and typed the number into her phone, praying that the person on the other end would answer.

CHAPTER FORTY-TWO

Halloween witching hour

The sun had long abandoned the day, and night spun its soundtrack. Matilda sat cross-legged in the center of her room, focusing her mind on the sounds around her. Owls hooted from deep within the woods and foxes cried out to one another, calling out to come and play; the humans had retreated from the darkness so the night belonged to the creatures and spirits.

It was hard to believe that less than forty-eight hours ago she had been on the cusp of handing Oliver the grimoire and losing her magic entirely. It was frightening, how close she'd gotten, how easily she could have been like any other seventeen-year-old girl, without a spark of magic inside her. How would that feel? Would it have been like the void Oliver had left inside her after siphoning her magic? The missing part made her feel like she was broken, like she couldn't connect the dots to perform even a basic magic spell successfully. Matilda shook the thought away. Not for much longer, she thought, not for tonight.

Oliver would arrive soon, and she left the warmth of her garden room to check the dozens of pumpkins she'd arranged on either side of the path up to her door, lighting the way for spirits who wanted to visit during the witching hour. Their flames beckoned inside the hollowed flesh, lighting a path in the darkness of midnight. Matilda closed her eyes; the Halloween night crackled with magic and mischief, and she could feel the witching hour beckoning, inviting her into its midnight embrace.

She circled the building and gave thanks to the sounds on the wind, holding on to the brambles to keep herself upright. The wind carried the smell of Nanna May's butternut squash soup, freshly baked bread rolls, and honey-glazed ham, just a fraction of the Halloween feast she'd spent all day preparing, but Matilda could only manage a few mouthfuls before she hurried back to her room.

Victor jumped up as she walked back inside. Matilda bent down and kissed his forehead.

"Not tonight, Vic. You go to the house. I'm sure Nanna May will let you snuggle up next to the fire."

He blinked at her, then turned and trotted through the door. She watched him go, her eyes widening as Oliver rounded the corner and bent down to stroke the goat. Victor kicked out his back legs and galloped down the gravel path.

"Here I am, before the stroke of midnight, as requested. You witches are obsessed with nighttime. But whatever, as long as I get what I'm here for, I don't mind staying up past my bedtime, just this once," said Oliver. He watched Victor trot out of sight, then turned back to Matilda. "You know, I don't think that goat of yours likes me very much."

Matilda stood at her doorway and folded her arms. "He knows what you did to Genie."

"Genie?" said Oliver, frowning.

"My grandmother's robin."

"Oh yeah," said Oliver, smiling as he swaggered between the row of glowing pumpkins leading up to her doorway. "You should have seen it. Was still flapping its wings and hopping around even after I'd stuck its head in the melted wax. Melted wax from the candles you gave me, by the way. Thanks for that."

"You're an asshole," said Matilda, fighting to contain her rage.

"Brought you to your senses, though, didn't it?" said Oliver.

Matilda nodded. "That and your witch's ladders."

Oliver smiled. "You found those, huh? Thanks for sharing that book with me. Those witch's ladders actually made it a lot easier to siphon your magic." Oliver kicked one of the pumpkins. "What's with all the empty pumpkins? Don't they need scary faces to keep away the spirits?"

Matilda shook her head, watching Oliver as he peered inside one of the pumpkins.

"Not tonight," she said, "tonight, we guide them."

Oliver rolled his eyes. "Whatever you say, Sabrina." He stopped in front of her and looked over her shoulder. "So? Where is it?" he asked.

Matilda stepped back. "In here."

Oliver pushed past her and raised his eyebrows at the dozens of pumpkins that were placed in a circle in the middle of the room.

"Jeez, you really do love your pumpkins, don't you?" he said, shaking his head.

Matilda pulled her shoulders back and walked past him, then crouched down at the side of her bed.

"Shit, that's where you keep your grimoire? Under the bed? Anyone could have found that, Matilda."

Matilda glared at him. "You didn't."

Matilda crouched down and pulled the trunk out. She could

feel Oliver hovering behind her, right in the center of the room. Her heart beat like a car's bass in her chest, shaking her stomach and making her sick, but she kept her breaths steady and tried to focus.

"You know, I'm going to miss you, Matilda."

"Yeah?" she said as her fingers fiddled with the lock.

"Yeah. I mean I know you think I'm, like, some kind of monster, but this is just what's owed to me. You took my life from me, and now I'm taking yours. Magic is all about balance, right? With the shit I'm going be able to pull now, I won't have to worry about any more names showing up on my skin. And who knows what sort of magic there is in this old book of yours. It's going to be *sick*."

Matilda unlocked the trunk and put her hands on the lid, glancing through the gaps in the thick brambles that crisscrossed her windows. She just needed to keep him talking and the shadows would do the rest.

"But I enjoyed hanging out with you, for the most part. It was an education, and I really got to see what I was capable of. Siphoning your magic was a necessity, but I am sorry I had to scare you as much as I did."

Matilda turned and looked up at Oliver, a serpentlike smile creeping across her face to match his.

"Oh, you weren't scaring me, Oliver," she said, opening the trunk. "You were provoking me."

Oliver looked down, his mask slipping as his eyes searched each corner of the trunk.

"Where's the book?" he said, his jaw tightening as he looked around the room.

Matilda took the jar of orange liquid from inside the trunk

and stood up, her hands shaking and her wide eyes blinking rapidly.

"The book is safe. But you're not." Matilda threw the jar's contents on Oliver's chest and stepped back from him. "Now!"

Matilda looked through the windows of the garden room as four green flames illuminated from each cardinal direction, flickering behind the cracks in the brambles that covered the windows. She turned to Oliver, who was too busy looking at his wet coat to notice the activity from outside or to hear the steady hum of the incantation that the candle bearers were reciting.

He looked up, fury making his eyes bulge. "Bitch. This is my favorite coat."

Matilda smiled and folded her arms as Oliver reached out to grab her. He blinked, his neck muscles straining.

"What have you done to me?" he said, his jaw clenched together. "I can't move."

Matilda smiled and put her hand on her chest. "Not what *I've* done to you, Oliver. What *we've* done to you. My coven out there is holding you still so we can have a little chat about your behavior."

The flames flickered and moved closer to the glass, close enough that Matilda could see four sets of eyes locked on Oliver, a string of magical words floating through the glass like a lullaby.

"Nanna May saw you coming a mile off, Oliver. *Wicked Tilly.* It's the only thing she's ever said after my dad took her voice, and I always thought she was talking about me. But it's not me who's going to a dark place; I know that now." Matilda nodded at the brambles covering the windows. "I thought all that was just some random weed growing outside my room, but Nanna May knew it was more than that. That it was a sign, a warning from Ivy and our ancestors that something was coming for me. That *you* were coming for me."

"What the hell are you talking about?" said Oliver through gritted teeth, his eyes wide as he tried to move. "What does your stupid grandmother, or Ivy, have to do with this?"

"You show some respect, Oliver, or you'll be even more sorry," said Matilda, pointing a warning finger. Oliver kept his mouth shut, and she went on. "It turns out that Nanna May really does have the gift of sight, because not only was she trying to warn me about you, but that brew she's been stirring on the fireplace for the last few months was exactly what my new coven needed to keep you still. I recognized the ingredients in an old book. You may have taken my magic, but you can't contemplate being as powerful a witch as my grandmother or those who came before her. You made a big mistake killing her bird, Oliver. A big mistake."

"You deserved everything I did to you, including that stupid bird," growled Oliver, his jaw clenching around each word as his muscles became tighter and tighter.

Matilda raised her eyebrow. "You shouldn't have come back here, Oliver. You shouldn't have come back to my town or back to Ferly Cottage. Yes, you stole my magic from me, but my family is happy to share, and this is the best time of year to do it. If you weren't such a bottom-feeding beginner, you'd know a few facts about witches, one of which is that we like to keep our dead close."

Matilda turned her palms upward and tilted her head back as if she were calling out to the moon.

"*Sisters of my sisters, mothers of my mothers, I call to you this Hal-*

loween witching hour. Share with me your love and power so I may punish one who has disrespected our ways and our magic. Lend me yours in the absence of my own, which he tore from me. Hear me, family, as I show you my face so you may pledge your power and I may put the balance right."

Matilda lifted her shaking hands to her face and closed her eyes, sucking down her breath as she prepared to drop the veil that she'd spent the last three years building to hide the things she'd done. She knew it was a fair trade, that the spirits of her ancestors deserved to see the true face of the young witch they might share their magic with, but she was terrified of revealing what was hidden beneath the facade.

"*I offer you my truth,*" she said into her hands. "*See me, sisters, see my pain so that I may draw from yours.*"

Relief rippled across Matilda's skin as though the pain seared into her face was blown away on a breeze. She'd forgotten what it had felt like before, to not carry the agony around with her, and for a moment she was overcome, until she felt a warm trail of blood trickle down her cheek and she remembered what the sudden absence of pain actually meant.

She lowered her hands. Oliver tried to scream, his frozen muscles making the sound even more terrifying as it screeched from within his throat.

"I may not be the wicked thing that Nanna May was warning me about, Oliver, but I'm pretty damn close," hissed Matilda. She shook her head, feeling a crimson waterfall trickling down her face as each of the names reopened her skin, pieces of flesh hanging between each letter. "I'm ashamed of what I've done to get these names on my face, but I'm not ashamed of who I am. You messed with the wrong witch."

The night took a breath. Animals stopped to listen, and the wind held still as the flames inside the pumpkins blinked out one by one up the path and into the garden room. Magic rushed through Matilda's veins, creeping up her neck and tingling at the end of her fingertips as Oliver panted, his eyes wide in panic. The shadow Oliver had made in Matilda's soul shrank as it refilled with magic. Not her magic; something much older, more powerful.

"The ground we're standing on is charged with the power and suffering of my ancestors and they *really* don't like you messing with one of their daughters. I can feel them, Oliver, I can feel them gifting my veins with pure, ancient magic, and right now I feel so powerful that if I had a broomstick, I think I could fly." Matilda tilted her head and smiled. "It's hard to tell because you can't move, but you're either pissed off or terrified. Maybe both."

"P-p-please . . . I . . . ," panted Oliver through clenched teeth.

Matilda put her finger to her lips.

"Shhh. The witch is talking."

Matilda felt unseen hands rest gently on her shoulders and arms, letting her know that she wasn't alone and those long buried had come to lend her the strength to stop Oliver. Tears fell from her eyes and her limbs shook as she embraced the new, old power inside her.

"Remember I told you what they did to us when they found out who we were? So scared of our power, they would hold a witch down, break every one of her fingers so she couldn't grind her ingredients for a spell, then they would take a sharp needle and sew her mouth closed so she couldn't utter a single charm. And then they would kill her."

Tears streamed down Oliver's cheeks as Matilda let her words sink in.

"So, I figured, what goes around comes around," said Matilda. "Don't worry, though, Oliver, not the killing part. Death is too good for you."

A gust of wind whipped through the open doors, sending books and glass bottles tumbling to the floor of the garden room, but Oliver couldn't move against the invisible forces that were still holding him.

"Hear me, sisters. I see this wickedness before me and I bind it from stirring a potion or grinding a powder beneath a rock." Matilda fixed her eyes on Oliver. *"A click for each of your fingers."*

She clicked her fingers once, not even flinching at the sound of cracking bones as Oliver screamed from within the prison of his body. She clicked again, and the screaming intensified as she glanced at his hands, both his thumbs and index fingers sticking out at unnatural angles. Sweat was beading on his forehead, and Matilda clicked a third time, then a fourth, and one final click so that every one of his fingers were broken.

Her coven watched as Matilda shook her hands out and then looked at Oliver again.

"I see this wickedness before me and I silence it so it may not utter a single word of magic. A needle through your lips."

Matilda pinched her index finger and thumb together on both hands, raising them up level with her eyes. She bent her head forward, so she was looking at Oliver from beneath her eyebrows, like an angry bull ready to charge. Slowly, she moved her fingers up and down, up and down as if she were sewing an invisible thread through the air.

Oliver whimpered as his lips slowly pulled together in an

unnatural grimace and his eyes squeezed closed as tiny pinpricks of blood sprang above and below his lips. Muffled sobs escaped through his nose as his mouth was sewn together by the invisible thread sending tracks of blood flowing down his chin. Matilda brushed her hands together and walked forward until she was almost nose to nose with Oliver, still with the firm weight of her ancestors' hands on her shoulders.

"*Use the weapons of our enemies against them.* I read that somewhere, Oliver. And take a close look," whispered Matilda, pointing to her face. "No new scar. Guess someone thinks I'm doing a good thing here."

Tears pooled in Oliver's eyes as he blinked at Matilda and dropped to his knees.

"One more thing, Oliver. This hand is for Ashley, and this one is for Genie." Matilda circled her fingers around Oliver's hands, his eyes closing tight in agony as she squeezed his broken bones together. "And silencing your cruel mouth? That's for everything you did to me."

Oliver slumped into a heap on his side. He stared back at her, the invisible stitches pulling his lips together and the blood trickling down his chin making him look like the monster he was, but she saw something new in his bloodshot eyes.

Fear.

She crouched down next to him and clasped her fingers together.

"You can stop now," she called to her coven, and the voices outside disappeared into the darkness. "For as long as your lips remain stitched and your fingers are broken, you can't do a spark of magic, but I'm going to offer you a deal. My coven has stopped holding you still, so you can move now, Oliver, but I want you to think very carefully about what your next move is going to be."

Matilda could still feel her ancestors behind her, nodding at her every word.

"I'll remove your fate from your face and your hands, but then you walk out that door and you leave my town, Oliver," said Matilda. "You leave and you don't stop going until you're far away from here and from anyone else. Do you understand?"

Oliver blinked and nodded.

"But know this," said Matilda, leaning in closer to Oliver so he could look into her eyes and see how much power she had at that moment, "if you even think about a spell or open a magic book, I will know. *They* will know."

Matilda looked up, and Oliver followed her gaze to the windows of the garden room. In the reflection of the glass stood dozens of women, crowding around Matilda and filling the room behind her. Some of them were hunched with age and some stood tall, wearing cloaks and holding broomsticks, their familiars perched on their shoulders or curling around their legs. The ones close behind Matilda had their arms outstretched and rested their hands on her shoulders.

Oliver gasped and shuffled backward on the floor, looking between Matilda and the windows as the women slowly lifted their hands and pointed at him.

"Do you understand what I'm saying, Oliver? Do you understand what *we're* saying?"

Oliver nodded, unable to tear his eyes from the generations of witches who had sealed his fate. Matilda stood up and lifted her hands.

"Undo this one's curse so that he may speak and use his hands once more."

Matilda clapped her hands together. The invisible thread tore from Oliver's mouth and his fingerbones snapped back into place. He threw his head back and a guttural scream filled the room as he was finally able to release his pain.

He pulled himself up, barely able to stand at his full height as he stared with wide eyes at the dozens of witches still watching him. He shuffled backward until he got to the doorway, then looked at Matilda, fear etched in his ashen face but sparks of anger still flashing in his eyes. He opened his quivering mouth a fraction, but Matilda lifted a finger and shook her head.

"Just because I've let you speak again, don't think it means you get to say what you want without consequence." Matilda folded her arms and Oliver closed his mouth. "Get the hell out, and don't trip over a pumpkin on your way."

Oliver glared at Matilda and the witches who stood behind her, then stumbled into the night, something unseen slamming the door behind him. The hands that had been guiding Matilda left her shoulders and the crackling possibility of the magic they had shared suddenly disappeared. She stumbled back and dropped to the ground.

They had taken back their magic, just as Maura said they would, and the shadow inside her was still there. Matilda lay on her back and put her hands to her forehead, staring up at the ceiling and hoping that the spirits of her ancestors could still hear her.

"Thank you," she whispered.

She hauled herself up and went outside to check on the others. The fairy lights on her roof began twinkling, and Matilda peered into the darkness as she sensed something coming toward her on the wind. Tree branches cracked together, the door slammed, and she was thrust backward into the air, panicking until she felt the wind embrace her, holding her light as a feather, stiff as a board a few feet above the ground. Something tingled from the tips of her fingers all the way to the magicless shadow inside her until it filled the void with energy, all over again.

The force that had levitated her brought her back down to the ground, resting her on the crunchy leaves of autumn. Suddenly, the barren cherry blossom trees awoke from their sleep, green leaves unfurling from their crooked fingertips, sprouting tiny green buds that burst open into pink flowers. Matilda watched the flowers blossom then burst from the ends of the branches, their petals drifting to the ground.

Daisies sprouted and daffodils bloomed before their petals puffed from their stems and drifted on the wind. The flowers' scent weaved through the autumn air as they went through their cycles in seconds.

Footsteps crept around the garden room and Matilda could feel the world slowing down as she watched four green hooded cloaks hurry toward her.

"Matilda?" said Erin, pushing her hood back. "You okay? What happened?"

Matilda smiled as Katrina and Sean pulled their hoods back, peering down at her with concerned eyes, both of them still holding their candles.

"It worked," whispered Matilda. "You did it."

"*We* did it," said Erin. "Gravewick Coven 2021, thank you very much!"

Erin held up her hand, and Matilda tried to do the same, smiling as Erin gave her a gentle high five.

"Oh my God, you're covered in blood!" gasped Katrina, kneeling down at Matilda's side. Her eyes flew across Matilda's chest and face. "Are you okay? I can't see where it's coming from?"

Matilda blinked. Her heart began clanging in her chest as she looked into Katrina's eyes, not seeing a single ounce of fear as she looked back. Matilda swallowed and slowly lifted a hand to her own face, her fingers shaking as they brushed against her skin, skin perfectly smooth and clear of a single letter to warn the world of what she was.

Matilda sucked in a breath as she looked around at Erin.

"Is my face . . . are they there?" she asked.

Erin smiled and shook her head. "There's nothing there, Matilda. Looks like you've been given a clean slate."

Matilda fell back and ran both hands over her face, remembering what she felt like as a young witch before all the scars, seeing the possibilities and the gifts in a world of magic. She bit her lip and whispered her gratitude into the wind.

"What the hell?" said Officer Powell, the fourth candle bearer, pushing her hood back and frowning at the brambles that covered the garden room.

A green shoot snaked out of the dirt and up through the brambles that had covered Matilda's garden room over the last few weeks. It wove through the branches, sure and steady, until it reached the top and worked its way over the roof. More of them shot up from the dirt and twisted around the brambles until it was submerged in the new plant.

The sky flashed with lightning, and they could all see tiny buds forming on the vines, growing into dark green star-shaped leaves.

"It's her," laughed Matilda.

"Who?" asked Sean.

"Ivy," said Matilda. "She's healed my scars and given me her magic. She's letting me keep it so I can start again and use it right this time."

Erin and Katrina helped Matilda up, and the coven watched as hundreds of ivy leaves unfurled from the vines, covering the entire garden house until there wasn't an inch of the brambles left in sight.

CHAPTER FORTY-THREE

Nearly a year later

"You two are hopeless at this."

Neither Erin nor Katrina looked up from the barrel, both of them frowning and sticking their tongues out of the corners of their mouths as they stabbed at the apples with the small knives in their hands.

"You do it, then, if you're such an expert," muttered Erin, sucking in a breath as an apple bobbed away from the end of her knife.

"I can't, not while I've got Ivy-May," said Matilda.

Katrina dropped her knife and held out her hands.

"My turn, then; I'll have her."

Matilda turned away and kissed the top of her baby sister's head.

"She's sleeping."

"Baby hogger," Katrina said. "We're still coming over to help babysit tomorrow night, though, right? I'm officially requesting lots of cuddle time then."

Matilda nodded. "Mom and Michael are out for dinner then the movies, so it'll be us, Ivy-May, and Nanna May."

Erin whipped around to Matilda, her eyebrows raised.

"And Nanna May's bread rolls, cheese-and-bacon potato skins, and toffee popcorn bark, right? *Right?* You did ask her?"

"Don't panic; I put your order in."

Erin's shoulders relaxed. "It's going to be the perfect Halloween night, in a real witch's cottage, stuffing our faces while we watch *Hocus Pocus* with Ivy-May, then *The Craft* after she's gone to bed. Oh my God," she sighed, "I'm in a food coma just thinking about it."

Matilda smiled at her friends and put her arms around the baby carrier, giving Ivy-May a little squeeze. Erin's description didn't sound that different from most of their other weekends, but she was still looking forward to it. She adjusted Ivy-May's little green pom-pom hat and turned to watch the rest of the festivities just as someone called her name.

Lottie and Michael, Ivy-May's dad (nicknamed The Beard by Erin), walked toward them with armfuls of steaming drinks and paper bags of deliciousness, followed by Nanna May hunched over a stroller that was nearly the same height as she was and crammed with fluffy blankets.

"Here you go," said Michael, handing Erin and Katrina their drinks as they muttered thank-yous and concentrated on stabbing the apples.

"Here's yours," said Lottie, holding out a cup to Matilda and frowning at her. "Are you going to take it?"

"I can't; I've got Ivy-May."

"Give her to me, then," said Lottie, handing Michael the drink and going to take the baby carrier off Matilda.

"But she's all snoozy and cozy on me."

Lottie rolled her eyes. "And she can be snoozy and cozy on her mommy. Come on, Matilda, you definitely get big sister of the year, but you can go off duty for one night and enjoy the festival with your friends."

Nanna May appeared in front of Matilda and began undoing

the straps with the nimble fingers of someone who spent her life adding pinches of secret ingredients to brews and potions. Matilda felt the warmth of her sister pulled from her body and watched Nanna May tuck the little baby up into the folds of the stroller, away from the biting autumn air.

"Right, we're going to wander around the rest of the festival and then get this little squish home. You have money?" said Lottie. Matilda nodded. "Text me when you're ready to leave, and I'll come get you."

"It's fine, Mom. We don't mind walking."

"And I don't mind driving you girls home."

Matilda nodded as Lottie and Michael, who was still giving Matilda just the right amount of respect and distance as they slowly found their footing with each other, walked alongside Nanna May pushing the stroller past the crowds. Despite knowing that her friends were safe right next to her and her family was heading home, the nagging sense of fear Matilda felt for those close to her nipped at her soul.

"Matilda?" said Katrina. "Shall we find somewhere to sit so we can eat this pile of food your mom bought for us?"

Matilda turned to her friends, trying to bury what she knew was an irrational fear. Oliver had disappeared after she'd threatened him with her ancestors' wrath. After he'd gone, she'd checked his social-media accounts and found they hadn't been updated, like they'd frozen in time, and Gravewick Academy was blazing with gossip about how he'd suddenly cleared out his bedroom and disappeared. She was satisfied that he was far away from those she loved, but every now and then at night she'd jolt upright, like someone had shaken her awake. Whether she liked it or not, she would remain connected to Oliver for as long as she needed to be, as her bloodline watched and waited in case he emerged from the gloom of his dark soul.

Matilda knew that her fear came from growing close to people and having them in her world, but it also meant that she was ready to protect them if she needed to. She looked at her friends, full of excitement and possibility, then smiled as she noticed something curling by their feet at the bottom of the barrels.

"Yeah, sure," she said, turning to watch her family walk beneath one of the festival's cloaked scarecrow figures holding a sign, an ivy vine lined with green star-shaped leaves curling around the post as they passed. "Let's go."

ACKNOWLEDGMENTS

A spell needs the right ingredients to make it successful, otherwise things can go awry. The same is true for writing a book, though instead of basil or belladonna, a book needs the right people.

Kirk Seymour. Thank you for your unwavering belief in me and for encouraging me to be my own Annie Wilkes (minus the hobbling, obviously). I couldn't have gotten to this point without your support, especially since we had our beautiful children, and definitely not through lockdown. You told me five years ago that you knew I was going to get published, and it turns out you were right.

Mum, I know you'll see these words somehow. Thank you for that time in the car when you pointed to the woods and told me that's where the witches meet. You sparked something in my imagination that day, and I've never been able to shake it. Dad, obviously I need to thank you, too, for everything, but also because you were probably driving the car at the time.

Cynthia Murphy. Cynthia, Cynthia, Cynthia. Thank goodness the universe brought our dark souls together when it did. I couldn't think of a better person to share this incredible writing journey with, plus the not so great other things we've had to endure along the way. You've been there for every single step, and I'm so thankful for your friendship. Thank you for your always spot-on feedback, for loving my twisted ideas, and for being my fellow weirdo.

Katherine Bowers, thank you for being the best bestie and the best SIL anyone could ask for. You've made so much time for me and for my writing, and I know how precious that time is. Your encouragement gave me the confidence I needed to pursue this dream, and your belief in me picked me up when I was down. I promise I'll write a romance one day to give your nerves a break.

Sue Shead. Thank you for being my office cheerleader and encouraging me to never give up whenever I got a rejection in my in-box. We can finally see my name on the catalog now! Also, I'd just like to let you know I'm available for library events.

Rachel Diebel. How lucky am I to have you as an editor? You've held my hand as I've taken my first steps into the world of publishing, and you never made me feel like I was asking a silly question. I couldn't have done this without your guidance and patience. Thank you for pushing me to make the ending better and for not letting me kill the horse. Also, thank you for the *Buffy* references in your notes; you truly know how to motivate me. Let us not have to change quotation marks ever again.

The team at Swoon Reads, who I know have worked hard to make this book a reality. Jean Feiwel, Lauren Scobell, Trisha Previte, Starr Baer, and Celeste Cass. Also, the incredibly talented Marcela Bolívar, who created the most perfect artwork for the book cover. It's honestly like someone reached into the dark depths of my imagination and painted what was lurking there in the shadows. It's a thing of beauty and I still can't stop staring at it.

My friends and family, and everyone in the Swoon community who read and voted for this book. Writing can be a very solitary place, and seeing your comments made me feel like I wasn't shouting into a void. I'm so lucky to have your support and enthusiasm, and I really can't wait for you to read this book again.

Public libraries and library staff. Where do I even start? I have so many memories of being nestled in the outstretched arms of bookshelves, the reassuring smell of shared books and muted sounds of others learning, enjoying, and inquiring. My mum took me to our local library as often as I wanted and probably watched proudly as I fell head over heels for books and reading. That love for books led me to a career as a librarian, and then a passion for writing. Every book I've written has been researched using library books or cuttings from the local studies section, the materials I read planting seeds and inspiring different scenarios. From devouring Point Horrors to sobbing over the dog in *I Am Legend*, I would not be the person or the writer I am today without access to those, and hundreds more, books through what has to be the greatest service on the planet.